Award-winning author **Yvonne Lindsay** is a *USA TODAY* bestselling author of more than forty-five titles with over five million copies sold worldwide. Always having preferred the stories in her head to the real world, Yvonne balances her days crafting the stories of her heart or planting her nose firmly in someone else's book. You can reach Yvonne through her website, yvonnelindsay.com

Maureen Child writes for the Mills & Boon Desire line and can't imagine a better job. A seven-time finalist for the prestigious Romance Writers of America *RITA®* Award, Maureen is the author of more than one hundred romance novels. Her books regularly appear on bestseller lists and have won several awards, including a Prism Award, a National Readers' Choice Award, a Colorado Romance Writers Award of Excellence and a Golden Quill Award. She is a native Californian but has recently moved to the mountains of Utah.

MARRIED BY CONTRACT

YVONNE LINDSAY

ONE LITTLE SECRET

MAUREEN CHILD

MILLS & BOON

First Published in Great Britain 2021
by Mills & Boon, an imprint of HarperCollins*Publishers* Ltd
1 London Bridge Street, London, SE1 9GF

www.harpercollins.co.uk

HarperCollins*Publishers*
1st Floor, Watermarque Building,
Ringsend Road, Dublin 4, Ireland

Married by Contract © 2021 Harlequin Books S.A.
One Little Secret © 2021 Maureen Child

Special thanks and acknowledgement are given to Yvonne Lindsay for her contribution to the *Texas Cattleman's Club: Fathers and Sons* series.

ISBN: 978-0-263-28313-6

1221

MIX
Paper from
responsible sources
FSC® C007454

MARRIED BY CONTRACT

YVONNE LINDSAY

I dedicate this to all the dreamers and lovers out there.
May all your endings be happy.

One

November

"**W**hat do you mean they canceled the order?" Rosalind mentally calculated the time back in Sydney, Australia, where Piers was calling from, and schooled herself to remain calm. "They can't simply cancel like that."

"They can and they did, Ros. They're citing long-term fallout from the pandemic and a need to cut back. I'm sorry—they see our product as being luxury driven at a time when people are being more careful with household expenditure. The arm of this thing is long. We both know that."

Her operations manager, Piers Benet, sounded calm, but then again, he'd had several hours to come to terms with the news that could easily derail Rosalind's entire business.

"Did you point out to them they signed the contract after the start of the pandemic?"

"I did, but they're cutting us loose. We get to keep the first payment, though, so there's that."

It was small consolation compared to the full contract value, not to mention the value of the exposure of her fashion label into every one of Australia's major department stores or her production costs to date.

"So, there's nothing we can do?" she said bitterly, pacing her hotel room.

"Nothing except hope your contacts in New York give us the uptake we need to remain afloat. How are things in New York, anyway?"

"I'm not actually in New York yet."

"You're not? Is there a problem?"

"No, not really. I…uh…thought I'd call in, say hi to Drake."

"Drake Rhodes? That Drake?"

Piers knew the full extent of the brief but fierce relationship she'd had with the Texan billionaire businessman during his six months in Sydney and he also knew that she'd walked away from Drake when he'd made it clear he was not into marriage. Wanting more than accepting happy-for-now, Rosalind had reluctantly ended their liaison when he'd had to fly home to Royal because his half-sister was ill. But time had given her a new perspective and she was willing to give them both another chance. It was why she was here in Royal, Texas, staying at the Bellamy, instead of already being in New York. A selfish choice, maybe, especially when her business currently teetered on a knife edge, but a necessary one. She had to know if she'd made the right decision because she could never forgive herself if she'd walked away from him too soon.

She couldn't quite believe that Drake had forsaken the busyness of Sydney and the exciting lifestyle they'd led there, to return to this small, so very *country* town. She knew that before he'd come to Sydney he'd lived in New York and she couldn't understand why he'd returned to his birthplace—a town he'd never spoken highly of. It made no sense to her that he'd come back here.

"Yes, that Drake," she said carefully. She knew Piers wouldn't be impressed.

"Are you sure about this, Ros? You were pretty upset when you broke up. Last thing you need right now is more emotional upheaval."

"I'll be fine," she responded firmly. "I can't help feeling I pushed him too hard, too early, on marriage. Maybe that was a mistake and all he needed was a little more time. Look, if things don't work out then I'll carry on to New York regardless. But I have to know, Piers. I can't live with 'what if' echoing in the back of my mind, forever."

Her operations manager sighed heavily on the other end of the call. "You take care. And let me know how it goes, okay?"

"I will. And send through the report on the loss we have to carry on that order cancellation. Looks like we're going to need get creative to shift that stock. Get one of the team to look into pop-up stores in both Australia and New Zealand, okay?"

By the time they ended the call, Rosalind was beside herself with frustration. This was to have been their big break. It had meant everything to her. Sure, she was American born but she'd lived half her life in Australia and taking the Australian leisure-wear market by storm would have been the fulfilment of a childhood dream.

Rosalind flicked a glance at the diamond-encrusted Cartier watch that adorned her wrist. It had been a gift from Drake for her birthday. Tonight she'd hoped it would bring her luck for what she had planned. Winning him back.

It was time to get ready for the gala at the Texas Cattleman's Club here in Royal. She'd been lucky to get a ticket at such late notice, but she knew Drake would be there and hopefully the knockout scarlet gown she'd packed would surprise him enough to agree to them taking a second chance on each other. After Piers's phone call, she needed some good news.

Housekeeping had steamed the gown for her earlier in the day and it hung in splendor in the bedroom of her suite. Rosalind took her time over her toilette and makeup. She smoothed on lightly scented body lotion with long strokes and applied her makeup with a practiced hand to emphasize her sculpted cheekbones and large blue eyes. She'd chosen to wear her long blond hair loose, but had curled it to give it more volume and bounce and, after brushing it out and spritzing with a light mist of hair spray, she was ready to don her gown.

The deep V of the crossover front of the bodice made it impossible for her to wear a bra and she felt a shiver of excitement course through her as her nipples brushed against the lining of the dress. The V wasn't salacious, but it certainly displayed more of her lightly tanned skin than her usual attire. The lower section of the dress hugged her hips and split at the left front, exposing her leg to lower thigh as she walked.

After slipping on her silver strappy heels, she took stock of her image in the full-length mirror on the wall. Yes, she thought with a nod at her reflection, she would most definitely do just fine tonight. Now all she had to do was knock Drake's socks off, and maybe a few other items of clothing along the way, and life could resume a better normal again.

When her bedside phone chimed with a message to say her car was waiting for her, Rosalind grabbed the faux silver fur coat she knew she'd need on this cold November night and slung it over her shoulders before picking up her silver clutch and heading for the door. Tonight had to work out. Given what was happening to her business right now, she couldn't handle another failure.

There was quite a crush in the ballroom at the club when she arrived and Rosalind felt a minor quiver of trepidation as she left her coat at the coat check and made her way to where everyone was gathered. Everyone was listening to the speeches and presentations to the first responders.

A passing waiter offered a tray loaded with champagne flutes and she lifted a glass with a smile of thanks, taking a moment to sip the wine and survey the room. She searched for a familiar dark head and broad shoulders. Drake was the kind of man who dominated the room and, to be honest, there were many other men here who also fit that bill. Both dark haired and fair and all darned attractive.

"Must be something in the water," she muttered under her breath.

"The water you say? I could have sworn that was champagne."

A deep and melodic voice from right next to her made Rosalind start. She turned toward the man and took in the humor reflected in his dark, almost black, eyes. And look at that, she thought, here was another ridiculously handsome, commanding specimen. Rosalind felt an unwelcome twinge of interest. A purely instinctive feminine response to an attractive, healthy male, she told herself. She wasn't interested in anyone here but Drake, but that didn't mean she couldn't appreciate a fine-looking man when she saw one.

"I was making an observation," she said and took another sip of her wine.

"First sign of madness, you know."

"What?"

"Talking to yourself. Or so they say."

"What do *they* know?" Rosalind responded.

"Indeed. I'm Gabriel Carrington. You're not from around here, are you?"

She took the proffered hand and felt that spark of interest flame to life as his broad, warm palm connected with hers.

"Rosalind Banks, and no, I'm not."

"Ah, a woman who doesn't feel the need to inform a total stranger of every detail about herself. Sensible," he commented as he let her hand go again. "Are you visiting Royal?"

She nodded. She had no idea if her plan would work. If it did, she might be here a short while before returning to New York where hopefully Drake would join her because he'd made the bustling, vibrant East Coast city the base for all his business interests prior to his time in Sydney. If it didn't, she'd be on the next plane out of the area tomorrow and connecting to a flight to New York on her own.

"Business, or pleasure?"

"Oh, pleasure, at least I hope so," she said with a small smile.

"Then I wish you luck," he said. "It's very nice meeting you, Rosalind."

"And you," she said, raising her glass in a small toast as he raised his whiskey glass in return.

She turned her gaze back to the crowd of men in black tie and women in a dazzling array of jewel-toned evening wear. With the speeches finished, the dance floor started to fill with couples. Through the throng Rosalind caught a glimpse of a very familiar profile. Drake. He was here. She felt her body alternately ease with relief that she'd found him, and tense in anticipation of what would come next. What would he say when she told him she'd made a terrible mistake and that she wanted a second chance? There was only one way to find out and that was to approach him but she wasn't about to cut in while he was dancing. No, she'd keep her sights on him and wait until he left the floor. Then she'd make her move.

Ros turned her attention to the woman he danced with. Tall and slender with beautiful red hair and delicately fair skin, she was dressed in a couture gown of dark forest green silk that complemented her skin tone perfectly. Low cut in the front and the back and held up with spaghetti straps that showcased her feminine shoulders and with sparkling beads decorating the edges and catching the light as she moved, she was quite a vision of perfection. Ros mentally costed the gown while appreciating its cut and construction at the same time. Definitely quality and class.

The couple turned, and Ros caught a glimpse of the woman's left hand which was adorned with a large diamond ring. She felt ice water run in her veins a moment before she schooled herself to consider that Drake may simply be dancing with a friend. Just because he was dancing with the redhead, it didn't mean they were an item, let alone an engaged item.

"See someone you know?" Gabriel Carrington asked.

He was still here?

"Yes," she said. "Over there, with the woman in the green dress."

"Drake? You know him?"

Intimately. "We met when he was in Sydney," she replied.

"Small world, huh? You're Australian."

"Australian American, to be more accurate."

"But you grew up Down Under, right? Your accent?"

She nodded, her eyes riveted on the subject of her entire reason for being here.

"Did you hear about their engagement?" Gabriel gestured toward the couple with his whiskey tumbler. "Took us all a little by surprise. Drake never made any secret about not wanting to settle down and start a family and yet, here he is."

The ice-cold sensation in her veins returned and Rosalind's hand shook a little as she lifted her champagne and downed it. Could tonight get any worse? First the news about her business and now she was too late with Drake, as well?

"No," she finally managed. "I didn't. Have they been engaged long?"

"Not long. Here, let me get you another of those."

Gabriel took her glass and gestured to a nearby waiter who immediately came over with a replacement. Gabe pressed the glass into her hand.

"Do you want to congratulate the happy couple?" he asked.

Ros noticed that Drake and his fiancée were leaving the dance floor. They were totally absorbed in one another. She clenched her teeth as Drake bent his head and whispered something in his fiancée's ear—something that made her blush delicately before they eased their way through the crowd and out the door.

"Not particularly," she bit out, before taking another long drink of her wine.

"Ah, like that, huh?"

She turned and looked at him. "He didn't know I was coming and doesn't know I'm here. I'd prefer to keep it that way."

"Noted. Shall we move somewhere a little more private?"

"Please."

He took her by the elbow and guided her to a smaller bar area with secluded seating spaces and settled her at a table.

"You okay?" he asked.

"I will be, eventually."

She had already dealt with the disappointment of losing Drake once and, to be honest, she hadn't really thought this through enough. She should have done more research before diverting to this out-of-nowhere town with too many cows and not enough bright lights.

"Good to know. Life sucks, right?"

"Sure does. I didn't think Drake would take up with someone else quite so quickly. I had hoped…"

"Hoped?"

"That I could convince him that we deserved another chance."

"What happened?"

She finished her second glass of champagne and gestured to a waiter for another.

"I wanted love, marriage and happy-ever-after. He didn't. Not with me, anyway."

Gabriel made a sound that was a mix of irony and humor.

"What you wanted is vastly overrated. In fact, I don't think it truly exists anymore."

"Why are *you* so skeptical?" she asked, suddenly genuinely interested in the man sitting beside her.

"People only really let you see what they want you to see. It's never the truth."

"Never?"

He shook his head. "My dad cheated on my mom more times than I could count. It broke her heart. And I guess I'm more like her than I thought because the woman I thought I loved cheated on me, too. It was enough of a wake-up call for me to realize that love and happy-ever-after are merely a construct of an industry dead set on selling fake dreams."

Okay. She could see why he was so cynical. Life had a way of screwing with you. It had certainly screwed with her today.

"I think you're probably right. I guess I should have expected this with Drake. It's pretty much the icing on the cake of my shitty day so far."

"Oh?"

She drank a little more champagne. Yes, she was definitely feeling a little buzzed. It was a good feeling. It loosened her inhibitions and made her feel things she normally kept tightly controlled. It was a feeling she vastly preferred to acknowledging the fact that she was now holding on to her business by a fraying thread and her plans for her romantic future had been crushed in Royal's dust.

"Before I came out tonight, I received news that a

business partner canceled their contract. We're down the tubes for close to a million bucks."

She shuddered a little. It wasn't until she'd actually admitted the true position out loud that it fully sank in.

Gabriel whistled long and low. "That's quite a hefty sum."

"Yeah, I need a cash injection and quickly, or my creditors will be baying for my blood."

"You know, it's a shame you're after the love-and-happy-ever-after thing because marriage to me would take care of your financial problems."

She reeled a little in shock. Marriage? To him? How had they progressed to that? She'd obviously had more champagne than she'd thought because she couldn't possibly have heard that right. Still, curiosity made her press him for more.

"Marriage to you? Explain."

"I want an heir—what man doesn't—but I don't want the mess that comes with it."

"Mess? What, like love?"

He raised his glass in a toast. "You got it."

"So, what are you planning? A surrogate or something?"

"I'm not averse to marriage entirely. I see what I want as more of a business arrangement based on physical compatibility and mutual respect. There's no reason why it wouldn't work. In fact, I've employed a specialist agency to find me just the right woman. Once we marry, she gets a settlement and, when my wife gives me the heir I want, she gets unfettered access to my wealth for as long as we're married. Simple."

Rosalind let her gaze roam over him. Thick, dark hair that curled slightly, but which was tamed by an expensive haircut. Broad shoulders and a handsome face dominated by dark, intelligent eyes. A full lower lip that was perfect for nibbling on. Whoa, where did that come from? But then she let her mind wander. She'd had it with love and disappointment. Not just today but before today, too. Here she was—still single and still fighting her own battles. A bit of financial help would be nice about now. Help without a hefty personal price tag.

"And do you plan to try before you buy this new wife of yours?"

He laughed and she felt something knot up tight deep in her gut before unraveling in a heated spiral of need. He really was easy on the eyes. And a girl could get drunk on that laugh. Mind you, she was heading that way already, wasn't she, and that was probably why she formulated her next words the way she did. She was the woman scorned, in both business and in her personal life. She demanded validation to soothe her wounded soul. Gabriel Carrington was hopefully the man to provide it.

"Maybe we're both what we need after all," she said with a smile and an arch of her brow. "Tonight at least."

TWO

Gabe looked at the beautiful woman sitting by him and felt every cell in his body spring to attention. Logic told him that this would be a very bad idea. She'd come here to Royal to rekindle her relationship with Drake, a man he knew and respected, and in the face of what she'd said, they'd been a serious item back in Australia. Serious enough to make her think she still had a chance with him.

That made him second-best tonight and that did not sit comfortably with him at all. And then there was her openly avowed wish for love and happy-ever-after. He wasn't in the market for that, at all. In fact, tomorrow he was meeting his latest match.

It was half the reason he had nursed a sum total of two whiskies on ice all night long. He needed a clear head for that meeting and if the woman proved to be a promising candidate, he sure as hell didn't want to scare her off by being hungover. No woman wanted a drunk for a husband and no child deserved one as a father, either.

Which left him with a difficult decision to make. The very beautiful Ms. Rosalind Banks was sending him all the right signals. She clearly wasn't in this for complications. So how wrong would it be to take advantage of what she was so carefully suggesting? He'd never made a habit of one-night stands. He respected both himself and his prospective partners too much to simply indulge whenever the whim took him. In fact, his cast-iron control was one of the things he was most proud of. Watching what his father's infidelities had done to his mom had been more than enough to drive home the message that casual sex could be very damaging to all concerned. But both he and Rosalind had needs and he had absolutely no doubt in his mind that they'd each fulfil those needs more than adequately.

"I apologize if my forwardness has offended you," Rosalind said as his protracted silence thickened the air between them.

"No, not at all," he replied.

"We Aussies can be a bit blunt at times, I guess. Although, it generally gets us what we want, or at least leaves us knowing exactly where we stand."

"I've been accused of being blunt a time or two, myself," Gabe replied.

He liked this woman. Not only physically attractive but she was straight up, too. Not like so many women he'd met and certainly not like his cheating fiancée Francine.

"I am sorry," she apologetically. "I should probably get to my hotel."

"No, don't go. I'm not at all offended. In fact, if anything I think we should dance."

Rosalind looked at him in surprise, a slow smile pulling her luscious lips into a delicious curve. She caught her lower lip between perfectly even, white teeth and bit down firmly, as if considering what he said carefully.

"Dance, you say?"

"We could see how well we move together," he answered with a smile and a quirk of one eyebrow.

Rosalind put down her champagne glass and stood, smoothing her gown over her curves. He could not help but appreciate the fine lines of her body. At the very least, tonight should prove interesting, he thought. Gabe rose to his feet and put out one hand.

"Shall we?" he asked.

She took his hand and he laced his fingers through hers before leading the way back into the ballroom. Her hand felt tiny in his much larger one and if he wasn't mistaken her fingers trembled slightly. Anticipation, he wondered, or regret at her bold suggestion. No doubt he would soon find out. The band played a slow two-step number and Gabe pulled her into his arms. She came willingly, with one small hand resting on his shoulder and the other clasped within his own. With his other hand at the curve of her waist, he guided her onto the floor.

They moved in perfect synchronization together. It was as if they had danced this way many times before. The crowd around them melted away from his consciousness as his sole focus concentrated on the woman in his arms. They could have been anywhere, anytime. He had found her attractive on first sight, but being together like this lit a flame of desire in him that demanded an answer. As her pelvis brushed against his he increased the pressure of his hand in the small of her back encouraging her to step closer. The tremor in her fingers had stopped, but as she felt the unmistakable evidence of his arousal her small hand tightened in his and her gaze flicked up to his face.

"I'm tempted to quote a very famous movie line right now," she said with a gleam in her eye. "But I'm pretty sure I know what the answer is."

He smiled back at her and smoothly changed step as the band eased into a livelier tune. Again, in perfect sync, she adjusted seamlessly to the new steps and they continued around the dance floor. If they moved like this in public, how much better would they be in private?

Gabe nodded to Jackson Michaels as he danced past him and his partner on the crowded floor, and considered the discussion they had had earlier before the formal section of this evening. Jackson had called him out on his hunt for the perfect wife. While he hadn't given Jackson an answer one way or another, he could see the cogs moving in his friend's mind as his gaze slid over Rosalind and back to Gabe. The short nod of approval made Gabe grin broadly in response and he turned his attention back to his dance partner.

"What's so funny?" Rosalind asked.

"A friend was asking me earlier about my marital plans and I think he just gave you a tick of approval."

"And do you, too?"

"Perhaps we should consider your try-before-you-buy suggestion, first."

She missed a step and stiffened slightly before recovering smoothly. "Perhaps we should," she said looking up from beneath hooded eyelids.

It was such a sultry look that the flame that had started earlier, deep inside him, roared into hungry, demanding life.

"We should get out of here," he said through gritted teeth.

"I thought you would never ask."

Gabriel took Rosalind's hand and led her from the dance floor, moving swiftly through the crowd and heading straight for the main doors.

"Do you have a coat?" he asked brusquely. At her nod he continued, "Let me get that for you."

She dug in her evening bag and passed him the coat check slip.

"I'll be straight back—don't go anywhere."

He was back in just a moment and helped her shrug into her coat. It seemed like a crime to cover her up but he consoled himself that he would be removing all her layers of clothing before long. He pulled on his own coat and took her by the hand again. Outside, his car was brought to the entrance.

"Your place, or mine?" he asked.

She looked at him for a full ten seconds before answering, giving him a moment to wonder if she had changed her mind.

"How far to your place?" she asked in response. "I'm staying at the Bellamy so if that is closer, I suggest we go there."

"The Bellamy is definitely closer."

He ushered her into his car and closed the door then walked around to the driver's side and settled behind the wheel. It took every ounce of control that he possessed not to spin the car wheels as they left the entrance to the club. While the Bellamy was close, every mile felt like torture. He flicked her a glance from time to time to try to read what she might be thinking, but she kept her gaze firmly forward as his car ate up the distance to the hotel.

Gabe left his car with a parking valet and with his hand on the small of Rosalind's back they stepped inside the hotel lobby. He drew her to a stop as she made a beeline for the elevators.

"Problem?"

He looked deep into her clear, blue eyes searching for any shred of doubt that might be reflected there.

"You're certain about this?" he asked intently.

"Definitely," she answered firmly. "Now let's stop wasting time."

His breath caught in his lungs and he could not have said another word to save himself at that moment. All he could do was follow her to the elevator and then, a few minutes later, down the corridor to her suite. There was no evidence of a tremor in her hand now as she passed her key card over the reader and the green light that glowed on her door handle seemed incredibly symbolic right now.

Rosalind opened the door and stepped into the suite then gestured for him to follow her in. The second he was over the threshold she shoved the door closed, grabbed him by the lapels of his coat, backed him up against the door and kissed him soundly. For a second he was taken aback at the unabashed sensual hunger in her kiss, but that was all it took before he answered in kind.

Her lips were soft and plump and no doubt he was doing a number on the lush red lipstick she'd worn but right now he didn't care. He simply wanted to taste her, all of her, and his hands slipped round to her buttocks and pulled her up hard against him—against the arousal that hadn't fully subsided during their ride to the Bellamy and was now making its own demands.

She tasted of champagne and an underlying sweetness. A flavor he couldn't quite get enough of even as his tongue teased her lips open and allowed him to deepen their kiss. She'd let go of his lapels and was pushing his coat down off his shoulders with short, urgent movements. They broke apart long enough to shed their coats and then she grabbed him again.

"I've been wanting to do this since I met you," she said, before biting softly on his lower lip.

"Just that?" he murmured against her mouth. "There's more of me."

She chuckled and the sound filled him with a combination of joy and desire. This was going to be fun as well as intense. He just knew it. The same way he knew tonight would be like nothing he'd ever done before with anyone else. She was different and with her he could be different, too. He could forget the heartache of his family. He could pretend the distance between him and his father did not exist. And he could relish the fact that while he knew next to nothing about this woman, she knew exactly the same amount of nothing about him, too. They could simply be together. Explore together. Find satisfaction in one another.

Rosalind tugged at his bow tie and her deft fingers made quick work of the knot. She yanked the strip of fabric that he'd so painstakingly tied this evening out from under his collar and cast it to the floor before adroitly flicking the buttons of his shirt open. The second she could pull the fabric away from his chest and bare his skin, she laid her mouth on one of his nipples, nipping gently before pushing his jacket and shirt off and then letting them drop to the floor also.

He wasted no more time. He'd already discerned the whereabouts of the hidden side zipper on her gown while they were dancing and he swiftly drew it down and then slid the garment off her shoulders and down her arms. The fabric slithered down her body, catching slightly on her softly rounded hips. It took the merest push of his hands and the dress joined his clothing that already lay on the floor. His tailor would freak out if he knew, Gabe thought with an ironic twist of his mouth, but then he found his attention magnetically pulled to the stunning vision standing before him.

He groaned as his eyes feasted on her skin. There were no tan lines on her bare breasts, which were exquisitely pert and round. He reached for her, his hands gently cupping her, his thumbs sliding over the taut buds of nipples the color of dark honey. Her pupils enlarged and a glazed look filled the blue depths of her eyes. Her chest flushed with a soft pink.

"I want to taste you." Desire thickened his voice, making it sound like more of a growl. "May I?"

"Oh, yes."

He bent his head and took one nipple between his lips, rolling it with his tongue and drawing the tight bead into his mouth before releasing it again. She trembled against him. Her fingers laced around the back of his head, holding him to her. His hand slid down to her hips, eased beneath the lacy scrap of underwear she wore and eased the fabric down her legs until it, too, dropped to her feet. His hands skimmed the globes of her buttocks, the backs of her shapely thighs. She parted her legs slightly.

"Touch me," she demanded.

He deftly moved one hand around to the front of her leg and then slowly drifted higher. He could feel the heat that emanated from her core and knowing she was hot for him made him desire her all the more. His fingers teased the crease of skin at the apex of her thighs as he brushed backward and forward. She was already wet for him. Her hands had moved to his shoulders and her fingers gripped hold of him so tightly he could feel the impression of her nails against his skin. It was exhilarating and made him feel almost invincible.

He wanted her more than he'd ever wanted anyone before and none of it made sense. They'd only just met and yet here they were. Desperate for one another. His erection was almost painful—he was so hard with the need to bury himself in her body and to feel that heat encase him and grip him hard. He forced himself not to think about it, to solely concentrate on what he was doing to her now. To listen to the sounds of her fractured breathing as he dipped one finger into her honeyed wetness and drew it out again to tease her clit before repeating the movement again.

Her hands were at the belt of his trousers, then slipping inside the band of his boxer briefs before easing the firm fitting fabric away from him. She took his length in her hand and stroked him from base to tip and back again. He groaned and let his head drop back, allowing sensation to ripple through him.

"I want you inside me," she ground out.

"Believe me, I want that, too," he growled back.

"Now, please!"

She lifted one leg over his hip and he shifted his hands to her buttocks, eased her higher until he could feel his tip at the heated entrance to her body.

"Gabe, now!"

"Protection," he muttered, straining to hold himself

back even while his body urged him to simply take her as she'd insisted.

"I'm safe. I'm on the pill—I have a clean bill of health. Please, Gabe, don't leave me hanging."

He knew he was clean; testing had been a pre-entry requirement with the marriage broker, and could wait no longer. Pushing her hard against the wall he entered her body in a single stroke.

"Yessss," she hissed against his ear.

It was madness and perfection all at once; he realized as his hips moved in the age-old rhythm of time, harder and faster until he felt himself on the edge of climax. But he wouldn't let go, couldn't. Not until she found her satisfaction. He opened his eyes and looked at her. Rosalind's cheeks were flushed, her eyes glittering with arousal, her lips parted on rapid breaths. A long slow moan ripped from her body and he felt her inner muscles clench around him, then tighter again as her orgasm poured through her. It felt as if she'd given him an incredible gift, this intimacy of watching her come and it was enough to send him over the edge as the waves of his own pleasure burst from behind the stop bank of his self-control and swamped him.

He wasn't sure how long they stayed like that. Their breathing hard and fast, their bodies slick with perspiration. Their legs trembling with the force of their joint release. Eventually though, she let her leg slide back down again and he reluctantly pulled free of her body.

"You okay?" he asked. Things had gotten quite tempestuous there.

She smiled at him like a cat that got the cream. "Oh, yeah. That was great, for a starter."

His lips quirked back in response. "Starter?"

"Well, there's still the main and dessert to follow, right?"

His grin widened. "Right."

He stepped from his pants and discarded his shoes and socks and watched as she walked across the suite to the bedroom. The sight of her, naked except for the sinfully sexy high heels she wore, was enough to bring him rapidly back to aching life again. He followed her into the bedroom and onto the bed.

Far from what he'd been expecting when he'd left the house to go to the club this evening, tonight was turning into a very good night indeed.

Gabe reluctantly let himself out of Rosalind's suite a few hours later. It had been tempting to stay and linger longer but he needed to get home to the ranch, get showered and dressed and return to town in time for his breakfast meeting at the Royal Diner.

All through his drive home he replayed the night he'd had with the exquisite and talented Ms. Rosalind Banks. They'd connected so intimately in the bedroom—and out of it too, he remembered with a broad grin. And even though he hadn't snatched more than an hour or two of sleep, he felt invigorated in a way he hadn't felt in a very long time. It was probably just as well they weren't suited as far as his Grand Plan for his future went. He already felt the kind of emotional pull to return to her that he'd sworn he wouldn't allow himself to feel again for any woman.

No, Rosalind Banks was good for one night—better than good—and that's where it began and ended. For them both. Their individual expectations were not compatible with what they each wanted out of life—a shame, really, but it couldn't be helped.

He turned his mind to the potential wife candidate he was meeting this morning. The matchmaker had only provided a photo and the basics of height, weight and employment, but nothing personal. Nothing like how she'd smell when he got close and lifted her hair to nuzzle her neck. Nothing like how soft her skin would feel beneath his lightly calloused fingers.

Gabe dragged his thoughts back to the road ahead of him. Nope, he wasn't going there. That way led straight to the woman he'd left in tangled sheets and a warm bed. By the time he'd reached the ranch, rushed through his ablutions, re-dressed and headed back out to the diner, weariness started to pull at him. Maybe this wasn't such a great idea, but it was too late to back out now. He'd paid his fee; he'd made his expectations explicitly clear and the matchmaker had promised to deliver.

And deliver she did. The prospective wife candidate was a beautiful, poised and accomplished woman. In fact, in many ways she was a feminine version of himself. Jaded by love but still hoping for stability and family. But no matter how perfectly they were suited—and if you'd asked him yesterday, he would have said she was hands-down exactly what he was looking for—he couldn't summon even a speck of interest. He'd at least hoped that his prospective bride would light some spark within him.

He pushed a piece of bacon onto his fork and swirled it around in the maple syrup that had poured off his pancake stack and wondered what Rosalind was eating for breakfast, before snapping his attention back to his date.

"I'm sorry, what was that you said?" he enquired, trying to inject something in his voice that would say he was anything but bored out of his mind.

"That woman over there, she keeps staring at you. And look, now she's coming over to our table."

Gabe looked up in time to see a petite, blond woman stride confidently toward their table.

"Friend of yours?" his date asked.

"No friend of mine."

He recognized her immediately. Sierra Morgan. The reporter for *America* magazine. She also freelanced for the Royal Gazette, recently doing a story about Cammie Wentworth finding a baby boy in his capsule, left on the trunk of her car. Ms. Morgan originally came to Royal to do a story on the tenth anniversary of the Texas Cattleman's Club finally admitting women, but she kept ferreting around for another story and had pestered him about his family history before. He'd put her off but now he had the distinct feeling she wasn't going to be put off a moment longer.

"Hi," she said with a wide grin as she reached the table. "Mr. Carrington, you remember me, don't you? Sierra Morgan, investigative journalist."

"A reporter?" Gabe's wife candidate stared at him in irritation. "I'm not talking to any reporter. My private life is exactly that. And, to be honest, I don't think you're what I'm looking for. Thank you for breakfast, but I'm out."

And with that, she rose to her feet, grabbed her bag and headed for the door. Gabe watched in stunned amazement.

"Was it something I said?" Sierra Morgan asked as she eased into the recently vacated seat.

Gabe turned his gaze on her. "Looks like it."

"I'm sorry, but I really wanted to catch you. You know I want to interview you about your family history and now's as good a time as any, right?"

Actually, no time was a good time as far as he was concerned.

"My family history is not up for discussion," he said firmly and pushed his plate aside, all appetite now gone.

"Look, let me at least run something by you. See if it rings any bells in the family-skeleton department."

She was nothing if not persistent. Gabe sighed and raised a hand to order more coffee.

"Fine," he said. Maybe the quickest way to get rid of her for good was to hear her out. "I'll listen, but that's it."

She smiled her thanks and added her coffee order when the waitress came over. When the coffee arrived, she took a gulp then put the mug down on the table in front of her, her hands cupping the ceramic, and leaning her elbows on the table.

"You know that baby Micah's mom, Arielle Martin, had been working at the Royal Assisted Living Center before she died, right? I understand you met her?"

Gabe nodded. He'd heard about the poor woman's passing and knew from their brief meeting that she'd been a budding photojournalist before her tragic death. Was that where Sierra was coming from? Did they have some professional link?

"Her diary tells us that she was fascinated by the centenarian who lives there, Harmon Wentworth. He told her a story that his powerful family had kept hush-hush, but that now he's decided that maybe it's time for someone to find out the truth. You know he discovered late in life that he was adopted by the Wentworth family. Well, it turns out that Arielle had some notes in her diary that suggest that Harmon is possibly connected to the Langley family."

Gabe felt a prick of concern. The Langley family members were long-standing Royal inhabitants, in fact they dated right back to the founding of the Texas Cattleman's Club many years ago. He knew Sierra was in town to write about the special anniversary of the club, but what the hell else had she unearthed?

"Carry on," he encouraged.

"Well, from what I can tell, Arielle tried to talk to the Wentworths about the link, but they clammed up, politely but very definitely telling her they would not discuss the matter. But she kept digging and she's mentioned another name in her diary, Violetta Ford, underlined three times, so it obviously was important to her."

Gabe had heard about the Ford woman. She'd been considered a rebel in her day, a confirmed spinster who'd run her own small ranch single-handedly until being joined by a young cowgirl, Emmalou Hilliard, who was now ninety-nine years old. As a rancher, Violetta Ford had demanded to be admitted to the newly founded Texas Cattleman's Club, but her gender had made her ineligible. Something she hadn't accepted well it seemed, because she'd sold up and left town permanently not long after her request for membership had been emphatically denied.

Sierra was still talking so he turned his mind back to what she was saying.

"I think this Violetta Ford could have been Harmon Wentworth's birth mother but I need to find someone who might have heard an old family story about her possibly having an affair with another rancher in the district. I know your family were neighbors of the Wentworths back then and I know from Arielle's diary that she spoke to you about your family history. Can you shed any more light on this for me? Have you heard of Violetta Ford and could one of your ancestors possibly have had an affair with her?"

Gabe slowly shook his head. This was getting so convoluted even he, who had a mind like a steel trap, was getting muddled.

"Everyone here has heard of Violetta Ford but you're barking up the wrong tree if you think she was Harmon Wentworth's birth mother. You can barely keep a secret in Royal these days—can you imagine how much more difficult it would have been back then with its much smaller population? Ms. Morgan, you really need to try again to talk to the Wentworths about this. I certainly can't help you and I know for sure that no one in my family would be interested in digging up old stories."

The journalist huffed a sharp breath in frustration. "What is it with you people? Aren't you interested in helping out an old man to find his true roots? Is no one here interested in the past?"

"You'll find we're passionate about protecting the past and our people. I'm sorry, but that's all I'm pre-pared to say."

"Fine, well, you haven't seen the last of me. I'm not giving up."

He watched her gather her things and leave. For a small woman she moved with huge energy. His coffee had gone cold so he flicked several bills on the table and got up to head back to the ranch. Outside, he saw the indubitable Ms. Morgan get behind the wheel of her car and drive away. She was nothing if not persistent. Trouble was, what the hell was she going to unearth with that strength of determination?

Three

December

Rosalind knew she'd been eating the right things and getting enough rest; goodness knew she needed naps and more sleep at night than she ever had before. She'd put it down to the frenetic workload she'd given herself once she hit New York, starting with finding accommodation that she could work out of in the short term, and continuing with meetings with buyers for various retail groups and smaller exclusive boutique owners who could feature her ranges.

They were running at a massive loss on the leisure-wear range, but Piers was optimistic that the pop-up stores through Australia and New Zealand during this whole month of December would be a huge hit. She could only keep her fingers crossed that he was right and hope that the new designs she'd worked up and costed would appeal to the new players she was targeting here in America.

All this travel and time zone changes and the demands of her work had really taken a toll, she thought as she dressed in one of her leisure-wear outfits and went to her automatic coffee maker which had her favorite brew ready and waiting, its aroma filling the tiny kitchen the way it did every morning. She took one step into the kitchen, however, and did an abrupt about-face and headed straight to the bathroom as a huge wave of nausea hit her. She managed not to throw up and the cold facecloth she bathed her face and the back of her neck with was a huge help, but when she looked at herself in the mirror, she knew she couldn't deny it any longer.

There was a distinct possibility she was pregnant. Admitting the news to herself wasn't quite as shocking as she'd anticipated. She'd always wanted kids, but she'd also always hoped for the love and marriage part, first. Having a baby now was the worst possible timing, especially here in New York on her own with no physical support network to help her out. And with her business holding on by a thread she had two choices—buy into Gabriel Carrington's marriage of convenience, if he was still available, or go home. To calm her mind, she started to make a list; at the top was buying a home pregnancy test and finding out if she was, indeed, pregnant. Then, if she was pregnant, she had to let Gabriel Carrington know he was going to be a daddy.

It shocked her to realize he'd never been far from her thoughts this past month, even more so than her disappointment that Drake had so clearly moved on without her. In fact, she'd barely spared Drake a thought. Shouldn't she have been more cut up about him? While they'd only been together a little under six months, she'd been prepared to spend her life with him and now it looked as though she'd have a lifelong contact with one of his peers instead. And for some crazy mixed-up reason, that knowledge sent a thrill of anticipation through her.

She and Gabe had experienced such a powerful connection, but could they build on that? She only hoped. What if he had already found his perfect wife candidate and entered into a contract? The thought pinged an emotion not unlike envy, which surprised her and made her reexamine her feelings for Gabriel in a new light. Ros had thought she'd been thinking solely in terms of the baby but it wasn't just about a child anymore, was it? She really wanted to see Gabe again, get to know him better, maybe even fall in love even if he said he didn't believe in such a thing—after all, they'd been bloody amazing in bed; surely they could find common ground in other areas, too.

From what he'd said at the gala, he'd expect her to marry him and she wasn't sure how she felt about that. She'd always considered marriage the penultimate goal of a strong and loving relationship, with a family coming next to seal everything. They barely knew one another, but they were going to be parents together. He wasn't looking for love and she knew she couldn't live with a loveless future. So where did that leave them? She had no doubt that with mutual respect they could make a marriage work, but would that be enough for her? She had to hope so or this entire situation became impossible, no matter which way she turned it. Ros snorted and looked at herself in the mirror. Here she was overthinking things when she didn't even know for sure if she was pregnant. One hand settled on her lower belly and she continued to look at her reflection. Pregnant. It felt oddly right thinking about bringing a child into her life even if the timing was all wrong. But a child shared with a man who didn't believe in love? It could make for a rocky future.

She tipped out the coffee carafe and made a cup of tea and some toast. While she ate and sipped her tea, she added to her list. One, find out if she was expecting. Everything hinged on that result. Then when she knew, it would either be life as normal, or she'd be searching flights to Royal.

At the drugstore she bought three tests, just to be certain. Twenty minutes later she had her answer. Positive. Positive. Positive. She was having a baby. The truth of it was exhilarating and terrifying in equal proportion. She hugged the news to herself for the rest of the day while she decided how best to approach Gabe. A phone call wouldn't cut it; she knew that. She had to tell him face-to-face.

Before Rosalind could change her mind, she looked up flights online and made her booking. That done, she reached deep into her wardrobe, hauled out her suitcase and began to throw things into it. She had no idea what she needed or how long she'd be there. That it would be cold was a given, but hopefully not as cold as New York. Her furnished apartment was paid up until the end of December and by then she'd know for certain if she was returning to it, or not. She tossed in her sketchbooks and art supplies while she was at it. No one said she'd have to stop working while she was there.

Three hours later she was on her way to the airport, that weird feeling in her belly one of nerves rather than nausea. How would he take the news and what if he'd already found that wife he was looking for? She just had to wait and find out.

Gabe looked up from his office desk as a chime warned him of a vehicle coming up the long driveway to his home. He didn't recognize the midsize SUV that travelled slowly as if the driver was unfamiliar with both the vehicle and the terrain. He rose from his desk and walked to the window and watched as the SUV pulled up outside his house and the driver's door flung open. Every muscle in his body pulled tight as he identified the curvy blonde figure that alighted.

Rosalind Banks. The last woman he expected to see either here or anywhere else, for that matter. He took the opportunity to study her carefully. It had been a month since he'd left her at the Bellamy. A month where he'd interviewed and rejected several potential candidates for what he now called Project Wife. And it was all her fault. For some idiotic reason, he hadn't been able to get her out of his mind and, equally stupidly, he'd held every other woman up to her image and found them wanting.

He thought he'd seen the last of her, so what the hell was she doing here and how had she found where he lived? She looked tired, paler than he remembered and the jeans she wore with a totally impractical pair of heeled ankle boots looked as if they'd been painted on her long legs. Something inside him hitched hard as he remembered those legs wrapped around his waist as he entered her body. He forced the memory from his mind. That was half his problem these days. Not being able to keep those sneaky thoughts of her from interrupting him at the most inconvenient moments. Hell, they'd barely known one another and yet she'd snuck under his skin like a burr under a saddle.

As he watched, she seemed to pull herself up a little taller and square her shoulders before making her way up the shallow stairs that led to the entrance to his single-story sprawling home settled atop a small hill. Gabe turned from the window and headed toward the entrance hall.

Rosalind looked a little taken aback as he opened the door.

"Oh, hi, I wasn't sure you'd be home, or out there somewhere." She gestured toward the range that spread as far as the eye could see.

"As you can see, I'm home. I didn't expect to see you again. How did you know where to find me?"

"I asked at a gas station just out of town. But…" She hesitated and chewed on that deliciously full lower lip for a moment before sucking in a deep breath and continuing. "Something came up. Something I needed to discuss with you, urgently."

"You'd better come in then. Follow me."

He closed the door behind her and led her to the inviting family room near his kitchen. The couches here were long and comfortable and bracketed the double-sided fireplace that also opened onto a casual dining area on the other side. The tall brick chimney that stretched to the top of the double-height ceiling featured a wagon wheel from his great-grandfather's first wagon. Gabriel liked the reminder of where and who his family had sprung from and the permanence of the Carrington family on the landscape here. One day this would all belong to his heir—provided he reached a satisfying conclusion to Project Wife.

"Take a seat. Can I get you anything to drink? A coffee, water, something stronger?"

"Water would be great, thank you."

He nodded and went to the kitchen where he grabbed a couple of water bottles and glasses. He brought them through, pouring Rosalind's out for her and handing her the glass. The moment their fingers brushed he was aware of that sizzling reaction he'd experienced the first time he'd touched her. Seems time had not allowed that primal reaction to abate at all. Obviously one torrid night with Ms. Banks had not been enough, but he wasn't into a short-term fling, he reminded himself. He was on the hunt for a wife and he and Rosalind were on different trajectories when it came to that no matter how compatible they'd been in the bedroom.

"What brings you back to Royal?" he asked, settling on the couch opposite hers. "You mentioned needing to discuss something with me urgently?"

For all she'd used the word *urgent* she didn't appear to be in a hurry to fill him in on the reason behind her unexpected visit. Instead, she gave him a weak smile and took a long gulp of her water. She set her glass down on the coaster on the table in front of her and hitched forward a little on her seat, her fingers clasped tightly on her knees. He didn't know her well but he was pretty good at reading people and she clearly didn't expect him to take whatever it was that she was here to tell him very well.

"Yes, a…complication relating to our night together," she said softly, her eyes dropping to the thick rug on the floor at her booted feet.

"A complication?"

Gabe pushed back the burr of irritation that made him want to urge her to just get on with what she'd come to say. He waited, his eyes fixed on the top of her head. When she looked up, their eyes locked and he saw the muscles in her throat work nervously as she swallowed.

"I'm pregnant," she said.

A roaring sound filled his ears and he shook his head slightly. "You're what?"

"Pregnant. With your baby."

"Are you sure?"

"That I'm pregnant or that it's yours?" she said with a slight bite to her tone.

"Yeah." For all he knew, she could have been with any number of men before or after that night they spent together.

"I am. To both. I must have made a mistake with my pill with the time zone changes and everything but I can assure you that the baby is definitely yours."

Her voice was clipped and she reached for her glass again. This time her hand shook a little as she tipped the liquid into her mouth.

"Well," Gabe said and then ran out of steam as to what to say next. A baby? *His* baby? Wasn't that what he wanted all along?

"Yeah, *well*," she repeated. "Obviously this is very inconvenient for both of us. I only just found out and I didn't think it was the kind of thing I could tell you on the phone, even if I had your number. But I wanted you to know before…"

"Before?" Gabe's blood ran cold. Instinct surged and the need to protect and provide for his child bloomed from deep inside.

She shrugged. "I don't know. Before I made my mind up about what I should do, I guess. To be honest, I didn't think much past telling you. Look, we got on pretty well that night we met and I think we could make this work. But if you're not interested, or if you're already married, then I'll go back to Australia. I can't bring this child up on my own."

Got on pretty well? The woman was a master of understatement. Even now, looking at her, all he wanted to do was take her in his arms and give in to the desire to kiss and taste every part of her body. But then the second part of what she said sank in. Head back to Australia? No way. If she did that he'd likely never see his child again—or her, a tiny voice tickled at the back of his mind. Ice ran in his veins.

"No," he said bluntly.

"No, what?"

"No, you're not taking this baby, if it is my baby, to Australia. He or she will stay here and be raised as a Carrington."

"It is your baby, Gabriel," she said softly. "I swear."

He looked deep into her blue eyes and saw the honesty that reflected back at him and knew, deep in his gut, she wasn't lying about this.

"We'll get married," he said firmly.

"I figured you'd say that. Are you sure that's the best thing to do? We don't even know each other. You're prepared to marry a complete stranger?"

"Not a *complete* stranger," he answered and watched as she blushed at his words.

"You know what I mean," she snapped. "This isn't a joking matter, Gabe."

"No, it isn't, and I am serious. Marry me. You'll be free to pursue your business interests and I will have the heir I wanted."

Her mouth twisted ruefully. "And what about us? As a couple? Will we be…intimate?"

He felt a thrill of excitement at the thought and quelled it rapidly. That wasn't what he wanted. He'd seen what unrealistic expectations of love did to people. If he could keep this clinical, no one would get hurt. "I wouldn't want it to lead to any misunderstandings or complications," he hedged.

"Complications like falling in love?" she asked bluntly.

"Exactly."

Ros fell silent and chewed on her lower lip again. He found his gaze fixated on that part of her, remembering the feel and the texture of her lips, her whole mouth, beneath his and on his body. Heat flared deep inside him and the urge to relive the night they'd spent together flared along with it.

He sounded so adamant—his single-word response reverberating through her. Love, to him, was a problem, not a joyful sharing of life and emotions and happiness. She didn't know how she'd cope without that. She flicked her eyes to where he sat opposite her, patiently waiting for her response. Or not quite so patiently, she realized, as she noted the vein pulsing rapidly on the side of his neck. Perhaps he wasn't quite so calm about this after all.

And nor was she. Seeing him again had reminded her of how beautifully they'd meshed and melded together that night. The passion between them had been off the scale. Even now, just looking at him, in casual jeans and a fitted black sweater that clung to every line of his torso like a lover's caress, made her heart rate pick up and her breasts feel full and heavy, longing for the touch of his incredibly talented long fingers. Of the touch of his lips and tongue.

Rosalind squirmed slightly on the couch but it offered her no relief from the discomfort that her arousal brought. There was only one thing that would assuage that, she thought ruefully.

Could she do it? Could she accept his crazy proposal? And what if they never made love—ever—because it, in his words, could make things complicated? This entire situation made no sense to her at all. She'd always wanted love and marriage and a family—in that order. Was it ridiculous of her to want what her parents and so many of her friends had? But the fact remained everything was happening in reverse. She was carrying Gabe's baby and she owed this little stranger inside her body the very best of everything and that included their father being a very present person in their life. There was no doubt that Gabe fully expected to be that person and that he could offer the best of everything to his son or daughter, especially if this home was anything to go by. And what of love? She didn't doubt that Gabe would love their baby with every fiber of his being. It was clear in the determined and implacable way he'd presented her with his solution to her current predicament. But could she live her life without at least the expectation of love? Would financial security be enough?

If she said no, she'd have to return to Sydney and try to pick up the pieces of her business there, which would diminish her chances of successfully breaking into the market here in the States and inevitably lead to staff losses and a massive drop in brand awareness—not to mention the complications of megalong-distance shared custody. If she said yes, she'd receive a cash injection to her business that would allow her to keep her employees on and to make an aggressive push to expand right alongside being an active daily part of her baby's life.

One thing was certain. There was no chance to potentially develop a relationship with her baby's father if she moved back home, and she wanted that opportunity. Accepting that truth left her with only one answer.

"Yes," she said.

Four

Gabe looked around him at the small group of guests he'd invited to celebrate his and Rosalind's nuptials here at the Club. Given the short notice, not everyone he'd invited had been able to attend but of those who could, it was great to see the lack of judgment as they'd been introduced to his new bride.

He rolled the word around in his mind a moment or two. He still couldn't believe they'd pulled this together in a little under five days but from the moment she'd said yes to him, he'd put things in motion with his lawyer and managed to find a local doctor who could care for Rosalind during her pregnancy. One of his dad's cronies, a judge, had been only too happy to marry them in his chambers after the requisite seventy-two hour wait time from when their application to marry had been approved.

Gabe's father, as usual, had been unavailable and his

grandfather was out of town. He'd only invited them as a matter of courtesy and had been relieved when Denver Carrington had sent his apologies, with an invitation to lunch at a later date. Gabe had accepted the invitation, happy to end the call to his dad as quickly as possible. He watched as Rosalind laughed at something one of his friends said and wondered what his mother would think of the whole situation. She had loved her husband dearly and he'd stomped all over that love with steel-capped boots. Would she be sorry that her only son had chosen a practical marriage versus one that might risk his heart?

He took a sip of the very fine champagne being circulated freely around the room and turned as one of their guests hailed him.

"Gabe, congratulations."

Carson Wentworth approached him with a genuine smile wreathing his face. The current president of the Texas Cattleman's Club, Carson had beaten the next-strongest candidate, Lana Langley, by a decent margin but his win had only served to feed the flames of the ongoing feud between the two families.

"I see you got your wish," Carson said as he stopped next to Gabe.

"Thanks, Carson. Glad you could make it to celebrate with us."

"To be honest, I thought you had a pretty tall order when I heard the rumors about you looking for a wife. I understood marriages of convenience went out with the horse and cart." Carson laughed and raised his glass in a toast. "But I mean it when I say congratulations. I met Rosalind just now and she's a keeper. Intelligent and beautiful. You two make a perfect pair. I hope you grow to be very happy together."

Gabe raised his glass in acknowledgment and took another sip. It seemed that Rosalind was winning everyone over. Even himself, which was something he neither anticipated nor truly wanted. He had no difficulty with liking her but, annoyingly, he found himself thinking about her all the time, even looking forward to seeing her when they'd met for their various appointments and wedding planning in the days preceding their ceremony.

"We suit one another and we're both committed to making this work," he said firmly. "Say, how's your great-grandfather doing? It's been a while since I've seen him."

Carson frowned. "He's doing okay. Frailer now, of course, but that's only to be expected given he's a hundred years old. If anything, though, his mind is even sharper than before, with the exception of this bee he has in his bonnet about being adopted. If it is true, I can understand why he wants to find closure before he passes away, but the chances of finding out anything new at this stage are pretty slim."

"I keep hearing about this diary of that photojournalist, Arielle Martin. Do you think she uncovered anything important before she died?"

"There are rumors and apparently he told her something in confidence, but you know as well as I do that all too often rumors are not based in fact, especially around here. Oh, and that's not all Harmon is obsessed with. He's been harping on about ending the feud between the Langleys and the Wentworths. Says it's gone on long enough. From my side of the fence, I'm more than happy to lay down arms, so to speak, but I doubt the Langleys are as keen. Especially since I beat Lana to the presidency here at the club. Trouble is, Harmon has made it clear that if there isn't some kind of truce soon, he's going to take the club out of his will."

Carson looked deeply concerned by this new revelation.

"The club's solvent enough without his bequest, surely?" Gabe asked.

"Yes, but we want to do bigger and better things for the entire community of Royal. That's going to take big money, too."

Before he could discuss the problem any further, they were interrupted by Rosalind. Gabe let his eyes roam over her, hardly daring to believe this enticing creature was not only his wife, but also carrying his child. It punched something deep inside him, making him feel a connection to her that he was ill equipped to handle right now. He hadn't expected to feel like that. Hadn't wanted to. And yet, she'd somehow begun to slip beneath his defenses and nestle somewhere within the fortress of his heart. He cast the idea aside as quickly as it bloomed in his mind. His heart was not engaged in this venture. That was not what this was about.

Even so, he'd barely been able to tear his eyes from Rosalind. Dressed in an ivory knee-length dress which had a floor-length overskirt of something light and filmy that caught the light and glittered softly as she moved and with her hair flowing loose over her shoulders, she had an almost ethereal look. And she was his. That knowledge fed something in him he didn't even know he craved. Craving was not part of their contract, he reminded himself firmly. For now, it was enough that she'd agreed to his terms and that he'd agreed to hers. Their marriage was an amicable legal agreement and he needed to remind himself to keep it that way.

"They're going to start the dancing soon," she said,

putting a hand on his arm and leaning up to talk to him more privately. "Are you up for it?"

They'd discussed this earlier but hadn't reached a decision. They'd had to pull everything together so quickly that thinking about a wedding dance had been the last thing on his mind. But now that the ink was dry on their marriage maybe it was time to relax and actually enjoy the evening.

"Always," he said, taking her hand in his and giving it a light squeeze. "Carson, would you excuse us? We have a dance to enjoy together."

"By all means," Carson said with a broad grin. "Don't let me stop you."

Gabe led Rosalind toward the dance floor of the function room and nodded toward the leader of the band the club had hired. The man nodded back and drew the set they'd been playing to a halt. Then, with an announcement to the crowd to welcome the newly wed Mr. and Mrs. Carrington to the floor, the band swung into a slow dance. Gabe pulled Ros into his arms and guided her around the floor. Around the perimeter, many of his friends applauded vigorously before, two by two, joining them. He knew no one had expected him to pull this off, in fact, many had counselled him against such a partnership, but a sense of exhilaration filled him as he and Ros danced smoothly together and he realized that his goal had been unequivocally achieved.

"You look pleased with yourself," Ros said, looking up at him with a smile.

"I am."

"It's all gone well today, hasn't it?" she said with a note of satisfaction. "And everyone has been quite welcoming. I didn't really expect such a turnout. Do you think they're all here because they're curious about me or because they wanted to take advantage of your generosity in throwing a big party?"

"Maybe they're just happy for us," Gabe said, but he couldn't deny that she was likely correct about their curiosity about her.

"We both know that is a big reach of the imagination."

"Well, there are always romantics in every situation. People who view the world through rose-tinted glasses and are always looking for the happy-ever-after."

"People like me, you mean?" she asked pointedly.

"But even you saw the practicality of our arrangement," he responded.

"I didn't really have a lot of choice, but yes. Our arrangement is practical, for both of us. By the way, thank you for the advance of funds. My operations manager confirmed receipt of it today. It will go a long way toward providing stability for my team."

"I'm glad it is going to good use. To be honest, when I first came up with the idea of this marriage arrangement, I expected whoever I ended up with would likely be more frivolous with the settlement. But you're not like that, are you?"

"We really don't know each other at all, do we?" she said, a note of concern in her voice. "This is going to work, isn't it?"

"Of course it is. We know exactly where we both stand. There are no messy feelings involved nor unreasonable expectations from either of us of one another. Most importantly, our child will be loved and provided for more than amply. What could go wrong?"

"Shh, don't tempt fate," she said. "Look, we both know what we entered this marriage for. Neither of us are children. It wasn't what I expected for my future but I'm going to give it my very best to ensure I hold up my end of the deal."

"Then we remain in agreement. See, it's not so hard. We've got this marriage thing down." He laughed a little but could sense she still suffered some concern about their situation.

She huffed out a short breath before replying. "We've been married for all of five hours. We can hardly use this as an example of how things will continue between us."

"But you forget, in the past few days we've spent many, many hours together working out the important things that most couples don't or won't face up to until it's all falling apart. We have everything bound up neatly and put in place to ensure our marital stability."

"Yes, we do," she agreed. "I'm a little tired—do you mind if we sit the next one out?"

"Of course we can. We can even slip away soon, if you'd prefer to head home."

Home. He meant his home, of course. She had no idea if or when the sprawling ranch house built of wood and stone where he lived would ever feel like home to her. It was so different from everything she'd ever known. The wide, open spaces that surrounded the house, the stock, the horses—it was a foreign land to this city girl and she felt thoroughly displaced.

To hold on to the last remnants of normalcy in her life, she'd remained at the Bellamy since her return to Royal. From there she'd arranged for the last of her personal items to be shipped from her New York apartment but she hadn't quite been able to bring herself to cancel the lease just yet. Realistically, she knew she didn't need to keep the place but a small part of her wanted to ensure she had somewhere to escape to, should she need it. A place that was still hers outside the life she'd been absorbed into here in Royal.

Wow, and as if that didn't sound dramatic, she castigated herself silently as Gabe led her to a quieter seating area just off the main function room. Before they could leave, however, a young woman with fine blond hair and a slight build walked up to them, a camera slung around her neck and a notebook and pen in her hands.

"Congratulations," she said with a big smile. "Would you mind posing for a photo for the local paper? I'd love to do a small feature on the two of you, if you have a moment."

"Ms. Morgan, this is a private function. Invited guests only. What are you doing here?" Gabe said in a forbidding tone.

The woman continued to smile but Ros noted that her green eyes didn't quite reflect the friendliness she was projecting.

"Mr. Carrington, you know I'm doing some freelancing since I'm in town. This is a bit of fluff for the local paper, not an attack on your family's integrity or asking you to haul any skeletons from the closet," she said patiently. "Please, just a photo, then."

"Gabe," Ros said softly to her husband. "We can do a photo, surely."

His arm was rigid beneath her hand but he turned to her and asked, "Are you sure?"

"Of course. Better that our marriage is publicized on our terms than as the subject of gossip, right?"

He took a moment to consider her words before nodding to the reporter who'd avidly watched the interplay between them.

"Fine, a photo."

"Great, thank you. If you two could stand a little closer...closer still. Yes, like that."

She continued to fire directions at them as she took several shots. Ros had curved her arm around Gabe's back, under his jacket, and the heat from his body suffused her arm and spread slowly through her body. He still held himself quite rigid, as though this entire thing was a torment. And maybe to him it was. She herself was used to being around cameras but not often the subject of them. By the time the reporter stopped taking pictures Ros was done with smiling and posing. It gave her a new appreciation for her models, who went through this every day of their working lives.

"These are great! Thank you both," she exclaimed brightly.

The woman turned and strode away, tucking her notebook and pen in her large bag as she did.

"There, that was relatively painless," Ros said with a smile at Gabe.

"For you, maybe. I prefer to keep my private life, private."

He led her to a smaller seating area away from their function room. The chairs were deep and comfortable and the room was uninhabited except for a staff member cleaning glasses at the bar off to one side.

"I'll get you some water," he said after she'd settled in a chair.

"A cup of tea would be nice. Hot tea, with a dash of milk. English Breakfast if they have it."

"In a land of sweetened cold tea drinkers that might

be a stretch but I'm sure I'll be able to rustle up something for you," he said with a teasing smile.

That smile sent a bolt of awareness deep into her core. The man was almost unlawfully good looking. And he was her husband! She looked down at the ornate diamond wedding ring he'd placed on her finger in the judge's chambers earlier today. It was a beautiful piece of jewelry but it felt heavy and foreign on her finger. His own ring had been far simpler and her fingers had trembled as she'd slid the heavy gold signet ring embedded with a single diamond and engraved with his initials onto his finger.

The importance of what she'd agreed to do had been underlined by the simple act of exchanging rings. The relief she'd experienced in that moment had been palpable. And, of course, it wasn't just knowing her staff would be okay, but the baby she was carrying, too. She had a responsibility to ensure her baby had the best life she could provide, something she was increasingly anxious about. After all, what did she know about raising a child?

Gabe was trying so hard to make everything feel normal, or as normal as it got when you'd just hitched yourself to a virtual stranger. But he hadn't forced her into this marriage, she reminded herself. She'd gone into this with her eyes wide open and her business would survive as a result of it. And their baby would want for nothing. Nor would she, financially at least. Gabe had been more than generous with the marriage settlement which had been designed to buoy her business through this difficult time.

But emotionally? Would she be able to live her life without the tenets of a long and happy marriage—love, commitment to one another, like minds—the way her parents had?

Gabe returned with a small tray.

"Just regular black tea, I'm afraid. But piping hot with not a touch of sweetener to be seen or tasted," he said, setting the tray down on the side table by her chair.

"Thank you. I'm sure it'll revive me in a minute or two."

"Seriously, I meant it when I said we could head home if you'd prefer. No one will blame us. It is our wedding night after all."

But would it be a normal wedding night? Ros wondered on an unexpected surge of desire that chased away her weariness and replaced it with a thrum of something far more primal. She made a decision.

"Okay, let me have a cup of this tea and after that we'll go."

"Good, I'll have my car brought round. Take your time over the tea."

He was gone again leaving her to watch his tall figure striding purposefully away. Even watching him from the back made everything ping in her body. There was latent strength in the way he moved, purpose in every step. He was utterly mesmerizing. Once he was out of sight, she poured the tea, added a dash of milk and lifted the cup to take a sip. She sighed with pleasure. The tea was perfect and just what she felt like right now. She was grateful for his consideration in getting it for her.

But that gratitude didn't stop a quiver of unease from rippling through her as she wondered anew how this would all work out. On paper everything had made sense, but her emotions were beginning to spiral on different tangents right now. She was fiercely attracted to him on a physical level and she knew that if they could enjoy intimacy together they stood a very good chance of making their marriage work, of developing strong feelings for one another. She wanted that to the depths of her soul and the optimist that dwelled inside her hoped they could achieve it. But could she crack the fierce control he had on his emotions? Could she get him to open up to her and let her into his heart the way she was willing to let him into hers?

As if she'd willingly conjured him up, Gabe reappeared striding back toward her and she felt a flutter of awareness as he approached.

"How's the tea?" he asked, sitting next to her and draping one arm across the back of her shoulders.

His fingers lightly brushed the top of her arm through the gossamer-fine overcoat she wore with her dress, making every nerve in her body focus on the sensations he created with his casual touch.

"Perfect. I'm feeling a lot better already. Seriously, if you want to stay longer, I'll manage."

"No, I'm all good to head home. I've already let a couple of people know we're slipping away."

Ros put her cup and saucer down and gave him a smile. "Shall we go, then?"

In answer, Gabe rose to his feet again and held out a hand to help her up. Their eyes met and there was that smile again, the one that made the corners of his eyes crinkle just a bit and made the almost obsidian darkness of his irises gleam. Again, she felt that tug of longing. She'd heard that pregnancy could make a woman more sexually responsive—was that what was happening here or was it simply his magnetism that had her all tied up in knots?

A club staff member brought Ros's wrap and bag for

her as they passed through the lobby. Through the main doors she could see Gabe's car gleaming outside. This was to be her life from now on, she reminded herself. She was used to wealth and privilege, after all she'd grown up as a child of a diplomat, but the rarified air of the club together with the obvious wealth so casually displayed by so many of its members was next-level. Life was getting very interesting, indeed.

Five

Ros hadn't paid all that much mind to the distance between Royal and Gabe's ranch when she'd arrived in town the other day but the forty-minute drive there now gave her some idea of the distance involved. Especially when the only lights she saw, aside from the roadside lighting, were from well-spaced ranch houses well into the distance.

"Doesn't the isolation bother you?" she asked, breaking the silence that had lasted between them since they'd pulled away from the club.

"Isolation? Nah, I never think of it that way. I have a ranch manager, Pete, and his wife, Doreen, who is my housekeeper, and their family that live on site as well as Cookie and my ranch hands, some of whom have wives and kids, too. We're our own small community within my own boundaries. I like that no one else can tell me what to do there."

She weighed his words and considered her reply carefully before speaking. "You don't like being told what to do?"

"Does anyone?" He laughed and spared her a glance before focusing on the road ahead. "You're your own boss. I bet you don't like being told what to do, either."

"You're right, I don't. It's one of the reasons I like to surround myself with 'yes' men," she teased. "But you're not a 'yes' man, are you?"

She turned slightly so she could watch him more easily. His face was faintly illuminated by the dashboard lights, throwing his strong features into relief. If anything, he looked even more handsome than he had the first time she'd seen him. Hard to believe it was only a little over five weeks ago. And look where they were now. His brows drew together slightly as he concentrated on his driving, his eyes flicking from the road to his rearview mirror and back again at regular intervals.

"Can't say anyone's ever accused me of that," he acknowledged. "Especially my father."

"Your dad's alive?" she asked, surprised. "When you didn't mention him being on the guest list today, I thought that maybe he had passed on."

"He's very much alive. Likes to think he still has a say in my life. I was relieved he couldn't make it to be honest. Dad and I rub each other the wrong way. Too much water under the bridge between us now for things to be any different."

"You don't think he'll want to be a hands-on grandfather?"

"I'm not sure I want his influence on our child. He wasn't exactly the best example of parenting back when

I was a kid. How about your parents? I'm sorry they couldn't come today. Do you think they'll visit often?"

"They probably will, as much as Dad's diplomatic schedule permits. We've always been close and I'm their only child so our baby will be special to them."

She smiled softly at the memory of the joy her parents had expressed when she'd told them she was getting married. But it had been tempered with concern at her not knowing Gabe very long. But they trusted her judgment and promised to visit as soon as possible.

Gabe slowed the vehicle down and turned into his driveway before traveling up the private road that led to his house. Discreet lighting on the sides of the driveway lit the way to her future home.

The enormity of what she'd done in marrying Gabriel Carrington hit home with all the subtlety of a Texas Longhorn on a tender toe and she drew in a long breath and held it a moment before letting it go. This would all work out. It just had to. She already had the money side of their agreement and it was already in place to do good things for her business. She was on the cusp of negotiations with a major midrange retail chain's head office with a view to introducing her leisure-wear clothing to them and branching out into her formal-wear ranges at a later stage. On the face of things, everything was working out. But tell that to the butterflies dancing in her stomach. The ones suddenly terrified by how all this would turn out.

It bothered her that Gabe had no plans to tie her to him in any way other than through their child and even then, that had been optional. It had been made patently clear that she could choose to walk away at any time. Equally clear was the directive that should she do so, Gabe would assume full custody for their child. Her lawyer had pushed back with a suggestion of shared custody but Gabe had been resolute. She knew visitation would never be enough. She already loved her baby. Because of that Ros was determined to make this marriage work, and last.

As the car approached the five-car garage, the door to one of the bays automatically opened. He drove straight in and stopped the car.

"Welcome home," he said warmly. "I hope you'll be happy here."

"Thank you," she said stiffly and undid her seat belt.

Gabe had already exited the car and was at her door before she could open it, his hand extended to help her out.

"I sent your rental back to the agency," Gabe said as she stood next to him.

"Oh, I thought I'd hold on to it a while longer."

Irritation at his high-handedness tinged her words and she was irked by the tiny smile that pulled at the corner of his mouth. The last thing she wanted was to be completely stuck here.

"Kind of unnecessary when you have a set of wheels of your own," Gabe answered her smoothly and guided her to turn around.

There in front of her was a brand-new midnight-blue Jaguar SUV with a great white satin bow tied on the hood. The inside was filled with white-and-silver balloons.

"A wedding gift," he said and reached in his pocket for a key fob, which he pressed into her hand.

Completely overwhelmed, Ros didn't know what to say or how to respond.

"You're welcome," Gabe said with an ironic twist

to his mouth. "If you don't like it, I can change it for something else."

"No!" she blurted. "It's incredible. I've never owned something like this. And I feel terrible. My gift to you is tiny by comparison. I honestly don't feel I should accept this."

"You need a car and for me it's important you have something safe and reliable. We travel long distances around here and cell phone coverage can be irregular. Think of it as my peace of mind for you and the baby."

"Thank you, Gabe," she said with genuine warmth.

"We can take it out for a drive tomorrow, if you like. Get you used to the feel of it and how it handles."

"I'd like that," she said with a small smile.

Her fingers closed around the fob. Did he understand how important her independence was to her? Was that part of the reason he'd made sure she had a reliable vehicle—so she wouldn't feel trapped here by the circumstances their passion had created?

"Did you want something to eat or drink?" he asked as he started to lead her to the door to the house.

"No, I'm fine. But I wouldn't mind a shower before bed."

"Oh, I think we can do better than that. Come with me."

He led her through the house, their way lit only by subtle downlights about a foot off the floor and positioned every couple of yards along the wall. As they walked farther into the house, the lights popped on as they neared them.

"You live alone in this great big place?" she asked.

"Not anymore now you're here," he answered with a smile and a light squeeze of her hand. "My staff live in their own accommodation on the property. Cookie mostly attends to the ranch hands but makes meals for me to reheat from time to time. I don't mind cooking for myself or eating out for the balance."

He stopped outside large double wooden doors and turned to open them.

"Our suite," he said.

He drew her inside and closed the door behind them. Thick plush carpet covered the floor and the private sitting room was decorated with a large television hung on the wall over a long lightly stained wooden sideboard. Comfortable-looking dove-gray leather easy chairs bracketed a two-seater sofa, and a coffee table that matched the sideboard sat in front of them with a large bowl of fresh fruit on top. Doors led off on either side of the sitting room.

"It looks nice," she said carefully.

"It's a good place to unwind. I haven't used it much, but you're free to use it as your own retreat if you need it." He gestured to the antique desk-and-chair set over by the window. "You can use that area as your home office if you want to—we have ultrafast internet to every room in the house. If this area isn't suitable for you, we can dedicate another room for that if you prefer more privacy. The light is very good in here during the day, so that might be helpful for your drawings."

She was surprised and warmed by his insightfulness. They hadn't even begun to discuss her workspace but it seemed he'd already thought of it.

"Thank you, I think that will do just fine for what I need." She remembered she hadn't yet given him his gift. "Do you know where I can find my things? I have something for you."

"Of course, your room is through here."

He led the way to one of the doors off the sitting

room and opened it wide before gesturing for her to precede him. She stepped into the room and eyed the furnishings with approval. Similar to the sitting room, the predominant tones were in soft dove-gray with lightly stained washed-ash furniture. The bed was immense, and looking at it reminded her anew of the night they'd shared at her hotel, making her insides tighten on a surge of desire, her fingertips tingling with the need to touch him.

Gabe opened another set of doors that led into a massive wardrobe. Ros shifted the direction of her thoughts and looked inside. Someone, his housekeeper, she supposed, had unpacked her clothes and hung them on the rails while the drawers held her tops and undergarments and her shoes were stacked neatly on purpose-built shelves.

"Looks like you'll need to do a bit of shopping. It's kinda empty in here," he teased.

"I don't see your clothing anywhere," she said, looking around.

"It's in my wardrobe."

"We're not sharing a room?"

"I thought you might like to have your own space, while we figure this marriage thing out."

"Oh-kay," she said on a drawn-out breath.

This wasn't quite the start to married life she'd been anticipating but she was prepared to work at it. Just then she spied the wrapped gift she'd had Piers buy for Gabriel and urgent courier to her. It had arrived only this morning and she'd shoved it in her case ready to be sent to the house. Whoever had unpacked for her had left it in easy view on a small shelf in the wardrobe. She reached for it and suddenly felt horribly nervous. He'd bought her a car for goodness sake and all she had for him was this?

"I…ahh. I bought this for you, as your wedding gift. From me."

Gabe took it from her and turned it in his hand, an odd expression on his face. She began to wonder if she ought to have bothered at all, but then he looked up at her and she saw genuine gratitude on his features.

"Thank you," he said warmly.

"You don't know what it is, yet. You might not like it."

"I'm sure I'll love it. Thank you for going to the trouble of getting me something. I know these past few days have been incredibly busy for you."

His long fingers made quick work of unwrapping the box and he opened it carefully, his eyes widening as its contents were revealed. He lifted one platinum cuff link from the box and held it to the light.

"These are beautiful. I've never seen anything with such fire in it. Opals, right?"

"Yes, black opals. Symbolically they're supposed to bring good fortune and the color inside, harmony."

"A prophetic start to our marriage, then."

She hadn't meant to tell him about the symbolism behind the opals. She didn't usually believe in that stuff but it felt right and, let's face it, they needed all the help they could get.

"They're quite stunning. Thank you so much," Gabriel said and carefully put the cuff link back in its case, closed it and slipped it in his pocket. "Now, let me show you your bathroom." He led her into another room off the bedroom.

Ros was wide-eyed as she observed the massive bathroom. A three-yard-long glass-screened shower hugged one wall, adorned with multiple showerheads and a tiled seat for good measure. Certainly big enough for two, she thought, eyeing her husband. A large well-lit vanity unit with twin basins ran along the wall opposite the shower and, at the end of the room in front of floor-length glass, stood a large freestanding tub—again big enough to comfortably accommodate two.

"The glass is privacy tinted and the window looks out onto a walled courtyard so no one can see in. I could draw you a bath if you like?"

"Will you join me?"

She saw his pupils widen and his nostrils flare slightly on a sharply indrawn breath and felt a flicker of hope.

"If you want me to."

She stepped closer to him. "I do."

He took a step back. "This isn't going to be a marriage in the romantic sense, Rosalind. Just so we're clear on that."

His voice was strained and his pupils had dilated, almost consuming the darkness of his eyes. His breathing had quickened. She had no doubt he wanted her right now as much as she wanted him and her body warmed in response, her nipples growing tight and aching for his touch.

"Perfectly," she answered succinctly.

But even though she'd agreed to what he'd said, she was going to do her level best to persuade him differently. And if she couldn't use words, she'd use her body to show him what they could mean to one another.

In response, he shrugged off his jacket and his hands went to the tie at his neck, unknotting it and then swiftly yanking it from under his collar. Next, he undid the buttons of his shirt, which he discarded also before turning on the faucet over the tub. Water rippled from a waterfall-style spout and poured into the large tub. Steam quickly began to fog the window behind. Ros found herself mesmerized by the play of muscles across his back as he bent and swirled something fragrant and foamy in the water.

When he stood and returned to her, she was still frozen in place. Caught by the beauty of this man— this stranger—that she'd married. Gabe moved behind her, removed her sheer overcoat and began to undo the pearl buttons that fastened her dress down the back. One by one, slipping each from its keeper and exposing another inch of skin along the way. As he went, he pressed warm kisses to her spine, making her heart race in anticipation.

Once her dress was undone, he gently slid it from her body, leaving her standing in her heels and her underwear, which consisted of a lacy strapless bra and matching bikini undies in the palest of grays, together with matching garter belt and sheer stockings. Her legs trembled as he ran his hand down one leg and bent to remove first one shoe, then the other. Then, he unsnapped the garter loops, one by one, his fingers strong and gentle and each brush of his fingers on her skin bringing more tingling sensation to her body. Gabe gently rolled down, then removed each stocking with painstaking care before standing again and divesting himself of the rest of his clothing.

The last time she'd seen him naked had been by the dimmed light of her bedroom at the Bellamy and, to be totally honest, she hadn't been that fixated on what he looked like. Only on what he offered at the time which had been a respite from the grueling disappointments of the day. But now, she took her time to look her fill. To admire the shape of his shoulders and the latent strength visible there. To reach out and touch the breadth of his chest and smooth her palms over the sculpted shape of his muscles then the ridges of his abdomen and lower still to the well-defined V that led from his hips and arrowed to his arousal.

Boldly, she took his length in her hands, sighing a little at the heat and smoothness of his skin. It felt like forever since they'd last made love together. Every part of her thrummed to a demanding beat, wanting to touch him all over. Wanting him to touch her.

Gabriel reached around to the back of her bra and unsnapped it, tugging it away from her full and sensitive breasts and tossing the garment to one side. She felt an ache build inside her. Deeper and more insistent than the last time because this time she knew what delights awaited them both. But Gabe seemed to be content with taking his time with her tonight, and why not. They had all night and tomorrow and whatever the future held.

He removed her panties next and held her hand as she stepped free, then he led her to the tub and helped her in. The water was perfect. Not too hot, not too cold, and the silky texture of the foaming bubbles felt divine on her skin. The water rocked a little as he joined her, sliding in behind her and pulling her back against his chest. He lifted her hair and draped it over her shoulder.

"Comfortable?" he asked.

"Very, thank you. And you?"

"I'll be fine for now."

She could still feel his arousal pressed against her lower back and wondered just how comfortable he could be with her leaning against him, but she had to learn to trust him and if he said he was okay, then he must be. It felt decadent to simply lie with him like this and be supported by the warm embrace of his body and the water that surrounded them. Gabe picked up the bottle of liquid he'd added to the bath and poured a little in his hand before massaging his hands together and stroking it over her shoulders and down her arms.

The scent was slightly sweet and slightly spicy and made her feel super sexy and pampered all at the same time. Gabe continued to stroke her, from her arms now to her breasts, then her tummy and lower. The tingling sensations she had experienced before all coalesced in that one point where he touched her now.

"Okay?" he murmured against her ear.

"Better than okay. Way better," she answered and let her legs drop open farther to give him better access.

He was barely touching her but the combination of the warm water and his touch combined to have her panting in seconds as demand grew inside her.

"More, please?" she asked.

He increased the pressure of his fingers as they swirled around her most sensitive point, his other hand cupping one breast and rolling her nipple between thumb and forefinger. She let her head drop back against the solid strength of his shoulder and gave herself over to the sensations that poured through her, rode each wave as it intensified until she suddenly crested—a gasp of sheer delight escaping her as she orgasmed.

Gabe continued to hold her to him. Never before had she felt so protected and satiated at the same time. It was a feeling she could definitely get used to. But what of their marriage? What they shared physically was without par but marriage needed more than sex to survive. Could she hope that maybe they'd become friends, and more, as time progressed? He'd said no romance and he'd been adamant about that. And she'd accepted it, but now she began to wonder if this incendiary connection they had would be enough. If *she* would be enough.

Six

It had been only two days since he and Rosalind had married. Two days where they'd barely left the master suite except to grab some food and drink from time to time. He thought he'd sated himself on her after their wedding night but it appeared he only continued to want her more. And wanted to please her more, too.

It was a worrying trend. He hadn't expected to find himself thinking about her all the time, nor wanting to be with her as much, either. Even today, a day where he was calling on one of Royal's oldest inhabitants before he was scheduled to meet his father for lunch, he'd suggested Ros drive them in her new car. He'd told himself it was because she needed the experience, but he knew it had more to do with his inability to be apart from her for too long.

Gabe directed Ros to turn into the next driveway so he could introduce her to Emmalou Hilliard. The retired cowgirl was still fierce about living independently at the ripe age of ninety-nine years old. He'd invited Emmalou to attend the wedding reception at the club, offering to arrange transport, but she'd refused citing her arthritis in the colder weather making it painful for her to do much more than be in her favorite armchair at home. But she'd insisted on meeting his new bride and invited them to call in at their earliest convenience.

"Are you sure she won't mind us dropping in like this?" Ros asked as she brought the car to a halt outside the old lady's home.

"She'll love it, especially since she gets to meet you before a lot of the other residents around Royal."

He linked his hand with Ros's as they alighted from the car and they approached the front door of the tiny four-room cottage where Emmalou lived alone. Others had suggested she'd be better off at an elder care facility but she stubbornly refused to move. That said, she had accepted help in the form of a cleaner who visited once a week and a team who brought nutritious meals to ensure she kept up her strength.

"Tell me again how you know her?" Ros asked as they approached the front steps.

"Emmalou was one of the early cowgirls in the area. She worked for a lady rancher, Violetta Ford. They were apparently quite a formidable team."

"And this Violetta Ford, I heard someone say at the reception that she left town after some stink about not being able to join the cattleman's club and followed her family back East?"

"Yeah, the same family who'd decided she was an embarrassment to them with her demands to join the club. She ended up selling her ranch to a guy named Vincent Fenwick. By all accounts he was a good rancher. Kept Emmalou on, too, which was forward-thinking of him for the time."

"Well, if she'd already proven herself as a good hand and had a strong working knowledge of the ranch, it would have made sense to keep her, surely."

"Yeah, but times were different then. In fact, it's only in the last ten years that the club allowed women to be members. Apparently, that was something Violetta was very hot under the collar about. When she started the ranch a lot of people laughed at her for being so bold as to step into what was considered very much a man's world, despite the fact ranchers' wives were always busy on the land, too. Despite the lack of support, she made it a success and felt she deserved membership with the club as much as any other rancher did. Regrettably, the old-school good old boys did not." He looked up at the house and smiled. "There's Emmalou now."

The old lady stood on her front porch and bellowed at them. "Are you two gonna stand about all day out there? Come in. You're makin' me let all the heat out!"

"Be right there, Miss Emmalou," Gabe said.

They ascended the stairs and he paused to introduce Rosalind.

"Miss Emmalou, this is my wife, Rosalind Banks."

"Banks, huh? Not taking your name, then? Given your family, I can understand that," she said bluntly with a finger poke at his chest. Emmalou turned and faced Rosalind and looked her up and down. "Yep, you look like you've got staying power. You're gonna need it with this one. I've known him since he was little more than a twinkle in his daddy's eye. He's always been a handful. You'll need to keep your wits about you."

"Thank you for the advice, Ms. Hilliard."

"Call me Emmalou or Miss Emmalou. None of that

Ms. rubbish. I made my choice to remain a spinster and I'm proud of it. No shame in being Miss anything."

Gabe fought a smile as he watched the look of bewilderment take over Ros's features. Emmalou turned around and stomped back into the house.

"Well, come on! You don't wanna keep an old lady on the porch in this cold, do ya?"

Ros bent her head in Gabe's direction. "Is she always like this?"

He grinned back. "Yeah, priceless, huh?"

They followed Emmalou inside and sat exactly where she told them.

"That's it," she said as Ros settled in a chair bathed in the morning light. "Can I get you two any coffee?"

"Not for me, thank you," Ros replied.

"Ros would prefer an herbal tea if you have one. I would love a black coffee."

"I'll see what I can find. People are always bringing round baskets of all manner of things for me. Can't stand most of it but it keeps the cupboards full."

She stomped toward the back of the tiny house and they could hear her muttering as cupboard doors were opened and banged closed again.

Gabe laughed. "I forgot how she can be so blunt. I should have known better. She's always been a pistol."

"Is that what you call it?" Ros said, raising one brow. "She's an original—that's for sure."

After a few moments, Emmalou came back into the sitting room, pushing a small tea trolley set with a lace doily, cups and saucers and a plate of cookies arranged on top. Gabe shot to his feet to aid her.

"No, no, young Gabriel. I can manage just fine, thank you. Used to be I could carry all this on a tray but my balance ain't so grand these days. Getting old is a bitch but it sure beats the alternative!" She cackled a laugh again. "Now, Rosalind, I found some red bush tea in the back of the cupboard. Smells good so I hope it's good for you. Gabriel, here's your coffee."

She handed the hot drinks and then the plate around before settling into her chair. Gabe could almost swear he heard her bones creak.

"Tell me about yourself, Rosalind. Gabriel, here, tells me you're a dressmaker?"

Ros smiled. "Kind of like that. I head up my own fashion brand in Australia and we distribute worldwide. Currently I'm aiming to branch into the market here in America."

"Australia, you say. You got cowgirls there, too, right?"

"Yes, we call them jillaroos."

"Jillaroos, I like that." Emmalou nodded. She turned her attention to Gabe. "Have you met that pesky reporter? What's her name…sounds like a mountain range. Yeah, that's right. Sierra something or other."

"Has she been bothering you?" Gabe asked, ready to do battle if necessary.

"Nothing I can't handle. She was asking about Violetta. I told her she was a good boss until she left and then I just kept on working for the guy who took over the ranch. She kept pestering me about whether or not I knew anything about some danged secret baby Violetta was supposed to have had. Frankly, I told her to mind her own business and leave the past where it lay. She didn't much like that."

"She wouldn't," Gabe said darkly. "About a month ago she asked me if I thought a Carrington could have been Harmon Wentworth's daddy. Ms. Morgan's mind sure goes on tangents."

"I promised Violetta I'd never tell a soul her secrets and she always told me everything. Said it was better than confession, ha! She had one helluva secret, excuse my language."

"And did she tell you that secret?" Ros asked, suddenly fiercely curious.

Emmalou nodded slowly. "She did, but that's in the vault. I ain't telling nobody what she entrusted me with, and that's that. And I know for darn sure she never slept with no Carrington," Emmalou said adamantly.

Which begged the question, did she know if Violetta had slept with someone else? Maybe Emmalou knew a great deal more than she was letting on. One thing was for sure, though. If Sierra Morgan's theories had any basis in fact, she wouldn't be finding that out from Emmalou. The old woman had held her secrets this long; she wasn't about to change now.

They visited a while longer before Emmalou appeared to tire. Gabe stood and reloaded the tea trolley with their cups and the cookie plate and took them through to the kitchen.

"Just leave 'em be," Emmalou called to him from the sitting room. "I'll get to 'em later. Give me something to look forward to."

"If you say so," Gabe said, returning to the sitting room. "Thank you for having us to visit."

"You know you don't need to stand on ceremony with me, boy. Call in any time. You, too," she said, directing her attention to Rosalind. "And take care of each other, y'hear."

"We will," Gabe assured her. "Don't get up. We'll see ourselves out."

"Thank you for the tea, Miss Emmalou," Ros added. "It's been lovely meeting you."

"Nice manners, that one," Emmalou said to Gabe. "You'd better keep your nose clean and hold on to her."

"Yes, ma'am."

They left the old lady sitting in her chair and once they were in the car, Ros turned to Gabe.

"What is that business you two were talking about with her old boss?"

"Just some rumor that's started up. Carson Wentworth's great-grandfather, Harmon, believes he was adopted as a baby, although there are no records to support his claim. A female photojournalist named Arielle Martin who visited Royal last year did some investigating and seemed to think that Violetta was likely his birth mom. It's all conjecture."

"What does that have to do with the reporter?"

"Ms. Morgan is like a dog with a bone on the subject. Thinks she can scent a news story there. It's upset a lot of people and threatens what we've all accepted and believed to be the truth for four generations, not to mention tears the very fabric of the founders of the Texas Cattleman's Club to shreds. She's gotten a hold of Arielle's diary and is following up on what she discovered and is trying to find out who Violetta may have had an affair with. Hell, it all happened a hundred years ago." He shook his head. "The past is best left there."

"Well, at least you know that your family isn't part of it," Ros commented.

"Yeah, there is that."

Ros dropped Gabe off at the RCW Steakhouse where he was supposed to meet his dad. Denver Carrington had been quite specific that he only wished to see Gabe. Gabe had been tempted to tell him to go to hell but Ros had encouraged him to talk to his father and said it would be a good time for her to look around the town while they had lunch. She planned to drive out to the Courtyard shops to browse the antiques shop and crafts studio there. On her return to town she had arranged a meeting with the proprietor of Natalie Valentine's Bridal Shop, with a view to providing some of her evening wear that would work as mother-of-the-bride-or-groom garments, to supplement the range already stocked there.

He admired Ros's drive to look for new opportunities and outlets for her designs. Her mind was constantly working. What he didn't admire, however, was his new and constant need to touch her, or be in the same space as her. Or be thinking about her when he should be doing something else. Like how he was going to get through this lunch with his father without losing his temper as he usually did.

Gabe walked into the RCW Steakhouse and spied his father at his usual table near the back of the restaurant. His father sat there, reading something on his phone, as if he had not a care in the world. Gabe wished he could say the same.

"Dad," he acknowledged as he approached the table.

His father stood and shook his hand. "Congratulations on your marriage, son."

"I thought you'd have wanted to meet my wife. Why didn't you include Ros in your invitation?"

"Can you blame a father for wanting a little one-on-one time with his son?" Denver said with a feeble attempt to look affronted.

"You've never been keen on spending time with me before, why start now?"

"Son, can we put your bitterness toward me aside for an hour or two? If you keep this up, we'll both end up with indigestion. Anyway, I want to say I'm sorry I couldn't make it to your reception."

Gabe had learned many years ago not to expect his father to make it to anything that was important to him. Not high school prize giving, not college graduation. Nothing.

"I saw a picture of your wife in the local paper. Pretty girl."

Even when paying a compliment his dad still managed to be condescending. Gabe counted to three before responding.

"Rosalind is a successful businesswoman. Not only is she incredibly talented in her field, but she's also extremely beautiful. I'm quite sure that *pretty* doesn't exactly cover it."

"Noted," his dad said with a smirk.

Gabe knew he shouldn't have risen to his father's bait, especially not with the number of restaurant patrons with their heads now turned their way.

"It helps if they're pretty, though," his father continued. "Especially if they're good in the sack. Makes a marriage last longer. I hope you have a watertight prenup set up. Wouldn't do to let a stranger get her hands on what's yours."

Gabe didn't respond to his father's crude comments. When Denver had finally left Gabe's mom, after years of cheating on her, he'd married again, only to cheat on that wife with the third Mrs. Carrington. His father was hardly an authority on the subject of a lasting marriage. He'd left each successive wife with little more than enough money to survive on, something that had driven Gabe to ensure he never relied on his father for anything.

He busied himself with studying the menu when

he became aware of someone approaching their table. Sienna Morgan. Again. The woman was as dogged as they came.

"Gentlemen," she said in acknowledgement as they both rose to greet her. "Please, sit down. I won't take much of your time."

"Ms. Morgan," Gabe's dad said with barely concealed dislike. "As you can see, my son and I are enjoying a private lunch together and would prefer to keep it that way. Private. I would also like to state for the record that you have been categorically told by myself and my father that my grandfather did not have an affair with Violetta Ford. If you continue to pursue that line of questioning with us, you will find a lawsuit on your hands."

"Oh, I'm not here to question you," the reporter said staunchly. "In fact, I just wanted to let you know that I've had confirmation that it wasn't a Carrington who had the affair with Violetta."

Gabe spoke up, deciding to take a different tack to his father's threats. "Ms. Morgan, I know you've been to see Emmalou Hilliard. I'd be grateful if you wouldn't bother her again."

"Bother her? I was only asking her to tell me about the good old days. She's bound to have some great stories about when she and Violetta Ford ran the Ford ranch. And Miss Hilliard is likely the only person left alive who can maybe put Harmon Wentworth's mind at rest about his true parentage. Don't you think Harmon has a right to that?"

There was an edge to Sierra Morgan's voice that told Gabe she was none too happy to be told to stay away from one of the only people still alive who'd known Violetta Ford.

"You might never uncover the truth behind Harmon's parentage and all this poking around other people's lives is causing tension. Is that your goal?" Denver Carrington snapped at Sienna Morgan.

"There's a story here—I know it. And if revealing the dirty secrets of Royal's elite is what it takes, then that's what I'll do."

Denver scoffed. "Sensationalism to sell more papers, more like. Now, is there anything else?"

"No, not at the moment," she said with a forced smile.

"Good, then perhaps you'll leave us to our lunch," he said dismissing her.

She nodded before pivoting on her heels and walking away from them.

"Not a fan of Ms. Morgan, then?" Gabe remarked.

"She's a reporter. I don't trust 'em and see no reason to encourage 'em. She's pretty enough, sure, but she certainly doesn't know her place. Now, what are you choosing today? It's my treat."

"Thank you, I'll go with the house special."

Denver looked up at the waiter who'd approached their table the moment the reporter had left. "Make that two house specials, and a bottle of your finest merlot to go along with it."

"Just mineral water for me," Gabe said firmly.

"Oh yeah, I forgot. You're on honeymoon. Need to keep your wits about you, eh? A half bottle then," Denver amended. "So, have you heard any other news lately?"

"Carson told me Harmon announced that unless someone solves the mystery of who his parents truly were and the feuding between the Wentworths and the

Langleys stops, he won't leave a red cent to the Texas Cattleman's Club."

"What? That's just wrong! Nothing matters more than that money in the club's coffers. Maybe that reporter-gal needs to get busy after all."

Not for the first time Gabe realized that his father's concern, first and foremost, was always money. And he might have agreed with him up to a point, except these past days with Rosalind had taught him something else—that other things mattered too, like people and relationships. Gabe felt a shock wave plummet through him at the thought. He'd believed he'd inured himself to the concept of love and happy-ever-after but here he was, wanting to tell his father that money wasn't the be-all and end-all of everything.

"What's the matter, son? You look like you swallowed a fly," Denver said with a bark of laughter.

"Nothing," Gabe said.

But it wasn't nothing. It was anything but. He was developing feelings for his wife. Feelings he hadn't counted on. Feelings he hadn't wanted, period. What the hell was he going to do about that? A spark of interest in the back of his mind told him he ought to simply relax and go with the flow, but then his more pragmatic side kicked in. He was the one who'd set the boundaries of his marriage to Rosalind. She'd agreed to them. Sex, well, that was an unexpected bonus but now that she was pregnant with his baby it wasn't absolutely necessary and, frankly, it was clouding the issue of the parameters of their arrangement. If they continued to sleep together, Gabe would continue to confuse sex with the messy feelings that were already intruding on him. Which was exactly what he'd expected to happen, but with Rosalind, not with him.

The sex had to stop.

Every cell in his body reeled in protest but the more he thought about it, the more he knew that was the road he needed to take. He needed to ensure that he held strong to his reasons for keeping his heart out of this. Looking at his father was a good incentive. He had no wish to become like him—to be responsible for the unnecessary hurt and pain caused to others with his selfish actions. The best way to do that was not to fall in love, nor to allow anyone else to fall in love with him. With the exception of his child, of course. For his son or daughter he would be the perfect loving father, completely the opposite of the example that had been given to him.

Their lunches arrived and Gabe applied himself to the meal with the concentration of an accountant with a spreadsheet. Anything to keep his mind on track and off Rosalind.

Seven

Ros left the bridal boutique with a new spring in her step. She'd had a lovely morning out at the Courtyard shops and a very promising meeting with Natalie Valentine who owned the bridal shop. Natalie had been enthusiastic about Ros's designs for special-occasion wear and had asked to see samples. Natalie had said that she lost a lot of formal-wear business to the major city boutiques because she simply didn't have the range here in her own store. With the Texas Cattleman's Club featuring so hugely in town and with the many formal and informal occasions it hosted, the demand for quality formal wear was a constant among the women in the area. It would be a win-win for both Ros and Natalie if they could work together on a suitable line to offer to the women of Royal.

Now all Ros had to do was get said samples promptly

sent over here. She made a note in her phone to follow up with Piers.

Her tummy growled, reminding her she hadn't had lunch yet. There were several places she could buy something to eat in Royal but Natalie had spoken highly of the Royal Diner. It wasn't too far from here but the wind outside was freezing so, remembering the instructions Natalie had given her, Ros drove there. Luckily there was a parking spot right outside. She went in and was delighted to discover the interior had a very retro 1950s feel about it with red faux-leather booths and a black-and-white linoleum floor.

"Where's Fonzie?" she muttered aloud as she made her way to an empty booth and settled there. She hadn't been seated long when a server came over.

"Hi, I'm Amanda Battle, the proprietor here. You're new in town, right?"

"Yes, Rosalind Banks."

"Say, aren't you the girl who married Gabriel Carrington a few days ago?"

"The one and the same," Ros said with a smile.

Seemed news traveled fast around here. She'd had a similar response from just about everyone she'd met in and around town today.

"Welcome and congratulations! But where's your new husband? Don't tell me he's left you to your own devices already!" Amanda Battle looked shocked.

"He had a meeting with his father so I'm flying solo today."

"Well, that explains it, then." Amanda smiled and passed Ros a menu. "Everything's good today but I have to say the chef's special, mac 'n' cheese, is sublime."

"I'll have that then," Ros said with a smile. "With a small green salad on the side, please."

"Coffee?"

Ros felt her stomach lurch at the thought. "No thank you. Mineral water, please."

"I'll send one of the girls over with your water in a moment. And, if you need a friend or just someone to talk to, you pop on by, y'hear? I imagine you don't know that many people here yet."

"Thank you, that's lovely of you."

Ros felt the sting of tears at the woman's kindness. The sense of isolation she'd felt when she'd left Gabe to meet his father had surprised her. She hadn't felt that way in New York, maybe because she remembered it from when she lived there with her parents, but in this town where everyone seemed to know everyone else, she felt like a rank outsider.

The food, when it came, was filling and wholesome and Ros left a generous tip with her payment as she exited her booth. She'd seen a few people she recognized from the wedding reception come and go while she was there and they'd acknowledged her with a nod, but for the most part she'd been left alone. As she got back in her car her phone rang. She used the hands-free option on the vehicle to answer and felt an unaccustomed surge of relief when she heard Gabe's voice.

"How're you doing?" he asked.

"I've had a good time—how about you?"

"I had lunch with my father."

"So not a great time then?"

"You could say that. He's not the easiest man to get along with."

"Would you like me to pick you up now?"

"Actually, I have a little business here in town. Do you think you can find your own way back to the ranch?"

She felt a surprising pang of disappointment, but then rallied her senses. It was a reasonable request, after all.

"I'm sure I'll be fine," she said firmly. "How will you get back?"

"I'll figure something out," he said vaguely.

"I can wait around town, find something else to do until you're finished," she said helpfully.

"No. I have no idea how long I'll be. Best you head back to the ranch. I'll see you there around dinnertime."

And with that, he severed the call. No goodbye. No indication of what time dinner actually was. If the past few nights had been anything to go by, it could be anywhere between six and ten o'clock.

Ros stared blindly out the windshield of her car. There'd been a different tone in his voice than when they parted. As if being apart had created a distance between them. The warmth that she'd grown accustomed to hearing when he spoke to her was gone. Not that he was rude, just detached. If that was what having lunch with his father did for him, she'd have to encourage him not to see his dad often, at all.

She started up her car and slipped it into gear and pulled out into the street.

"Who needs GPS?" she said to herself. "It'll be an adventure to find my own way back. How hard could it be in a place like this?"

Harder than she imagined, she discovered. She was glad for the full tank of gas in the car because she had to backtrack several times during her journey back to the ranch. But she knew she was on the right track when she drove past Emmalou's place. A curl of smoke drifted from the brick chimney and lights glowed from inside the tiny home. Seeing the lights in the windows made Ros realize just how long she'd been driving around. It had been several hours since she'd had lunch and she was beginning to feel ravenously hungry again. Still, she consoled herself, not far to go now.

By the time she pulled up in her bay in the garage, she was feeling the effects of that hunger combined with the hours of concentration and driving. Weariness pulled at every muscle in her body as she alighted from the car and her bladder was none too happy about the length of time it had been since her last toilet stop back at the diner.

"Where the hell have you been? You should have been back hours ago," Gabe demanded, looming from what felt like out of nowhere.

"I beg your pardon?"

This was a side of him she hadn't seen before and it was a stark reminder of how little she actually knew him. Oh sure, she knew how to make his entire body tense with anticipation and she knew how to make him growl with impatience as she took her time exploring that same body. But as to what made him tick, she knew very little.

"I got sidetracked when I took a wrong turn."

"You didn't use the GPS?" he demanded.

"I didn't think it would be that hard to find my way back, but turned out my sense of direction isn't that great when it comes to the back end of nowhere."

She couldn't help that last statement. She had been nervous when she'd lost her way more than once and hadn't been able to figure out using the GPS.

"Rosalind, this isn't the city where everything is laid out in blocks and there's someone to give you directions on virtually every corner. We're out on the range, here. A long way from town or help. Plus, there are areas where there is no phone coverage. You took a serious risk doing what you did, especially at this time of year. You could have put both yourself and the baby in danger. Don't be so reckless next time. The car is fitted with an excellent GPS—use it."

With that he turned sharply and stalked away, leaving Ros to stare at his retreating back feeling a mixture of shock and irritation. How dare he speak to her like that? Her hands curled into tight fists of frustration, at him and at herself for not standing up and telling him she'd do what she damn well pleased when it came to driving around. She started after him but changed her mind partway, deciding that giving him a piece of her mind while she was angry was probably not the best course of action.

This whole marriage thing was painfully new to them both and they needed to work at it much harder than she'd realized. It was all very well to spend their nights together, exploring all the things that made their bodies sing in perfect harmony, but they needed to find a middle ground where they could be friends during the day, as well.

After going to the bathroom, Ros detoured to the kitchen, where she discovered a covered plate in the oven. Just the one serving, which told her he'd obviously eaten alone while waiting for her return. She shrugged out of her coat and set it and her bag on a chair at the breakfast bar before getting herself some cutlery and bringing her plate from the oven to sit in splendid isolation at the granite counter and eat her meal. She was partway through when she heard a sound in the doorway. She looked up to see Gabe standing there, watching her.

"I was worried about you," he said bluntly.

"As you can see, I'm just fine, but thank you for caring."

His face tightened and he took a step forward. "I meant it when I said it—you took a serious risk. Anything could have happened to you."

"Like what, being mooed to death by a cow?"

"Like getting stuck on the side of the road with no phone reception and the temperatures dropping. Like running out of gas and not being able to keep the heater in your car running. Like an unexpected snowfall burying you in a drift before anyone could come along and find you."

She put up a hand. "Okay, okay. I get it. I'll use the GPS in future. I promise. I honestly didn't think it'd be that hard to find my way back. Usually, my sense of direction is excellent."

"But it wasn't today."

"No," she conceded. "It wasn't. I'm sorry I worried you."

"I'm sorry I raised my voice."

Silence fell between them for a full minute before Gabe spoke again.

"Rosalind, it's imperative you do everything you can to keep our baby safe—you know that, don't you?"

She flinched as though he'd slapped her. Really? Was that what all this was about? It really had nothing to do with him caring whether she froze on the side of the road or not. It was all about his darned heir. She'd thought they were making some progress in this crazy mixed-up relationship of theirs. They'd managed to be in agreement on every carefully constructed point in the contract they'd both signed prior to their wedding. They'd had the kind of wedding night that she'd always dreamed of even if their reasons for marriage hadn't involved love.

She knew they could make this work. But that would only happen if they were both equally invested in doing so. It seemed he hadn't been kidding when he said he only wanted a wife so he could have an heir. She just hadn't realized what that entailed.

"I knew I had plenty of gas. I wasn't in danger. And I object to you treating me like a child. You forget, while I was born here in America, I've spent many, many years in Australia, too. The Australian Outback is equally as challenging as your Texas ranges. Possibly even more so."

"But you weren't pregnant with my baby when you were in Australia, were you?"

His words took the wind right out of her. Why, why, why had she become pregnant? Her low-dose pill had never let her down before and she was accustomed to travel. So why this, why now, why *him*?

She looked down at the plate of food she'd been eating, suddenly losing all appetite. She got up and took her plate to the trash bin and scraped the contents into it before rinsing and stacking her plate and implements in the dishwasher.

"Did you have enough to eat?"

"I'm not hungry anymore. In fact, I think I'll head off to bed. Good night."

Gabe watched as she grabbed her coat and bag and headed toward the hall that led to the bedroom. Instinct urged him to go after her. To soothe the anger that he'd seen flash in her blue eyes. He'd knew he'd been over-the-top with his response, and while he'd told her it was because he'd been worried for the baby he knew it was far more.

He hadn't been able to get her out of his mind but he couldn't tell her that. It was contrary to everything he'd stipulated about their marriage. It had been easier to focus on the baby's safety than admit that his feelings for her were changing and growing, as hard as he fought against them, and he'd been terrified something had happened to her.

He took a step to follow her then drew himself up again.

Lunch with his father had reminded him of all the reasons why he hadn't pursued a normal marriage. He didn't want the complications that came with it or the hurt that came when it became clear the other person did not love as much as you did. Seeing his mother crushed by his father's cheating had left deep scars on his heart and her death in a car wreck not too long after he'd left them had added to them.

While the head-on collision with a drug-affected driver had clearly been out of his mother's control, he couldn't help but wonder in the years since that if she'd been in a better frame of mind would she have noticed the car barreling toward her earlier and been able to take evasive action? His gut clenched at the thought of something like that having happened to Ros today. A pain not unlike that he'd experienced after his mom's death shafted through him, robbing him of breath.

He reached a hand to the countertop, steadying himself. And reminded himself Ros had been fine. Lost, but fine. And she'd found her way home eventually. His night would not end the same way that it had so many years ago.

Gabe and his mom had lived alone after his father

had walked out to set up house with his latest love interest. Waiting for her to come home that night was still vivid in his mind. She'd been assisting with putting up decorations for a fundraiser at the Texas Cattleman's Club the next day. Even though the cops had told him she hadn't stood a chance when the other vehicle had crossed in her path, he still wondered. Gabe clenched his hands into fists. He would not let the fear and grief of that night be repeated.

Later, he entered their bedroom suite to find the sitting room in complete darkness. The last few nights they'd gone to bed together and it already felt foreign to him to come into the suite alone. He found himself standing in front of her bedroom door without even realizing he'd walked there. No light shone around the edges. She was very obviously in bed already. Asleep? He wondered.

He pressed his hand against the door as if he could feel her consciousness then uttered a small sound of disgust at himself. He was behaving like some lovelorn fool when love didn't even enter into the equation with the kind of marriage they had. Nor would it.

Gabe turned sharply and headed to his bedroom on the other side of the sitting room and got ready for bed. But hours later he found himself still staring at the ceiling, his arms empty and with an indefinable ache at the center of his chest. He rolled onto his side and punched his pillow into shape. He couldn't miss something he'd never had and never wanted, he reminded himself.

But even though he told himself this, it was almost dawn before he drifted off to sleep.

The next morning, he rose later than usual, feeling groggy from the combination of lack of sleep and the too deep sleep he'd finally succumbed to. He showered quickly and dressed in jeans and a flannel shirt. It was time to show Ros around the ranch. Not on horseback, which was his preferred method of transport around the ranch, but on one of the four-by-fours he kept in the shed for the ranch hands to use while rounding up.

It was quiet on the ranch this time of year, with stock moved in closer to the buildings. They'd experimented with calving a number of their cows in the fall and he wanted to ensure the supplemental feeding regime to keep the herd healthy and ensure the best prices for the calves come spring was doing everything they'd hoped for. He also hoped that Ros would enjoy the trip out to see the cows and their calves, but realized he knew so little about her that he had no idea if she even had a pair of boots suitable for walking out on the pasture.

She wasn't in the kitchen when he got there, but a few crumbs on the countertop gave evidence that she'd had something to eat already. Probably not enough to eat, if her lack of appetite lately was anything to go by. He knew she suffered from nausea from time to time and it worried him that pregnancy was making her uncomfortable. She had enough to get used to right now without adding feeling sick into the bargain.

Gabe checked the other rooms of the house but couldn't find any trace of her until he caught a glimpse of light at the end of the hall that led to the garage. He followed the light and was surprised to find her in her car staring intently at the dash and tapping on the screen with an increasing look of irritation on her face.

"Problem?" he asked, standing by the open car door.

She jumped visibly. "Jeez, Gabe. Talk about scare a girl to death."

"Sorry, you looked like you were having trouble."

"I'm trying to figure out the GPS. If I save this point, I should be able to navigate back here from wherever I end up at any stage, right?"

"That's the theory. You want me to give it a try?"

"I wanted to work this out for myself, but whatever."

She sounded utterly defeated. Gabe walked around to the passenger side of the car, settled in the seat and looked at the screen. An error message flashed determinedly, preventing the input of any new data.

"First, we need to clear the message."

"Really? You think I don't know that? You must think I'm an absolute fool," she said in a withering tone.

"I don't think you're a fool and I'm sorry if I made you feel that way last night. I was worried about you."

"You didn't have to worry."

He knew that unless he opened up a bit, she'd never understand why he'd been so anxious.

"Look, I respect that you feel that way, but I lost my mom when she was involved in a crash on the road home one night. I waited and waited but she never arrived."

He heard Ros's sharply indrawn breath. "Oh, Gabe. I'm so sorry. I had no idea."

He shrugged. "It was a long time ago but when I'm expecting someone, I tend to be a clock watcher. Add to the equation that you're unfamiliar with the roads around here and that you're probably used to driving on the other side of the road—"

"You don't have to say any more. Honestly, it's why I'm here trying to set this darn thing up correctly in the first place. Except all I seem to be able to get is that."

She gestured to the error message on the screen.

"Let's see if we can fix this together. Have you checked the owner's manual?"

She rolled her eyes. "No, I haven't. Shouldn't this kind of thing be simple and intuitive?"

He grinned back at her. "Well, I've always found that when simple and intuitive fails, it pays to check the manual."

"Seriously? A man who uses a manual?" she asked incredulously.

"Well don't tell everybody or I'll lose my man-card," he said with a quick grin.

She smiled back at him and he felt as if he'd been rewarded with a gold star. The tension inside him begin to ease. He popped the glove compartment open and extracted the manual.

"How about I read the instructions out loud and you do the programming, that way you'll get more familiar with what menu selections to choose?"

After a few minutes they had several destinations programmed into the GPS and Ros was satisfied that she could operate the functions without any problems.

"Okay, it looks like you're all set up."

"Thank you, it was driving me crazy."

"You'd have figured it out eventually. Do you have plans for today?" he asked. "I was hoping to show you around the ranch, if you're okay with that."

"What do I need to wear?" she asked.

"You'll need a thick, warm coat and boots and a few layers of warm clothing. Oh, and a hat if you have one. Wool would be best, but any kind of beanie will do."

She pulled a face. "I don't think I packed anything like that. I was planning to be in New York, not the back end of civilization."

While she laughed as she said it, he couldn't help but be offended. They might be remote here on the ranch but it was hardly the back end of civilization. But then she was unashamedly a city girl. Maybe when she understood more about the ranch, and the running of it, she'd have more appreciation for things out here.

"No problem, you can wear one of my beanies and I know I have a spare jacket you can borrow. It'll swim on you but you'll be warm."

"Okay, warm is good. Come on then, let's go gear up and you can show me your ranch."

She looked eager to see what his world entailed and that ignited an unexpected spark of hope within him. One he rapidly dashed. He didn't want hope when it came to Rosalind. He just wanted an amicable relationship where they raised a child together. Was that too much to ask?

Eight

Ros felt grossly cumbersome dressed in Gabe's sheepskin-lined coat as they walked out the back of the ranch house and toward the stables and outbuildings. A light sprinkling of snow was already melting on the ground and her boots were more suitable for hard pavements than the rapidly forming mud that was beneath her feet right now. She felt herself start to slip but Gabe was quick to catch her with one arm around her waist.

"Thanks," she said, gratefully. "If we're going to do this kind of thing more often, I'm going to need to invest in a better pair of boots. Does it snow here a lot?"

"This is about as much snow as we're going to get this winter. Are you warm enough? We can go back inside if you think you'll be too cold."

He sounded disappointed and she wanted to make it up to him for the misunderstanding over her being so late last night. If she'd have known about the situation with his mom, she would have called him. There was no way—even if her toes were already likely turning blue in her fashionable but synthetic socks—that she was going to turn him down now.

"I'm fine. Really," she said, attempting to inject as much enthusiasm as she could into her voice. She looked at the stables they were walking toward. "We're not going on horseback, are we? I might have neglected to tell you, I can't ride."

"After the baby is born we can remedy that. I have plenty of gentle-natured horses you can choose from."

"I also neglected to tell you that I'm terrified of the beasts. One end for biting, the other for kicking, right?"

He laughed and she felt herself light up inside at the sound.

"Yeah, something like that, with the ornery ones anyway. But my horses are gently bred and kindly raised and trained. You generally won't see a nip or a kick out of them. Come on in and meet them."

He guided her to the main entrance of the stables and swung the massive wooden door open. She was assailed with warmth the moment she stepped in, along with an array of scents of sweet hay, oats, wood, leather and horses. Gabe closed the door behind them. The scents grew stronger.

"Is it temperature controlled in here?" she asked, beginning to feel warmer straightaway.

But with feeling warmer, also came a sense of being overwhelmed by the smells and the heat, all combining to make a swell of nausea rise within her. She determinedly swallowed against it.

"Yes, these are working animals and we need to keep them at their peak at all times."

One horse, with its head hanging out of a nearby

stall, whickered softly as Gabe came closer. She watched carefully as he stepped toward the animal and put a hand to its head, then his forehead to the horse's, as well. She heard him murmur something softly, the sound little more than a deep rumble and, as if the horse agreed with him, it nodded gently.

"Communing with nature?" she asked, staying well and truly back.

"Sure, come on over. You can give Ulysses a treat."

"Do I have to?" she said with a small laugh to conceal her nerves.

"He won't hurt you I promise."

She forced herself to put one foot in front of the other until she was level with Gabe. The horse lifted his head and looked at her as if he were sizing her up for his next meal. The nauseous sensation grew stronger.

"Gabe, I—"

"Here." He took a small carrot from his pocket and pressed it in her hand. "Hold it out like this."

He demonstrated with his own empty hand held out flat, palm up. Ulysses nuzzled Gabe's empty palm and tossed his head in disappointment.

"Your turn," he encouraged.

Ros forced herself to uncurl her fingers and held out the carrot on her palm, as Gabe had shown her. Ulysses wasted no time checking it out. She flinched as his mouth nuzzled her hand. Soft, she realized, and incredibly gentle. Finding the carrot, Ulysses snatched it up in his teeth and chomped happily. Ros took a step back, a rush of adrenaline coursing through her. She'd done it. She'd fed a carrot to a horse. She should feel elated; instead she just wanted to be sick.

She couldn't hold the nausea at bay any longer and headed for the door.

"I'm sorry, I need some fresh air," she managed before pushing open the stable door and staggering outside where she promptly lost what was left of her breakfast.

This was worse than the other times she'd been sick. So much worse. The smell of the stable continued to wrap around her like a thick miasma until she was vaguely aware of Gabe coming through the door, closing it firmly behind him.

"Ros, are you okay?"

"No, I think I need to lie down for a bit. Can we postpone today's tour for another time?"

She turned abruptly away from him and dry retched some more.

"I'll call the doctor," he said, stepping forward and taking her by the arm.

"No need. Just morning sickness. It should pass, I hope."

"If it doesn't I'm taking you to the doctor, no arguments."

"Fine," she said, feeling too weak right now to argue.

Gabe walked her back inside the house and bent to remove her boots and helped her out of the heavy jacket before taking her to her room. He pushed back the covers of the freshly made bed while she went to the bathroom to brush her teeth again and when she returned, she gratefully lay down and put her head on her pillow. She felt utterly wretched and exhausted.

"I'll be fine in a bit. Just let me get some sleep. The sickness seems to be worse if I get overtired."

"You didn't sleep well last night?" he said, concern obvious in every line of his face.

"Not particularly."

He pulled the covers over her and hovered, obviously unsure of what to do next.

"Can I get you anything?"

"No, thank you."

He turned to go but was stopped by her calling his name.

"Gabe?"

"Do you need something?"

"Will you lie with me?"

He felt torn. Every instinct told him to climb into the bed with her but he had to draw a line somewhere and that line was drawn here and now.

"No, I need to go out on the ranch for a while but I'll stay within easy reach of the house. Phone me if you need me, all right? And I'll ask Doreen to check on you in a short while. And, Ros, I think it's best if we don't sleep together anymore. It's confusing things."

"This is just a bit of morning sickness," she argued.

"Whatever, you need your rest and we need to keep to the terms of the contract."

She closed her eyes then, her fingers clutching the sheets tight around her. "Right, the contract."

Gabe left her room and closed the door quietly behind him. She'd looked terrible and he felt even worse for forcing her to go out when she obviously wasn't feeling great. She'd mentioned morning sickness before, but he'd seen little evidence of it and, to his shame, had blithely put it to the back of his mind and forged on.

He thought about Ros's reluctance to go into the stable and his insistence that everything would be okay. Her frightened face as he'd encouraged her to come closer and give Ulysses his treat should have made him realize how uncomfortable she was in his world. It was an alien space for her and, if she was like that around horses, how much worse would she be around steers?

All of this brought home to him even more clearly how vastly different their worlds were. Hers was one of concrete and noise and skyscrapers and his was one of peace and animals and sky. They couldn't be less compatible if they tried. And yet, she'd agreed to stay here and have their baby. Agreed to at least try to make working from Royal a viable thing.

She'd made all the sacrifices and what had he done? Thrown a bit of money around, that's all. And that was no hardship for him. He'd given up nothing. Changed nothing. Guilt slammed into him. But what could he do? They'd made their bed and lain in it. He grimaced at the metaphor and the swift rise of arousal that escalated through him, but doing what he did best, he pushed it aside and went through to the mudroom and geared up again before heading out the back door. Outside, the air was still crisp and cold and he filled his lungs with the cleanness of it. This wasn't the fume-filled city. Here a man could breathe and dream. This was his life, his home, his everything. It clearly wasn't Rosalind's.

So where did that leave them? Would she stay? Or would she be gone the moment their child was born? A pang of loss struck him as he thought about Ros leaving. And while he told himself that, ideally, he wanted his child raised by two parents it wasn't mandatory. But the thought of losing her didn't sit as easily with him now as it had before their wedding. When they'd drawn up the marriage contract, he'd been adamant that any children born to them would be raised by him should their marriage dissolve. He had firm ideas about how he wanted his child or children raised and it would be with love and care and stability. Not the kind of careless and casual parenting his father had observed where he'd left everything to Gabe's mom and on those rare occasions when he'd taken Gabe out for a day all he'd done was splash money about and pass judgement on others.

That wasn't what Gabe wanted for his son or daughter. He wanted them to know they were loved and safe, always, and although it made him sound like a control freak and maybe even an asshole, the only way to ensure that was to have sole custody if his marriage didn't last. He refused to allow his child to ever be hurt, to be a part of a tug-of-war or be used as a weapon against their other parent. And he absolutely refused to be as absent and as cavalier about his child's emotional wellbeing as his father had been with him. But now the idea of not having Rosalind be a part of his life, together with the baby they'd created, made him feel an element of loss he hadn't experienced since his mother's death.

He shook his head at his thoughts. He didn't have time to dwell on maybes. Right now he had a day's work ahead of him and that's what he would do.

They fell into a routine after that. One where he did his work on the ranch by day, as she did hers inside the ranch house. Evenings they usually ate together before heading to their separate sleeping quarters. She'd taken to staying in bed in the mornings and he'd asked the housekeeper to take her tea and plain toast or crackers before she rose. She'd thanked him for it and admitted to feeling a lot better during the day if she just started slow. That was fine by him. She wasn't due to see the baby doctor for another couple of weeks and he planned to be right there along with her. In the meantime, it was easier to keep some distance between them because the more time he spent with her, the more time he wanted to spend with her and that wasn't part of his plan.

Gabe was in the stables, brushing Ulysses down after a morning ride when his cell phone rang. He didn't recognize the number on the screen and was tempted to send it to voice mail, but an edge of curiosity prompted him to accept the call.

"Gabriel Carrington," he said with a touch of irritation in his voice.

"Gabe, it's Rafael Wentworth. How are things going? Congratulations on your marriage, by the way."

Gabe smiled at the all-too-familiar voice. He and Rafael had been friends back in their high school days where they'd bonded over their mutual disgust with their fathers and, while they'd mostly lost touch after Rafe had left town when he was seventeen after a particularly tough time with his dad, they'd sporadically gotten in touch with one another. Rafe had made his fortune in Miami and had a bit of a reputation as a ladies' man. Despite that reputation, Gabe knew him as a man who, while always proud and ambitious, also valued integrity above everything else.

"Thank you. I saw you at the TCC gala, but with so many people, I couldn't get near you. I'm glad you're still in Royal. What's keeping you here?"

"I'm scouting out a new business opportunity."

"Have you seen your dad?"

"Briefly. But I've seen a lot of Cammie. That's a cute baby she's fostering."

"Yeah, your sister is doing a great job, although no one seems to know who the baby's daddy is."

"Well, despite the rumors filtering around the club, I can assure you it isn't me," Rafe said with a laugh. "In fact, I've pretty much had enough of all the rumors and questions. I've asked Cammie to organize a DNA test to prove that Micah and I are definitely not related."

"Good idea. Should stop the gossip train in its tracks. Say, why don't we catch up for a drink now you're back?"

"Sure, not the club, though. Too many ears for my liking at the moment. What about Sheen or that new place set up by Lauren Roberts…what's she called it?"

"The Eatery," Gabe supplied.

"Yeah, that's the one. Shall we meet there? Say, seven tonight?"

"I look forward to it."

They ended the call and Gabe found himself looking forward to catching up with his friend in person. It had been a while but if Rafe was back in town for good maybe they'd get to see one another more often.

Later that day, Gabe pulled up in a parking lot not too far from the restaurant and sprinted through the light rain to get there. He spied Rafe immediately over by the bar and crossed the floor to meet him.

"Good to see you, buddy," he said enveloping Rafe in a man hug.

Rafe clapped him on the back in return. "Good to see you, too. It's been too long."

"Well, I wasn't the one who left town."

"You weren't the one who had to," Rafe said with a crooked grin. "What can I get you to drink?"

"A zero alcohol beer would be good. Driving and all that."

Rafe gave his order to the bartender.

"So, what's brought you back to town?" Gabe said, taking a sip of his beer when the barman put the brew on a coaster in front of him.

"Cammie's nagging about the gala, but mainly it's

a new business idea. Something I've been thinking about for a while but just need to find the right property, y'know? I never thought it'd be in Royal, but it's looking that way. How about you, still running the ranch?"

"Yeah, not a lot changes there. Although I've had some ideas about expanding it into more of an educational and training facility. Something to get city kids off the streets, out of trouble and into gainful and rewarding employment."

Rafe looked surprised. "That's quite an undertaking. What made you come up with that?"

Gabe shrugged. "Just an idea that pinged into my brain during my last trip to Houston. Seems to me there are a lot of disenfranchised youth about and not just in the cities. This might help set a few of them on a better path."

"That's philanthropic of you. What does the new wife think of all that?"

"Rosalind? I haven't discussed it with her yet. We don't really have that kind of marriage."

Rafe looked surprised. "What kind of marriage is it?"

"One of convenience, mostly. I wanted an heir and I needed a wife who wouldn't want all the messy crap that comes with relationships to help me achieve that goal."

Gabe grimaced. Stated bluntly it didn't sound very appealing or kind, which wasn't something that had bothered him before. So why did it now?

"Jeez, buddy, that sounds clinical. What happens if she falls in love with you, or you with her?"

"Not going to happen," Gabe said firmly. "It's a contracted agreement. She gets a financial boost to help her business out of a tight spot—I get my heir."

Rafe laughed. "You know how feudal that sounds, right?"

"I know but we went into it with our eyes open. I don't expect complications."

If that was so, why did he have to fight the urge to cross his fingers behind his back?

"Tell me about her."

"She's blond, petite, beautiful, has her own busin—"

"Not that stuff. What's she like?"

"Tenacious, she has to be to be successful in the fashion industry. She's also a city girl through and through."

"Doesn't sound like she'll fit on the ranch. Does she like animals?"

"Not as far as I can tell."

"Man, you'll have your work cut out for you. Your ranch is your life. I've always kind of envied you that. Being a man of the land and all. Even as a kid you always knew exactly what you wanted and went for it."

"What about you? And those rumors at the club? Has Cammie booked the test yet?"

"She's organized it all for me already. I damn well hate having to dignify the rumors but they've got to stop. You know yourself how these things get out of hand. Even though we were both in Miami, I never met Arielle Martin, Micah's mom. Apparently, my name is mentioned in some diary of hers and maybe she wanted to talk to me at some stage but I sure as hell never heard from her. I just want all the conjecture to stop. It's not fair on me but mostly it's not fair on the baby, either.

"I can understand why it's important he know who his daddy is but it isn't me."

"I get it," Gabe empathized.

Rumor and speculation had led his mom to the truth about his father's infidelities. It had been tough for her, a genteel woman, to continue to hold her head up after that. She'd always been proud of her position in her husband's life—proud of his achievements and her son's, of the life they'd built together. But all that had come crashing to the ground when she'd discovered everything that she'd held dear had been an illusion. She'd been devastated by the betrayal and seeing her like that had made Gabe even more determined to never hurt another human being that way.

Surely it was easier not to allow your emotions to become engaged than it was to try to piece yourself together when everything fell apart. Hell, even in his adult life, his own attempts at relationships had ended miserably. The last ending when he'd discovered Francine, his girlfriend and a woman he'd thought he loved and could make a future with, was cheating on him. It seemed he was just like his mother, too trusting and wanting to believe that others had the same dreams and aspirations as he did, when nothing could be further from the truth.

And Ros? He knew exactly where he stood with her and she with him, also.

Liar, his conscience whispered.

No, he slammed the door on that voice so hard the echoes reverberated in his mind. He cared about her because she was carrying his baby. It had nothing to do with attraction or love or anything complicated. Absolutely nothing.

Nine

Rosalind ended the call feeling a massive buzz of excitement. Things were looking up. The conference call she and Piers had just completed with a New York based retailer, who had stores nationwide, promised the lift their business needed. The company buyers had enthused over the samples Piers had couriered to them and were already talking about an exclusive supply contract. At this rate everything would be back on the same track it had been before the letdown in Australia. Better even, because the potential market reach here in America was so very much bigger.

She did a little happy dance across the living room of the master suite before coming to a halt in front of a hard unyielding male figure. Gabriel. Her body responded instantly and she felt her cheeks flush with color.

"Sorry, I didn't see you there," she said and stepped back.

"You look happy. That's good."

"Yes, I am happy. Piers and I just had a call with a company that will potentially be my biggest customer very soon. We just need to prepare the contracts and send them to their legal department."

"That's great news," he said, but she noticed his eyes didn't light up quite the way she was sure hers were.

"It means I'll be able to pay you back your money," she continued.

"That money is yours—it's part of our contract."

She pulled a face. The whole business of that marriage contract, and his subsequent withdrawal from any intimacy between them, had begun to make her feel like she was little more than a womb for hire. Sure, he was solicitous and ensured that her every need was met, but there was no affection or tenderness between them anymore. Even so, she found herself reacting to him every time he entered the same room she was in, as if just being in his presence heightened her every sense.

"What did you come to see me for?" she asked, rapidly changing the subject.

"I wondered if you were ready to meet my dad. He'll be visiting with my grandfather at the club later this afternoon. I thought we could call by for half an hour or so."

"Just half an hour?" she asked. "That doesn't seem a long time for you to catch up with your family."

"Long enough. I wouldn't inflict them on anyone any longer than that. They're…" he hesitated a bit, choosing his words carefully. "Very old-fashioned with their ideas. Don't be offended—it's just the way they are."

"That's fine—I've had to deal with people operating with outdated concepts my entire adult life."

"Well, I can only hope it will have prepared you for this, then," he said with a faint smile.

"What's the dress code? If we're at the club I imagine I'll need to do better than this." She ran her hands down the long, loose-fitting cream-colored woolen sweater she wore over a pair of camel-toned merino leggings that showcased her slender legs to perfection.

"You look great as you are and I hate to suggest something slightly more formal but—"

"What time do you need me to be ready?"

"Is thirty minutes cutting it too fine?"

She raised her brows at him. "I'll do my best."

She spun on her heel and headed for her bedroom and threw the doors to her walk-in wardrobe wide open. She had something in mind; she just needed to find it. Ah, there it was. The plain black crew neck knitted dress with its clinging long sleeves was perfect for a situation like this. It was the kind of thing that transferred well from office to evening wear with the mere addition of a few choice accessories and the right shoes.

Given they were heading to the club at this end of the day, she chose a pair of black pumps with slender heels and a twisted gold belt and matching necklace and bracelet to complete the ensemble. She assessed her hair in the mirror, deciding an updo would lend a little more gravitas to what she was wearing and swept the thick tresses into a sleek chignon before removing the light makeup she'd worn since this morning and applying a more distinctive eye-and-lip look. When she stepped back from the mirror she was well satisfied with her appearance. She only hoped she'd do Gabe proud.

Maybe if he was happy with her, he'd lighten up a little. She could understand that their marriage was essentially a business deal but he'd said he wanted their child to have a good life with two parents. But the way he kept shutting her out made her think that the whole concept was nothing more than a platitude.

She stepped back into their sitting room and caught Gabe sitting on the couch, leaning back with his eyes closed. Even though he was in repose, his face held unexpected lines of tension, as if he had a bad headache or, more likely, wasn't looking forward to the upcoming meeting.

"Everything okay?" she asked.

His eyes flicked open and he took in her appearance. "Wow, that's quite the transformation."

She did a twirl. "You approve?"

"Wholeheartedly."

She'd never considered herself the kind of person who craved male attention and acceptance but knowing he thought she looked good was a balm to her soul right now. She'd begun to feel nervous about meeting the two senior Mr. Carringtons, but knowing she was okay in Gabe's eyes went a long way to soothing her anxiety.

"Shall we go?" he asked. "You'll need your coat."

"Just a sec," she said, nipping back into her bedroom and grabbing a white wool coat from her wardrobe.

It was a cape-shouldered style that folded over her chest and belted with a matching sash. Its wide arms had always made her feel like some kind of 1940's glamor queen and right now it bolstered her confidence up a notch.

"Perfect," Gabe said as she returned.

The trip to the club went smoothly and, on the way, Gabe peppered her with questions about her talks with the new client. Despite the fact his business was all about cattle and land, he had strong business acumen and she was grateful for his insights, which aligned very closely with her own. He seemed to understand her excitement and her desire to expand her business, not for expansion's sake, but for the sake of her staff and their families, too. It felt like they were very much on the same page when it came to providing safe and encouraging employment opportunities. So why then were they miles apart on pretty much everything else?

Everything else but the bedroom, maybe.

What was with that? It was almost as if he was afraid to get closer to her. To her way of thinking, that would solve a lot of the tension between them. She knew she wasn't imagining it. Every accidental touch seemed to make him withdraw from her even more and even though he had a huge team of ranch hands and a manager, he was still very much hands-on and busy all day with the ranch itself. If she didn't know better, she'd say he was hiding from her, but surely that wasn't the case.

Her thoughts prompted her to ask a question.

"Gabe?"

"Hmm?"

"Just how hands-on do you plan to be with our baby?"

"What makes you ask that? You know I plan to be very present in their life." He sounded defensive.

"Well, I just wondered. You're out on the ranch all day long and I know as we come into spring your time will be even more eaten up. By the time summer and the baby come along, I was just wondering where we will fit into your day."

"Obviously I will make changes so I can be there."

She shook her head. "In the beginning maybe, but what about when it really counts. Like on the days the baby might be fractious or I might need a break."

"I plan to hire help—it is in our contract, remember?" he said, shooting her a frown. "Why are you asking all this now?"

"I'm just trying to clarify things. You want an heir, to be a dad, I get that. But there's more to baby rearing than simply popping in every now and then and leaving others to the mundane tasks."

"Trust me, I know how not to be a father. My own was a perfect example of that," he said with a quelling glance.

She let the subject drop but she couldn't help feeling that their expectations of their parental journey ahead of them were poles apart. She couldn't remember a time when her father hadn't been available to her. Even during his work with the diplomatic corps, he still made a point of being accessible. Her mom had quit work to be able to travel with her husband's postings and had been satisfied with creating a home wherever they went and acting as his hostess. But that wasn't the life Ros wanted for herself. Her career was important to her. Right up until she became pregnant, it had been everything.

Now she was going to have to find a new way of juggling her need to work and create and share her creations, with being a mom. Her need to excel at what she did would no doubt put additional pressure on her, but she'd find a way to come to terms with it. She had to. She settled a hand on her flat belly. It was still so hard to believe a new life was growing there. A life that happened due to chance. A life unplanned, unexpected, but cherished nonetheless.

They drew up outside the club and they left the car with a valet and went to check their coats in. Gabe took her hand and led her to the bar where they were meeting his dad and grandfather. The bar was tastefully decorated in modern hues but the influence of the past remained in the dark wooden floors and hunting trophies hanging from the walls. She suppressed a shudder at the many glass eyes staring at them as they crossed to meet two older men who stood as they arrived.

"Dad, Granddad, I'd like to introduce you to my wife, Rosalind Banks."

"What? Not Carrington? What's wrong with you, girl?" the older man barked before taking her hand to shake it.

Ros noted he only took the tips of her fingers and gave them the barest touch and the gentlest shake before quickly letting them go. It was the kind of handshake that always irritated her immensely. As if she wasn't an equal, or worthy of a decent handclasp.

"Pleased to meet you, sir," she said with a smile that belied the irritation that also arose at the expectation that she would automatically take Gabe's name. Then again, it wasn't as if he hadn't warned her. "As to my name, it's been good enough for me for thirty years, I figure it'll be good enough for at least another fifty or sixty."

"Hmph, would never have happened in my day. And he's got you knocked up already?"

"You'll have to excuse my father," the other man said. "He has no social filter and tends to hold on to old traditions. He doesn't mean to be offensive."

Ros wasn't so sure of that but smiled and shook Gabe's father's hand anyway. At least he had the courtesy of actually clasping her hand firmly in the handshake.

"Pleased to meet you, Mr. Carrington."

"Call me Dad, or Denver. Welcome to the family."

"Thank you, Denver."

"What can I get for you both to drink?" Denver asked.

"I'll get the drinks. Same again for you two?" Gabe said. The two men nodded and walked on ahead as he turned to Rosalind. "Hot tea, or something chilled?"

She smiled and felt a curl of warmth in her lower belly. There was that solicitous side of him all over again.

"Tea, please," she answered.

He dropped his head to murmur in her ear. "Will you be okay with these two?"

"I'm sure I'll be fine. How much trouble can they get into in a few short minutes, right?"

"You have no idea," he muttered before heading to the bar.

Denver and his father waited for Ros to sit before resuming their seats. Denver leaned forward, his elbows on his knees and his hands clasped before him. Ros wondered if Gabe realized he had the exact same mannerism as his father when he sat and engaged in conversation with someone. Looking at the two older men was an interesting insight into how Gabe would age, too. No doubt he would continue to be a vital and handsome man for many, many more years yet, if his father and grandfather were anything to go by.

"Gabe tells me you make frocks?" Denver said with a challenging glint in his eye.

"Oh, I'm sure he told you I do a bit more than that," she said with an equally determined glint in her own. "Yes, my company does make special-occasion wear for women, but we're also well-known for women's leisure wear. In fact, we are on the cusp of branching out into the American market, which we're very excited about."

"You'll stop working once the baby is born though, right?" said Gabe's grandfather.

"No. I won't," she answered firmly.

"You're going to leave your child to be raised by strangers?" he persisted.

"Not at all. With a mom and a dad both working from home, there's no reason why we can't share our responsibilities."

"Hmph, never did that kind of thing in my day. Never saw why a man needed to do a woman's work. I s'pose you expect our Gabe to cook and clean as well after a hard day on the ranch?"

"Mr. Carrington, we do have a housekeeper and Gabe is quite adept in the kitchen. In fact, I think he enjoys cooking from time to time. We both do. We'll find our normal, I'm sure."

"Babies are woman's work."

"Well, it takes two to make them so I'm pretty sure that they benefit from two to raise them, too," she said firmly.

She was beginning to understand why Gabe had next to no idea of what was involved in baby rearing if his grandfather was any example. She had little hands-on experience when it came to babies, but even so she knew that it had to be easier working as a team of two than leaving everything just to one parent.

"You talk funny. You're not American, are you?" he continued doggedly.

"I have dual nationality, both American and Australian."

"Dad, stop misbehaving. You'll have Rosalind thinking we're from the dark ages," Denver interrupted.

"Gabe's gone and married the girl without a proper vetting from the family. A man needs answers to certain questions," the elder Carrington said gruffly.

"I'm happy to answer your questions, Mr. Carrington."

"Well, you can start by calling me Granddad."

"Granddad, then."

"Can you handle a horse?"

"No, sir—Granddad."

"What kind of ranch owner's wife can't handle a horse?"

"The kind who has never needed to or wanted to," Rosalind said, keeping a determined smile on her face.

"Dad, not everyone was born in a saddle," Denver said smoothly. "How long have you been back in the States, Rosalind?"

Grateful for the turn in direction, Ros quickly filled Denver in but was deeply grateful to see Gabe's return.

"I hope you haven't been grilling my wife in my absence," he said as he took the seat next to Ros and took her hand.

She squeezed his hand gratefully. "Not at all," she said breezily. "I was just telling your dad how we met in November."

A waitress arrived with a tray with their drinks. She set a small teapot and cup and saucer down by Rosalind, together with a small milk jug, then the whiskeys in front of the gentlemen.

"Tea? Oddest way to celebrate a wedding I've ever seen," Gabe's grandfather grumbled.

"You forget," Ros answered. "I'm carrying the next Carrington heir. It's my responsibility to ensure they get the best care and opportunity to develop that they possibly can."

"Humph." The old man looked at her and to her surprise gave her a wide grin. "You'll do."

"I beg your pardon," she said.

"What? You hard of hearing, girl? I said, you'll do. Welcome to the family."

Not even realizing how tense she'd been through the exchange with Gabe's grandfather, she felt herself relax.

"Well, I guess you'll do, too," she replied tartly and poured her tea.

The old man laughed out loud and winked at her.

"I was just testing you. Sorry if I came across as unkind."

"No, just rude."

He roared laughing again and beside her she now felt Gabe relax, too.

"Right, now we have that out of the way, can we visit together like civilized human beings?" Gabe said dryly.

Talk quickly turned to ranching and without anything to offer to the conversation, Ros merely watched the interplay between the three generations of men. She drifted off mentally, until she heard Gabe suggesting that as Ros tired easily they would be heading back home. Ros didn't know whether to be grateful or annoyed that he'd made the decision without even asking her but she had to admit that she was tired and that the head-to-head with Gabe's granddad had taken more out of her than she'd expected.

They got in the car and headed toward the ranch but as the tires ate up the miles Ros couldn't help feeling that things were more off-kilter than they'd been before. She'd thought that maybe meeting with Gabe's dad and grandfather might bring them a little closer, make their marriage feel more real somehow even given their circumstances around getting hitched. Instead, it was as if the distance between them now stretched in an echoing chasm and she was at a complete loss as to what to do to resolve it.

She wanted this to work. She'd agreed to Gabe's terms but she wanted so much more. Was she destined to failure? It certainly felt like it. A real marriage involving intimacy, closeness, friendship and passion. They'd had intimacy and passion until Gabe had removed himself from that equation and now Gabe's behavior toward her was like that of a work colleague. She needed…more than that. For both herself and for their child.

But was Gabe capable of it? Having met his father and grandfather and seeing the examples he'd been led by, she seriously doubted it.

Ten

Gabe focused on the road ahead trying to remain oblivious to Ros sitting quietly in the seat beside him. Trying and failing. The subtle scent she wore seemed designed to torment him, to remind him of what it was like to bury his nose in the warm inviting curve of her neck where it met her shoulder. It made him want to do it again. But he'd chosen not to, he reminded himself firmly.

She'd leave eventually; he knew she would. Oh, she might stay a while for the baby's sake, but he knew this was not her world. She was like a butterfly needing color and stimulation, hopping from one exciting venture to the next. Life on the ranch was not like that, which made it easier to keep his feelings firmly locked in their airtight compartment, safe from harm. It was clear as day that she did not fit in his world and he would not risk having his heart dashed into a million pieces as his father had done to his mom when he'd left her. Unfortunately, that did nothing to alleviate the desire he felt for her.

He just had to try to keep himself clear of her as much as possible, which had been working since that episode she'd had at the stables. If anything, it had driven it home to him that he'd likely made the biggest mistake of his life that night they'd first made love after the gala. But it had led to what he hoped would be the best thing he'd ever done—created a child to love and cherish and raise to love the land as much as he did.

It was dark as they came up the drive, but even so, he knew what every shadow on the landscape represented. Every dip and hollow in the land, every fence line, every building. It was all his. He loved the ownership of it, the management of it, the challenges the animals and the weather brought him. And it would belong to his son or daughter after him. That had been his goal ever since he'd been a young boy and he was achieving it.

So why didn't it feel right?

He had no answer to that. When they entered the house, they went to their master suite and Ros went to take off her coat. He fought the urge to assist her, to peel the stylish garment from her shoulders, because he knew that if he did that, he wouldn't want to stop there. He'd want to go all the way, to slowly strip her naked and to lose himself in her. To wipe his mind clean of the taint he always felt after spending time with his father. But it wouldn't be right or fair to use her like that, even though he sensed she'd welcome him into her arms.

Gabe threw his coat on his bed and spun around and headed for the kitchen, determined to put some space between him and Rosalind before he did something incredibly dumb, like give in to his feelings. Feelings led to pain. How often had he seen that and been forced to learn his lesson? He didn't know if it was a curse on his family or not, but there hadn't been a single happy marriage in all the years there had been Carringtons in Royal. At least not one that he'd ever heard of.

All the way back to his great-great-grandfather, the Carrington men had been hard men of the land and focused on one thing: making money. And they'd been damn good at it. Womenfolk had been an accessory to a successful life and there had always been rumors of infidelity along the way. Rapidly hushed-up rumors, but they left their stain nonetheless. He would not be that person. He would not cheat on Rosalind but he would not give in to the allure that she presented to him, either.

A sound behind him made him realize he'd been standing at the kitchen counter for the past several minutes without doing anything.

"Everything okay?" Ros asked as she entered the room.

She was still wearing the black dress and he could not ignore the way it clung to every inch of her, highlighting the roundness of her breasts and the curve of her waist. She'd taken off the heels she'd worn earlier and was wearing a pair of slippers with an odd-looking animal on the tops of them.

"Are you wearing koalas?" he asked incredulously.

"I am. And they're a great deal kinder on my feet than the heels I was wearing earlier. My feet are oddly puffy this evening for some reason."

"Why didn't you tell me earlier?"

"Because it's just a little puffiness. No need to worry. By the time I get up in the morning it'll be all gone. Maybe you can give my feet a rub for me later on?"

He bit back the instant refusal that leapt to mind. Touching her, any part of her, would only lead to wanting her even more. But it was for her well-being, he reminded himself. She was the mother of his child.

"Sure," he answered abruptly. "Cookie has left dinner in the oven for us. Are you hungry now? We can wait until later if you'd prefer."

"No, I could eat now. Shall we take trays through to the TV room and watch a movie together?"

She started to move around the kitchen, gathering plates and cutlery and setting two trays before he could even respond. If theirs was a normal marriage they'd be dining together and watching a movie before retiring to bed—together. The realization sank like a stone in his stomach.

"No. I've just remembered I need to do some work in my office. I'll take mine through."

She didn't bother to hide the disappointment on her face. He hated hurting her like this—forcing more distance between them. But it was vital for his peace of mind. If he gave in, it would leave him vulnerable, weak. He could not be that person. Unable to look at her a moment longer, he turned and brought the covered dishes out of the oven, set them on pads on the countertop and lifted the lids. Cookie had done a potato gratin with green beans and a beef casserole with mushrooms that smelled like heaven.

"Shall I serve for you, too?" he asked.

"No, thank you. I'll take care of myself."

Her voice sounded small, as if she too had withdrawn emotionally from him and the situation they were in. He should be rejoicing in it; instead he felt a sling of guilt hanging around his neck. He could change all that in a minute, but he remained resolute.

"Here," he said, passing her a set of serving spoons and a ladle for the casserole. "You go first."

She gave him a weak smile of acknowledgment and scooped a small portion of each dish onto her plate. While she did so, he poured her a glass of sparkling water and added one for himself to his tray, too. Ros lifted her tray and turned to leave the kitchen but hesitated and turned back to face him putting her tray back on the counter top.

"Gabe, can I ask you a question?"

"Of course."

"Do you hate me?"

"No. What the hell? What makes you ask that?"

"It's just that you seem to be doing everything you can to create distance between us. I don't get it. You parade me out to your father and grandfather and then we get home and you're distancing yourself from me, literally. We're married. It's up to us to make the best of it. I know you don't want romance and all of that— I get it. And I accept that we entered into a contract. But does it have to be like this—so separate? Can we not find a happy medium somehow?"

"I don't believe there is a halfway, Ros," he answered gently. "I don't want to hurt you."

And he wouldn't let her near enough to hurt him, either.

She laughed and it was a bitter sound devoid of any implication of mirth or joy.

"You think I'd let you hurt me?" she said with a twist of her lips.

"Sometimes I don't think we mean to let others hurt us. Other times, we can't help but let it happen."

As he had with Francine before he'd decided on a marriage of convenience. Learning of her infidelity had cut him deeply. He, who thought he was more observant than his mom had been. More careful with his heart. Less trusting. Turned out it was those last two things that had driven Francine to seek another man's love and trust. The betrayal had cut deep but rather than devastate him, it had only served to make him more wary.

"You sound as though you're speaking from experience," Ros said carefully, giving him an assessing look.

"Both as an observer and as a participant," he answered and heaped generous portions of the casserole and potato dish onto his plate.

"*Participant*, that's a strange term to use for being in a relationship."

"It fits."

"It explains a lot."

He stiffened and gave her a hard look. "What do you mean by that?"

"That you don't see yourself as being partner *with* someone, but merely a contributor to a mutual joining."

Gabe shrugged. "I guess. Whatever, it doesn't change our position. I made it clear to you from the outset what would be involved. It's a little too late to be getting cold feet now."

His words sounded harsh, even to his own ears, but they needed to be said. She lifted her chin and stared at him with eyes that were now an icy blue.

"Who said anything about cold feet? I was merely having a conversation with the man I married. The man who is the father of my child. Is it too much to expect civility and friendship?"

She was gorgeous at any hour of the day or night but right now? With fury making her eyes snap at him and a flush of color in her cheeks? Well, she was stunning. His body stirred to unwelcome life but he wouldn't give in to desire. Desire led to emotional entanglements and with emotional entanglements came problems. He did not want to be hurt.

So, you'll just be bitter? A voice at the back of his mind said perversely. No. He wasn't bitter. He was careful. He would love his child, in fact, he did already. But he knew he could fall in love with Ros all too easily. Already he was drawn to her in ways he hadn't anticipated. Ways that would complicate things all too well when she left—and he knew she would in time. He'd seen her reaction to the ranch, the wide-open spaces, to Royal itself. Staying here was stifling her in ways he'd never considered. He couldn't expect that she would stay when it clearly was impacting her creativity and with that, her career.

She was the kind of creature who needed the buzz of bright lights and the big city. Something he'd never fully experienced or understood aside from the occasional visit to Houston or Dallas or a trip to New York to catch a show. While he hadn't minded the cityscape, he'd told himself it was only because he knew he didn't have to stay there. Didn't have to put up with the noise, the people, the smells. He would always have the chance to return here to clean air and to family.

Family. There was the rub. His mother was gone, he barely spoke with his father and his grandfather was cut from the exact same cloth as his dad. So maybe family wasn't what kept him here but now there would be a new generation. A son or daughter to raise to appreciate the land and the animals he farmed here, to teach the business side of ranching effectively—to love.

Was that what he truly wanted? Yes. It was. Someone to love unconditionally who would love him the same way in return. Someone he could trust—and who couldn't trust a child, right? They were a clean slate from birth. No preconceived ideas, no deceit. They loved without restriction.

He realized that while he was lost in his thoughts, Ros had settled at the breakfast bar and picked up her fork but was merely pushing her food around on her plate, not eating.

"Are you feeling all right?"

"I'm fine," she snapped. "You don't have to keep asking me that every five minutes."

"I wasn't aware that I did," he answered calmly.

"I'm sorry. I'm just out of sorts. I'm tired, I'm not hungry and I just feel so frustrated by everything."

He was at a loss for words. She wouldn't want any kind of placebo statement from him but he felt guilty that he had planned to leave her to her own devices this evening when she obviously would appreciate some distraction.

"Look, I can do my paperwork tomorrow. Why don't we choose a movie and eat in front of the TV like you suggested before?" he offered.

In response she pushed her plate away and got down from her stool.

"No, I think I'll turn in early. You do what you need to."

She tipped the contents of her plate in the trash and rinsed her plate before putting it in the dishwasher and leaving the room without a backward glance—leaving him standing there feeling all kinds of idiot. He hated that she had the capacity to do that to him, that he *let* her. It shouldn't have been a problem to him. They'd both gone into this marriage with their eyes wide open and it wasn't as if she wasn't benefiting financially from the arrangement.

But he could see it was taking a toll on her. Bit by bit she was losing the vivacity and vibrancy that he'd seen in her from the first moment he'd laid eyes on her. And it was his fault. She'd been plucked out of her chosen environment and planted here on Texas soil— a place that was as foreign to her as the moon. Okay, so he hadn't forced her, but she'd been between a rock and a hard place. Her choices limited by the events that transpired after their first night of passion together. Passion that was shared equally, as the result of that passion needed to be, too. Passion he was doing his level best to ignore.

She'd make a great mom, he realized with a twist of his heart. He only hoped he could be as good a father.

He picked up his plate and cutlery and forced himself to walk in the opposite direction of the master suite and down the hall toward his office. He would not go after her. They were married, yes, but that didn't mean anything other than a couple of signatures on paper. What was more binding was the contract they'd agreed to and he would hold up his end of that contract because he was an honorable man.

Honorable? When you let an unhappy, lonely, pregnant woman go to bed alone? There was that blasted voice again. He growled and kept going to his office. He would not give in. Giving in was a sign of weakness and he was not a weak man. He was not ruled by lust, as his father had been and still was by the ever-changing women who appeared on his arm, nor by love, as his mom had been. He was rational, sensible, loyal and hardworking. Not bad traits in any man, he told himself. But as he settled at his desk and booted up his computer, he began to wonder what he was doing this all for. He ate his meal without tasting it and found himself studying the projections his ranch manager had emailed through to him without paying them the attention they deserved. In the end he closed his eyes and, elbows on the desk, rested his head in his hands while he massaged his temples.

This was supposed to be easy. Straightforward.

So why then was his mind in complete turmoil? Why then did every cell in his body urge him to go to Rosalind? To simply hold her. What difference would it make?

Every difference, he warned himself. It would be a sign of giving in to the weaknesses that destroyed his parents and he would not, ever, go there.

Gabe sat upright, shoved his empty plate away and forced his mind to the facts and figures on the computer screen. Everything looked promising for the development of his ranch into an educational facility. It would merely be a matter of applying for the right consents and then starting marketing and he'd be able to reach out to help disaffected and directionless youth from all around the region. Kids that needed a chance to find satisfaction in what they did all day, rather than fall victim to peer pressure and the trouble that boredom inevitably led to.

It was ambitious, this plan of his, but no more ambitious than what Rosalind had wanted for her own business. He grimaced, thinking about how he hadn't had to change anything in his life or his business and how she'd made all the sacrifices. He'd find a way to make it up to her, somehow, because while he didn't want to do marriage with all the usual trimmings, he didn't want her to leave, either.

Eleven

Rosalind woke the next morning still filled with a helpless empty feeling she just couldn't shake. She'd always exercised regularly until her move to Royal and knew Gabe had a well-equipped gym near the garage. Swimming had always been her preferred exercise but a brisk walk on a treadmill would probably help her clear the cobwebs away.

She dressed in leggings and a fitted long-sleeved T-shirt, both from her leisure wear collection and featuring a quintessential Australian print on the shirt, and went to the kitchen and grabbed a bottle of water from the fridge before making her way to the gym. Behind the closed door, music pounded out from the sound system inside. She hesitated at the door, her hand poised over the handle. The walls virtually rocked to the beat of Metallica at high volume and she couldn't help but smile. It was one of her favorite tracks. She opened the door and went inside and spied Gabe working out on a bench press. Dressed in shorts and a tank top, he exposed a great deal more skin than she'd been accustomed to seeing lately and by the way his clothing clung wetly to his skin he'd been at this awhile.

He was also oblivious to her presence and she took the opportunity to observe him, to relish the play of his muscles as they flexed with each press. He made it look so easy but one look at the weight he was pressing and she knew he was managing this through sheer strength and determination.

He completed one more repetition then let the bar rest in its stops and came up to a fully sitting position. It was then he saw her and she noticed the way his eyes sharpened as they raked her. Her breasts were fuller than they'd been before her pregnancy and while it was still such early days, she knew there was a new lushness about her figure that hadn't been there before. She took her time walking toward him, feeling a sense of satisfaction that he was so captured by her right now. But then the shutters came down on his gaze and he grabbed a nearby towel and wiped the perspiration from his face.

"Good workout?" she asked.

"Hard, but good," he replied before spraying the equipment with sanitizer and wiping it down. "Planning to do some exercise?"

"It's something I haven't done enough of recently. I thought it might help."

"Help?"

"Clear my head."

He nodded. "I know what you mean. I've been slack lately. I feel like I'm getting out of shape."

Her eyes flicked over his body and the words blurted from her mouth before she could stop them.

"Nothing wrong with your shape as far as I can see."

The air thickened between them and for a moment time stood still as their eyes met. Ros's body reacted instantly, a curl of desire warming and spreading from the pit of her belly, her breasts feeling fuller and tighter than before, her nipples hardening into taut points that became very obvious through her sports bra and the fabric of her top. Gabe's gaze dropped from her face to her chest and his nostrils flared as he noted her physical reaction to him. But then the spell between them broke as he shook his head once, abruptly, and, with a sound of disgust, snatched up his towel and walked away.

"I'll leave you to it," he said brusquely.

"You don't have to leave on my account," she called after his retreating form.

He muttered something indistinct, which she thought sounded a lot like, *Yes, I do,* and then he was through the gym's door and gone.

Metallica still boomed through the sound system in the gym and she left it going as she started on the treadmill. It suited her mood perfectly and helped her stay focused on her steps as she slowly increased speed and then incline. He'd said last night that he didn't hate her, but lately he couldn't wait to put distance between them when they were home alone. It was infuriating and it made her feel doubly lonely here.

Okay, so sure, she had no one living with her in New York, but at least there had been a bustling metropolis outside the door. She could go for coffee or a meal or to the park, or shopping—basically anywhere her whims might take her. But what did she have here? Land and cows? She shuddered. It would all be so much easier if Gabe would just allow them to be closer. Why couldn't they be friends with benefits? Surely it would have served to bring them closer as a couple, then as parents when the baby arrived. This yawning emptiness between them was driving her crazy.

It made her want to leave.

But she couldn't leave. She'd made a promise and she'd signed a contract. If she left, Gabe would have full custody of their child and all she'd have was visitation rights. A financial obligation hung between them that meant she needed to honor her agreement or face having to let her staff in Australia go. Just thinking about it made her feel sick to her stomach. Her staff were an extension of her family. They relied on her to keep work coming in so they all had jobs and their families had roofs over their heads and food on the table.

As awful as it might get here—and right now she felt pretty trapped—it was what it had to be. And she'd have to work her way through it. Maybe after spending some time sketching today, she'd go visit Miss Emmalou again. Ros knew the old woman was keeping something back. If she could befriend her, maybe she'd want to share her secrets with Ros, or at least unbend a little on the enigma that was Violetta Ford. Ros could see why that journalist, Sierra Morgan, was so fascinated by the story. The intrigue had her hooked as well, but first she needed to get showered and dressed for work and have some breakfast.

The walk on the treadmill had helped her mind to reset, though, and she felt like she was better prepared for whatever the day might throw at her. Probably cow poop, she thought with a wry chuckle as she stepped into the master sitting room.

"Care to share the joke?" Gabe said as he came through from his bedroom.

"Not really. You probably wouldn't appreciate it," she said smoothly and continued to her room.

She sensed him behind her but she continued walking and she could feel his affront coming off him in waves. So what, she decided as she firmly closed her bedroom door behind her. He was the one who decreed they should remain physical strangers in an affectionless marriage. To her mind that meant not sharing jokes, either. Okay, maybe that was petty, she conceded as she stripped down and stepped into her shower, letting the warm jets of water course over her body, but there was no doubting he wouldn't have found the joke funny and despite everything, she really didn't want to offend him.

Gabe was in the kitchen when she came through and he looked up at her for a moment before rising from the kitchen table and clearing his things away.

"You don't have to leave on my account," she said. "Again."

"I'm not," he said in that same brusque tone he'd used in the gym. "I have a meeting at the club. I'm not sure when I'll be back. Will you be okay on your own today?"

"You don't need to babysit me, especially when you've made it patently clear that you don't want to spend any more time with me than absolutely necessary."

"Look, I'm sorry about that. Obviously, I've offended you."

"Yes, you have."

There, she'd leave it at that and see what he came up with.

"Again, Rosalind. I am sorry. We blurred the lines

when we consummated our marriage. We shouldn't have done it. It's…muddied things."

"Really? How? Are you afraid you'll fall in love with me or something?" she prodded.

His face froze into harsh lines. "I don't do love."

"Then I feel sorry for you, Gabe. You're missing out on one of life's best experiences."

"And its worst."

And with that, he stalked from the kitchen. Ros sank into a nearby seat, realizing she was shaking after the encounter. She didn't know why it affected her so deeply. After all, they barely knew each other. But she also knew that she was attracted to him in a way she'd never felt with any other man for that matter. She wanted to get to know him better, to understand him and, with time, maybe love him as she was sure he deserved to be loved.

Clearly his upbringing had been different from hers. So different that they obviously had strongly differing views on love. Who honestly thought that love was one of the worst experiences life had to offer? But it gave her pause for thought. If he couldn't see love as a good thing, what would that mean for their baby? Sure, he said he'd love and care for his heir, but if he didn't understand what love was, how fulfilling it was but how demanding it could be, too, then how could he be a good dad? What if he simply gave up when the going got rough, which it inevitably would. It was a sobering thought.

Gabe drove to the club with only half a mind on the road ahead of him. The other half was firmly trapped back at the ranch with a certain blond. He couldn't rid himself of the image of her in her workout gear this morning. She looked stunning in evening wear, as she had on the night he'd met her, and she'd looked knock-out gorgeous yesterday to meet his dad and grandfather. But dressed in casual wear there'd been something elemental about her that called to him on a deeper level. As if she were some kind of siren and he an unwitting victim of her siren's call.

But he wasn't unwitting, was he? He knew what danger lay ahead if he went down that path and, despite her obvious attraction to him and his answering one to her, he'd removed himself from temptation and walked away. He should be proud of himself. But all he could think about was what it would have been like to close the distance between them and kiss her the way he craved. Kiss her, undress her and make love to her.

He growled out loud, immensely irritated by the train of his thoughts and how, no matter what he did, they always circled back to Rosalind Banks. And every darn time they did, he was left feeling out of sorts and physically uncomfortable. If he were a man like his father, he'd find an outlet for that discomfort. A willing woman who'd ease the demands of his flesh. But he wasn't that kind of man and, even more daunting, he doubted that it would make him want Ros any less.

Gabe was so deep in his own mind he almost missed the turnoff for the club but by the time he'd parked and walked through the entrance he'd almost convinced himself he had his thoughts firmly under control. The members' meeting itself was routine and, hanging around again like a bad smell, was Sierra Morgan. Gabriel wondered what it would take to make her go away. She had an unerring knack of pushing people's buttons while she investigated her stories.

Once the meeting was over, he sauntered to the bar

area to order a coffee. While a few members began imbibing early in the day, Gabe was not one of those and as he waited at a table for his hot drink and a slice of pie, Sierra Morgan slid into a chair opposite him.

"Mind if I join you?" she asked once she was already seated.

He merely raised his brows at her.

The waiter brought him coffee but before he could take a sip, their attention was drawn by the sound of voices. Not loud, but certainly not in calm conversation, either. Gabe looked over his shoulder and spied his friend, Carson Wentworth, in a fierce discussion with his former opponent in the race for club president, Lana Langley. Words, like *bylaws* this and *rules* that, filtered to them before Carson made a dismissive gesture with his hands and walked away. Lana stared at him, obviously still seething, before turning on a high heel and heading in the opposite direction.

"Those two need to kiss it out already," Sierra observed. "Sparks fly whenever they're around—and not necessarily in argument, either."

"No way. Their families are mortal enemies. They've been feuding for generations."

"Mark my words. I'm right—you'll see. One of the things I've learned to be good at in this job is observing people and understanding what makes them tick. Those two, they're attracted to one another. They could make a concrete wall melt with all the energy they create when they're together."

Sierra rose from the table. "Better go. Stories to write."

After she'd gone Gabe took his time over his pie and ordered another coffee for himself, then asked himself why he was lingering here when he could be home working. But being home meant being in proximity with Rosalind and he wasn't sure if he was strong enough to continue to do that and not give in to the ever-growing urge to step into intimate waters with her again.

Why was it so darn hard to simply be together without the complications that emotions brought? He'd drawn his line in the sand and made his decisions. He didn't want love.

But suddenly the thought of an empty life stretching out ahead of him without it seemed a very long time, indeed.

Twelve

The next morning Ros followed the same pattern as the day before—to the gym for a brisk walk on the treadmill followed by some light weights this time, then shower and breakfast before settling in to work. Gabe was nowhere to be seen today and he'd been scarce all day yesterday, too. Despite the housekeeper's presence, the house pretty much echoed in silence.

Not wanting to spend another day completely alone, Ros drove into town after breakfast and browsed some of the stores. The range of goods you could buy was certainly varied, especially when it came to the baby, she realized as she entered a store that specialized in baby gear. Her hand hovered over a tiny onesie in pale gray with a baby elephant embroidered in white on the chest. She'd barely stopped to consider her pregnancy in terms of an actual infant, a tiny human being to love and to hold. Everything else around her had moved so fast from the moment she'd discovered her pregnancy, but right now the reality of her situation hit her hard.

She reeled a little, feeling slightly light-headed and put out a hand, but there was nothing there and as darkness consumed her, she fell to the shop floor.

"Are you all right, ma'am?" she heard one voice say close by her.

"Call an ambulance. Better safe than sorry," said another.

"Probably just low blood sugar—pass her a candy," suggested someone else.

Rosalind opened her eyes and struggled to sit up, only to be firmly encouraged to remain down.

"Don't rush up, honey, you fainted. How are you feeling now?" the first voice asked her.

"I'm okay. I just got light-headed and then…"

"Let me help you to a sitting position, then we'll see if you're up to standing in a minute or two."

The woman, about her own age, guided her up and requested the other two women hovering about to move away. After a couple of minutes Ros said she wanted to stand and the woman led her to a chair in an office out back and got her a glass of water.

"I'm Francine, owner of the store," the woman introduced herself.

"Rosalind Banks, potential shopper," Ros said with a wry smile.

"Oh, you're Gabe's new wife, aren't you?" Francine said.

"I am. Do you know him?"

"Oh, everyone knows everyone around here, and we were an item for a while."

Ros's gaze sharpened on the woman. She was certainly attractive. Slender and tall with shoulder-length glossy brown hair and dark brown eyes, she would have looked good with Gabe. And, from what Ros could tell so far, she had a sweet nature.

"I didn't know that."

"Well, our Gabe likes to play his cards very close to his chest. How's married life?"

"It's interesting."

Francine nodded. "I went out with Gabe for two years and I don't think I ever really knew him."

There was a wry note to her voice that made Ros sit up a little straighter and take notice.

"Well, we didn't exactly marry under regular circumstances," Ros said. "It was more of a business arrangement."

"I heard he'd hired some fancy high-profile international matchmaker to find him a wife. I thought it was just rumor. But is that how you guys hooked up?"

"No, actually, we met at the gala."

"And you hit it off straightaway?" Francine asked in surprise.

Ros thought of her physical reaction to Gabe the moment she'd seen him. It was a reaction that certainly hadn't dulled in the time since they'd met.

"You could say that," she said with a quirk of her lips. "It's why I'm here looking at baby clothes, after all."

"No kidding. Well, that's great news. I'm really happy for Gabe that he's finally getting what he wanted. We didn't part on the best of terms. I, uh, fell in love with another man while we were going out. Troy just swept me off my feet and I quickly realized that that was the kind of relationship I wanted. Oh look, here I am, hardly knowing you and just about telling you my life story. I'm sorry, that's all probably far more than you wanted to know."

Ros shook her head. "No, please, don't stop. I don't have any friends here yet and I'm feeling a bit isolated."

"Where are you from? I can't pick the accent."

"Sydney, Australia, but I had been hoping to settle in New York for a while, at least."

"And you ended up here?" Francine laughed out loud. "Girl, you have some issues with reading a map."

"Well, getting pregnant wasn't exactly on my short list of goals, but here I am."

"Gabe's looking after you, all right?"

"He makes sure everything I need is there for me," Ros said.

And it was true. She didn't want for anything in a material sense. But physically, emotionally? That was a whole other story.

"But you're lonely, right?" Francine pressed.

"Yeah, I am."

"I was that way with him for two years and we lived together for twelve months of that. I kept thinking he'd change, that things would improve between us, but he's a closed book when it comes to his emotions. Happy to be part of a couple without actually *being* part of a couple if you know what I mean."

She'd hit the nail smack on the head. Ros nodded. "I don't really know what to do, to be honest. I thought I could do this, that my work would keep me busy enough that I wouldn't miss the rest. But being here and not really knowing anyone, well, it does make it all a lot harder and, well, Royal… It's not New York, is it?"

"No, it sure isn't. But look, you've made a friend today. I'd be happy to have coffee with you or do lunch. Not so sure Gabe would approve but who cares, right? You don't need his approval."

Ros smiled. "I'm glad I met you, Francine. Thank you for your help today and the conversation."

"Any time, Rosalind. Here, I'll give you my card and pop my cell number on the back for you. Call me when you need a chat or company. We'll work something out."

Ros got to her feet and was relieved to find she felt normal again. As she left the store she stopped and looked at the onesie again and resolved to return to buy it and a whole swag of other things for her baby. While its mom and dad might not have a traditional relationship, the baby would always get the best of everything else.

As she drove back to the ranch, she thought a bit more about what Francine had so openly shared. Gabe was an enigma, one she desperately wanted to unravel. A man of the depths of passion such as they'd shared was only living half a life if he wouldn't allow himself to love. Sure, sex had been great, but sex within a loving, caring relationship was another step above that and could help sustain a relationship for decades. Ros desperately wanted that with him and, with that realization, came to understand that even though she'd been unable to chip through his walls, he'd somehow inveigled his way through hers. She was falling in love with her husband. In itself, not a bad thing, but when it was complicated by the fact he wouldn't love in return, it made for a very unhappy future.

The hands-free function on her car rang and she answered the call. Maybe it was the prospective client in New York. She could do with some good news about now.

"Hello, this is Rosalind Banks."

"I heard you fainted. Stay where you are—I'm on my way to get you."

"Well, hello to you too, Gabe. How are you today?" she said with a touch of asperity in her tone he couldn't fail to miss.

"I was fine until I heard about you fainting. I've made an appointment for you to see the doctor and I'm coming to get you. Just tell me where."

"You can turn right around and cancel that appointment. I'm fine. I just got a little light-headed. That's all."

"Ros—" he started in a voice that told her he wasn't used to someone else countermanding his orders.

"Gabriel Carrington, I'm a big girl and I'm fully aware of the precious cargo I'm carrying. If I thought I needed to see the doctor I would have made an appointment myself. Now, stand down, big guy. Everything is fine. Besides, I'm nearly at the ranch and you can see for yourself that I'm okay."

He huffed out a breath of obvious frustration. "Fine, but if it happens again, promise me you'll get checked out."

"I promise. And how the heck did you find out anyway?"

"This is Royal, Ros. Someone heard from someone at the shop you were in and they rang me."

"Good to know the jungle drums are in full operation. I would have told you myself."

"Would you?"

"Of course I would. I wouldn't keep something like that from you. I'm just about home. See you soon."

She ended the call before he could say another word and she allowed herself to replay their conversation in her mind as she started up the long driveway to the main house. He'd sounded worried, frightened even. For her, or for the baby? She couldn't be certain, but given his emotional distance she had to suspect it was for the baby. Sudden and unexpected tears pricked at her eyes.

He'd been gruff because he cared. What would it be like to have that care and attention focused on her? Maybe, just maybe she could find a crack in that carapace he kept around him. He was essentially a good man and he was missing out on so much in life by keeping himself locked up like that.

Gabe was standing in the garage waiting for her as she pulled up in her stall. Dressed like a quintessential cowboy, he made her heart flutter and her girlie bits tighten on a swell of longing when she saw him there looking so strong and so concerned at the same time. She fiercely wanted him and she didn't know if that was pregnancy hormones or the fact that her feelings for this locked down man were escalating. The latter, she suspected.

He stepped forward and opened her car door, his dark eyes raking her as if to see if she'd been telling the truth about feeling okay.

"You're all right."

It was a statement, rather than a question.

"I told you I was." She got down from the SUV and grabbed her bag then reached up to cup his cheek with one hand. Operation Soften Gabriel's Heart started now. "I'm sorry I worried you."

She followed up with a kiss, pressing her lips to his with every intention of keeping it short and sweet, but the moment her lips touched his she was overwhelmed with the need to be closer to this complicated man. She let her bag drop to the floor and put both arms around his neck, the fingers of one hand spreading through his short-cropped hair. She felt the bolt of shock plummet through him at her touch, but then felt his body ease against hers, felt his lips begin to move in response to her kiss.

In seconds her body was on fire for him and judging by the hardness she felt at her groin he felt the same way. Why then couldn't they just keep going? But then she felt his hands on hers, gently pulling them from him as he lifted his face away. She could see it in his eyes; he wanted her every bit as much as she wanted him. His cheeks carried a flush of desire and his breathing was more rapid than usual.

"Ros, I thought we were clear on this," he growled.

"*You* are clear on this," she said stepping closer again. "I, however, am more than a little murky on the subject. Gabe, I want you. We are consenting adults. We made a baby together. Can't we please just let ourselves find joy in one another?"

He shook his head. "I don't want to hurt you. I won't love you, Ros. Not the way you want me to."

"Then let me take what I can get."

She kissed him again. This time tracing the seam of his mouth with her tongue and yanking at his shirt so her hands could slide over his belly and around his waist to his back. She put everything she could into the kiss. All the yearning she had for him at this point in time and somehow, some way, it worked. Suddenly she was lifted off her feet and then Gabe was carrying her swiftly down the hall and toward their master suite.

He kicked the door closed behind him and went to her bedroom in long strides, closed the door there also and put her down on the bed. He sat down and leaned over her, propping his arms on either side of her body.

"I will do this with you because you want it so much."

"You want me, too. I know you do," she insisted firmly, suddenly desperate to hear him admit it.

He looked conflicted, turmoil clear on his face and reflected in his obsidian dark eyes.

"Yes, damn it."

"Then say it. Say you want me."

"I want you."

She reached for him then, before pulling him down on her and wrapping her arms around him, kissing him with everything she had in her. He was big and solid in her arms and she reveled in the truth he'd finally uttered, the truth she'd ached to hear.

She kicked off the heels she'd been wearing and Gabe lifted his body from her. Seconds later she felt his hands at the waistband of her jeans. She raised her hips so he could slide them down her legs then sat up as he tugged her sweater and long-sleeved tee from her body. Her breasts spilled over the lacy top of her bra, her skin hot and flushed, aching for his touch. He stared at her as if he'd never seen her before, then ripped his shirt over his head, not even bothering with his buttons, before shedding the rest of his clothes and then rejoining her on the bed.

"You are temptation itself," he muttered as he traced the tops of her breasts with one knuckle.

She shivered under the gentleness of his touch.

"Trust me," she whispered. "I try my hardest."

She smiled and reached behind her to unsnap the hooks of her bra. It took a mere shrug of her shoulders for the straps to slide down her arms and the cups to fall away, revealing her full breasts tipped with dark honey-colored nipples. Gabe groaned and reached for her, his hands gentle as they cupped and kneaded her tender flesh before he bent his head and took her nipples, first one, then the other, in his mouth, rolling the taut buds with his tongue. Sensation speared through her, sending jolts of need straight to her core and making her wet and hot for him.

"Gabe?" she all but purred.

"Mmm?"

"Don't stop."

She felt his lips curve in a smile as he continued to pour all his attention on her breasts before slowly lowering her down onto her back. She clenched her hands on his shoulders, relishing the warmth of his skin and the strength of the muscles beneath it. He was a finely built man, every inch of him, and she was finding herself lost in tenderness. Surely this was their way forward. Surely he could not keep his heart locked away when they were so very perfect together.

She dragged her hands down the length of his back, sliding her fingers under the waistband of his boxer briefs and clutching his taut buttocks, holding him to her, against that part of her that begged for his touch.

"Patience," he said, his voice thick with desire.

"I don't want to be patient."

He lifted his head and cocked it, looking at her with lust-drugged eyes. "Are you sure about that?" he asked.

With one hand he cupped her between her legs, the pressure of the palm of his hand directly on her clit and sending a spark of intense pleasure through her. Pleasure she knew would only intensify the longer he spent giving it to her.

"Okay, maybe I do want to be patient," she gasped as he renewed the pressure on that sensitive spot once more.

"Glad to hear it, because I've a mind to take my time."

She laughed softly. "Then you do that. I'll just be your willing partner."

"I like the sound of that."

She did, too, but for a very different reason. For Ros, being his partner meant being his partner in everything. Not just housemates. Not just parents of their child. Partners in every sense of the word. Not that she could make him see that, just yet. But maybe, just maybe, he'd come to see it if they could rebuild the intimacy that had brought them together in the first place.

Gabe hooked her panties with his fingers and dragged the lacy garment down her legs before dropping it to the floor beside the bed. Then he let his fingers drift back up the length of her legs before resting at the tops of her inner thighs. She squirmed against the bed, wishing he would speed things up again but telling herself at the same time he was taking as long as he needed.

Even so, it was sweet torture as he kissed her thighs with little nips and strokes of his tongue to torment her even further. She pushed her hips up toward him, silently urging him to touch her at that point of her body where she craved his touch with a physicality that was making her mind unravel. And then, finally, he was there. His lips and tongue deftly touching and stroking. She was so ready that the orgasm that hit came hard and fast, a culmination of wanting him so much for what felt like so long and finally having him here in her bed with her.

Trembling in the aftermath, she eagerly reached for

him as he moved up and over her body, settling between her legs, his hard length nudging at her entrance.

"I can feel the heat of you, your wetness," he murmured as he bent to kiss her. "Do you have any idea how sexy that is?"

"It's all because of you and what you do to me," she answered. "Do it to me some more."

He smiled and locked his eyes with hers as he pressed his hips against her, his erection sliding into her even as her body still clenched on aftershocks of pleasure from her climax. He began to move and Rosalind could feel her body responding again, felt the building swell of need and pleasure coalescing into a maelstrom of feeling. How was it possible he could do this to her? One touch, one look, and he had her virtually panting for him.

She needed him on a level that was daunting but right now he was exactly where she needed him to be. As the sensations building inside her reached their peak, she cried out his name giving herself over to the sheer wonder of their joining. Gabe, too, climaxed, his body rigid, driving deep within her as his own pleasure punched through him making him thrust inside her two, three, four times more. Her inner muscles tightened around him, holding him when he made to withdraw and she felt him shiver in response to her actions.

He wrapped his arms around her and rolled them onto their sides, holding her close. She nuzzled against his chest, inhaling the scent of his skin—a combination of the fresh soap he used, a light touch of cologne and the sexy maleness that was essentially his alone. Ros felt him relax, heard his breathing slow, felt his heart begin to return to a steady, less frantic beat.

"I love you," she whispered against his skin in a voice pitched so softly she was sure he couldn't hear it.

But the words needed to be said. In her heart of hearts, she knew that what they shared was so special she would never reach this level of bliss or this sense of connection with another man. Gabe was it and she was lucky enough to have found him. Lucky enough to be bearing his child. Now if only she could persuade him of that and encourage him to let her into his heart, too.

Thirteen

Had he heard that right? Gabe wondered, as he felt Ros's body soften as she drifted into sleep in his arms. He waited a few minutes and carefully extricated himself from the tangle of their legs and the loosening hold of her arms.

He put a soft blanket over her sleeping form and picked up his discarded clothing before making his way to his bathroom. He'd heard it right; he knew it. And it was his worst nightmare. He'd told her over and again that he didn't want to hurt her, but he wouldn't be able to help it now. Why had she gone and ruined everything by falling in love?

Love brought expectations and pressures he had no desire to yield to. He should never have given in to her coercion to make love. It had led to heightened emotion and a declaration he'd had no desire to hear. And it was his fault. He'd given in. Hell, he'd been so relieved to see she was okay when she returned from town, it was all he could do not to pick her up and lock her away in her room for the duration of her pregnancy. The idea of something happening to Ros had terrified him, gripping his chest with an icy hand until he could see for himself that she was okay.

He hadn't wanted to examine why it was so important to him that she be all right. It was simple biology, he told himself. She was carrying their baby and for that child, his heir, to come to fruition she needed to be well and safe.

They had to talk about this; they had to reestablish the boundaries of their marriage and they could not make love again. It opened up corridors that needed to remain firmly closed.

He stepped into the shower stall and turned the water to full cold, bracing at the shock against his body. Was he a madman, choosing this over curling up in bed with his wife? Some would likely say so, but given the words his wife had uttered this was the only response. He didn't shower long and was soon dressed and back in his office.

Hours later as he entered the kitchen he heard sounds in the formal lounge and, curious as to their origin, went to look. The sight that greeted him made his blood run cold. There was Ros, on a stepladder no less, arranging a string of fairy lights on a large artificial Christmas tree.

"What the hell are you doing?" he barked.

The instant he spoke he regretted it because Ros's attention came off what she was doing and went straight to him. The stepladder teetered a little, before righting itself, but that didn't stop him moving swiftly over the distance between them and lifting her down.

"Well, thanks for giving a girl some warning," she grumbled at him. "I was doing okay until you shouted at me."

"Do you have a death wish or are you just trying to be the death of me?" he retorted.

"Neither, I just wanted to put up the tree. I asked Doreen where to find everything. Christmas is just around the corner. I wanted to surprise you."

He felt churlish for having yelled at her but looking around the room at the boxes on the floor—boxes carefully labeled in his mother's clear handwriting—sent a shaft of loss and pain through him.

"Well, consider me surprised," he said bluntly and turned to walk away. "Stay off the ladder. I'll get one of the hands to help you."

"I can't get to the high points without it. Wouldn't *you* like to help me?"

"Frankly, I wouldn't care if you didn't put the tree up at all. I haven't had one up in years."

"But why not?" Ros asked, looking stunned. "It's Christmas. I thought it would be fun for us. Our first Christmas together. Don't you celebrate?"

"No, but do whatever makes you happy."

He left her then, determined to put distance between them. A good hard ride might be what he needed to blow the cobwebs away and to prevent the memories of the last time he'd seen that tree and those decorations standing in his mom's front room. It had been the night she died and seeing them dragged out and the boxes open on the floor of his living room brought it all back again. The anxiety about her not being home yet, the darkening night, the unexpected snowstorm that blanketed the roads. The knock at the door by the police.

Gabe was at the stables before he realized he hadn't

grabbed a coat or hat but he didn't care. He saddled Ulysses and led him out of the stables, swung up into the saddle and headed the gelding out to wider pastures. Several of his stock lifted their heads as he and Ulysses rode through, gaining pace the farther they got from the ranch house. It was only when he drew Ulysses to a halt that he realized that the reason why his face felt so chilled was because of the tears that had frozen on his cheeks. He scraped a hand over the evidence of his grief and vowed anew not to let her get to him, not to let her see the chinks in the armor that he'd so carefully constructed around his heart.

That tree, those decorations—all of them combined to remind him of one of the worst times in his life. A night made worse by the arrival of his father and grandfather and their platitudes and expressions of grief over the loss of his mom. Crocodile tears, all of it. If his dad had ever truly loved his mom, he'd never have treated her so badly, but then again, with the example his own father had given him, it was no wonder. Gabe had vowed then to never become like either of them.

Then why did it sting so much to realize how much it had hurt Ros when he'd refused to help her and had walked out? Hell, he hadn't even stopped to ask one of the guys working near the house to give her the help he'd promised. He turned Ulysses back toward the stables, the horse eager to head home in the cool air. At the stables he took care of Ulysses's needs before going back into the house.

He should apologize to Ros, maybe explain why he'd reacted that way, but wouldn't that lead to him having to open up about those messy things, feelings? Maybe it was better to simply keep his past firmly where it belonged. Locked up tight and never to see the light of day again. He went through to the living room only to discover the tree had been packed up and the boxes were gone. Everything was exactly as it had been when he'd risen this morning. Before he'd heard about Ros's fainting spell, before he'd driven himself mad with worry for her, before he'd made love to her with an intensity that had shaken him to his very core.

Before she'd told him she loved him.

He still had to deal with that. Nip it in the bud now. He'd already crushed her with the business over the Christmas tree, though. It would be like kicking a puppy when it was already injured to discuss her softly whispered declaration now, wouldn't it? But if he didn't face it down, didn't draw those lines in the sand, where would it lead? Would she too, like his mother, wounded in heart and spirit, make a fatal mistake one day? He couldn't let that happen.

He carried on down the hallway to the master suite. Her bedroom door was open and he could hear her moving around inside, humming a Christmas carol sweetly off-key. He pushed himself to go inside her room. The bed was still in disarray, a stark reminder of their passion earlier, but that wasn't what made his blood run cold. No, that would be the half-filled suitcase she had open on the bed.

"Oh, you're back," she said as she came out of the walk-in wardrobe with an armful of clothing. "I got a call from Piers and I wanted to share the news with you. My New York connection has connected. We're going under contract."

She sounded so delighted he knew he'd have to put this discussion on the back burner for now.

"That's good news, but why the packing?"

"I have to go and meet with my lawyer and we're

having a joint meeting with the new distributor. The sooner the better. I've booked a flight out from San Antonio first thing in the morning and I thought I'd drive there tonight and stay over in an airport hotel so I can be fresh when I get to New York tomorrow."

"Weather's not great—I'll drive you."

"Oh, there's no need."

"Yes, there's need."

She shrugged and dumped her clothes on the bed before picking up individual items and folding and rolling them neatly before placing them in her suitcase.

"If it makes you feel better," she acceded. "I'll be glad of the company during the drive. You could stay with me in the hotel, too, if you like."

She took a step toward him and laid one hand on his chest with a mischievous glint in her eye. "In fact, *I'd* like that very much. We could revisit what we did together."

Gabe's entire body clenched. If theirs were a regular marriage, if she hadn't used a specific four-letter word—then sure, maybe he'd do that but given how she felt about him, he couldn't do that to her. He couldn't take from her what he wasn't prepared to give in return.

He put his hand over hers, forcing himself to hold strong and not to give in to the urge to agree to her suggestion. Even now, with her palm pressed against his shirt, feeling the warmth of her, it was so tempting. But he would not do it.

"No, I won't be staying." He lifted her hand away from his chest. "What time do you want to leave?"

"I'll be ready in about forty-five minutes," she said.

Her voice had lost a lot of the excitement that had shimmered from her only moments ago. He'd done that. He'd sapped her joy. And he had to bear the responsibility of it, too, along with the responsibility of getting them both into this lopsided marriage. He'd known when he met her that she was full of dreams and sunshine and fairy-tale endings, whereas he was the flip side of that being grounded in hard reality. He should never have slept with her, never gotten her pregnant, never married her.

But he'd done all those things and now she was a butterfly trapped in a glass case. Its beautiful, colorful wings batting helplessly and futilely against the barriers of its existence. He was that barrier. He took another step back from her.

"I'll leave you to your packing. Please, don't lift your case. I'll come and get it when you're ready to go. Have you eaten?"

Damn, he sounded like her mother again. Not like the man who'd brought her to two cataclysmic orgasms only a few short hours ago. He shoved that thought to the very recesses of his mind. It was not a good idea to go there. Ros rolled her eyes at him.

"No, I won't lift my case and, yes, I have eaten. Cookie made us something. Yours is probably still in the fridge. I'm assuming *you* haven't eaten?" she said with a supercilious quirk of her eyebrow.

"No, I haven't. I'll get on to that now." He started to walk away but stopped and turned and looked at her. "I'm sorry about the tree."

She shook her head. "No need. I should have discussed it with you first, I guess. This is your home, after all."

And yours too, he wanted to add. But it was clear she didn't feel that way and he wondered just how long this marriage of theirs was going to last. Not long by the looks of things. A sharp pang hit him in the chest and he rubbed his breastbone as he walked away. He'd been cold while riding out with Ulysses but that was nothing to the cold that permeated him to the bone, now.

She wasn't going forever, he reminded himself. She was attending business meetings and then coming back, wasn't she? Right now, he wasn't so sure and he had no idea of what to say to ensure she did return other than reminding her of the contract she'd signed. It wasn't as if he were offering her the love and affection she so clearly craved. Hell, he hadn't even let her set up a Christmas tree.

He muttered an expletive and retrieved his sandwich from the fridge. But he didn't feel like eating. Not when she was going away. Not when he was feeling all the things he'd been trying so hard not to feel. Maybe it was a good thing she was going to New York for a visit, he told himself. It would give him a chance to reset. To get his head straight. To maybe move to a bedroom in another part of the house so he didn't feel the temptation to stop in at hers every night when he went to bed.

He shook his head. He was a hopeless case. He got up and put the sandwich back in the fridge before going to his office. Maybe he could do some paperwork in the time he had left before taking Ros to San Antonio. Whatever, he had to find something to distract him. Because his own thoughts were taking a very disturbing turn, indeed.

Ros sat down on the bed with a sigh. She couldn't understand the yawning chasm that had opened up between her and Gabe since they'd made love earlier today. He'd been so tender, so caring, so absolutely attuned to her needs. And then nothing. Nothing but coldness. Not so much as a speck of the warmth and passion they'd shared together.

She got up and went to her wardrobe, gathered a few more items to pack. New York was cold, colder than here, but she was certainly looking forward to going back. There was an energy about the city that she loved and the opportunities there were endless. She inserted the last items into her case and closed it before changing into a fresh set of clothing for traveling in. When she was ready, she went looking for Gabe.

Ros found him in his office, but he wasn't working. In fact, he was probably the most still she'd ever seen him. He'd swiveled his chair to face the window behind his desk and not so much as a hair on his head moved as he sat there.

"Gabe? I'm ready."

He started, as if he'd been asleep but when he turned around, she saw that he'd been holding a photo frame.

"Who's that?" she asked, taking a step closer to his desk.

"My mom. Those were her decorations you were using today. She loved Christmas."

He didn't say much, but his words pretty much said it all and compassion bloomed through her.

"Gabe, I'm so sorry. I didn't mean to drag all that back up for you."

"It was a long time ago. I shouldn't have reacted the way I did. Maybe when you get back, we can do the tree together."

She nodded but the compassion she'd felt a moment ago was swiftly replaced by another emotion that was harder to define. She was sorry she'd hurt him, but if he didn't open up to her, how would she ever be able to avoid hurting him again? Before she could say anything else, he had risen from his chair and was walking to the door.

"Come on then, let's get on the road."

Ros followed him to their suite and then to the garage where she settled in his vehicle while he stowed the case in the trunk. He got into the car without saying a word and they left the ranch in silence. The silence stretched out between them for the entire duration of the journey and the longer it continued the less she was inclined to break it. There was so much unsaid between them and she ached to tell him again that she loved him, that everything would be okay.

But she didn't and, deep down, she didn't believe it would be, either. Maybe when she returned, they'd talk—really talk—but even the thought of how different they were and how differently they saw marriage still loomed between them. She was city and he was country. She loved bright lights, people and noise. He craved solitude, wide-open spaces and the sounds that came with the peace of the land. And despite all that, she loved him anyway.

She didn't know when she'd fallen asleep but she was stiff and her neck sore when she finally woke as they pulled into the front entrance of the hotel she'd booked.

"Gabe, I'm sorry to have slept so long."

"You looked like you needed it," he said and got out of the car.

She did the same and walked around the back where he was taking her case out of the trunk.

"Well, here you are," he said, standing back and looking more remote than he'd ever done.

A bellhop came forward to take Ros's case and she

gave him her details, wishing he'd just go away so she could talk to Gabe. But what was there to say?

"Thank you for driving me. Are you sure you don't want to stay the night with me?"

His face hardened, looking as if it had been carved from granite. "No, thank you. I'll head straight back. I have a lot to attend to in the morning."

She nodded. "All right then, well, goodbye."

Ros stepped closer and reached up to kiss him but at the last moment he turned his head slightly so her lips did no more than brush his cheek. So, it was to be like that, she thought with a disappointment that struck her so deeply she couldn't speak. Instead, she gave him a short wave and then followed the bellhop through the entrance. She didn't turn and look back, she couldn't, because if she did, she couldn't trust herself not to run back to Gabe and beg him to take her back to the ranch. She needed to do this trip. The future of her business hinged on it and with that the employment of all her staff.

Maybe when she came back, things would be different. But as she completed registration at the front desk and booked her ride to the airport for tomorrow, she knew that even wishing for things to alter between them was grasping at straws. Nothing would change, because Gabriel Carrington was exactly who and what he was. He hadn't pretended to be any different. She was the one who'd spoiled things by letting her heart rule the very practical arrangement they'd agreed on.

And she loved him.

Fourteen

Rosalind had felt different the moment she set foot in New York a week ago. It was as if the city sang to her, making her blood rush excitedly through her veins and her mind fill with possibilities. On the day she got back, her lawyer had collected her from the airport with a driver and begun discussing the contracts that had been proposed by her new client. Overall, it'd looked perfect and the first-stage payment from them would set her company back on an even keel. Everything had been signed late that afternoon.

She picked up her pencil and focused on the new drawings she'd begun this morning, because that meeting had ended up going so well, the new customer had also asked her for concept designs for an exclusive range for their firm alone. From where she was at the beginning of November, to where she was now, were poles apart. This was the life she'd craved.

The ambition, the creativity, the hard work and the rewards. Everything she had worked toward since her very first design.

After serious discussions with Piers and the rest of her management team in Sydney, Rosalind had reached a decision. This was her home now, New York. It fed her soul in ways she couldn't even begin to describe. There was nothing for her in Royal. Nothing except a man who was incapable of loving her. It was an incredibly difficult decision to reach and it tore at her, knowing that her decision would create even bigger problems between them, not to mention the legal fight she had ahead regarding custody of their baby, but between his emotional distance and the stifled feeling she'd had living on his ranch, there was no way she could consider returning.

Aside from a Skype session with her parents, she'd spent Christmas Day alone with her thoughts and wondering about Gabe and what he was doing. Maybe things might have been different if he'd have been open to loving her in return, or even liking her enough that she could pretend it was love. She shook her head sharply. No, that was a ridiculous way to think. Why should she accept a half measure when she was prepared to give it all, herself? And even though it would crush her, she had to do this.

They'd always be bound by the baby she carried, and they'd have to find a legal way to deal with living in different states and co-parenting this life they'd created, but she was confident they could remain civil about it.

She looked at the old-fashioned calendar on her wall. He should have received the letter from her lawyer by now. It had been sent by express courier. She'd expected a call, an email, anything. But there'd been nothing from him at all. Maybe he was relieved she was gone. That way he wouldn't have to deal with her messy emotions or demands on him.

She pulled herself up. That was unfair. He wasn't born that way. The raw grief she'd briefly seen on his face when she'd found him with his mother's picture was evidence of that. Grief he'd rapidly masked, she remembered. Was that what it was that held him back from loving anyone? Had the pain of losing his mom been too much to bear? So much, in fact, that he'd shut himself off from the joy of loving anyone ever again?

Fifteen

Gabe turned the legal papers over in his hands as if he might see something different on the backs of the sheets. He'd been expecting it. There'd been an invisible divide between him and Rosalind when she'd left that he'd felt with a physical ache. He knew what she needed, but he knew equally well that he wasn't capable of giving it to her. Would it have made a difference even if he had, or would it have set him up for even greater disappointment if he'd loved her and she'd left anyway?

He shook his head. A contract between two consenting adults who were in agreement. It had all seemed so simple, but it had turned into a hornets' nest.

He missed her, as stupid as that sounded, and she'd only been gone a week. Who'd remind her to eat on time and well enough now? No, stop, he told himself. She didn't need a mother telling her what to do. She needed a partner, supporting her in what she did. She'd come to him as vulnerable as a woman could probably get and he'd taken the opportunity with both hands, capitalizing on it without compunction because it fit into what he wanted.

Deep down he'd always known he'd trapped a butterfly and he'd learned as a child that they didn't do well in captivity. He shook his head again. And here he was thinking about the ranch as if it were a prison when it had always been his life's dream to have his own spread and when his father had agreed to apportion half of the Carrington Ranch to him completely, he'd never once dreamed that he'd want to walk away from his dreams.

But he wanted to now. And why? Because he'd lost something that he'd seen as his? Could he ever have imagined that Ros was his completely? No, of course not. Especially not when he wasn't prepared to give her the emotional support she so clearly needed to feel at home in his life, too. She'd tried, he had to give her that. She'd given him the openings, the hints, the encouragement. But he'd been too bullheaded to listen to any of it. All because he hadn't wanted to get hurt or to hurt her in return.

And look how well that turned out, the voice in the back of his head jeered silently.

The phone on his desk rang, jerking him out of his contemplations. There was only one person who continued to insist on trying to reach him on his landline before trying his cell phone. His father.

"Carrington," he said tersely.

"Sounds like you need a drink, my boy."

Gabriel fought back a sigh at the sound of his father's voice. "I'm afraid if I start now, I won't stop for a few days," he answered honestly. "How are you, Dad?"

"Better than you by the sounds of it. Why don't you join me for a drink and dinner at the club tonight, say seven? I'll see you there."

His father hung up before he could refuse. The last thing he really wanted was to spend time in his father's company, right now. But what else did that leave him? His own? He looked at the papers he'd received from Ros's lawyer and made his decision.

"See you there, Dad," he said out loud as he replaced the phone in its cradle.

He set the papers on his desk. He'd deal with them tomorrow.

He looked at the gold ring on his finger and wondered if he should take it off. Was Ros still wearing hers?

At the club Gabe parked his car and went inside to find his father. Denver sat on his own in one of the bars.

"Dad," Gabe said in greeting as he perched on the chair beside his father.

"Son." Denver nodded to the bartender who brought two whiskies on ice. "Get that inside you," he said to Gabe as he picked up his glass and held it up in a toast. "To you and your blushing bride."

Gabe put his glass down on the counter without taking a sip.

"What's wrong? You two fighting already?" Denver said in a tone that teased but needled at the same time.

Gabe decided the easiest way through this was to just be up-front with his father. No point in fudging the truth.

"No, she's gone back to New York."

"Business or pleasure?"

"Permanently."

For a moment his father was speechless, not something Gabe had witnessed very often in his thirty-one years. Denver put his glass down on the counter, too, and swiveled to study Gabe carefully.

"You all right?"

Again, honesty seemed the best policy. "No, I'm not. And I'd rather not discuss it."

His father's face settled into serious lines. "You know, you could go after her."

"What? To drag her back by her hair, kicking and screaming because of a stupid contract? I have far too much respect for her to do something as archaic as that."

"Well, I wasn't suggesting that, exactly," Denver said ruefully. "But why don't you go, talk it out, find a middle ground."

"What? Like you did with Mom?" Gabe shot back.

His father was hardly the man to be giving anyone relationship advice.

"I guess I deserved that," Denver acknowledged. "I'm sorry my choices made you so bitter, Gabriel."

"You treated her like an accessory to your life."

"I did, and it was wrong. We probably should never have married. I always knew what she wanted but I didn't think it mattered. My own mother had always been happy with her lot—I never expected any different when your mom and I married."

"How can you say you never expected any different?"

Denver shrugged. "I guess that's the lazy man's way out. I didn't want to face up to the fact that my decisions hurt your mother."

"Why the sudden turnaround? Your choices never bothered you before," Gabe said bitterly.

Denver sighed heavily. "I know it probably looked

that way to you, but you can rest assured that I have had my own cross to bear with respect to my marriage. I had hoped that by staying away from you the way I did, it might give you a chance to be a better man than I was."

"I am a better man than you were."

Gabe saw his father flinch as if his words had been arrows flung straight at him.

"I deserved that and, yes, you are. I'm really proud of you and all you've achieved, but you're just like me at the same time."

Gabe felt a surge of belligerence rise in his chest and he was that argumentative teenager who'd gone toe to toe with his father more times than he could count.

"No, I'm not."

"Then why aren't you following your wife?"

"Because she doesn't want me."

"Doesn't she? I know I said I am proud of you, but you know, you can be real dense sometimes."

"Dad, I didn't come here to be insulted."

Gabe picked up his drink and downed it in a few short gulps. "Thanks for the drink. I've lost my appetite for dinner so if you'll excuse me—"

"Don't you dare run away from me when we're having a conversation."

"A conversation? Sounds more like flinging abuse to me."

"You are so like your mother. Too quick to take offense and so guarded that no one can reach you when you really need them to. I bet that's what Ros did, too, right? Try to reach out to you, to touch your heart, and you kept it all clammed up like the bullion depository at Fort Knox. Any fool could see she was in love with you, not that you deserve it."

"I beg your pardon?"

"I said you're like your mother, and you are, but you're a lot like me, too. I didn't deserve her devotion or her love. I treated her as if she was an employee, not my wife. You, too, a lot of the time. I guess I just wasn't cut out to be a husband and a father the way a regular man is. But you still have the chance to fix that. Go after her, Gabe. Tell her how you feel about her."

"Dad, I don't even know how I feel about her."

"You do, you just don't want to admit it. Son, I let the right woman slip through my fingers by not being the man she deserved. Don't be like me."

As Gabe drove home later that evening, he replayed his conversation with his father in his head. They'd talked, honestly talked, for the first time in his life, and he'd found himself actually enjoying his father's company by the end of the night. Sure, none of that turned back time—it didn't bring his mother back, but it had laid the path to a new beginning with Denver. One not based on bitterness and recriminations.

So where did that leave him, he wondered. He had the ranch, sure, but while he told himself he needed it, his spread certainly didn't need him. He had employed the best of the best and the place ran like a well-oiled machine with or without him.

What did he really want? Rosalind. There was no question. But why? Had she inveigled her way into his guarded heart despite his best efforts to keep that part of him intact? He thought about his father's comment, about dying a lonely old man and it made his gut clench in fear. It didn't have to be that way. All Gabe had to do was open up. To admit to his feelings for Ros. To love her the way she deserved.

This had to do with far more than the child they'd

made together. He'd been drawn to her from the moment he'd first laid eyes on the sultry blond siren at the gala. He wasn't the kind of man to have a one-night stand. And yet he'd done so with her and the moment she was back in his life he'd done what he could to lasso her to his side in marriage. They could have still had an agreement to live together and raise their child together without marriage, but he'd wanted her tied to him in every way possible, even if he hadn't wanted to admit that to himself.

Could he do it? Could he walk away from the ranch, from everything he'd ever strived for and worked toward his entire adulthood?

Could he do it for love?

More important, would she let him back into her life?

Sixteen

Ros looked up from her design board at the kerfuffle going on in reception of her new workplace. She could see her new receptionist's back ramrod straight and heard her remonstrating with someone just slightly out of view.

"And I told you she's not seeing visitors today. What part of 'no' don't you understand?"

LaToya's hands went to her hips and, if anything, she bristled even more. Ros caught a soft Texan drawl, a voice she knew all too intimately. She dropped her pencil and walked swiftly to the door between her workroom and reception.

"It's okay, LaToya. He's my husband."

"You didn't tell me you were married," her staunch receptionist accused her.

If the woman weren't quite as good at her job as she was, Ros might have snapped a reply; instead she ex-

pressed her thanks for her excellent vetting skills and
led Gabe through to her room.

"I suppose you'll be wanting a hot drink?" LaToya
said following behind them.

"Thank you, I'll have my usual and Mr. Carrington
will have coffee, black with one sugar."

LaToya snorted. "Man needs more sweetening, if
you ask me."

She turned on her heel and disappeared in the direction of the kitchen. Rosalind closed the door to her
workroom and gestured to the seats she had over to
one side.

"That's quite the conquest you made there. Do you
want to sit?"

She felt ridiculously nervous, skittish even. She
hadn't expected Gabe to come all the way here and to
turn up unannounced like this. She also felt that all-
consuming tug that she'd almost managed to convince
herself she'd forgotten in the days since she'd left Royal.

"Thanks," he said and folded himself down on the
two-seater sofa she had positioned opposite two arm-
chairs.

Her workroom at the top of a warehouse conversion
was large and airy and the winter sun through the tall
windows behind him bathed the room in a clear light.

"Nice place. You worked fast," he said carefully.
"I didn't expect you to have space and staff already."

"In fairness, I had started the ball rolling before we
married and LaToya is from an agency. I just hadn't
expected to be working from here, myself."

An awkward silence fell between them and Ros had
to force herself not to shift in her chair. He had come
to her. She'd leave the floor open to him if he wanted
to discuss the paperwork she'd had sent to him. LaToya

came in with their hot drinks and set them down on the table between them, giving them each a hard look before raising a brow in question to Rosalind.

"Everything okay here?" she asked, looking fierce.

Ros fought back a smile. Her new receptionist knew she was pregnant and looked like she was prepared to eject Gabe personally if he was bothering Rosalind.

"Everything is fine, thank you."

LaToya sniffed and with a final glare in Gabe's direction she returned to her station.

Gabe looked at Ros with a puzzled expression on his face. "Did I say something to offend her?"

"Probably not," Ros answered. "She takes her role as gatekeeper here very seriously. That's all."

Gabe grunted. "Good to know you're surrounding yourself with good people."

"What are you doing here, Gabe?"

Damn, she'd failed at waiting him out but surely asking him directly was easier than sitting here, staring at him, remembering what he smelled like, how he tasted, what his skin felt like beneath her fingers. The sooner she knew what he wanted the sooner he could leave and the sooner she'd get back to work and her new normal, even if she knew she would always imagine him here, sitting sprawled on her little sofa, every time she came in. He had a way of imprinting himself onto her memory that was indelible.

She'd hoped she would have more time to inure herself to him before she saw him again. She'd hoped in vain.

"You're keeping well?" he asked, ignoring her question.

"I'm fine. Please, Gabe, tell me why you're here."

"I wanted to ask you out to dinner."

"What?"

"Yeah, dinner. You know, where people go to a restaurant, sit at a table, choose from a menu, get served their selection."

"Don't patronize me, Gabe. If you want to argue the terms of the dissolution of our marriage, please take it up with my lawyer. Now, if you haven't got anything else to discuss I really need to return to work."

"No, wait, please. I'm serious. I want to take you out for dinner. On a date."

"A date."

"We skipped a few steps. I thought I'd like to take some time to recover that lost time with you, if you'll let me."

She sighed sadly. "Gabe, it won't make any difference. You're still Mr. Texas and I'm Ms. New York."

"Humor me?" he asked. "Look, give me your address and I'll pick you up. Seven thirty? Eight? What suits you best?"

She stared at him a full ten seconds before answering. "Sure, fine, whatever it takes. Make it eight."

Ros gave him her address.

"Thank you. I'll see you then."

He swilled down his coffee. "Damn, she must have put half a cup of sugar in there."

Rosalind giggled in response. "I'm so sorry."

He shrugged and his lips quirked into a half smile. "I can change," he said before downing the sweet brew and placing his mug back on the table.

With that he left and Ros stared at his departing back, wondering exactly what he'd meant by that. Out in reception, she heard him thank LaToya profusely for the coffee before leaving their office space. The receptionist came back into Ros's workroom.

"That man all right in the head?" she asked.

Ros laughed again and it felt good. She couldn't remember the last time she'd found anything humorous.

"I'll have to get back to you on that," she answered and lifted her cup of herbal tea. "Just don't try any of that on me, okay?"

LaToya beamed in return. "Oh no, I like you."

"Thank goodness for that." Ros grinned back.

She was in a chronic state of indecision in the lead-up to eight o'clock. In the end she opted for the black wool dress she'd worn the last time she and Gabe had gone to the club together and accessorized with a blue patterned scarf that accentuated the blue of her eyes, and wore her hair loose. High-heeled pumps and sheer stockings completed the ensemble. She'd just slung her coat around her shoulders when the concierge buzzed up to say Gabe was waiting for her downstairs.

She let herself out of the apartment and took the elevator to the ground floor. Gabe waited for her in the lobby, flowers in his hands. The blooms were glorious and completely unseasonal, as if they'd been flown in directly from an Australian rain forest, in fact.

"You look great," he said, stepping forward and passing them to her. "These are for you."

"Thank you, they're beautiful."

The concierge cleared his throat. "Shall I keep them in water for you until your return?"

"Thank you, I'd appreciate it."

Gabe led her out to a cab waiting by the sidewalk. He ushered her into the backseat and followed close behind before giving the name of the restaurant to the driver.

Ros was startled. The eatery, near Bryant Park, was

popular and she thought the wait list to get a table there was weeks long.

"How did you get us a booking there and on New Year's Eve, too?" she asked.

"I know a guy who knows a guy," he said enigmatically.

"He must have some influence," she said in return.

"Actually, I went to college with the owner. I told him I needed to impress a girl and, hey presto, a table opened up for us."

She sat back in her seat and pondered his statement. Impress her? Why now? Why, when they were already married? They'd been there, they'd done that and they'd failed. If anything, living together had exposed all the reasons they shouldn't have married in the first place. What exactly was on his agenda?

They'd worked their way through appetizers and their main course and were lingering over dessert before she found out.

"Enjoying dinner?"

"Yes, very much. Thank you. It sure beats baked beans on toast."

For a moment he looked horrified but it dawned on him that she was teasing him.

"You got me, there," he said.

"I did, didn't I? Now, tell me, why are you here?"

He instantly looked serious. "I'm here because you're here. It's as simple and as complex as that."

She didn't understand. "What do you mean?"

"I mean Royal is a great place, but it's not home if you're not there with me."

She shook her head. "Gabe, you love Royal. You love your ranch. You don't love me."

He speared her with a look. "Don't I? Then why have

I not been able to sleep since you've been gone? Why does every day stretch out before me like an interminable loop in time? Why do I miss you so much I can barely finish a sentence without thinking of you, wondering how you are or what you're doing? Sure, fine," he said, cutting the air with the palm of his hand. "That sounds stalkerish, I know. I'm sorry. But I can't help it."

Gabe drew in a long breath and exhaled just as slowly. "You see, I want to be where you are. I want to be your husband, in every sense of the word. To be by your side in everything. The good, the bad, the not-so-pretty. I want to be hands-on with our kid, not stuck out on the range working my guts out for some dream that I don't even want anymore. I need to be with you, if you'll let me."

"But what about the ranch? You can't just leave it."

"I can manage a lot of things from here just as easily as I did from there. I have a great team in place and the education center I told you about during dinner a couple of weeks ago is on track to begin in the spring. Obviously, I'd like to be there for the start-up and for each new intake, but I don't have to actually live there. Why would I when you're here?"

"But New York is nothing like Royal. It's crowded, it's noisy, it's go-go-go all the time."

"You know, I wondered what it would be like so I came here a few days ago. I've done some of the tourist stuff, but I've spent more time just walking. Feeling the city. Seeing what it is that drew you here in the first place. And I get it. There's a vibrancy that catches you here," he put a fist at his chest. "It fed something in me I didn't even know existed. But most of all, it's where you live and even if you don't want me back in your life full-time—just yet, or ever—I know I could make my home here. It feels familiar and yet so different from what I know all at the same time. It's wild and crazy and full of light and people, and it's solemn and interesting and has dark places and strangers, but all of it speaks to me in a way I never thought it would."

"You would run the ranch and the program remotely?"

"Pretty much. Pete is an excellent manager and he has a solid team behind him. Doreen is chafing at the bit to be a housemother to the youths we anticipate bringing to the property. To be honest, Ros, it'll be a win-win for everyone, but I need to know it'll be a win-win for you, too. You sacrificed so much to move to Royal and I was too stupid to understand that. Too stupid to see that your openness and your love weren't things to be afraid of, but things to cherish and protect. But now it's my turn—not just to make it up to you but to allow us to figure out what works for *us* and how we work together."

"But why, Gabe? I don't get it. Why are you turning your entire life upside down for me and our baby?"

"Because I love you. Because my world begins and ends with you and I don't want to ever live without you."

"But what if you find yourself to be a total fish out of water, like I did back in Royal."

"I won't. I know it deep in my heart that if I'm with you, and you're happy, I'm where I need to be. Look, I'm sorry I'm laying it all on you tonight. But it's my turn to try. My time to make it up to you for pushing you away. I had this grand plan of wooing you for however long it took to win you back and then asking you to marry me again."

"That sounds fun," she said carefully, still in a state of disbelief at what she'd heard from his lips.

Lips she ached to kiss again. She clenched her napkin in her hands to stop herself from reaching for him. How could she trust that he was telling the truth? *Isn't it enough that he's walked away from everything he knows to come to you?* Well, yes, there was that, she conceded.

"But how do you know you love me?" She cut straight to the chase. "You didn't want to love me before."

She couldn't help but sound accusatory. He'd hurt her with his closed emotions. He'd pushed hers away as if they'd meant nothing and now he expected her to believe he'd had a complete change of heart? She said as much, fighting to keep tears from choking her throat and flooding her eyes.

"I'm sorry, Ros. So sorry. It was never my intention to hurt you. In fact, I held back because I didn't want to hurt you. I'd seen how my mother coped—or more importantly, didn't cope—when my father cheated on her. I'd seen how much she hurt and I remember all too well how I felt when I realized that neither of us was enough to keep him home. I saw my Mom risk everything for her love for him and he just threw it back in her face. I hated him for it—I swore I would never be like him but I had the awful sobering realization after you left that I have been no different after all.

"That fear of being vulnerable has colored every relationship I've ever had. I've allowed myself to become a victim to it, and it's left its scars. But I want to heal. I want to love. I want to live and not keep that vital part of me locked away any more. Look, I know this is a lot to take in, and it's a lot to ask. I'll give you all the time and the space you need but I'd like to ask you just one thing."

"And that is?" she asked as evenly as she could. It was no mean feat with her heart hammering in her chest the way it was.

"To give me, us, another chance. To let me love you. To let me accept your love for me, if you still love me that is."

"Love isn't something you can turn on and off like a faucet," she said fiercely. "It consumes, it becomes everything."

"I know. I am consumed. You are my everything."

He said the words so simply, so without artifice and with such conviction she knew she had to believe him. She sat back in her chair and stared at him, noting the lines of tiredness around his eyes and the tension in every line of his body. He felt this, deeply and honestly, and he deserved honesty in return.

"Yes."

He blinked. "Yes?"

"Yes, I still love you. I will never stop loving you. But, no, at the same time."

His face, which had begun to glow with hope, froze. "No?"

"No, I don't want time and, no, I don't need space. I want us to be together. I want to be able to tell you every minute of every day how much I love you. I don't want to be apart. I want to know everything about you and I want to share everything about me, too. I want to start the New Year and every year after that with you, forever."

Gabe reached for her hands across the table. "I love you so much, Rosalind Banks."

"Rosalind Banks-Carrington, I believe," she said

with a smile and a sense of joy that she felt rise from the tips of her toes and fill her entire being with light.

"I like the sound of that," he said. "Let's get out of here."

"I like the sound of that, too."

He settled the check and hailed a cab as they left the restaurant. The moment they returned to her apartment and they were inside her front door they were on each other. Hungry for one another as if they'd been apart for years, rather than days. Hungry to express in touch and embrace, exactly what they meant to one another. And when they crested the wave of their desire together, and the skies outside filled with the cascades of color from fireworks being let off all over the city, Rosalind knew she was exactly where she needed to be.

In Gabe's arms for the rest of her life.

* * * * *

ONE LITTLE SECRET

MAUREEN CHILD

My first book was dedicated to my husband, Mark, and now this one, too, goes to the man who first believed in me, supported me and loved me always.

I miss the hugs, the laughter, the midnight chats and the road trips. I miss knowing that you're just in the next room. I even miss the whistling that used to drive me nuts. And I'm blessed to have had you for so many years.

I hope the fishing is great where you are, honey. Save me a seat. I'll get there eventually. I love you.

One

Justin Carey looked around the conference room and told himself *this* was why he usually skipped family meetings.

He'd been sitting at the Carey Corporation for a half hour already and they were no closer to ending the meeting than they had been at the beginning. Maintaining the Carey legacy required a family meeting at least once a month and Justin avoided them as often as he could. Not that he didn't want to spend time with his family. But he definitely wasn't interested in becoming a link in the Carey family chain.

The Carey Center, basically a palace to the performing arts, was the grand dame in their holdings. But there were also five star restaurants and an upscale shopping center called FireWood and dozens of real estate holdings and none of it interested Justin.

He wanted to make his own way. Build his own contributions to the Carey legacy. And he'd felt as if he might suffocate if he'd fallen into line and taken an office here at the "mother ship."

Still, he had to admit that the last few months had brought changes. His sisters, Amanda and Serena, couldn't seem to talk about anything other than their upcoming weddings. And the oldest Carey sibling, Bennett, seemed almost...*relaxed.* Which was just unnerving.

Bennett had always been the most driven of them all. He ran his life on schedules and lists—and yet, since he'd sat down for the meeting that morning, the man had had a small, self-satisfied smile etched on his face. Leaning back in the black leather chair at the head of the table, Bennett watched the family like a benevolent old uncle. Amazing, Justin told himself, what finding love with Hannah Yates, contractor extraordinaire, had done for Bennett.

While he waited for the meeting to get going again after a short break, he watched his sisters. Amanda and Serena had their heads together over a bridal magazine, flipping madly through the pages, with the occasional sigh or muffled shriek of approval.

Only his parents' relationship hadn't changed. What he and his siblings were calling the Retirement Wars were still in full swing. His father, Martin, had promised his wife that when Bennett took over the Carey Corporation, Martin would retire and the two of them would do all the things they had talked about. But that time had come and gone, and Martin still couldn't let go. So Justin's mother, Candace, had moved out of their house and into Bennett's.

Justin smiled to himself remembering how hard Bennett had worked to get his mother out of his home—unsuccessfully. Though now that Hannah had moved in, too, Bennett didn't seem to mind as much. Just one more perplexing change among the rest. Hell, maybe he should attend more meetings. It might be the only way to keep up.

"Candy," Martin Carey said, "it's time this is over. We've got two daughters getting married, Hannah's moved into Bennett's house and they probably want some privacy..."

"Don't bring me into this," Bennett said.

Justin kept quiet and watched the byplay.

"Candy, you come on home and we can talk about the retirement plan."

Candace tapped one finger against the tabletop and shook her head until her short, chestnut hair swung at her jaw. "No, Marty. I'm not coming home now. I'm comfortable at Bennett's house. As a matter of fact, Hannah and I are having a wonderful time turning that beige palace into a home."

"Hey..." Bennett broke in again and now even Justin's sisters looked up, listening.

"I'm sorry, dear," Candace said with a wave of her hand. "But you know it's true. And Hannah is so talented at bringing homes back to life."

Bennett sighed and scowled.

"The kitchen is being redone as we speak and the living room has already been painted a wonderful, dark forest green..."

"I don't care what you're doing to Bennett's house," Martin grumbled.

"Well, you should. It's just lovely."

"Candy, I miss you," Martin said, gritting his teeth. "It's time you came back to me. Talk to me."

"We've done all the talking we're going to do already," Candace said softly. "You know what has to happen if you want this to end."

Justin winced on behalf of his father. He knew how much his parents loved each other, but he also knew his mother wouldn't give up if she thought she was right. His father had to know that, too.

"You're being unreasonable," Martin said.

"And you broke your word to me."

He looked insulted. "I did not."

"I'm sorry," Candace said, glancing around the room. "Are we on a cruise ship right now and I just missed it?"

Martin ground his teeth together and Justin wanted to tell his father to simply surrender. Candace Carey always found a way to win. None of her four children had ever been able to get around her, and her husband wouldn't have any luck with it, either.

While the family talked over and to each other, Justin sat back in his chair and looked at the room as an outsider. Because basically, that was just what he was.

In a world of tailored suits and high expectations, Justin was an Armani black leather jacket and charting his own course. He didn't take orders well, and didn't have the slightest interest in the family business—none of it.

And no one in the family understood that.

All his life, he'd had the Carey legacy hanging out in front of him like a hoop he was expected to jump through. Some people, he supposed, would have looked at that as a promise of a future. A path stretched out in front of him, all tidily laid out.

For Justin, though, that path led nowhere he wanted to be. He loved his family, but the thought of spending every day of his life behind a desk felt like a jail sentence. And he'd learned early that trying to please the family was, for him, a lesson in futility. As the youngest Carey sibling, he found that everyone had an opinion on what he should be doing. Despite loving his family, the only way he wouldn't eventually resent them for trying to rule his life was to strike out on his own.

To find his own way to contribute to the Carey Corporation.

And now he had it. He was almost ready to show his family that he was more than simply "the youngest."

"Okay, let's talk about the summer concert series," Bennett said, and slowly, the conversation began to quiet down.

Sunlight filled the room, but thanks to the wall of tinted windows, the light was muted. On the walls were framed family photos, plus pictures of the Carey Center, the restaurant and the shopping center. One day, Justin told himself, there would be framed pictures of *his* contribution to the family business. He was looking forward to that.

"Everything's on track, Bennett," Amanda said, still flipping through the bridal magazine.

"Thanks for your attention, Mandy," Bennett said wryly.

She lifted her gaze to his. "This is not the first time I've run our summer concert series, Bennett. I've got every evening filled. Our returning acts are happy to be here and the new ones are eagerly anticipating performing at the famed Carey Center.

"Ticket sales are through the roof, and I have to say…we've got the blueprints done for the pub and mall walk between the center and the new restaurant we're planning, and they're fantastic."

"When does work start on the new project?" Bennett watched her.

"Hannah did the first go-through, as you know…" Bennett nodded.

"And since she's busy building Alli's castle and the retaining wall at Jack's place, we found another contractor to handle the beginnings of the job. We should break ground next month."

"Good news," Bennett said. "Hannah's going to be finished with the castle in a couple of weeks, but she's got jobs lined up now for the next two months. Not to mention that she's got some of her guys at my house, adding a breakfast room to the kitchen and painting every wall in the place."

"Hurray," Amanda said. "No more beige."

"Funny," Bennet countered.

"Anyway." Amanda nodded at their sister. "Serena's got a few new points about the Summer Stars program, but as for me, things are rolling." She took a breath, narrowed her eyes on him and reminded him, "I'm also getting married in a few months and I need time to plan the wedding."

"Right," he said, and shifted his gaze to his other sister. "Okay, then. Serena. The Summer Stars winners. Have we got them set up to perform this summer?"

She nodded her head at him and her butterscotch-blond hair flew around her shoulders. "Of course we do, Bennett. Do you think I'm incompetent?"

"What? No. Of course not." Bennett looked around the table and Justin couldn't help but think he looked like a man searching for a way out. "I'm just trying to be—"

"Controlling?" Serena asked, slowly pushing to her feet. "What is it about men that makes them think they have all the answers and the rest of us are just their cheering sections?"

"I don't think—"

"You're all alike," Serena said and Justin winced when he saw his softhearted sister's eyes fill with tears.

"Hey," Bennett said, standing up himself. "I'm not trying to control you, Serena. But I can if you want me to."

"Honestly, Bennett, you could *try* to be supportive." Amanda jabbed her index finger at her brother. "You all stick together. No matter what."

"What's going on?" Martin asked.

"No idea," Candace said and looked worriedly at her daughter.

"Bennett…" Justin looked at his sisters and then said, "maybe we should all calm down for a second and—"

"You stay out of this," Serena said and swiped a stray tear off her cheek. "You're never here, Justin, and now you just take Bennett's side against me?"

"I'm not taking sides," he protested, glancing at his brother as if looking for help. But Bennett was just as confused.

"Whose side am I supposed to be on?" Bennett demanded, confusion stamped on his features. "What are you talking about?"

"Jack," she said shortly. "Of course it's Jack. He wants to get married this summer and there's no time. It's *already* summer, for heaven's sake. I want to wait until Christmas…"

"Sure, because you don't have anything to do around Christmas," Justin muttered.

"You're on Jack's side, too," Serena said.

"Sweetie," Candace said softly. "This isn't a tragedy. We'll come up with something."

"I just can't deal with any of this today." Serena walked out of the room and Amanda watched her leave.

"See what you did? I can't believe you're this insensitive, Bennett. Has Hannah seen this side of you?" Amanda picked up her bridal magazine. "It's very unattractive."

She flounced out after Serena and Bennett looked at Justin. "What the hell just happened? How the hell did I go from asking about the Summer Stars to being insensitive?"

"Damned if I know." Justin looked at Candace. "Mom, do you have a clue what's going on?"

Slowly, Candace pushed to her feet, looked at both of her sons, then shifted a brief glance at her husband. "What's going on is that once again, you men refuse to hear us. And sadly, that includes Jack and most probably Henry, as well. I suppose none of you can help it. It's simply your gender."

"Wait a minute," Martin said, standing. "How did I get lumped into this?"

"You're a man and you don't listen. How are you

not in this?" Candace turned and left the room behind her daughters and Martin was just a step or two behind her.

Justin looked at Bennett. "What the hell did *we* do?"

"We were born male. Happy you were here to share the heat this time."

"Right," Justin said. "*Really* glad I made the time to come to this family meeting."

Scowling, Bennett said, "Maybe if you came more often, you'd be able to help me deal with our sisters."

"Yeah, no thanks." Justin grinned, shoved his hands into his jacket pockets and said, "You're the CEO. It's your job to handle the crap."

"I didn't see that in the contract," Bennett mumbled.

"Dad made you sign a contract?"

"Never mind." Bennett shook his head, eased one hip against the table and asked, "Why did you come to the meeting today, anyway? Which just so happened to turn into the shortest family meeting in history, thank-you to all the tiny business gods."

Justin laughed shortly. This was a side of his older brother he hadn't known existed. "Damn, Bennett, I've never known you to *not* like those meetings. What's happened to you?"

One corner of Bennett's mouth lifted and his gaze softened. "I found Hannah and discovered what having an actual *life* is like."

Hannah Yates, contractor and, apparently, *brother tamer*. He'd only met her the once at a big, splashy dinner at The Carey—the family corporation's flagship restaurant that Hannah and her crew had completely restored after a fire. But even meeting her only that night, Justin had seen the change she'd brought about in his brother.

And hell, if Bennett Carey could change, anything was possible.

Smiling to himself, Justin said, "I only came to thank you in person for loaning me that money a few weeks ago. I had the accountant cut you a check today to pay you back." He handed it over and was silently grateful to the grandfather who had left each of the Carey siblings a substantial trust. Still, there were hoops to jump through when you needed to draw on that money. He hadn't had time to wait and Bennett had come through for him when he'd needed it most. Justin wouldn't forget it.

Bennett dropped the check onto the table, crossed his arms over his chest and said, "Uh-huh. Do I get to know why you needed it?"

Justin grinned. He'd been working this deal for three months. Hell, longer, if you considered he first tried to pull it off a year and a half ago.

But it didn't matter how long it had taken, he told himself. The point was, it was a done deal now. He'd turned over the cash payment just a couple of weeks ago and there was no going back. His course was set; now he just had to prove to everyone that he knew what he was doing. That starting a new branch of the Carey Corporation was the right thing for him.

"Earth to Justin."

"What?" He'd drifted off.

"I asked," Bennett said, "do I now get to know why you needed the money? Why you've been so damn se-cretive the last few months about what you're doing?"

He still wasn't ready to tell the family.

Bennett sighed. "It's a no. I can see it on your face."

"Yeah, it's a no. Today," Justin hedged. "But soon, Bennett."

"Yeah." Bennett laughed. "I've heard that a lot from you. Yet nothing changes."

Justin bristled a little. "It will, though, Bennett. You'll see soon enough."

This was the problem with being the youngest in the family. Everyone felt like they had a say in his life. They wanted to "help," but too often it ended up simply that they tried to steer him onto what they considered a safe path.

Well, Justin wasn't interested in "safe." He didn't care about doing the expected thing. What he did want was to carve out his own path. To prove to his family, at last, that in spite of not toeing the company line, he was a Carey.

Right down to the bone.

A couple of hours later, Justin was exactly where he wanted to be.

He stood on a slate patio and stared out at the wide sweep of the Pacific stretched out in front of him. Heavy, gray clouds hovered on the horizon and were busily sailing closer. And behind him was the hotel that would be his link in the Carey family chain.

Everything was riding on this. He'd taken a stand years ago—not against his family, but against being dragged into the family business. And this was his chance to prove to everyone that he'd been right to do it.

Here in La Jolla, just a few miles from San Diego,

he was a good two hours from Orange County, California, where the Carey family had centered their world. Here, he wasn't the youngest Carey sibling. Here he was whoever the hell he wanted to be.

He was never going to be satisfied with sitting behind a desk and moving from meeting to meeting. That kind of life felt more like a cage to Justin than anything else. It suited his family completely and they shone at running the corporation and growing it, as well.

He loved his family but he'd always felt like the proverbial square peg trying to find his way into a round hole. Eventually, he'd stopped trying and made the decision to go his own way.

His family didn't understand; they still saw him as the black sheep. The rebel. But once he told them what he was doing, maybe that would change. Maybe.

While the cold ocean breeze blew past him, ruffling his hair, tugging at the black leather jacket he wore, Justin heard the echoes of the last of that morning's conversation with his older brother.

"You've been avoiding the family for months, Justin. It's time to tell us all what you're up to."

"I will. Soon."

"That's what you said last month."

As the youngest of the four Carey siblings, Justin was used to the family trying to either rein him in or give him "advice" about how to run his own damn life. This time, he wasn't going to tell them anything about his plans until they were already set in stone.

He loved his family. All of them. But this he had to do for himself.

"I'm almost ready, Bennett," he said. "Believe me, I want you all to know."

"Fine." Bennett's sigh was both patient and irritated. Justin didn't know how he managed that. "I'm glad you came today. You might try coming to more family meetings."

Now it was Justin's turn to sigh. "I'm not part of the Carey Corporation, Bennett."

"You're part of the Carey family, Justin. Time you started acting like it."

Remembering the exchange, Justin rolled his shoulders as if shrugging off Bennett's last barb. It had stung, because there had been plenty of truth to it. He did miss the family. And he wasn't trying to cut himself off from them. But until he was firmly entrenched in his own business, he would steer clear. As he had been.

Justin stared out at the churning sea and watched waves crash against the shore, then ripple along the sand, leaving damp, lacy patterns in their wake. Sandpipers scuttled along the wet sand, leaving tiny footprints behind until the water washed them away.

Why the hell would he want to be at a meeting in Carey corporate headquarters when he could be standing here, between the sea and the hotel that would be his contribution to the Carey legacy?

No fabulous Carey Center for him. He admired what his family had built—basically a temple to the arts—but it wasn't *his*. It had never pulled at him the way it had his siblings. Hell, even his sister Serena had eventually become a part of the company, and from what he was told, she was damn good at it. But Justin wanted—needed—to make his own mark. And in that way, he realized, he was just like his father and older brother. They might not see it, but he did.

They'd made their mark *on* the Carey Center. He'd make his on the outside. Each of them did things their own way.

And here was where he was going to do it.

"Hey," a voice called out from behind him. "I've been looking for you for a half hour."

Thoughts shattered, Justin turned around and smiled as Sam Jonas walked up to join him. Tall and lanky, with long blond hair, wearing worn jeans and a faded red T-shirt, Sam looked just what he was: a surfer. Of course, he was also half owner of Jonas and Son Builders and was currently running the restoration of the hotel.

"Hey, Sam."

"Should have known I'd find you out here," Sam said and lifted his face into the sea wind, letting his hair stream out like a white blond flag behind him.

"Hard to resist," Justin admitted. On the ocean, there were a few surfers, and a couple of small sailboats skimming the surface, gem-colored sails ballooned out with the wind. And those storm clouds hustled even closer. "A hell of a view."

"It is that."

Five years ago, he'd met Sam outside a pub in Ireland, when they were both on solitary backpacking trips across Europe. As the only two Americans around, they'd bonded pretty quickly and spent the next couple of months traveling together.

Their friendship endured long after the trip had ended. Sam had gone into business with his father and now Jonas and Son Builders operated out of San

Diego. While Justin had no interest in his family's business, he found himself sometimes envying Sam for being able to do what he loved and still please his family.

"Why were you looking for me?"

"What? Oh." Nodding, Sam said, "I wanted to let you know the designers are at work in the finished hotel rooms."

"Good news." With the front half of the hotel—the ocean-view side—nearly ready to open, and the rest of the rooms being upgraded quickly, the whole place would be ready for the public by the end of the month.

Damn good thing, since it felt as if he'd been building toward this moment for more than a year.

"Here's more," Sam told him. "The treatment rooms are finished, too, but for the light fixtures, and those are going in this afternoon."

"Seriously? Damn, man, you don't waste time," Justin said, smiling. He leaned his forearms on the iron railing and stared into the cold wind.

"You don't pay me to waste time, buddy," Sam pointed out. "We'll need another week or two to get the saunas and the pool where we want it, but everything else is up and about ready to shine."

"I'm going to owe you a bottle of scotch, aren't I?"

"Damn straight." Sam gave him a light punch on the shoulder. "Single malt, at least fifteen years old and preferably from the Highlands."

Justin laughed. "Got it. Anything else?"

"Actually, yeah," Sam said thoughtfully. "Once you're open, I want one of your best rooms for a long weekend."

Still laughing, Justin looked at him. "Seriously? You want one of the rooms?"

"Not for me. For Kate."

Kate O'Hara, OB nurse and Sam's fiancée. "For her? You got it, man. Best room in the house." Grinning, Justin added, "I still don't understand how she could have picked you over me."

"A woman of excellent taste," Sam quipped, then rubbed one hand against the center of his chest. "Can't believe the wedding's in three weeks."

"You're not nervous, are you?" Justin grinned.

"Hell no." Sam shrugged. "Nervous doesn't cover it. Scared half to death. What's wrong with eloping? Why do I have to stand in front of a couple hundred people?"

"Because that's what Kate wants and you're crazy about her."

A second or two later, Sam nodded. "I really am." He shot Justin a look. "So, as best man, you have the bachelor party all worked out?"

"Oh, yeah. It's going to be epic." As soon as he set it up. Damn it, he'd been so busy he'd forgotten all about that. But that was easily enough taken care of.

"And it's not the night before the wedding, right? Kate's being picky," he added. "Doesn't want me getting married with a hangover."

"Women." Justin slapped his friend on the back. "Don't worry about it. I'll have you at the wedding stone-cold sober."

"Yeah, that might not be a good idea, either."

Laughing, Justin half turned at a sound, a scent, some sense of motion. He swore every nerve ending in his body stood straight up the moment he spotted her. The bottom dropped out of his stomach and a slow burn started a bit lower.

Sam shifted to look at whatever Justin was staring at, then said, "Okay, then. Guess I'll get back to work."

"What? Oh." Hell, one look at her and Justin had forgotten his friend was standing right beside him. "Okay. Talk to you later."

Sam left and on his way past the woman headed Justin's way, he said, "Morning, Sadie."

She smiled but once he'd gone past, that smile slipped away and she faced Justin with the same cool expression he was getting used to.

Sadie Harris.

The one woman he'd never been able to get out of his mind. The one woman who still made guest spots in his dreams. The one woman who looked at him with a dismissive stare that Justin was just contrary enough to enjoy.

Sadie.

"Hello, Justin."

That soft, husky voice rippled through him and set off a ripple of heat he was pretty sure would immolate him any second.

It would be a hell of a way to go.

Two

"Hello, Justin."

Her voice was low, and made him remember all the nights they'd spent together. Just a year and a half ago, they'd been together during long nights when she would whisper his name while she wrapped those long legs around him.

"Sadie," he said.

She took a spot at the railing, keeping about two feet of space between them. Justin had to ask himself why her indifferent attitude was so damned attractive. Tall, she stood almost five foot ten and, he swore, most of that was legs. Long, shapely and tanned, it had been her legs he'd noticed first and he knew that every straight male would say the same.

But it was her eyes that held him. Big, brown with tiny flecks of gold in their centers, they were wary, watchful, suspicious even, and damned if he wasn't intrigued every time they met his. Her hair was thick, the color of good whiskey—brown with sun-kissed, amber streaks, and right now, that heavy mass of waves tumbled free to the middle of her back. He knew what it felt like in his hands and he wanted to feel it again.

She'd changed since he'd first met her. Her breasts were fuller, hips rounder, as if she'd gained a little weight in all the right places. He'd been back here the last few months and from the first time he'd seen her again, she'd been tormenting him. Whether she meant to or not. Just looking at her kindled a fire in the pit of his belly. This woman had always turned him inside out and made him hunger for the heat they'd once found together.

But now Sadie was a hell of a lot pricklier than the first time they'd met. She wore pale, cream-colored shorts, a tight, mint green T-shirt and sandals. And she made that simple outfit look staggering. He waited until she turned to look him in the eye and when their gazes locked, he felt the snap of heat like a gut punch.

She closed her hands over the damp, icy railing and shifted her gaze to the sea. Almost, he thought, as if she couldn't bear looking at him. She hadn't always been that way, though. When they'd met more than a year ago, they hadn't been able to keep their hands off each other.

Back then, there was nothing cool in her eyes when she looked at him. It had been heat. The kind of soul-swamping heat that made a man believe in heaven.

But apparently, things had changed.

"We've been working together now for a couple

of months," Justin said. "You want to tell me why you still treat me like the enemy? All of this—this whole project—is because of you. And your father," he added. "You're the one who came to me, remember?"

She tipped her face into the ocean wind and he watched that breeze lift her hair into a dark cloud, swirling around her. Tempting, that was what she was. Just pure temptation brought to life.

"I remember," she said finally. "That doesn't mean I'm happy about it."

A man with two sisters knew how complicated and yet, Justin had to admit that what was between him and Sadie was even more so. He hadn't seen her for a year and a half when she'd called him three months ago with an offer he couldn't refuse. Sounded like a movie plot, but it was the truth. But from that unexpected phone call to this minute, she'd been so coldly polite Justin spent most of his days with frostbite.

And he had no idea why she was so clearly furious. He'd left it alone until now, figuring that at some point, she'd tell him why she was so angry. But she hadn't and he was tired of living with an ax hanging over his head.

The worst of it was, he still wanted her.

"Is the attitude because you needed help?" he finally asked, honestly curious. "Or because you needed help from *me*?"

"Good question," she murmured and then slanted a look at him. "I think it's you."

"Great. Progress." He leaned his forearms on the railing and kept his distance as he asked, "And why's that? You're still pissed because I left?"

"Please." She laughed a little, but didn't sound amused. "Don't think so highly of yourself."

One eyebrow lifted. It wasn't much of a conversation, but at least she was talking to him. "Okay, fine. Then why?"

"Really, Justin? You can't figure out what I'm experiencing here?" Sadie's eyes flashed and that was the most emotion he'd seen from her since he'd come back to San Diego. Hell, even if she was mad, at least he knew she was feeling *something*.

She slapped one hand on the iron railing and turned to face him. "Let's think," she said tightly. "Maybe it's because I didn't want to sell our family hotel but had no choice?" She whipped her hair back behind her shoulders and glared at him. "Could that have something to do with it?"

"Like I said, Sadie. Nobody forced you to call me, right? Coming back here wasn't my idea, remember?"

"Oh, trust me, Justin," she countered. "I remember that you never came back."

"Here we go," he muttered.

"No." She interrupted him with a quick shake of her head. "It's you coming in and making all these changes…"

"You wanted to renovate."

"Of course, but I want to keep some of the history, too. This is my family's place. My great-grandfather's legacy and too much of it is changing."

He sighed, scrubbed one hand across his face and quickly tried to find a way to say what needed saying. Without also pushing Sadie even further away than she was already.

A year and a half ago, Justin had tried to buy the

beautiful old hotel and after a couple of weeks of talks and negotiations that went nowhere, she and her father had turned him down flat. Justin had been searching since for the kind of place that could compete with the Cliffside, but he'd never found another one like it.

Then out of nowhere, three months ago, Sadie had called him to open negotiations again. He hadn't understood what had changed her mind, and truthfully, at the time, all he was thinking about was getting his hands on the Cliffside so he hadn't cared. Now, though, he wanted a few answers.

"We are keeping some of the history. But faded wallpaper has got to go. Besides, again," Justin reminded her, "you called me with the offer."

"Because I had no choice." She sighed, and briefly turned her gaze to the ocean before facing him again.

Justin understood that. Her father had been sick and she'd needed money fast to get him settled and pay off some of the bills that were coming in. Had Justin taken advantage of the situation? No, he didn't think so. She had needed him, and the deal they'd finally hammered out was more than fair.

Still, he knew what the hotel meant to her—and her family. As she'd said, it was the Harris legacy. The old place had been in her family for decades, and as a Carey, he knew what that kind of tradition could mean. It wasn't only a responsibility but a burden of sorts, weighing her down and making her consider and reconsider every decision she made.

"I get that. Had to be hard to swallow, but we all do what we have to do." He watched her. "With that in mind, how's your dad feeling?"

She sighed and he didn't know if it was exasperation or resignation. "He's much better. Thanks."

He liked her dad a lot and he was worried the man had been hit with a medical issue. But Justin wasn't sorry he'd gotten the hotel. And he couldn't regret being back here. With Sadie.

"We're a team now, Sadie," he finally said. "Whether you like it or not."

"A team." Her lips twisted into a sardonic smile that tore at him.

He took a step toward her and stopped when she looked at him as if she were going to turn and bolt. "You realize that you'll have to get used to having me around. Dealing with me."

"Oh, believe me," she muttered, turning her face toward the sea rather than look at him. "I know."

A year or so ago, she'd been in his bed and hadn't seemed to have a problem with him being around at all. Hell, just remembering the nights with Sadie could make him hard and hot, in spite of that icy sea wind whirling around him. Staring at her profile now, Justin was forced to admit that it didn't seem her memories were as pleasant as his.

Or she was lying to herself.

Scowling at the thoughts tumbling through his mind, Justin half turned to look over his shoulder at the reason he was willing to put up with Sadie's bad attitude and the memories that wouldn't leave him alone.

The Cliffside Hotel. It was practically an institution in La Jolla, California. Just eleven miles from San Diego, La Jolla boasted some of the best coastline in the state. The world-famous Torrey Pines Golf Course was close by and sat on the edge of cliffs overlooking the pounding ocean. Just beyond the hotel, the village of La Jolla was filled with art galleries, five-star restaurants and exclusive boutiques. That tiny town drew tourists from all over the world, and soon, the Cliffside Hotel and Spa would be able to compete with the best resorts the village had to offer.

Along the shore there were tide pools to explore and La Jolla Cove, a small, deep-water bay that drew experienced and novice snorkelers from all over to explore the sea caves.

The Cliffside itself sat right on the beach. Landscaping that needed some care lined the front of the sprawling building, and the restaurant was a wall of glass that faced the sea. Three stories of rooms spread out from that restaurant and formed a horseshoe so that each room had a balcony with either a view of the ocean, or one of the village and the spacious gardens that filled the hotel courtyard and lay behind it in a riot of color year round.

The Cliffside had stood on this spot for more than sixty years, and while it was still spectacular, it was beginning to look a little haggard. Sea air and salt spray had done a number on the paint, and the wide porch needed to be redone in cedar so it would stand up to the dampness.

All it needed was some freshening and redesigning of the rooms to make them more contemporary while still holding on to the history the hotel had earned. Which was why Justin had first come to the hotel more than a year ago. And why Sadie had called him back.

"Damn it, Sadie, we both know this is a good deal for both of us." He took a step closer and stopped when she shifted to face him. "We can work together or you can keep up the ice woman treatment."

She laughed a little, but the humor didn't reach her eyes and that was a little disappointing. Because he remembered what a great laugh she had, and how her eyes would shine with it.

"Ice woman," she repeated. "I sort of like that."

"Of course you do." Reaching out, he almost touched her hand, but she slid it back on the black railing and Justin sighed.

"Fine," he said. "But if that's the way you want to play this it's going to make for a hard partnership."

"Partners?"

"We both own the hotel, so yeah. Partners."

Shaking her head, she looked at him for a long moment before saying, "You with seventy-five percent and me with twenty-five isn't exactly an equal partnership."

"I didn't say it was equal," he pointed out and gave her a smile that got zero reaction from her. "Look, paperwork's been signed. You got your cash payout a couple weeks ago, so why the attitude today?"

Sadie slapped one hand on the railing lining the slate patio. When she looked at him, she said, "Because I didn't want to make the deal."

"Yeah," Justin said with a half smile. "You made that pretty clear when I was here a year and a half ago."

"Fifteen months," she corrected.

Three months made that big a difference? One eyebrow winged up. "That's very specific. Do you have it down to days and hours, too?"

"You might be surprised."

Her face was unreadable, and still he stared at her. Those eyes drew him as they had from the first moment they met. And even at times like now, when she was coldly angry, he couldn't deny the craving she caused. And he had to wonder, if he reached for her now, pulled her in tight and kissed her, would she push him away? Or kiss him back?

He wasn't sure he wanted to know. For the moment.

Changing the subject, he said, "The designers are finishing up with the ocean-view rooms."

"Yes, I know. I walked through a few of them before I came down here."

Wryly, he said, "Tamp down the excitement, Sadie. It's embarrassing." He laughed shortly. "We used most of your ideas on those rooms. I would have thought you'd sound more pleased with the results."

"Of course I'm pleased about them," she said. "I've wanted to fix up the rooms for a long time. Dad and I talked about this for years, too, you know. It wasn't all your brilliant idea to come swooping in with plans. We just couldn't do it earlier." She looked into his eyes and said simply, "As for using my designs? They were good and you know it, so don't act as if you were doing me a favor."

"I wasn't…"

She cut him off. "Fifteen months ago, you came here and made an offer for our hotel."

"And you said no," he added, before she could. "Things change."

Swiping one hand through her hair, she held it back from her face. "Yes. This time we sold it. But it wasn't by choice. There was no other option."

"Maybe not. But you were happy enough about the

cash payout," he reminded her. "You liked the indoor pool and the swim spa you talked me into."

She waved at him. "That was brilliant and you know it. Clients will love it."

He'd already acknowledged that she was right about the swim spa.

"My point," he ground out, "is that you've had plenty of say in what we're doing. Hell, you sold the place to me and still managed to hang on to twenty-five percent of it," he said. "*That* should make you happy if nothing else does."

He hadn't liked her terms, Hadn't thought to have a partner. But they'd been set in stone as far as she was concerned, so he'd accepted it because this hotel was going to be the start of something for him. Once the Cliffside established itself, he'd start over on another hotel that had been left to age less than gracefully.

Justin was going to prove that he'd done the right thing in walking away from the Carey Corporation and paving his own way. If that meant having to bargain on this, the first hotel of what would be many, then so be it.

"Oh, yes," Sadie said wryly. "Twenty-five percent of a hotel that was one hundred percent my family's up until a month ago." She shook her head. "Wait. Let me get the balloons."

Justin stared at her for a long minute. Putting aside the fact that she could set him on fire with a glance, she was a damn mystery. He'd liked that about her when they first met because he hadn't been looking long-term anyway. If she wanted to keep her secrets, then fine. Worked out better for both of them. Nothing wrong with a lot of lust and heat. Neither of them had been after hearts and flowers, after all.

But now they'd be working together. Joined by a contract that would make it impossible to *not* deal with each other. So the time for all the mystery was over.

He tucked his hands into his jacket pockets, braced his legs wide apart and tipped his head to one side to study her. "We used to like each other, Sadie."

"Like?" she repeated. "That's what you think? We liked each other?"

"Didn't we?" Now he was confused and maybe more than a little irritated. "I liked you and the way I remember it, you seemed pretty fond of me, too."

"More than fond and you know it." She inhaled sharply. "At least until you disappeared."

He remembered. But he'd done what he'd had to do. "I *left*. There's a difference."

"Sure," she said, sounding way too amiable for the glint in her eyes. "You *left* my bed to take a shower, you said, and then you *left* without another word."

He scrubbed one hand across his face. She was right, but he hadn't seen it that way at the time. He'd had to go because if he'd stayed any longer he might never have left. She'd been too important to him and he hadn't been able to embrace that because he'd had to make his way. Find his path before he indulge himself in a relationship. "Damn it, Sadie. I didn't want to hurt you. But I couldn't stay."

"Well, that's okay, then. Thanks so much."

"We had an affair, Sadie. Hot. Sexy as hell and *temporary*," he said tightly, defending himself against the accusation he saw in her eyes. "Neither of us made promises."

That was certainly true, Sadie told herself. No promises, just the magic of being with him. The thrill of his touch and the hunger he aroused in her like no other man ever had—or would. And then it had all gone to hell.

"No. We didn't." Sadie Harris sighed and realized that talking about this wasn't doing any good. It surely wasn't making her feel any better. But she'd been holding on to these feelings for a long time. Was it so bad to dump some of them on him now that she had the chance?

Just looking at him made her blood burn and her heart beat faster. Harder. She remembered every minute of every night she'd spent with him what felt like a lifetime ago. The sensation of his hands sliding over her body. The heat of his breath as he suckled at her breasts and the amazing friction when his body slid into hers. She trembled and Sadie locked her knees so she wouldn't simply sink to the pavement.

Justin's light brown, sun-streaked hair was a little too long, curling over his collar, making her want to touch, to wind her fingers through it. His pale blue eyes shone like ice chips, yet she knew exactly what they looked like when they were reflecting the heat burning between them. His jaw carried a couple days' worth of scruff, only adding to the ridiculously attractive package.

He wore that black leather jacket—Armani, of course—that he loved so much, over a black T-shirt and black jeans. His black boots were scuffed and scarred and somehow just right. He was tall, well over six feet, ensuring that she had to look up at him in spite of her five feet ten inches of height. She suspected he enjoyed that.

God, she'd missed him.

And that was a dangerous thought to entertain, however briefly.

Fifteen months ago, she'd spent two weeks with Justin Carey and they'd been the best two weeks of her life. He was funny and smart and there was an innate kindness in him that had attracted her from the start. Of course, the fact that he could set her hair on fire with a kiss didn't hurt anything, either.

But when he left that last morning and didn't even bother to *wave* at her, she'd been crushed. No, they hadn't made promises to each other, but they'd been so good together that she'd allowed herself to hope—to believe—that there was more between them than simple heat.

She was wrong.

"Here's the deal," he was saying and she looked into the blue eyes she'd never forgotten. "We don't have to be friends, Sadie. But damned if I'm going to have a partner I'm at war with every day. So why don't you just tell me what's bugging you and get it over with?"

God, she thought. Where to begin? With the lie? Or the truth?

She took a deep breath and steeled herself for what was to come. "You need me to satisfy your curiosity?"

He shrugged. "Why not?"

"Because I don't owe you anything, Justin." At least, she'd been telling herself that for the last fifteen months. She hoped it was true. Hoped she'd done the right thing.

"Didn't say you did, but you might want to reconsider since we *are* partners now."

She shook her head and when her hair flew across

her eyes, she impatiently plucked it free. "Only as far as the hotel goes."

"Well, yeah. What other way is there?"

Sadie laughed lightly. "Fifteen months and you haven't changed a bit."

"What's that supposed to mean? Sort of sounds like I should be insulted."

"The hotel was all you could see then and it's the same now."

"That's why I'm here," he pointed out. "The hotel is why you called me. What the hell else am I supposed to be seeing?"

"Never mind, Justin," she said and half turned to leave until he laid one hand on her arm to hold her there. The heat of his touch sank into her bones and drifted crazily throughout her body.

"Just wait."

She lifted her gaze to his and stared into those pale blue eyes, wishing things were different. Wishing they could start over somehow. Wishing...never did anyone any good.

"What the hell is wrong here, Sadie? The way I remember it, we got along great a year and a half ago."

"Fifteen months," she muttered.

"Fine," he said flatly. "Fifteen months. My point was, we had a good time together."

"And then you left," she countered.

"Well, yeah." Justin let her go, then pushed one hand through his hair. "I wanted your family's hotel. You wouldn't sell. Why would I stay?"

Sadie tipped her head to one side and studied him. She wouldn't have thought it possible, but he looked even better than he had fifteen months ago.

"Right," she said finally. "You had no reason to stay. We were just together every night for two weeks."

"Is that what this is about?" He shook his head and gave a half laugh. "Damn, Sadie. We both knew what we were doing. It was an affair. A damned hot one," he added with a wink that she guessed was supposed to be charming, "but an affair. Nobody said anything about me staying forever."

"Who asked for forever?" Sadie demanded. She'd known going into those two weeks with Justin Carey that it wouldn't last. How could it? He wasn't in La Jolla looking to build a life. He'd only been there trying to *buy* her life. Yet, even knowing that, she'd dreamed a lot of what-ifs. "How about a simple *Bye, Sadie. It's been fun.*" She pushed her windblown hair back from her face with impatient hands. "You couldn't even manage that. One morning, you were just…gone."

"Is *that* what's been bugging you for weeks now?" He shoved his hands into his jacket pockets. "I had to go. Family crap I had to deal with."

"And you couldn't tell me that?"

He sighed. "Yeah. I could have. Maybe should have, I don't know." His gaze speared into hers. "But there was no reason for me to stay, Sadie. You know that. You and your dad refused to sell the hotel and my reason for being here evaporated."

"We had something, Justin," she said. "Even if all it deserved was a goodbye, we had *something*."

"We had a good time," he said and lifted one hand to touch her, but Sadie stepped back.

Fifteen months without him and now he was back. She'd sold him the hotel, so he wouldn't be going anywhere. With her father so sick, she'd needed the money Justin paid her. And maybe she could have gotten more from someone—anyone else. But she hadn't had time to shop around for a buyer. Instead, she'd called the man she already knew wanted the hotel. It was time for Justin to understand just what had happened while he was gone.

"We did," she said. "And now you're back."

"Not going anywhere."

"Right. So." She took a breath, shifted her gaze briefly to the ocean before turning back to him again. The man she'd never forgotten. The man who visited her dreams and left her every morning aching and wanting. The man who had changed her life.

"So?"

"We should talk, Justin."

"Thought we were," he quipped.

She ignored that. "You haven't asked me how I am. If anything's new."

He frowned, clearly confused. "Okay. How are you, Sadie? What's new?"

Here it was. Time to rip off the Band-Aid. She blew out a breath and said, "I'm fine, thanks for asking. As for what's new? Well, he's six months old now, so not really new. But newish."

Justin went still. When he spoke again, his voice was tight and low. "*Who* is six months old?"

"Your son," she said, watching those pale blue eyes. "*Our* son."

Three

He held up one hand. "I'm sorry. *What?*"

"Our son. Ethan." Just saying her baby's name brought a smile to Sadie's face, but it dissolved quickly enough in the flash of heat in Justin's eyes.

"*Our* son. Ethan," he said.

She took a breath. "This is going to take forever if you just keep repeating what I'm telling you."

"Six months old?" he demanded.

"Yes."

He scrubbed both hands across his face. "You had a baby. *My* baby."

Since she could see Justin in her son's face, there would be no denying it even if she wanted to. And yet. "Yes. Well, *my* baby."

He shoved both hands through his hair, then just held his head as if afraid it would explode. "What the hell, Sadie? You didn't bother to tell me that I'm a damn father?"

"No, I didn't. And you didn't bother to say good-bye when you left."

He choked out a laugh. "Seriously? You're comparing those two things and saying it's what? Fair?"

She'd struggled with whether to tell him or not. Those long months of pregnancy had been some of the loneliest of her life. Oh, she'd had her parents who were supportive, though her father had wanted to confront Justin on his own and only Sadie's fast talking had stopped him. But she'd experienced the joys, the fears, the magic of those nine months as the single mother she would be. Maybe she should have told him. Maybe. But when they were together, he'd made it very clear that he wasn't looking for a long-term relationship.

And to be fair, she hadn't been looking, either. At first.

But after the first week with Justin, Sadie had begun to want more.

After he left, she'd discovered that was exactly what she'd gotten.

God, she hadn't meant to just blurt out the truth like this. The plan had been to ease him into knowing about Ethan. But the truth had been gnawing at her for the last two months. Not to mention the difficulty of keeping Ethan out of Justin's way. Being this close to Justin again, knowing what he'd missed, knowing what she'd kept from him, it had to come out.

In her defense, she thought, not telling him about the baby had made her feel terrible. But should she really have tracked him down to tell him she was pregnant, when he'd left so quickly and made it clear she wasn't important to him at all? And if she wasn't important, how could her son be?

No. She'd done the right thing.

Justin Carey's family had more money than she could even imagine. If he'd wanted to, he could have taken Ethan. He could have hired the best lawyers and she'd never have been able to afford a long court battle. She might have lost her son to a man who'd walked away from her without a second thought. And there was still a chance he would do just that—though she would fight him with everything she had.

So in the midst of her guilt, there was also a nugget of acceptance that she'd done the right thing.

"Where is he?"

Brought up out of her thoughts, her gaze snapped to his. "Safe."

"Seriously? Safe? That's all I get?" He threw both hands up. "You live here at the hotel. I've been in your suite. I didn't see him."

"I didn't want you to. Not until we'd talked."

"And 'talking' took you two months? We've been together nearly every day since this project started, Sadie. Yet, you never mentioned Ethan."

That hadn't been easy for her. So many times, she'd almost said it. Almost told him what they shared. With the hotel closed for renovations, Justin had paid their employees to take some time off, which was why no one had been able to spill her secret. Maybe knowing that she was safe from him finding out accidentally had given her the opportunity to keep quiet, to see if he was the man she remembered. "I had to find the right time."

"Sure. I'm not playing games with you, Sadie." Justin took a step toward her and stopped again. "If I have a son, I want to see him."

"If?" Of all the things she'd imagined him saying to her at this moment, that hadn't been one of them. "Why would I lie to you about that?"

"Good question," Justin snapped. "But you've been lying to me for... *fifteen months.*"

"I didn't lie," she muttered thickly. "I just didn't say anything."

"A fine distinction."

The fact that he was right made her cringe a little. "Justin, I don't want to fight with you about this."

"That's a damn shame." He stepped still closer and Sadie just managed to keep from stepping back. But she wouldn't look weak even if she *felt* weak. She wanted to walk away from the entire situation.

She stared up into those eyes of his and thought she could actually see chips of ice floating in those pale blue depths.

"I want to see him."

"You will," Sadie said and lifted her chin slightly. "But not until you've calmed down."

He laughed, but there was no humor in the sound. "I just found out I have a son I knew nothing about and you want me to calm down?"

"Justin," she said, fighting for calm herself, "do you remember how you left last time you were here?"

"What's that have to do with anything?"

She gritted her teeth, took a deep breath and said, "Every night for two weeks, we were together."

He stared at her but didn't speak, so Sadie kept going. She still couldn't believe how she'd reacted to him.

Looking back now, it seemed that the moment they'd met, there had been some invisible force drawing them together. She'd never experienced anything like it before and hadn't since, either.

She wasn't a one-night-stand kind of woman, but with him, she hadn't been able to help herself. It was heat and passion and the best sex of her life, and she'd fallen, foolishly, in love. Thankfully, she'd gotten over that.

"I remember."

"And do you also remember that when my father finally said no to the sale, you disappeared?"

"I left. There's a difference."

"Not really," she argued, running with the chance to say what she'd been feeling for the last year and more. She'd loved him, allowed herself to dream of being with him always. She'd let herself believe that his touch, his whispers in the night meant that he loved her, too. She was wrong. "You left my room in the middle of the night and in the morning, you were just gone. Like you'd never been there at all." The sting of that could still bring a slow burn to the center of her chest. "No call. No note. No fond farewells. You just left without a backward glance."

He pushed one hand through his hair. "I never said I was going to stay, Sadie."

"No, you didn't. And I'm not even saying I wanted you to." Now she was lying, but he didn't need to know that.

"What are you saying, then?"

"That if you couldn't be bothered to even say goodbye to me, why would I think you would care about a surprise pregnancy?"

"Okay." He ran one hand over his face and nodded. "You might have a point there." He shook his head. "Two completely different things. And while we're at it, we used condoms. How the hell did you get pregnant?"

"They're not perfect."

"That's just great." He threw his hands up. "They've got one job and can't manage it." Still shaking his head, he walked away from her, stared out at the ocean for a long minute or two, then turned back to face her. "You had plenty of time, Sadie. You shouldn't have kept this from me. You had no right."

"I have every right," she argued. "He's my son and I'm not going to have him hurt by a father who might decide to just walk away one day."

He gave her a fierce scowl. "I wouldn't do that."

"Really?" She tipped her head to one side and looked at him. "You already did." She saw a quick flash of insult in his eyes and when he spoke, she heard regret in his voice.

"Damn it, Sadie. You should have told me."

Probably. She wrapped her arms around herself and held on as if giving herself a comforting hug. "I don't know, Justin. Maybe I should have. But if I could do it over, I don't know that I'd do it differently. Ethan's mine to protect."

"He's mine, too, Sadie. And I want to meet my son." He stared at her with speculation. "That's why you insisted on keeping twenty-five percent of the hotel. Because of the baby."

She sighed. "Mostly, yes. As long as your idea for transforming the hotel into a world-class spa resort works out, I'll never have to worry about taking care of Ethan."

He took the few steps separating them with a couple of long strides. She always had admired how he could look so fierce, so confident, sure of himself and what he wanted. Now those emotions were stamped on his features as he reached out and grabbed her upper arms.

"Did you really think I wouldn't take care of my son?"

"This isn't about what you would do, Justin. *I* take care of Ethan. *Me*." She pulled free. "This is just what I was worried about."

"What?"

"That you would sweep in here with your family name and money and try to take over. I don't need you to take care of Ethan," she said and jabbed her index finger at his chest. "We've been doing fine without you."

"Yeah, well. It doesn't matter what you want." His gaze narrowed on hers and she read fury and determination in those pale blue eyes. "I know the truth now and you're not keeping him away from me."

That sounded like a threat, and even if it wasn't, she knew it could have been. With the kind of money Justin's family had, she was at a serious disadvantage.

"So, where is he?"

The wind was icy, but it was not the source of the chill sliding up and down Sadie's spine. "In my suite."

"Let's go." He took her arm and turned her toward the hotel.

The burn of his touch filled her and yet still it wasn't enough to take away the chill of fear. Fear for her son. For her. For the life she'd built for them both.

Sadie had known that asking Justin to come back to the hotel would be dangerous. That he would somehow tangle her up again, twisting her emotions into knots. But knowing that didn't make it any easier.

And even with those thoughts filling her mind, she looked at the hotel as they walked closer and noted all the changes Carey money had already made. New sun umbrellas in a bright red-and-white stripe over brand-new round tables and iron chairs with cream-colored cushions. The flagstone patio had been re-mortared and power-washed so that it sparkled in the sunlight.

New accordion doors opened from the patio into the main dining room so that it brought the outside in. The building itself was going to be painted in a few days and the terra cotta Spanish tiles on the roof had been replaced by the same kind of tile, but in an aquamarine color that mimicked the sea.

He'd made so many incremental changes that had ensured, on the whole, the hotel was sparkling. Her great-grandfather had built the place and for years, it had done good business, mostly because of its location. Not many hotels could boast of being right on the beach in La Jolla. But now people wanted more than just easy access to the ocean. They wanted an *experience* when it came to their hotel. They wanted to be pampered, and with the Cliffside's location, it was prime for just such a makeover.

Of course, her father had turned down Justin's offer fifteen months ago. He'd wanted, hoped, to make these changes himself. But then her dad got sick. He needed a heart operation and he needed to move somewhere warm and dry and relax for the first time in his life.

Which had left Sadie with few options, so she'd

called Justin and reopened negotiations herself. His offer this time was substantially more—including the cash bonus she'd insisted on for her father's sake. Plus she'd kept an interest in her family's hotel, ensuring Ethan's future and hers. Not to mention being able to have a say in how her family's hotel was remade.

He had a tight grip on her upper arm and stalked along beside her while her brain kept spinning. Maybe because she was trying to not think about him and Ethan together. About having to trust Justin with her son's heart. Of having to trust Justin, period.

To give him his due, though, Justin hadn't wasted any time, once he owned the hotel. He'd been in San Diego off and on for the last three months, pouring money into the Cliffside and working with designers and with Sadie, to enhance their gym and to build "treatment rooms" for what would be the spa element.

When Justin Carey wanted something, nothing would stand in his way. He'd wanted her that way once and remembering his determination to get her into his bed was enough to shake her soul. Which was just another reason to be wary. If he decided he wanted his son—what was there to stop him?

Still holding on to her, Justin made his way to the elevators. Sadie finally pulled free, glanced at him and said, "I know the way. You don't have to perp-walk me."

"Fine. Let's go, then." He pushed the button, and when the elevator doors swished open, waved her inside.

She hit the button for the top floor, then stepped

to the rear of the car, keeping a safe distance between them.

Justin watched her, and in spite of the circumstances, felt that familiar burn in his body. Sure, a lot of that heat at the moment was anger. But he couldn't deny the sexual pull he felt for her. It had been there from the moment he'd looked into those gold-flecked eyes and shook her hand fifteen months ago. There had been an electrical jolt of something undeniable the moment their hands met—and it was still there.

Being around Sadie had a way of putting pure lust in charge of the thinking for him. He wanted her. Even now. Even knowing that she'd lied to him for almost a year and a half.

Studying her, he finally understood why her body looked riper, fuller than he'd remembered. She'd had a child. *His* child. That realization planted itself uppermost in his mind and even managed, briefly, to shove lust onto the back burner.

He was a father.

That thought was enough to send fear racing along his spine. Most men had nine long months to get used to the idea of having a tiny human depend on them. He'd had five minutes and it wasn't nearly long enough.

Assuming she was telling him the truth. But why would she lie now after keeping the whole thing a secret all this time? He'd have to do some checking on this. He'd want a DNA test—to be sure. But looking at her now, seeing the gleam of what looked like worry in her eyes, he was ready to believe her.

The doors opened and he waited for her to precede him into the hall. He knew her corner suite well. There were views of the ocean from both sides of the main room and both of the bedrooms. Those views were staggering enough that she used to never draw the drapes. Even at night, they were open to the flickering lights of La Jolla and the moon that dazzled the sea.

He didn't speak and neither did she on the walk to her rooms. Hell, he didn't have a clue what to say. A father. The thought was terrifying and…intriguing, as well.

He'd always thought that someday, in the far distant, nebulous future, he would have children. A wife. A home. But it wasn't even on his radar now. He was still trying to forge his own path within his family. This was about doing what he needed to, to build his future. And he wondered if he'd be able to do this. Be a *father*? A *dad*? What if he screwed it all up? What if he was so bad at the parenting thing that his kid turned into a mean little bastard? Or worse? And that wasn't even considering the fact that now he would be tied forever to Sadie. That continuous, sexual pull he felt for her was going to be a permanent part of his life.

His sister Serena had always wanted to be a mother and now she had his niece, Alli, and was newly engaged to Jack Colton. Amanda Carey was engaged, as well, to Henry Porter, so he expected that at some point she would have a child, as well. And hell, even their older brother, Bennett, had fallen in love and was now engaged, and Hannah made no secret of the fact that she wanted a lot of kids.

Strange to realize that Justin was the one to provide the second grandchild to the Careys. Strange—and he wasn't ashamed to admit, a little terrifying.

Sadie used her key card, swung the door into the

well-appointed set of rooms and called out, "Mike. I'm back."

"Mike?" Justin stared at her. She had some guy in her suite? Some guy watching *his* son? She trusted some other guy to know Justin's son? To have a relationship with him? Was he also in a relationship with Sadie? Hell, he didn't like that at all. "Something else you want to tell me?"

Before Sadie could say anything, a young woman came out of one of the bedrooms holding a baby close. She had short blond hair, brown eyes and a suspicious gleam in her eyes as she looked at Justin. But he had eyes only for the tiny boy grinning and babbling incomprehensibly.

"Mike, this is Justin Carey." She paused. "Ethan's father. Justin, this is Michelle Franks. Mike works here at the hotel and helps me out with the baby."

He barely heard Sadie. The words sounded like those old Charlie Brown cartoons, where the parents' voices were just noise. That was what he heard while Sadie and Mike talked to each other. Justin couldn't tear his gaze from the baby. He walked closer and stared into a miniature face so like his own Justin couldn't think of a damn thing to say. Except the obvious, of course.

DNA test or not, this was his son.

There was simply no denying it. The boy even had Justin's pale blue eyes and one dimple in his left cheek. He was a mini-me, Justin told himself.

The question now was, what to do about it?

He didn't like not knowing. He much preferred having a plan.

"I don't even know what the hell to say," Justin

admitted, and the minute the words came out of his mouth, he wanted to bite them back. He was rarely at a loss for words and on those few occasions, he hadn't admitted it. Especially to an adversary. And at the moment, that was exactly what Sadie Harris felt like.

"Justin, I know you're shocked," she said. "It's a lot to take in. But I don't want anything from you. Ethan and I are doing just fine. I only thought you should know."

"Because it was getting too hard to hide it with me right here?"

"Mostly," she admitted. "But not entirely."

He swiveled his head to give her a hard look. Hell, he'd thought he knew Sadie Harris. Those two weeks with her were what fantasies were made of. She was sexy and kind and funny and smart and, all in all, the perfect woman. Which was another reason he'd left so damn fast. He hadn't been ready for her. Hadn't been ready for that whispered *"I love you"* that had slipped from her their last night together.

Love? Forever? He'd had too much to prove. Too many things to do. So he'd left while he could.

"Fifteen months later," he said. "That's when you figured I should know." Justin fought to get a grip on the anger churning inside him. Looking from her to the boy they shared, he tried to sort out the myriad emotions racing through him. How could he not have known he was a father? Shouldn't he have *sensed* it on some level? Hell, he'd helped create a new human and hadn't realized it.

His gaze locked on the baby and he felt his throat tighten. He and Sadie had made a child and he hadn't had a clue.

There had been times over the last year and a half when he'd thought about calling her. When he'd regretted leaving. When he'd wake up in the middle of the night aching for her. But he hadn't made that call because—hell, the reasons why didn't matter. Not now. Not when he was faced with a child who had his eyes. His smile. That dimple.

"Damn it, Sadie," he muttered, never taking his gaze from the tiny boy in front of him, "you had no right to keep this from me."

"Mike, you should go downstairs. See if they need any help."

"Are you sure?" the other woman asked as she handed the baby over to Sadie.

"We're fine. Thanks."

Justin waited until the woman was gone, then he speared Sadie with a glare and waited for some kind of damn explanation.

"Justin, you left." She met his gaze squarely and lifted her chin a little in defiance. "You never called. You never came back. Why should I have thought that you'd be interested in my child if you clearly weren't interested in me?"

"Not just *your* child, Sadie."

"You made him, Justin, but you're not raising him."

"Whose fault is that?" he demanded. "I didn't know he existed. Until now."

He watched her eyes go wide, then narrow with suspicion even as she cuddled Ethan closer to her. "What's that mean?"

"I think you know what it means," he muttered and reached out to take the baby. Sadie hesitated, but finally released Ethan to him.

Justin held his breath as he settled his son on his arm. He half expected the tiny boy to let out a howl at having a stranger hold him. But he needn't have worried. Ethan stared at him for a long, breathless moment. Father and son studied each other and Sadie might as well have not been there. It was as if Justin were alone in the world with his son. Looking at *his son* was a staggering experience that he wouldn't have been able to describe to anyone.

The child was a solid weight that smelled of soap and baby powder. He wore a tiny red shirt with navy blue shorts over his diaper. His knees were dimpled and his bare feet kicked excitedly as if he was trying to run. Clapping his hands together, Ethan looked at his mother, then turned back to Justin and happily patted his daddy's cheeks.

And suddenly, something…happened.

Staring into his son's eyes—so much like his own—Justin felt his heart actually turn over in his chest. His pulse was pounding and his mouth and throat were so dry it felt as if he were choking. And maybe he was. The baby gave him a wide, toothless smile and slipped into Justin's soul with an ease that was breathtaking. How could a man steel himself against this kind of feeling? This wide, deep emotion that suddenly swamped him. He didn't know what to do with it. How to think past the raw surge of emotion charging through him. Justin had never been the kind of man to show what he was thinking, feeling. But this one tiny boy was changing all of that in a heartbeat.

Silence stretched out in the room, and he knew that he wasn't ready, not yet, to deal with Sadie and what she'd just thrown at him. It was as if the world he'd known only hours ago had been ripped out from beneath him. The ground he was standing on now felt wildly unstable. He had to think. Had to talk to someone. Straighten out his own thoughts and decide what the plan would be, going forward.

"He's a good-looking boy," he finally said, to no one in particular.

Sadie laughed a little. "Since he looks just like you?"

He shot her a look and, helpless to prevent it, smiled. "That did sound a little self-serving, didn't it?"

"It's true, though. I see you whenever I look at him."

Her voice was soft and quiet, as if she'd confessed something she obviously hadn't really wanted to say. And all he could say in return was, "I should have known about him."

"I can't change that now, Justin," she said, just as quietly. "But for what it's worth, I'm sorry."

He looked at her and wondered if she meant that or if she was only now regretting the lie that had kept Ethan from him. Either way, she was right. Nothing could change the past. Nothing could give him the memories he might have had of his son being born and the first months of his life. All they could do now was chart a course from this point.

Justin hadn't held a baby since his sister Serena's daughter, Alli, was small. Funny how it came back and felt…natural. But there was a lot to think about, before he allowed himself to talk to Sadie about what the future would hold. All he knew for sure was that he had a son and now more reason than ever to succeed. To bring his plans and ideas to life.

First, though, he needed time to think. Needed to set things straight in his own mind and get some damn advice—from someone he trusted—about what to do from here. Handing the baby to his mother, he watched the two of them together and saw the love shining between them like a damn beacon.

Suddenly, he was both father and outsider and he didn't know how he was feeling about being either of those.

"I've got to go."

"Go?" Sadie repeated, staring at him in surprise. "Are you serious? You're going to leave now?"

"You dropped this on me, Sadie." His gaze flicked to Ethan briefly before meeting Sadie's again. "I'm going to need more than ten minutes to figure out—"

"What? What is there to figure out? We have a baby."

A son who would depend on both of his parents. Depend on them to get along. To work together for him. And right now, Justin was so angry with Sadie he could hardly speak to her. It was more than anger, though, he admitted silently. What he'd felt for her a year and a half ago had been seeping into him since his return to San Diego. And now, it was as if an invisible wall inside him had crumbled, allowing the feelings he'd been running from for so long, to come crashing back.

"What I need to figure out," Justin told her, "is what I'm going to do about it."

Four

After Justin left—she couldn't believe he'd left again—his features grim and tight, Sadie picked up her phone and hit the speed dial. When her mother answered, Sadie let out the breath she'd been holding.

"Hi, Mom," she said, swinging her hair back over her shoulder and smiling at her son. "I told him. I told Justin about the baby."

"Oh, honey. How did it go?"

"Just like you told me it would," she admitted and wondered if, as Ethan grew, she would become all-knowing, like her mother. "He was furious. Then stunned. Then he saw Ethan and the fury came back."

Her mother sighed softly. "He's bound to be angry, sweetie. You hid his son from him."

"*Hid* is a strong word."

"Have a better one?"

"Not off the top of my head, no." Sadie carried Ethan to the French doors leading to a small balcony and stepped outside. As she held him close and welcomed the cold rush of wind, Ethan laughed.

"What was I supposed to do, Mom? Go running to the man who walked away and say, 'Oh, by the way, I'm pregnant and you're the father'?"

"Well..."

"No, I couldn't do that." It had been humiliating, having him walk away from *her*. What if he'd walked away from Ethan, too? Well, she would find out soon enough if that was his plan, wouldn't she? But even that wasn't the whole truth. If Justin had ignored her or told her to get lost despite being pregnant it would have hurt right down to her soul. Yet, it was a different possible reaction that had worried her so much, and her mother knew it. "Mom, he's a Carey. They have more money than God. If he wants Ethan, he can find a way to take him."

Sunlight, the scent of the sea and the icy cold wind combined to soothe her as they always had. And still she walked back into their suite, protecting Ethan from the cold air. She carried him into his room while her mother talked.

"He's your son, honey," she said. "No judge is going to take Ethan from you."

"If the judge is friends with the Careys, he might." And that fear was the real reason she'd kept quiet about the baby. She put her mom on speaker so she could lay Ethan down and draw up his blanket. "Nap time, baby boy," she said and her son kicked his legs, waved his arms and in general told her he really wasn't in the mood.

Scooping up her phone, she closed Ethan's door and walked back to the balcony that would always call to her. Taking her mother off speaker, she said, "I had to tell him, even though I'm still worried about what will happen next. The last two months have been a nightmare, trying to keep Justin from finding out about the baby. And frankly, it's exhausting."

"I imagine," her mom said.

"We're going to be working together and we're both living at the hotel for now, so sooner or later, Justin would have discovered the truth on his own. Might as well take charge of it," Sadie grumbled. There had just been no way to keep Ethan a secret forever. She'd known that the moment she'd invited Justin to come back and bid on the hotel. "And as soon as I told him... he left. Again. And he's probably gone off to get one of the three-piece-suit lawyers his family keeps on staff. God, Mom," she whispered, "what if he does take Ethan from me?"

"We won't let him."

A small smile curved Sadie's mouth. Good to have support even if her mother couldn't actually *keep* that promise.

"Honey, you're reaching out for things to worry about and they don't exist yet," her mother soothed. "So instead, why don't we change the subject and you tell me what the hotel looks like now?"

Sadie walked back inside, dropped into a blue, flower-spattered chair and curled her legs up beneath her. Oh, she hated to admit it, but she said, "It looks wonderful. He's doing all the things you and I and Daddy used to talk about doing. The rooms are decorated beautifully and he's added French doors to the suites with balconies. Makes a heck of a statement."

"Oh, wish I could see it."

"You'd love it," Sadie admitted, because she loved what had happened so far, too. Not for the first time, she wished her parents weren't in Arizona. But it was best for her father, so she would deal with it. "The building's being painted this weekend."

"What color?" Her mother asked eagerly, then less enthusiastically, "Not the same brick red, is it?"

"No." Justin was too smart for that, she conceded silently. Whatever issues she had with him, she could admit that he was on top of things. What he didn't know, he found out. What he wanted, he got. Which brought her back to remembering how he hadn't wanted her—and worrying about him deciding he wanted their son.

Instantly, Sadie pushed that concern aside and went back to the subject at hand. "Justin has been 'researching' hotels along the coast and has decided that the 'coastal' color scheme was the way to go."

"Okay," her mother said, "I think I know what that means, but define it for me."

"It's going to be a bright white with navy blue trim and a lighter blue as an accent color on the posts along the porch and on those French doors."

Her mother sighed and Sadie knew she was picturing it all.

"He's still working on the treatment rooms—though those are almost finished and the new indoor pool is gorgeous."

Her mother clucked her tongue. "Why an indoor pool? The hotel's at the ocean's front door."

Sadie laughed because that had been her first reaction, as well. "Justin said there will be plenty of rich women coming to the spa that aren't going to want salt water in their hair."

"But chlorine's okay?" her mother asked.

"I suppose. He wanted a couple of hot tubs, as well, but I talked him into going for a swim spa instead."

"And he went for it?"

"He did." Sadie remembered being surprised at how open he was to her ideas.

"Sounds like it's going to be beautiful."

"It is, Mom. I just wish it wasn't Justin doing it all."

Her mother sighed and Sadie winced.

"Honey, I know you don't want to hear this," she said patiently, "but this is happening because he's a Carey. He's got the money to give you that cash buyout and still pull the hotel into the twenty-first century."

Sadie knew all of that was true. She hated that it was true. Hated that she needed Justin as much as she wanted him. Just as she knew she'd needed that cash payment to send to her parents. "How's Daddy?"

"He's better." She could hear the smile in her mother's voice. "Much better, actually. He started arguing with the doctor yesterday, so that's a good sign."

Sadie grinned. "That *is* a good sign. So his heart will be all right now?"

"It will. He's on medication and since he's traded in worrying about the hotel for driving a golf cart, his blood pressure has really dropped."

"Okay, good." Relief swamped her. She hated that her parents were now living in Arizona, so far away, but if it meant that her father stayed healthy and worry-free, then she could live with it. Arizona wasn't a bad drive from San Diego, so she would be driving out for visits all the time.

Once this situation with Justin was resolved or ended or escalated, or whatever was going to happen.

So this was what she had to do, Sadie told herself. She had to remember that entering this partnership with Justin—telling him about Ethan and handling that fallout—was for her father's sake.

When Max Harris had a heart attack, it had been a giant wakeup call for Sadie. Her father had been running and working and worrying over the hotel all his life and it was time for him to take it easy. Especially since the doctor had said that the heart attack was a small warning sign.

It hadn't been easy, but Sadie and her mother had finally convinced Max that retiring to Arizona was the right call. His brother lived there and Bullhead City had the Colorado River, so it wasn't just a desert landscape. He'd fought it every step of the way, but now, three months in, he was making friends, golfing a few times a week with his older brother and, in general, enjoying his life. Which made it possible for Sadie's mother to enjoy herself, too.

All it had taken was for Sadie to call Justin, swallow her pride and make a deal.

"Now, enough about us," her mother said. "Tell me everything new about my grandson."

Sadie grinned and settled in to talk about her favorite subject.

Justin drove like a bat out of hell.

The traffic on the freeway didn't slow him down any; it was more like the other cars were forming an obstacle course. He switched lanes, passed, switched again and stepped on it. He had to talk to the family. To Bennett. Hell, he had to talk to *somebody*.

He was a father and he didn't have the slightest clue what to do about that. The memory of holding his son rose up in his mind, then lodged in his throat, a hot ball of emotion that confused him. Hell, he'd been a father for an hour and his whole world was undone.

"Damn it," he muttered, "this was *not* in the plan."

Marriage and family had always been in the back of his mind, but somewhere in a very nebulous future, shrouded in mist. He hadn't been looking for a relationship, let alone a *family*. There was too much to be done. Too much left to prove. To both himself and the rest of the Careys.

But it seemed he didn't have a choice anymore. Ready for it or not, he had a son.

"Why didn't she tell me?" He fumed at that thought and passed a Camry like it was standing still. "The kid is six months old and I knew nothing about it?"

What would you have done if you'd known?

Well, he didn't know the answer to that, did he? He hadn't been given the opportunity to find out.

He punched in Bennett's number and waited impatiently while his brother's phone rang.

"Justin? Twice in one day? What's going on?"

"I've got to talk to you," Justin practically shouted to be heard over the roar of the wind racing past his BMW convertible. "Are you at the office?"

"No. I went home early."

"A very strange day," Justin muttered. His big

brother leaving the office early. The world really was upside down. "I'll be there in a half hour."

"What's this about?"

"You won't believe me." Justin hung up before he could blurt out the truth. He wanted to do that in person and on his feet, so he could pace off the temper still chewing on his insides.

When he reached Bennett's house in Dana Point, Justin was stunned for the second time that day. He'd never much cared for Bennett's place. It was, he supposed, an architectural statement, but for him, it had always looked like a concrete box. But since Hannah had come into his brother's life, it looked like more had changed than just Bennett's attitude.

The building was still the same, but Hannah and her crew had done all they could to add some interest, some texture to the place. There were dark green shutters at the windows, window boxes filled with brightly colored summer flowers tumbling from them, and a new, gabled roof with cedar shingles over a wide, brand-new front porch that boasted gliders, chairs and tables alongside more potted flowers. The house itself was painted a softer green than the shutters, but nothing pale or ordinary. It reminded Justin of the color of moss when the sun shone on it. All in all, it looked a hell of a lot better than it had.

He climbed out of his car, took a breath, then headed across the flower-lined drive to the front door.

It swung open as he approached and Bennet was standing there, wearing blue jeans, a red crew shirt and black boots. "You wearing jeans?" Justin shook his head and walked past his brother into the house. "Don't know if I can take one more surprise today."

"I've worn jeans before," Bennett argued and shut the door. "What's going on with you?" he asked as he followed Justin into the great room.

"It's different in here, too," Justin muttered, shaking his head.

Bennett looked around at the deep green walls, the white crown molding and the gleaming wood floors, that somehow looked brighter now than they had when the walls were beige. "Yeah. Hannah and Mom are turning the place upside down."

"Beats beige, I guess," Justin said as he walked to the wide hearth, where he leaned his forearm on the heavy oak mantel.

"What the hell is wrong with beige, anyway?" Bennett murmured, then joined his brother. "You want to tell me what's happening now? Are you okay?"

"No." Justin took a deep breath, hoping it would steady him. "Nope. I'm really not."

"Just tell me. What kind of trouble are you in?"

Barking out a laugh, Justin said, "Thanks for the vote of confidence. Although, maybe it is trouble. That's the problem. I just don't know."

"Spit it out, Justin. I'm going to die an old man, watching you talk to yourself."

"Okay, then." Justin turned to face his brother. "Turns out I'm a father."

"What?"

"This is going to take a while," Justin said, dropping into one of the maroon leather chairs. "Can I have a beer?"

Bennett stared at him for a long moment or two. "I think we're both going to need one."

Sadie didn't know what she'd expected, but somehow it hadn't been Justin taking off the minute he found out about Ethan. She shouldn't have been surprised, though. He'd disappeared once before. Why not now?

If only she didn't still want him every bit as much as she once had. Those two weeks with him had been the best in her life. She'd fallen in love—that she hadn't expected—and when he left, her heart had shattered.

Until she'd discovered she was pregnant.

That had been like a gift. A miracle.

Sadie smiled, remembering, as she walked into one of the new treatment rooms at the hotel and stopped just over the threshold to admire it. Justin had taken what used to be small but tidy hotel rooms and turned the whole row of them into treatment rooms for the new spa. Aromatherapy, massage therapy, manicures and pedicures, exfoliation wraps…and so much more. It was going to be lush and beautiful.

In this room the walls were a soft meadow green, with sparkling white trim and soft lighting. Windows stood open to the ocean view now, but there were shades that could be drawn if the client preferred darkness. A small refrigerator would hold fruit juices and spring water. There were speakers on the wall to provide soothing music, and a dozen candles to fill the space with the scent of lavender or chamomile. Feather-light blankets and pillows that would soothe clients into sleep were stacked on a top-of-the-line massage table.

It was, in short, perfect.

"Boy, I hate to admit that," she murmured. Justin, with all of that Carey money at his disposal, was doing to the hotel all the things she'd dreamed of doing. So she was both pleased and irritated. An uncomfortable jumble of emotions.

"Oh, hi, Sadie."

She turned to the man in the doorway behind her. "Hello, Sam." She gave him a smile. "I was just checking out the treatment rooms."

He took a long, approving look around. "Turned out nice, didn't it?"

"They all did." She surveyed the room again and gave a satisfied sigh. "And I love that every room is just a little different."

"That was your idea, wasn't it?" he asked.

"Yes," she admitted. "Justin wanted them all to be the same so there was continuity." She glanced at the lovely furnishings and said, "But I thought that having them be different, each of them luxurious in its own way, would encourage our clients to want to try every one of them."

She'd fought Justin on that and it wasn't the only argument they'd had over style. Well, Justin was a man and, sexist or not, most of their clients would be women. Not only was Sadie female, but she'd studied interior design in college. Plus, for years, she'd dreamed and planned and fantasized about what she would do to the hotel if she ever had the chance and the money.

Over the years, she had done what she could. But usually, the money she and her parents had been able to come up with had gone to repairs that really didn't show. New stoves in the restaurant. New elevator. New plumbing. Now, having the opportunity to do what she'd always longed to do, she was eager to do the rest. Even if that did mean accepting a partnership with Justin Carey.

"I think your idea was the better way." Sam shrugged. "I think my favorite is the dark green room. Makes me think of a forest."

"I like the blue one for the ocean," she confessed, then smiled again. "And we're proving my point, aren't we?"

"Guess we are. Have you seen Justin?" he asked and Sadie immediately tensed.

"No. He left a couple of hours ago." And that worried her. Minutes after meeting his son, Justin had left. Did that mean he wasn't coming back? No. She'd seen the look in his eyes while he held Ethan and it was enough to tell her that whatever else was going on in his mind, Justin wasn't walking away from their son. Which worried her in another way.

She wanted Ethan to know his father, of course. Of course. Her mind niggled at the wildly different scenarios that could play out and she wanted to reel back from all of them.

Truthfully, she didn't want to share Ethan. Not with a man who could pick up and walk away so easily. How could she trust Justin to *not* leave Ethan? To not hurt him as he had devastated her when he turned away from her fifteen months ago? But she didn't have a choice, did she? Because of the son they shared, she and Justin would be linked forever.

And the way she felt about the man was going to make that more and more difficult.

But that wasn't all of it. With the Carey family money and influence, Justin could, if he decided to, come in and find a way to take Ethan from her. And she couldn't risk that. What mother would? God it seriously felt as if her head might explode.

"Well, hell," Sam said. "Do you know when he'll be back?"

"No, I don't. Why?" Sadie asked. "Is there a problem?"

"Not really a problem. Just something I needed to talk to him about."

"Tell me."

Sam gathered his long blond hair and tied it off with a leather strip at the back of his neck. "You know they've been working on the indoor pool for a couple weeks now."

"Oh, yes." She and Justin had gone back and forth over the pool and the placement of it. Of course, at the end, Justin had won that round.

"Well, we're putting in a spa separate from the pool."

"Yeah, I know that, too," she said and followed Sam as he headed out into the hall. "I won that battle with Justin. He'd wanted a pair of hot tubs on either end of the pool."

"Well, we've got that swim spa you ordered all set up."

"Already? That's great." The swim spa was pool and spa combined and Sadie was sure it would be a big hit with their clients. It could seat up to twenty people, and had more than sixty jets. There were lights and Bluetooth for music and it could also be used for swimming against a current caused by heavy-duty jets.

"We're building the cedar decking and stairs now. Then we'll fill the spa. I was wondering if you wanted us to build a couple of cabinets you could use down there for towels and whatever else you might need."

"That's a terrific idea, Sam, thanks."

"No problem. The wet bar has two refrigerators, so you can have wine or your waters and whatever."

Sadie grinned. It was so much easier to talk to Sam. He actually *liked* her ideas.

"Anyway, I wanted to check with you and Justin to see if there were any last-minute changes you wanted to the decking around the swim spa."

"No, I loved the design you showed us."

"You think Justin's okay with it?"

She paused to think about it. "I think if Justin wanted a vote, he should have stuck around."

Sam rocked on his heels and bit back a small smile. "Power struggle?"

She shrugged. "Maybe a little." *A lot.* "Why don't you show me the spa setup?"

He led her through a door, across the courtyard that also needed work, Sadie thought, to the building that was once used as a conference area. Well, with the emphasis now on building the Cliffside as a spa resort, they wouldn't be needing that space.

They walked inside and the cavernous room actually echoed with their footsteps. The new pool gleamed like a pale sapphire in the overhead lights. The new patio furniture was stacked at the back of the room and once they opened, this indoor pool room would be ready to help their clients relax and be waited on. Both sides of the rooms boasted floor-to-ceiling windows and the skylight overhead flooded the room with natural light.

"As you can see, the pool's completed. Finished filling it just this afternoon," Sam was saying as he pointed. "I thought the swim spa should be its own area." He turned to wave one hand at the opposite end of the room.

The swim spa, naked but for the casing it came wrapped in, sat, waiting to be filled and enjoyed. "I think it looks great there, Sam. When are you and the guys going to build the decking and stairs?"

"We're hauling in the cedar today, and we'll get started first thing in the morning. Shouldn't take more than a few hours."

"Perfect." Sadie's head was spinning. So much happening. So quickly. Was it too much? No, it was just happening so fast that she was having a hard time keeping up. She'd wanted to give the hotel a serious overhaul for years, and now that it was happening, she was both excited and irritated that she had Justin to thank for it.

The Cliffside was going to be reborn. And that was a very good thing. Meanwhile, she felt as if maybe her world was trembling on the edge of…something. She just wasn't sure what.

And she wouldn't know. Until Justin came back.

If he came back.

When he did return, they had to have a talk. She and Justin were going to have to work together. They were both living in the hotel, so there was going to have to be communication. There was no reason they couldn't work well together, once they got past the initial bumps of being around each other again. And sharing Ethan.

Of course, she promised herself sternly, there would be absolutely *no* sex. Under any circumstances. They would not be going to bed together. That wouldn't solve anything and would only complicate *everything*.

Nope. Been there, done that, and not going back.

No matter how good it sounded.

Five

Back in La Jolla, it took Justin about ten seconds to spot Sadie.

Sunset was over, but the moon hadn't risen yet, so the world was in that twilight stage where everything looked just a little softer. Streetlights were on, and small, white fairy lights were strung along the railing that ran the length of the hotel restaurant's outside patio.

But he wasn't interested in the atmosphere. He didn't give a damn about the pedestrians strolling along the shore or the music drifting to them from a group of kids gathered around a beach fire ring. All he cared about was Sadie.

She was sitting alone at a table far back from the boardwalk. She was in shadows and still he would have known her anywhere. Because there was a buzz in his bloodstream that only happened when he was close to Sadie.

Alone at the small round table in the soft glow of the pale lights, she looked...vulnerable. And she wouldn't thank him for thinking that.

He took a deep breath and released it, hoping to ease the knot of tension that had been with him since he'd left here a few hours ago. Talking to Bennett had helped—though it hadn't solved anything. He hadn't actually expected it to. What he'd really needed was just to talk to family. To get his brother's advice— which he wasn't sure he would follow anyway.

Bennett, after the first shock of finding out he had a nephew, had talked Justin down, made him swear to get a DNA test and had promised not to tell the rest of the family. Justin really didn't need the entire Carey clan descending on La Jolla to check out his son. Not before he had a chance to work this through with his son's mother. And who the hell knew how long that would take?

"Are you just going to stand there and look at me?"

His lips twitched. Sadie never had been the shy type. A man never had to wonder what she was thinking. Feeling. "I always liked looking at you, Sadie."

"And you always had something pretty to say."

Regret rose up inside him because of that tone of her voice. He didn't need to see her face to know she wasn't happy. And he really didn't like being the cause of her pain. Hell, all he'd ever wanted, from the moment he'd first met her, was to see her smile. To feel her touch. To taste that tempting mouth.

"I never lied to you, Sadie."

"I know." She dipped her head and her hair slid across her shoulders. "I think we should talk, Justin."

"Agreed." He walked closer, saw she was having a glass of wine and asked, "You have another one of those?"

"I do." There was a second glass on the table and as he walked closer, she poured pale gold wine into it. "I've been waiting for you."

Nodding, he took a seat beside her and asked, "Where's the baby?"

She took a sip and said, "Ethan is sleeping. Mike is with him."

"You seem to trust her with Ethan," he said.

"If I didn't trust her, she wouldn't be near my son." She took another sip of wine and said, "You're going to have to let that one go, Justin. Mike's a good person and she loves Ethan. He's safe with her."

"Fine." He lifted one hand as if in surrender. "I'll take your word for it." *For now*, he told himself. He could have good ol' Mike checked out with a single phone call. He'd take care of that tomorrow. For tonight… "Anyway, I wanted to say that I'm sorry I left."

"Which time?"

"Nice shot." He slid a glance at her. "But is that really how you want to start this off?"

"No, it's not." Now Sadie lifted one hand and shook her head. "That was a knee-jerk response, sorry."

"Yeah, I guess we both do that too often."

"Probably," she said, then added, "I wasn't sure you'd come back."

"You can't be serious," he said. He sat up straight and leaned his forearms on the table. Cupping his palms around the wineglass, he spoke softly. "Not only are we remodeling this hotel and not finished yet—I just met my son. Why would I leave and not come back?"

"I don't know, Justin." Sadie sipped at her wine, pushed her hair back from her face and sighed a little. "For all I knew, meeting Ethan pushed you over the edge and you backed off."

"Not hardly," he muttered. "I just needed to clear my head."

"So, where did you go?"

This was the best conversation they'd had since he'd come back to San Diego. And he didn't buy for a second that she'd thought he wouldn't be coming back. Sadie was too smart for that. So maybe she'd just wanted him to explain where he'd gone. And why. Well, hell, he could give her that.

Nodding, Justin sat back in the chair, stretched his legs out in front of him and lifted the wineglass to take a drink. "I drove up to Orange County to talk to my brother."

"You told your family about Ethan?" Her voice was tight and her entire body went rigid. Tension radiated from her in thick waves and Justin wanted to know why.

"I told my *brother*. Why is that a problem for you?"

"I didn't say it was," Sadie countered, sipping at her wine again. "But why is it that the minute you find out about Ethan, you go off to your family?"

"Why wouldn't I?" He still didn't get it, though he could see that she was really off-balance about all of this. "They're my family. Who the hell else will I tell about Ethan? Why does this bother you so much?"

"It doesn't," she said, in a tone that shouted *Yes,*

it does! Shaking her head, she said, "Why should I worry about you going to see the incredibly wealthy Carey family about *my* son?"

"So it'd be okay with you if my family had zero money."

"Yes. Maybe. This is coming out all wrong," she murmured.

A flicker of anger kindled in the center of his chest, but Justin deliberately ignored it. "Yes, it is. So you're trying to say you don't like my family because they're rich."

"I don't know if I like them or not. I've never met them. They could be totally nice people," she said, then took another sip of wine. "I just don't trust them because they're rich," she said.

"Wow. At least you're honest about it."

"Well, come on, Justin, when we were together before, you didn't exactly make me think your family was all Norman Rockwell or something. All you could talk about was how your family made you crazy."

"*Everybody's* family makes them crazy, Sadie. It's not just rich families. In fact, money has nothing to do with any of this."

"You know who says that? Rich people." Sadie rolled her eyes. "That and 'Money can't buy happiness.' You'll never hear someone living paycheck to paycheck say that."

"I suppose not," he had to admit. "That doesn't mean every guy with money is a jerk."

"I didn't say *every* rich person…"

"Didn't have to," Justin said with a half laugh. "The problem is, Sadie…you're a snob." He congratulated himself on his placid tone. "A reverse snob, but basically the same thing."

"That's ridiculous. I never—"

"Sadie," he said, still keeping his tone even—and good for him, "I wanted to talk to my brother. That's all." He shrugged and tucked his hands into his pockets. "If it makes you feel any better, he swore he wouldn't tell the family until I was ready."

"And when's that going to be?"

"I don't know." He shook his head. "You hit me with something that's going to take more than twelve hours to come to grips with."

She sighed, and most of the tension she'd been carrying around seemed to slide off her shoulders. Then she was quiet for another moment or two before muttering, "I'm not a snob."

He laughed shortly. "Fine. Leaving my family out of it for now, let's talk about the baby."

Her fingers tightened on the stem of her glass. "Okay. You start."

"I want time with him, Sadie," he said. That was the one clear thought he'd had all afternoon. "With Ethan. That's nonnegotiable."

"Nonnegotiable?" She took another drink of her wine before saying, "This isn't a contract, Justin."

"Not yet it's not."

She frowned so slightly that if he hadn't been watching her closely, he might have missed it. "We don't have to go to war over our son," he said quietly. "Look, Sadie. I've already lost six months of his life. I'm not going to lose any more."

"I don't want you to, Justin. That's why I finally

told you about Ethan." She set her wine down and quietly asked, "What did your brother say?"

"After he picked his jaw up off the floor, you mean?" He laughed shortly. "He told me to get a DNA test."

"He's your son, Justin," she said. "If you don't believe me, just look at him. He's a mini-you."

"I believe you and yeah, he does look like me. But for legal reasons, Bennett wants that DNA test."

"*What* legal reasons?"

"Nothing to worry about."

"People who say that never realize that those are the magic words that *start* the worry."

"Sounds like you're primed to worry no matter what I say."

"Maybe," she admitted. She leaned in toward him and he caught her scent on the air. Not cloying or heavy, it was softly floral and reminded him vaguely of peaches. And for the last year and a half, that scent had chased him through his dreams.

Justin looked at her, and in the glow of the white lights, her eyes shone as her gaze locked with his. She pulled the mass of her hair around to her left side and, as he watched, began to braid it, to contain it while the wind continued to swirl around them.

He reached out and caught her hand. His fingers burned at the contact with hers, and his voice was just a little tight when he said, "Don't tie your hair down. I like it loose."

Sadie ran her fingers through the loose braiding to undo it and kept her gaze fixed on him while she did. He couldn't look away from her. The night seemed to close in on them as it got darker, as if they were being closeted away from the rest of the world.

She took a deep breath, lifted her chin and said, "Okay. How are we going to handle this? I mean, Mike watches Ethan for me when I'm downstairs working with Sam or you or the others."

"That'll still work," Justin told her. "Or, sometimes I can take him with me while I talk to Sam or you."

"You want to take Ethan into the construction zone?"

"The heavy work is done now, Sadie. What's left is the finishing, the painting, the decorating."

"True. Okay, we can start off that way and see how it goes."

He took a drink, then smiled at her. "See, not so hard for us to talk without arguing."

Her lips curved briefly and he felt an answering tug inside him. This woman was burned into his blood. He'd never gotten past her. Never been able to forget her. And now she was here. Back in his life. With his *son*. He didn't know where that was going to lead them. Didn't know what was coming beyond the opening of the hotel that was going to be the first of many in the legacy chain Justin wanted to build.

All he really knew for sure was that he still wanted her.

The wind lifted her hair and Justin watched, hypnotized by the wild movement. Until she spoke again and he met her gaze. "Anything's possible, I suppose."

"Hope so," he said and reached out to cover her hand with his.

Her breath caught even as she slid her hand free of his touch. It was too late, of course, to prevent the sizzle and burn that simply touching her engendered. He took her hand again, yearning for that burn, and stroked her skin with his thumb, making both of them breathe faster.

"Justin," she said warily, "that's really not a good idea."

"I missed the feel of you, Sadie." He leaned closer, set his wine aside and looked into her eyes, enjoying the sparkle of those gold flecks. "We've been working together for nearly two months now, and you're all I can think about. Can you really say you haven't thought about…us?"

She licked her lips and almost killed him.

"Of course I've thought about it, Justin. But…"

"No buts, okay?" He stood up, then pulled her to her feet. Rubbing his hands up and down her arms, he said, "We're here. Together. Moon's starting to rise and the whole scene is too damn romantic to waste."

She looked up at him. "Romance? That's what you want to talk about now?"

"Who said anything about talking?" He smoothed his thumb over her bottom lip and she inhaled sharply. "Problem?" he asked.

"No," she said. "Just…kiss me, Ethan"

He did and she sank into him as if she'd been waiting for this moment for a lifetime.

She linked her arms around his neck and parted her lips for his tongue. At that first sweep of intimacy, she gasped and the sound set Justin's heartbeat galloping. For the last two months he'd been tortured every day with being around her and not being able to touch her. Tormented every night by dreams that were so real, so vivid he woke every morning in agony.

Now he had his hands on her at last. Was tasting her, at last. And all he could think was that it wasn't enough. He wanted—needed—more.

His hands fisted at her back and everything inside him did the same damn thing. God, he'd missed her. The taste of her. The feel of her, pressed up against him. The sigh of her breath, the whispered moans that slipped from her throat.

Everything about this woman pushed him to the edge of sanity. And she was the only one who could hold him there and make him enjoy the madness.

Her fingers stroked through his hair, tugged at the back of his neck, silently demanding more—and he gave it to her. He held her tighter, closer, ran his hands up and down her back, following the line of her spine down to her butt, then he pulled her tightly to him so she could feel exactly what she was doing to him.

An instant later, she groaned, pulled her head back, and struggling for air, said, "This is a mistake, Justin."

"Doesn't feel like one," he murmured, dipping his head to run his lips and teeth and tongue up and down the line of her throat.

She tipped her head to one side, sighed and held on to his shoulders as if she were hanging off a cliff face. "It feels…amazing. But—"

"No buts, Sadie. Not now. Not tonight." He slid one hand from her back to her breast and she groaned. He tugged at her nipple, and even through the fabric of her shirt and bra, it was enough to jolt them both.

"That's cheating," she whispered.

"I'm just getting started," Justin told her, then pulled back. "But even if it is dark out here, I think we'd do better inside."

"Oh my god," she muttered, clearly horrified. She looked past him, past the shadowy outdoor patio to the boardwalk and the beach beyond. "I can't believe we almost…"

"Yeah, we've got an entire hotel at our disposal. Let's pick a room." Justin took her hand in his and tugged her toward the entrance.

"What about the wine?"

"We'll get it in the morning."

She blew out a breath as she hurried to keep up with him. "Justin…"

"You're thinking," he said. "Cut it out."

She laughed and the sound of it rippled along his spine. "Justin, I didn't wait outside for you, hoping for…well, this."

"Too bad," he said, tugging her in his wake toward the elevator bank past the reception desk.

"I just wanted us to not fight anymore."

"Not planning on it." He punched the up button and waited impatiently, keeping a tight grip on her hand. When the elevator dinged and the doors slid open, he pulled her inside and had her against the wall while the doors slid closed again.

"Don't want to wait," he muttered as this time, he swept one hand up under the hem of her shirt, then under the silk of her bra to cup her breast in his hand. And the moment he touched her, she sighed and he was forced to bite back a groan.

"I've been thinking about this for the last two months," he admitted, burying his head in the crook of her neck. He inhaled that scent that was purely Sadie, and let himself drown in it.

"So have I, damn it," she said and arched into him as

his fingers pulled at her hardened nipple. "I didn't want to want you so much, but I simply couldn't help myself."

"If you think I'm going to feel bad hearing that," Justin said, pausing long enough to give her a wink, "you're wrong."

The elevator dinged again and the doors slid open. "My room," Justin said, cupping her face in his palms and kissing her with everything raging inside him.

When he lifted his head, she looked up at him and whispered, "Yes. Now."

Nodding, he grabbed her up, tossed her over his shoulder and grinned when she yelped in surprise. Then he was out of the elevator and striding down the hall toward the corner suite he'd claimed for himself. Black wall sconces that would soon be replaced by brass ones lit the way down the hall. Justin dug into his pocket for the key card, got the door open and when it closed behind him, he set Sadie on her feet and grinned into her smiling face.

"You're the only guy who's ever been able to just pick me up and walk off with me." She shook her hair back, then cupped his face between her palms. "I shouldn't admit how much I like it when you do that."

"I'll pretend I didn't hear it," he said as he pulled the hem of her T-shirt up and over her head to drop it on the floor. Then she reached out and did the same for him. The air in the room kissed his skin with a soft chill that did nothing to quiet the fires inside.

When she ran the flat of her hands over his chest, Justin sucked in a gulp of air and let it slide from his lungs on a sigh. Sadie flipped the front clasp of her bra and let it fall to the floor beside her shirt.

Justin smiled, set his hands at her hips and bent

to take first one of her nipples, then the other into his mouth.

Sadie's back bowed as she moved against him. She speared her fingers through his hair and held him to her—an unnecessary move, Justin thought wildly. He wasn't about to stop.

He backed her up against the wall and feasted on her, sliding his hands down to the waistband of her shorts, undoing the zipper, the snap and then pushing them and the wisp of black silk beneath them down her amazing legs. She stepped out of her sandals and kicked off those shorts. Then he cupped her center and groaned at the jolt of heat.

"Justin!" Her short, neat nails dug into his back and he felt every tiny stab like a match flame.

His gaze locked on her face as he pushed one finger, then two, deep inside her body, stroking her incessantly as she twisted and writhed in his grip. He watched as those beautiful eyes of hers flashed with every emotion and sensation crowding through her. And when she came a moment later, he saw those eyes glaze over as she held him tightly and rocked her hips into his hand, riding the climax shuddering through her.

When the tremors stopped, Sadie slumped against him and he heard the shakiness in her voice when she said, "That was so good, Justin…"

He grinned, tipped up her chin so he could look into her eyes and said simply, "Just getting started, Sadie."

"I was hoping you'd say that," she admitted.

He smiled, swung her up into his arms and headed for the main bedroom in the two-room suite.

"I *can* walk, you know," she said, smiling.

"I like holding you," Justin told her.

Sadie wrapped her arms around his neck and asked, "What am I supposed to say to something like that?"

"You don't *have* to say anything. But..." His eyes met hers and he grinned. "How about *I love your manly muscles*?"

She laughed and Justin watched her eyes shine with humor. "Yes, that sounds just like something I'd say."

He laid her down on the bed, then stood back and stripped quickly.

"This time," she said as she lifted both arms to him, "I'm on the pill, so as long as you're healthy, too, we're covered."

He paused. "And is the pill a hundred percent effective?"

"I think it's more like ninety-eight percent," she admitted.

Justin scrubbed one hand over his face, swept his gaze up and down her body before settling on her gaze again. "I'll risk it."

"Me, too," she said, still holding her arms out to him in welcome. He moved into her arms, covered her body with his, and she wrapped her long legs around him, to keep him close.

Running her foot up and down his leg, she whispered, "It's been a long time, Justin."

"Fifteen months," he said and one corner of his mouth tipped up.

"Funny man." She slapped his shoulder and grinned at him. She ran her fingertips down his cheek and asked, "What're we doing, Justin?"

"What we do best, Sadie." He rolled, taking her with him until she lay stretched out on top of him and her gorgeous hair fell like a curtain on either side of their faces.

Staring into his eyes, she said, "Sex won't solve anything. Won't change anything."

"Does it have to?" he asked, running his hands up and down her body, following every line, every curve. "Why can't this just be what it is?"

Briefly, she closed her eyes and sighed softly. "What exactly is it, Justin?"

He looked up at her and smiled. "Magic, Sadie. Pure magic."

She didn't answer him and he tried to see what she was thinking by reading her eyes, but then she kissed him and he was surrounded by Sadie—her taste, her scent, the silken slide of her hair on his skin, the heat of her body soaking into his. When she moved, sitting up to straddle him, Justin's breath caught in his lungs. She looked like a goddess in the moonlight streaming through the windows. Her body was full and ripe and more beautiful than he remembered.

He reached up, covered her breasts with his hands and she covered his hands with her own. Tipping her head back, she shook her head and her glorious hair drifted from side to side like a sensuous curtain of silk. Looking at her, Justin's heartbeat hammered so loud it echoed in his mind. His mouth was dry and his throat clogged with a knot of need so huge he thought he might never draw an easy breath again.

"Magic," she whispered, and bracing her hands on his chest, Sadie lifted her hips and slowly lowered herself again, and as she did, she drew him into her body. The tight, wet heat of her had Justin gritting his teeth in a desperate attempt to control the need pounding through him. He looked up into her eyes and wondered how he'd gone so long without seeing her, being with her.

For those fifteen months they'd been apart, he'd thought of her often and had been tempted time and again to return to San Diego…to her. And he'd kept himself from surrendering to his want in favor of staying true to his plan.

Now he couldn't imagine why.

"You're thinking," Sadie said. "Cut it out."

He flashed her a grin, tightened his grip on her hips and held her still so he could savor that sensation of being deep inside her body. "Right. Not thinking."

She scooped her arms under her hair and then lifted them high, letting that glorious hair of hers slide over her skin, playing peekaboo with her breasts. While she watched him, she swiveled her hips, creating an amazing friction that pushed him further along the road to completion.

"You're driving me crazy, Sadie," he murmured and watched her smile blossom along with a shine of pleasure in her eyes.

Rocking her hips against him, she fought against the anchor of his hands and finally, he released her. Running his hands up and down her thighs, he listened to the rasp of her breathing, felt every move she made and gave himself up to the rush of sensations racing through him.

As a staggering climax came closer, he reached down to where their bodies joined and used his thumb to stroke and rub that one sensitive spot at the very heart of her. "Let go, Sadie. Just let go and fly…"

She reacted instantly, with a groan and a twist of

her hips, moving into his touch even as she moved on him, driving him on toward a climax that hung just out of reach.

"Justin!" She moved faster, harder, hips rocking while he matched the rhythm she set and lost himself in watching her. And still, he rubbed and stroked her core. "Don't stop," she whispered brokenly.

"Never," he answered on a groan.

She was amazing, he thought wildly, looking at her in the soft light pooling in through the open widows that faced the sea. Lithe and beautiful, she was the very definition of sex. And he couldn't imagine *not* wanting her.

She gasped, cried out his name and shuddered on top of him as her body erupted. He held her while she rode the wave of her release, and moments later, Justin leaped into that same abyss so that the two of them were locked together in a thundering, triumphant moment of completion.

When she slumped forward to lie across his chest, Justin wrapped his arms around her and rolled to his side, keeping her close so that they lay face to face on the pillows and he could watch every emotion that crossed her features.

"That was," she said, "really amazing."

He winked and grinned. "Thanks."

Laughing, she slapped lightly at his chest. "Fine. Take a bow. You earned it."

"Funny," he said, leaning in to taste that mouth of hers again, "I was going to say the same to you."

Sadie sighed. "This was never our problem. In a bed or on a table or against a wall, we were always great."

"Still are. Think we just proved that."

"But, Justin, sex isn't everything."

"Maybe not," he allowed, "but it's right up there at the top of the list."

"Justin…" She paused before admitting, "I promised myself that I wouldn't have sex with you again."

"Well, then," he mused, "you either lied to yourself, or can't be trusted with a promise."

"That's not funny."

"It's not the end of the world, either," Justin told her and cupped her face in his palm. "Hell, maybe it was a good thing."

"How do you figure that?"

"It sure got rid of some of the tension that's been humming between us for the last couple of months." He slid a hand down to cup her breast and stroke the tip of her nipple with his thumb.

She shivered, swallowed hard and said, "Justin, this morning we were shouting at each other. And tonight, we're doing…this?"

"Better than arguing, don't you agree?" He bent his head and tasted that nipple while he heard her gasp and sigh.

"Yes, but—"

He lifted his head, stared down at her and said, "Let's not question tonight, okay? Let's just accept it for what it is and be grateful for it."

Her eyes met his and he tried to read what was written in those golden eyes. She remained a mystery, though, and a part of him enjoyed that.

"Okay," Sadie finally said, then skimmed the tip of her finger across his chest, outlining the sculpted, tanned skin that she'd missed so much. "Tonight was… wonderful. But… I've got to get back to Ethan."

"Stay," Justin said. He covered her mouth with his, tangling his tongue with hers until neither of them could breathe. When he finally broke the kiss, he looked deeply into her eyes and smiled when she said, "I'll stay. For a while."

Six

Two hours later, Sadie was shaken. No other word for it.

She was still in love with Justin and that terrified her.

Nearly a year and a half ago, she'd whispered, "I love you," one night, and the next morning he was gone. The humiliation, the tears that followed had taught her a very valuable lesson. While the sex between them was, just as he said, *magical*, that was all there was. For him, anyway.

As for her, she couldn't seem to keep her heart from getting involved. And right now, her heart was racing and every single nerve in her body was buzzing. It had been that way from the first with Justin. He'd said it was magic and he wasn't wrong.

But that didn't change anything, did it?

She loved him.

He didn't love her.

"You're thinking again," Justin said. "Cut it out."

She laughed a little, as he'd meant her to, though her laugh had sounded strained to her. Then she looked at him and asked, "What do we do now, Justin?"

"About what? The hotel? Our son? More sex?"

"God." She stood up, pulled her shirt on over her head, then scooped her hair out and let it fall. "Just this morning, you were furious and now you're joking?"

He frowned up at her. "Would it make you feel better if we were screaming at each other?"

"No—of course not." But at least then, she'd know where she stood. As it was, the ground beneath her feet felt shaky. And if she lost her footing, it might cost her everything that mattered to her.

"Nothing's changed, Sadie." He crooked his arm behind his head. "I still want time with Ethan. Still want you. Still want the DNA test. Still want this hotel to be up and running in three weeks."

"And us?" she asked. "What do you want from *us*?"

"Well, now," he mused, his mouth in a slow curve, "that's a very good question."

She looked around the room, stalling for time. This room, like her own, was one of the few that hadn't yet been remodeled. All they really needed to do was paint, get a new bed in there, replace the bathroom counters and the shower and... Okay, there was a lot to do in both of their rooms. But there would be time for that later, wouldn't there? Once the hotel was open and guests were clamoring for space in a beautiful spa hotel with glorious views of the ocean.

Sadie had known for a long time that she couldn't

continue to live at the hotel. Her son would need a yard. And friends. And room to run. She knew what it was to grow up living in a hotel, and though she'd had good times there and had made countless great memories, she wanted more for her son. She wanted him to have a tree house and a dog and—but this wasn't the time for those plans. Right now, she had to deal with Justin. How did *he* fit into those plans for the future? Heck, she didn't know if he would even want to be a part of them.

"It is a good question, Justin," she said, and gave in to impulse. Bending down, she planted a quick kiss on his lips, relished that quick, sharp buzz and said, "Let me know when you have an answer."

She made it to the door, and opened it before his voice stopped her. "What exactly do you want from me, Sadie?"

Looking over her shoulder at him, she said, "I'm not really sure."

By morning, Sadie had shoved the night before into a dark, dark corner of her mind. She hadn't slept, because whenever she closed her eyes, she saw Justin's smile. Felt his kiss. His touch.

And she couldn't focus on wants. It wasn't only her heart she had to protect. It was Ethan's. Loving Justin didn't mean that she was going to find a future with him. What it meant was that she was more vulnerable than ever. And she couldn't risk her son. If Ethan loved his father and that father left him, then what? No. Much better to wrap away what she was feeling and bury it deep inside her. Protect her son. Protect her own heart.

For now, what she had to do was work with Sam on the paint for the pool room and then talk to the designers working on the manicure-pedicure stations. She had some ideas on making the room the restful, warm, inviting place it should be.

Mostly, though, she had to go check on Ethan. Justin had picked him up early that morning and had planned to spend the day with their son. She'd been nervous ever since. Maybe Justin meant the very best, but Ethan was only six months old, which meant he needed naps and a bottle and to be changed and she was sure Justin wouldn't have the slightest clue what to do with a baby for hours at a time. Maybe she should have given him a schedule. Although, Justin probably wouldn't have paid any attention to it. He was too much the kind of guy to do things his own way.

But she also knew Justin would never admit when he couldn't handle something. So she had to find him and her son. She walked all over the hotel looking for him and finally found him out front, holding the baby close to his chest and pointing toward where the crew was painting. Leaning against a doorjamb, Sadie folded her arms over her chest and watched her son and his father.

"You see, Ethan?" Justin said, looking into his son's eyes as if expecting the baby to be taking all of this in. "If you need a job done, you always get the best people for it."

Of course, she thought, teaching their son how to hire people. The sun was pouring down around them and she smiled to herself to see that Justin had Ethan wearing his hat, to keep his baby-soft skin from burning. Ocean waves swept toward shore and sounded like the heartbeat of the world.

"But you can learn how to do some things for yourself," Justin was saying as Ethan slapped his palms together, applauding. "For example, your father happens to be a great painter." He grinned at the baby. "Not like an artist kind of painter, but I did help Sam paint his house a few months ago."

Ethan grabbed a fistful of his father's hair and yanked.

"Ow!" Justin winced and Sadie muffled a laugh as she watched him trying to pry his son's fingers open. But he didn't get angry. Didn't lose patience. He looked a little out of his depth, sure, but he also looked...happy.

She should be glad to see that happiness, for her son's sake if nothing else, but instead, she was worried. If he enjoyed the time he spent with Ethan, he'd want more. He'd want custody. Maybe *full* custody. And she'd never be able to win a court battle with him. He could afford to hire a whole herd of lawyers and the only way she'd be able to do the same was if the hotel took off right away and started making profits.

She didn't have any spare cash lying around. Certainly not the kind she'd need to fight a custody battle against the Careys.

Sex last night had softened her up. Had smoothed off the hard, jagged edges of suspicion and hurt. Had he done it on purpose? Who knew? But the point was, it had worked. She'd smiled with him, laughed with him and shared intimacies with him that she'd sworn she wouldn't. Now Justin was clearly trying to ingratiate himself with their son while keeping her mollified with magical sex. She let her head drop against the wall behind her. God, she was an idiot. She'd stepped right back into the trap of loving Justin and having her heart walked on. Well, screw that. She wouldn't make this easy on him. No more sex. No more being soothed by his charm or sense of humor. She couldn't allow herself to let down her guard. Because the moment she did, she risked losing her son.

After all, Justin had walked away once before. If he did it again, he could take Ethan with him.

For the next week, they worked together to get the hotel ready, but it was as if Sadie had erected a wall between them. Justin hadn't been able to get past it. He had asked himself countless times if he really wanted to. The answer was, damn right he did.

That first night with her had whetted his appetite for what he'd only ever found with Sadie. Oh, he'd been with other women since walking away from her nearly a year and a half ago. But every time he felt a little buzz of interest for a woman, it had fizzled out before the evening was over.

Because she wasn't Sadie. And Sadie was always there for comparison. In his mind. In his dreams. Hell. Sometimes he thought that she'd imprinted herself on every cell in his body. She was so deep inside his soul, he'd had to run from her.

And the night they'd spent together a week ago had only awakened everything he'd spent the last year and a half trying to bury.

He wanted her.

Justin could admit that to himself without acknowledging anything else. Sadie hit him on levels no one else ever had and he was done pretending that wasn't true. And now, there was Ethan. That tiny boy was a link between them and Justin knew that link would be forever. So he and Sadie would have to find a way to make this work.

He checked the time on his phone and realized he had to leave or he'd never make the family meeting. Today was the day he'd tell the Careys about the Cliffside and what he was trying to build.

"Hey, Sam," he called out. "Have you seen Sadie?"

"Yeah. She's in the relaxation suite. Said she needed to make some changes."

"Seriously?" He shook his head, said, "Thanks," and headed for the treatment rooms. The relaxation room was something he had jokingly called the "recovery" room. It was set aside for clients coming out of treatments to take a few extra minutes to unwind, to savor a last little bit of pampering before leaving.

"And they're finished, so what's she changing?" The woman was driving him right over the edge. Not just physically, but in the fact that she challenged him on every decision regarding the hotel. It only made it worse when she was so often right.

He found her in the expansive room filled with comfortable chairs and chaises, soothing music piped in from overhead speakers and flowering plants on every surface. He spotted Sadie against the far corner, wielding a measuring tape like a sword.

"What're you doing?" he asked as he walked closer.

"Measuring." She glanced at him and then made notes on her phone.

"Sadie…" He wasn't in the mood for another battle.

"Fine." She glanced at him, then pulled the tape

out again and laid it on the floor. "I'm measuring the space for the dual refrigerators I'm installing in here."

"*Two* refrigerators?" he repeated, stunned at the idea. "We talked about adding one," he said, realizing that a battle might happen after all. "And we decided that it wouldn't exactly fit with all the woo-woo relaxation stuff that's already in here."

"Woo-woo." She shook her head. "That's a pitiful statement. And no, Justin, *you* decided. I said you were wrong." She made another note and with a quick *zip*, the tape measure slid back into its case.

"Fine." Justin looked at her and waited until she turned to face him before asking, "Why is it we need a fridge—or two—in here?"

"Of the two of us," she asked, hitching one hip higher than the other, "which one has been to the most spas?"

His lips quirked. "If I said me, would you think less of me?"

"No." She grinned and shook her head. "But I wouldn't believe you. My point is, Justin, when women are relaxing, taking that extra half hour before they get dressed and get back on the freeway, they could use something to drink. Mainly I'm, thinking of flavored waters, juices, mineral water." She tapped one finger against her chin and spoke again, more to herself than to him. "We can have a barista of sorts stationed here, serving our clients, giving them that little taste of luxury. One more indulgence before returning to the real world."

He looked around the room, saw that she'd really poured herself into the decor. Pale lavender walls, gleaming oak floors scattered with rugs in jewel-toned colors. There were chaises and chairs and everything coming together to look exactly what it was. A sanctuary.

She'd been right about the colors. Right about the rugs. Right about a hell of a lot, though it cost him to admit it.

Scowling, he thought it was hard to take anyone's advice on this place. Justin had wanted this for so long, and he had planned to make all of the decisions. Make the calls on the look the hotel would offer. But he had to acknowledge that Sadie's input had been… invaluable. Whether he liked it or not.

He'd wanted to make his own statement. To break away from the Careys and build his future alone. Depending on no one but himself. But things had changed. He was building what he'd planned, but he wasn't doing it alone. The woman he'd once walked away from was now a huge part of the legacy he was creating and that fact wasn't easy to swallow.

Especially because somehow, she'd become…important. All over again. And he wasn't sure how he felt about that.

"Are you okay?"

Sadie's voice drew him up out of his thoughts. "What do you mean?"

"Well, I've called you three times." She shrugged and made another note on her phone. "Looked like you'd slipped into a fugue state."

Both eyebrows rose. That was embarrassing. "Well, I didn't. I was thinking."

"About how to get rid of the refrigerators?"

Reluctantly, he said, "No. More like I hate that you were right. Again."

She smiled, tipped her head to one side and studied him. "Well, that was honest anyway."

And she had no idea how much it had cost him to say that.

"Was there something you wanted when you came here? Or were you just checking up on me?"

He took a good, long look at her and his gaze sort of settled on the swell of her breasts even as he told himself to stop. When he lifted his gaze, he saw her narrowed eyes on him. Oh, yes, there was something he wanted. *Someone.* But he couldn't very well say that. Not after the distance between them over the last week.

"Yeah." He tucked his hands into his pockets. "Wanted to let you know I'm headed up to OC for a family meeting."

Her warm, whiskey-colored eyes instantly went cool and distant. Even though she was standing just a foot or so from him, she might as well have been across the room. Hell, he could feel the chill in the air around her.

"Great. Have a good time."

He choked out a laugh. "Yeah. It's always fun. Anyway. I'll be back later today."

She stared at him and he knew she was remembering, as he was, what had happened the last time he'd come back from Orange County. That one night of blistering hot sex had stayed with him every minute of the last week. Even now, that need hummed inside him and Justin fought down his own instinct to reach for her.

"I'll see you then," she said. "Drive safe."

When she turned away, he told himself to let it

go. Once the hotel was up and running, they'd have to talk. About how they would work together. About Ethan. About what was still between them and what they were going to do about it.

Sadie didn't think about Justin while he was gone. Well, not more than four or five times an hour. But every time he popped into her head, she pushed him out again. Right now, he was going to talk to his family. And she had no doubt that this time, he'd tell them about Ethan. Because the hotel would be opening soon and they'd be coming down en masse to see the place—so they would naturally see Ethan.

Her nerves were jumping. Ethan was a Carey grandchild. That wasn't something Justin's family would ignore. So she had to be prepared for whatever was coming.

"And how do I do that?"

Ethan shrieked, slapped both hands on his high chair tray and grinned up at his mommy. Sadie's shoulders slumped, her heart melted and she smiled, helplessly. "You are the best thing that ever happened to me, baby boy."

He threw his head back and giggled as if to say, *I know that.*

Sadie filled a spoon with baby veggies and Ethan gobbled it down. As he played and crowed and laughed, Sadie's mind spun down all kinds of avenues. She had worked alongside Justin for a week now. And they'd done well enough together, though she had to fight to have her opinion heard. "But he does have the ability to admit when I'm right, too, so that says something."

Not enough, but something.

They shared a child.

They shared a bed—or had.

But they didn't share a life and she didn't see that happening, either.

And yet she loved him still. Couldn't change that, but she didn't have to let him know how she felt, either. That would only give him more power in their relationship than he already had.

There was no future with Justin beyond him being Ethan's father. She knew that. And she wasn't sure what he and his family might do about Ethan. So she couldn't risk letting her guard down. Couldn't chance believing this little interlude with him would last beyond the opening of the hotel.

"Hey, Sadie?"

She turned to face Mike standing in the open doorway. "What's up?"

"Your mom's on the hotel phone. Said she couldn't get through on your cell."

"What?" Sadie checked her cell and saw she'd forgotten to charge it. Fabulous. "Can you finish feeding Ethan for me?"

"Sure. Go ahead." As she left, Mike asked, "Is Justin coming back today?"

"He says he is," Sadie told her. "So we'll see."

"You really don't trust him, do you?"

Sadie stopped, and rubbed her hands up and down her arms as if fighting a chill. She wanted to say she did. But how could she? So instead, she smiled and said, "Don't let Ethan fight you on the veggies."

At the Carey Corporation building, Justin stalked through the halls. For the first time, he was looking forward to facing his family. Because for the first time, he was sure that he wasn't going to be facing a life behind one of these tinted windows.

It was a beautiful glass-and-chrome building in a pretty office park, with tidy greenbelts and views that showed off the 405 freeway and offered a smudge of blue that was the Pacific. He knew the Careys had done well here. Knew that this building was just a symbol for how successful his family had been over the years.

And he knew, deep in his soul, that he would never be closed off in this beautiful building. He was finally in a position to go his own way. Make his own mark. For years, his plans had built and grown and changed, but there'd been nothing solid to show for it. That wasn't true now, though. The hotel was real. The re-model was almost complete. And the Carey Cliffside was just the first of what he planned to be a chain of Carey Spas—so the worry about having to cave in to family and live his life their way was finally gone.

As long as the hotel was a success—and he knew it would be. Because it *had* to be.

"Justin." Bennett rushed up from behind and stopped him with a hand on the arm.

"Where'd you come from?" Justin looked around, the long hall flanked by tinted windows and dozens of desks where employees busily ignored the Carey brothers. "I was just headed to your office."

"Yeah." Bennett scowled a little. "I was in Serena's office when I spotted you. Wanted to give you a heads-up."

"About what?" Suspicion colored his tone as his eyes narrowed on his older brother.

Bennett cringed uncomfortably. "They know about the baby."

"What? You said you wouldn't tell them." Justin gave another quick look around to make sure no one could overhear. But Bennett took his arm and drew him a bit farther along the hall.

"I didn't," he said, shoving one hand through his hair. "I told *Hannah*. Hannah told Mom. Mom told Amanda, Mandy told Serena and there you go. Chaos."

"That's perfect." Justin threw his hands up. "Just perfect. Thanks. What happened to keeping the baby news to yourself?"

"There's a rule about wives," Bennett muttered in disgust. "You're supposed to tell them this stuff."

"You're not married yet."

"Details," Bennett mumbled. "Besides. We're close enough."

"Isn't there a brothers' code, too?"

"I don't think so," Bennett told him. "And if there were, it would lose to the wife code, I'm pretty sure. But is that really the point?"

"No," Justin said on a heavy sigh, then asked, "How'd they take it?"

"Are you kidding?" Bennett shook his head, shoved his hands into his pants pockets and said, "It was all I could do to keep Mom from hauling ass to San Diego to meet her new grandson."

"Oh, that would have been great." Justin walked three steps away and came back again. "Sadie would have loved that. She and I can't agree at all on what the future's going to be like, how to do this whole co-parenting thing... Yeah, Mom showing up out of the blue would be the frosting on this particular cake."

"Hey, I talked her out of it," Bennett said like a man looking for gratitude.

"Congratulations." Scowling, Justin grumbled, "Look, I don't even have the results of the DNA test back yet."

"But you took one," Bennett prodded.

"Yeah. One day last week," Justin muttered. "Mine and the baby's, and Sadie wasn't happy about that cheek swab, either."

"If she's worried about it, that's even more reason to take the damn test." Bennett tugged at the edges of his suit jacket, then buttoned it. While Justin watched, the new and improved Bennett turned himself back into the tightly wound Bennett that Justin had known all his life. "What if she's lying to you about him?"

"She's not." Bringing Ethan's happy little face to his mind, Justin sighed as his heart seemed to double in size. "He looks just like me, Bennett. He's mine. I'm sure of it."

"Okay, say that's true," Bennett said quietly. "What're you going to do about it?"

"Be his father," Justin told him. "What else is there?"

"What about... I don't know...marrying his mother?"

Justin frowned. Nobody had even mentioned the word *marriage*. That wasn't on his radar at all. Not yet. The main reason he'd left Sadie a year and a half ago was because he'd known that she could be the one and he couldn't commit to anything more than the dream that was driving him.

Well, now that dream was closer than ever. He was on his way, but until he had his slice of the Carey Corporation stable and growing, he wasn't in a position to make promises to anyone. Not even the woman who haunted his every thought.

"If you don't want to marry her," Bennett said smoothly, "then I suggest you call the family lawyer. Make sure your rights as a father are covered."

Justin sighed and frowned into the distance. He really didn't want to bring lawyers into this. Not until he and Sadie had a chance to meet in the middle. To figure this tangled mess out themselves. "Since I found out about Ethan, she hasn't tried to keep me from being with Ethan."

"Not yet. But you're both living in the same hotel while you remodel, right?"

"Yeah." Instantly, memories of the night she'd gone to his room with him filled Justin's mind. He'd been aching for her ever since. And even living in the same damn hotel didn't guarantee that he'd have another night with her.

That thought was depressing as hell. He scrubbed both hands across his face, then looked at his brother.

"So what happens when you move out?" Bennett watched him, waiting. "Unless you plan on always living there."

"I haven't thought that far ahead," he admitted. "But the hotel will be open in another few weeks, and having room service twenty-four seven doesn't sound like a bad deal."

"Right." Bennett smirked. "And every kid deserves his own hotel hallway to play in."

Justin gave him a dirty look. "Hannah's been a bad influence on you. I don't remember this wise ass side of you."

"She's opened a lot of new doors for me." A soft, satisfied smile curved Bennett's mouth, and Justin found himself envying his brother's happiness.

"But my point is," Bennett said, coming back to the subject at hand, "kids grow up. Hell, look at Alli. Jack's building her a castle in the backyard and they're looking at shelters for puppies."

Justin frowned to himself. His brother was right. When Ethan was a little older, things would change. He and Sadie would have to change, too.

"Sooner or later," Bennett added, "that kid's gonna need a house. Then what? You and Sadie live in separate wings and hand off the kid in the foyer every other week?"

Seriously, Justin's head was spinning. Not that living with Sadie, sharing a home with her sounded like a bad thing. It was just all coming at him so fast. He hadn't had time to think of any of this. "I've only known I'm a father for a week. Give me a break."

"You think Mom will?"

Not a chance, Justin thought.

Seven

With the hotel set to open in three weeks, there was a lot to do.

And with Justin in Orange County, saying God knew what to his family, Sadie buried herself in the work just to keep from driving herself insane with speculation. Her organizational skills were legendary and she was drawing on them heavily at the moment.

The courtyard of the Cliffside had always been a pretty spot. But since the remodel, it had taken a sharp turn toward Heavenly. The three-story hotel made a square as it surrounded the courtyard. Each hotel room boasted a balcony from whose iron railings hung lush ferns and flowering vines, which gave the building a lush feel that soothed the eye and scented the air.

Slowly, Sadie turned in a circle, studying the hotel's central courtyard. The flagstone patio had been pressure-washed and, like the front of the Cliffside, looked brand-new. For years, there had been massive terra cotta planters housing shade trees that dipped and swayed in the ocean breeze. Now, though, there were flowers at the base of the trees and tiny fairy lights strung in the branches. A fountain at the far end of the courtyard had been scrubbed and repainted, but the plumber still had to align new hoses and check the reclamation basin. She made a note to call him and confirm tomorrow's appointment.

Glass-topped tables with iron-backed chairs had been freshly painted a gleaming black, but the new cushions weren't in place yet. Stone planters stood empty, but tomorrow afternoon, the local nursery would be delivering the plants Sadie had ordered.

It was all perfect and yet somehow, she couldn't really enjoy it. Instead, she was thinking about Justin. Wondering where he was and more importantly, when he would be back.

"You don't look happy," Mike said, and Sadie heard the smile in her friend's voice.

"Happy enough," she allowed, then shrugged. "It's just there's still so much to do. And I haven't even started looking through the registration area to make sure the computers are online and—"

"I'll take care of that, Sadie," Mike said, and threw a glance at Ethan, who was blissfully chewing on a teddy bear.

With his playpen set up in the shade of the courtyard, Ethan was safe and happy, giving Sadie the time she needed to take care of business. "Okay, thanks, Mike," she said. "That would be great. Make notes of anything you see that has to be fixed before the opening."

"You got it. Uh, is your mom okay?" She winced a little. "When I spoke to her this morning, she sounded sort of...tense."

Sadie laughed, remembering her conversation with her mother. "That's a good word for it. Apparently, my father is feeling so much better he wants to buy a camper and hit the road."

"How fun!" Mike grinned. "So what does your mom not like about that idea?"

"Oh," Sadie said with a grin, "all of it. My mom's idea of camping is a two-star hotel. She doesn't do the great outdoors and now she's feeling pressured."

"Why?"

"Because she moved to Arizona with my dad to make sure he relaxed and took it easy. Well, he wants to relax on a really long road trip and she doesn't want to do it." Sadie completely understood how her mother was feeling.

After all, she had gone into business with the man she loved, even knowing that there wouldn't be a future for them. She'd risked custody of her son and her own heart—to ensure her son's future.

"Maybe they should get an RV instead of a camper," Mike mused. "More like camping in your house."

"And seriously expensive," Sadie pointed out.

"Yeah, but they could rent one first. See if they like it." She shrugged. "Worth a try."

Sadie thought about that for a minute. It might make a difference for her mom, and her father would seriously love driving a huge RV. "You're right. I'll suggest it and see what happens."

When Mike headed inside, Sadie was still smiling. At least her mom and dad were doing well. Dad's health was improving and mom was happy enough to be complaining about camping of all things. Which meant that no matter what else happened between Sadie and Justin, she'd done the right thing. She had to keep reminding herself of that.

Accepting his offer for the Cliffside, taking that cash payment, had made all the difference for her parents. If that deal had also made life more difficult for Sadie, it was still a price worth paying.

"Isn't that right, Ethan?" She leaned over the playpen to tickle her son's chubby chin. He laughed up at her and Sadie's heart soared. There was nothing she wouldn't do for Ethan.

"You and I are going to be just fine, sweetie," she promised. "You'll see. Now, chew on Teddy while Mommy goes over the nursery order. And every other thing on her list."

He flapped his arms, swinging Teddy in a wild arc. Sadie laughed and moved off to check her orders. Flipping through her phone, she went over the order from the local nursery. For the concrete planters, she'd ordered what gardeners liked to call *filler, thrillers and spillers*.

Thrillers were the tall plants, sure to catch the eye, and Sadie had ordered Tuscan Sun sunflowers. To be surrounded by sweet potato vines in a nearly fluorescent green as a filler and lobelia in a dark blue to spill over the edge of the planters. In others she had pink hydrangeas, blue lobelia and creeping Charlie ferns. The garden was going to be more beautiful than ever, from the fountains, to the flowerpots, to the arbor, where deep lavender clematis was already entwined. Everyone without an ocean view would step out onto their balconies to be greeted by the sound of dancing water in the fountain and a rainbow of color and scent.

It was going to be…well, she hated to use the word *magical* again, but it was the only word that truly fit.

Sadie made a quick phone call to the nursery and was reassured that everything was on schedule to be delivered the following day. She'd have plenty of help for the planting, since the hotel gardeners were eager to get back to work. With that thought in mind, she sent the head gardener, Tom, a text letting him know he should gather the troops for tomorrow.

There were still finishing touches to be done for some of the rooms and the restaurant kitchen was being set to rights by the chef. And the new menus were being printed. They had ads ready to run in California outlets up and down the coast, advertising the reopening of the Cliffside. "And fingers crossed, people will come."

They had to come, she thought. Justin had pinned his ambitions and dreams on the success of this hotel. But for Sadie, it was even more personal. More important. She needed this partnership with him to succeed because her son's future depended on it.

Yes, the Harris family had owned this hotel entirely, and for decades, it had supported them. But as bigger and more plush hotels grew up around them, business had fallen off. Their only hope had been a remodel her family couldn't afford. There were plans for bank loans and equity lines of credit, then her father got sick, and suddenly, there was no more time to waste.

Then along came Justin. He'd waved his millions at her, and this time, Sadie had gone for it. But holding on to that twenty-five percent ownership had been even more important to her than the cash payout she'd needed so badly. Her partnership would ensure her son's future, with or without his father.

"Sadie?"

She turned and smiled. "Hi, Sam." Then she noticed his expression. Fighting a sense of dread, asked, "What's wrong?"

"I just got off the phone with Kate."

Sam's fiancée, Kate O'Hara, was in the last two weeks of planning before her wedding and was probably on her last nerve by now. So if they'd had a fight, Sadie was ready to defend her friend's general crabbiness. "Is she okay?"

"Physically? Sure. Emotionally?" Sam shook his head, plowed one hand through his long blond hair and finished, "Hysterical."

Sadie took his hand, pulled him down to sit beside her on the iron chairs and said simply, "Tell me."

Justin looked around the conference room at his family. He was expecting to be ambushed by not only his mother, but his sisters, as well. According to Bennett, they all knew about Ethan. Yet, no one had said a word, and they simply watched him as he began to speak. And that was a little creepy. Knowing they knew. Knowing they were going to say something but not knowing what or when. So he hurried to tell them what he'd come to say before everything shifted to the subject of the son he didn't want to talk about yet.

"Well," he said, "I wanted to finally tell all of you what I've been doing down in San Diego."

"About time, too," his father, Martin, said, slapping one hand to the conference table, before leaning back in his chair.

"That's enough, Marty," his mother, Candace, warned. "Let's hear what Justin has to say." She paused, narrowed her gaze on Justin and added, "*All* of it."

He cleared his throat, looked away from his mother's accusatory glare and said, "I bought a hotel in La Jolla and I've been remodeling it into a luxury spa hotel."

"You what?" his father said, looking horrified.

Well, Justin hadn't expected anything less. The Carey Corporation was the Carey Center for the arts, the upscale Firewood shopping center and real estate holdings all over the state. If you didn't make your mark in one of those areas, Martin would not be happy.

Martin Carey was of the opinion that if his family wasn't part of the Carey Corporation, then whatever they were doing was wrong. But Justin was through trying to placate his dad or convince him of anything.

"It's a great place," he went on as if Martin hadn't spoken at all. His father was never going to be all right with this, so Justin was determined to convince everyone else that what he was doing was brilliant. "Right on the beach. It's been there for sixty years and is practically an institution in La Jolla."

"An institution," Martin muttered.

Justin ignored him. "We've been working on it now for nearly three months—" He paused as he realized that he'd only just met his son at six months old. If

Sadie had told him the truth sooner, he could have been spending the last three months getting to know his child. Funny that hadn't occurred to him before, but now that it had, he was angry all over again.

Even while he was *there* at the hotel, she'd kept up the lie, hiding Ethan, keeping Justin from discovering the truth. What the hell was the point of all of it anyway?

But the moment those thoughts crossed his mind, he had to acknowledge that part of this mess was his own fault. He was the one who had walked away. Why should she have trusted him to stay now?

"That's what you've been doing all this time?" He turned to see Amanda watching him, and was grateful to his sister for bringing him back to the subject at hand.

"Yeah." He nodded, brought images of the hotel up in his mind and said, "The rooms needed a lot of updating and we sectioned off a dozen of them to turn them into 'treatment' rooms…"

"Treatment," Martin mumbled, shaking his head.

Justin simply kept talking. He really wanted to impress on the family how much he'd accomplished in a few months. How he'd set himself on the path toward the future *he* wanted for himself. "We've added an indoor pool and a swim spa—"

"What the hell is a swim spa?" Martin wanted to know.

"Marty, stop it," Candace said tightly.

Justin swallowed hard. "Every hotel room has a view of either the ocean or the courtyard. And both views are amazing. We've had crews working nearly round the clock for three months—" He looked at

Bennett. "Remember how you had Hannah and her company working solid for four weeks to remodel The Carey?"

"Not likely to forget," Bennett mused. "It was because of the fire and the need to remodel that I met Hannah."

Justin nodded and saw similarities between himself and his older brother. The Carey restaurant fire had brought Hannah Yates into Bennett's life. And the Cliffside hotel had given Justin Sadie. "Well, I'm working with Sam Jonas— You remember Sam, don't you, Mom?"

"Of course I do," she said, waving that away. "Weren't the two of you thick as thieves for years? And I'll remind you that the whole family's attending his wedding in two weeks."

"Right," he mumbled, realizing that all of the Careys would be gathering at Sam's wedding, where they would definitely meet Sadie and Ethan and...he'd better well have a handle on what the hell was going on in his life before then.

He knew he cared for Sadie. He always had. But a year and a half ago, he'd left her because she was becoming too important to him. He'd had a mission to fulfill for his own sanity. To build his dreams apart from the family business.

And that hadn't changed. He was further along the road, but could he really give Sadie—and Ethan, for that matter—the kind of attention they deserved when he was so determined to forge a future for himself? And if he wasn't ready...was he willing to lose her? And his son?

God, his head was pounding suddenly and he needed peace to think. To figure things out.

But his mother wasn't finished speaking. "So what else is new in La Jolla?" she asked, with a knowing gleam in her eye.

"What else?" Martin looked at his wife, dumbfounded. "What? The fact that your son is starting up a business that's not part of the Carey Corporation isn't enough news?"

"Actually," Justin interrupted his father and avoided answering his mother. "Since Bennett invested in the hotel, you could say that technically, the Cliffside *is* part of the company. And I am changing its name to the Carey Cliffside, so..."

"Bennett?" Martin turned a hard stare on his oldest son and Bennett shot Justin a look that said clearly, *Thanks a lot.*

"So you're in this, too?"

"It was a good investment and Justin paid the loan back as soon as the trust money came through."

"You used your *trust*?" Martin's outraged face turned an interesting shade of red.

"That's what it's for, Dad," Justin told him. "Besides, I didn't use it all, and once the hotel is open for business, it won't matter."

"Won't matter..." Martin's grumbles were drowned out by the raised voices of all the other Careys.

"And while we're on the subject, Dad," Bennett added, "Justin's told me that he plans to build a line of luxury spas up and down the California coast, to start. He says he's planning one in Newport Beach next. Eventually, he'll take the idea nationwide. And you should know, the Carey Corporation will be investing in him."

Justin grinned and Martin slapped one hand on the table. He looked at one son, then the other, hurt, the stamp of betrayal carved into his features. "Without discussing this with me?"

Bennett gave his father a patient smile and Justin mentally applauded. His older brother had found himself with Hannah. He was even more confident than he'd once been and that was really hard to believe.

"Yes, Dad," Bennett said quietly. "I'm the CEO now. I make the decisions for the Carey Corporation."

"And you just step over the old man to do it?"

Bennett shook his head. "Dad, you're supposed to be retired, remember? You passed the company on to us to take care of and grow. Just like your father did for you. It's our time, Dad."

Martin's mouth worked furiously, as if he were physically fighting to keep from saying what he'd have liked to. Justin had to give his dad points, too, for his hard-won control. Maybe Martin was finally coming to grips with his own retirement.

"When is the hotel opening and when can we see it?" Serena's question stopped him cold.

Justin didn't want the family trooping down to see the hotel ahead of time, because that meant they'd be seeing the baby and he wasn't ready for any of that yet. He needed to work things out with Sadie, and so far, Justin hadn't seen a way to make that happen.

"We're going to be opening in three weeks," he said, avoiding the rest of her question. "And actually, Serena, I'd like your opinion on some marketing ideas I've got. We have ads ready to go a week before the opening, in papers, online, in neighborhood magazines…" He laughed a little. "Hell, I've even got a billboard going up on Pacific Coast Highway, announcing the changes and the grand reopening."

Serena smiled and patted his hand. "It doesn't sound like you need my help at all, but I'm happy to listen."

"Thanks," he said.

"Does no one besides *me* care that Justin is stepping outside the family business?" Martin demanded, looking from one of them to the other.

"Apparently not, dear," Candace told her husband and smiled while he blustered. Then staring at Justin, she asked, "What about my grandson?"

"What *grandson*?" Martin shouted.

"His name is Ethan," Amanda said.

"Oh, man…" Bennett rubbed his forehead and Serena tugged at the sleeve of Justin's black leather jacket to get his attention. "Did you bring pictures?"

"He had better have pictures with him," his mother said.

No way out now. Hell, the minute Bennett told him that Hannah had spread the word to their mother, Justin had known that there'd be no holding Candace Carey back.

"His name is Ethan Harris and he's six months old." Justin pulled out his phone, called up photos and handed the phone to his mother.

"Oh my goodness." Candace immediately teared up and cooed at the pictures as she swiped through. Amanda and Serena jumped up to stand behind her and were muttering, "Slow down, Mom."

"*Your* son's last name is *Harris*?" Martin bellowed.

"Now you're not even using the Carey name for your child? What the hell, Justin?"

Temper spiked, then subsided. He knew his dad. Martin felt cornered. Justin had left the family business; Martin's wife was living with Bennett and Hannah; and the old man thought he was slowly being edged out of the company he'd helped build. So Justin was willing to cut his father a little slack. For now.

"I didn't know about Ethan until about ten days ago," he admitted.

"Oh, Justin…" His mother looked up at him, disappointment and sympathy shining in her eyes.

He winced. "Now that I do know about him, things will change," he said. "Including his last name."

Since discovering Ethan, Justin had had that thought in his head. His son would carry *his* name, whether Sadie liked it or not. He didn't care if he had to officially adopt the boy he'd helped create.

"That's something, I guess," Martin muttered.

"And how are you going to get his mother to agree to that?" Bennett demanded.

"I haven't figured that out yet," Justin conceded.

"There's one very simple way," Amanda pointed out cheerfully. "We've already got three Carey siblings planning weddings. Why not make it all four of us?"

He shook his head. "Married?"

"Why not?" his mother asked. "You have a son. Do you have any feelings for his mother?"

"Of course I do—"

"Well, then?"

Damned if he'd be coerced into marriage by a mother looking to solidify a relationship with her grandson! Just because his brother and sisters were getting married, it didn't mean it was the right thing for him. He'd left Sadie once because she had been too important to him. Now, those feelings were even stronger. Back then, he'd had to focus on his future. On the goals and plans he'd set for himself. Now she was back in his life, with a son he already loved, and he had to ask himself if he was any more settled now than he had been then.

And the answer was no.

He couldn't risk a marriage when he didn't know if he was going to be successful or not. It had taken him a long time to figure out what he wanted to do in his life. And he hadn't proven himself yet. How could he risk Sadie's happiness and Ethan's safety? No. He had to make it. Had to succeed. Then and only then could he take a chance on marriage.

"I'm not talking about this here with all of you." He looked at each of them in turn. "That kind of decision is up to Sadie and me. I'm only here to tell you about the hotel and invite you all down to San Diego for the grand opening."

Bennett rolled his eyes and sat back in his chair. Martin drummed his fingers against the tabletop while the three women continued to scroll through baby pictures. Justin noticed a single tear roll down his mother's cheek and knew that he was in deep trouble. Candace Carey was not going to be put off. She would want and expect to meet her grandson and she wouldn't be waiting for an invitation.

"If that's all the new business," Bennett said, rising.

"It's not," Martin said flatly and Bennett dropped back into his chair with a sigh.

"What time is it?" Bennett asked.

Serena looked at Justin's phone. "Almost noon."

"Where's your watch?" Justin asked him.

Bennett shrugged. "Hannah doesn't like it."

"This is too much," Martin announced to anyone willing to listen. "Too much is changing. Everyone's getting married. Bennett gave up his damned watch. Justin has a son. And a hotel." He shook his head as if waking up from a dream that was still clouding his thoughts. "My wife is living with our son and goes to lunch with a younger man."

"Really, Martin..." Candace frowned at him. "You're feeling sorry for yourself now."

"And who has a better right?" he argued. "Candy, it's time you moved back home and stopped this nonsense of living at Bennett's."

She handed the phone back to Justin and glanced at her husband. "Are you ready, at last, to retire then?"

"I've told you I am retired."

"Then why are we at this meeting?" Her eyebrows lifted. "We should be on a cruise ship sailing our way toward England right about now."

Martin scowled. All four of his children held their breath and kept quiet.

"No answer to that, I see," Candace muttered.

"Damn it, Candy, we can go on a cruise anytime. Hannah's moved in with Bennett. Why don't you give them some privacy?"

She laughed and stood up. "So you want me home because you're worried about Bennett, is that it? Well, I can tell you that Hannah and I are having a wonderful time eliminating all shades of beige from Bennett's house."

"Wasn't that bad," Bennett muttered.

"Yes it was," Amanda and Serena said together.

Justin was just glad the focus was off him.

"Damn it, Candy...what happened to our life?" Martin stared down at his empty hands as if wondering how everything had slipped from his grasp. "I've got two sons going against me now..."

"Oh, Martin."

"You're only staying with Bennett to punish me," he added, "and now we've got a grandson who doesn't even carry our name." Shaking his head, he looked what he was. A man in his sixties, watching his family pull away and lead their own lives. The problem was, he didn't know what to do about it.

No one in the room looked comfortable with the turn the meeting had taken. But Candace stood, laid one hand on Martin's shoulder and said softly, "Marty, when you realize what's really important...you know where to find me."

Then she looked at Justin, and there were tears in her eyes when she said, "Your son is the image of you as a baby. Don't keep him from us."

Justin opened his mouth to say...something. But he was saved from stammering some half-assed reply when his mother turned on her heel and left the conference room. Amanda and Serena gave him their often seen, sometimes-brothers-are-just-idiots looks and followed.

Martin sat in his chair, staring at nothing. Bennett stood, gave his brother an elbow nudge, then nodded toward the door. Leaving their father in the quiet, they walked out, and Bennett didn't stop until they were far down the hall.

"You realize that Mom's not going to sit around waiting for you to bring your son for a visit."

Justin pushed one hand through his hair. He knew his mother. And more, he knew Sadie and was afraid that the way she felt about the Carey family, she wouldn't be happy if Candace showed up out of the blue and laid claim to her grandson. "I know."

"If it makes you feel any better," Bennett said with a grin, "Hannah and I are doing our best to produce another Carey grandchild."

Justin laughed. "Work harder."

"I can promise to do that." Bennett slapped him on the back and said, "Come on. I'll buy you lunch before you head back. You can tell me all about the hotel and your son and the woman you're avoiding talking about."

"If I'm avoiding talking about her, which I'm not—" Lie. "—what makes you think I'll tell you about her?"

"Because you need to talk and I'm what you've got," Bennett said with a shrug as they headed toward the elevator.

Justin hated that his brother was right. But more, he was fascinated by the changes in the man that Hannah had wrought.

Their father was right, Justin decided. The Carey family was rewriting itself.

Would it turn out to be a comedy? Or a horror novel?

Eight

"Are you sure about this?"

"Absolutely," Sadie said, reaching out to give Sam a hug. They'd been talking for a couple of hours, going over and over everything, but Sadie had finally convinced him. Now Sam held on to her for a minute longer, and when he let her go, he was smiling.

"I seriously owe you for this, Sadie."

"No way. It's going to be fun." She opened up a new page on her phone notepad and said, "Let's get down to it. I love a good list, so we'll just write down everything we can think of right now and then add to it as we go."

"Did I miss something?"

Sadie and Sam both turned to look at Justin as he walked across the courtyard. She studied his face for some clue as to how the Carey family meeting had gone, but Justin's expression was deliberately neutral.

Which told her one thing. It hadn't gone well.

"Miss something?" Sam asked, shooting Sadie a quick glance. "Well, what you saw was a relieved celebration, but it really sort of depends on you agreeing."

"Agreeing to what?" Justin looked from him to Sadie and back again. Confusion sounded in his voice when he asked, "What's going on?"

"Kind of a long story," Sam said, "but I'll give you the Cliffs Notes version."

"Since I just got off the freeway, I appreciate it," Justin said.

"Kate called me this morning, crying," Sam said.

'What happened?" Justin stepped closer.

"Our wedding venue happened," Sam said and scrubbed one hand across his face. "You remember, Justin. I took you to that Victorian house in Old Town, San Diego?"

"Yeah," he said, "I remember. Kate found that place for you guys to get married in."

"Exactly." He glanced at Sadie. "She really loved the grounds for the reception and I didn't care where we got married, as long as we did."

Sadie grinned. "I love that."

"Right," Justin said. "So what's wrong?"

"Kate called me in tears this morning. A water heater blew out and flooded the whole place." Sam shook his head. "They're going to be closed for a month while the disaster crews come in to clean it all up."

"Oh man, that's terrible," Justin said, shoving both hands into his pockets. "How's Kate handling it?"

Sadie stared at him. "How do you think she's handling it? It's two weeks before her wedding."

Justin rubbed his forehead. "Yeah. Of course. Sorry."

"Anyway," Sam said. "The venue called her this morning and she's been crying ever since."

"Can't blame her," Sadie said.

"No, but I tried to help." Sam shrugged. "Told her it didn't matter where we got married and we could just get our families and go to the courthouse."

"Oh, Sam," Sadie muttered.

He sighed. "Yeah. That's when the screaming started."

"Okay, I get the disaster. What I still don't get is why you were celebrating when I got here."

"Because," Sam said, "as long as you go along with it, Sadie saved the day. And probably my life."

"Well, you are my friend, so I'd prefer you alive," Justin said. "What's the solution?"

"We hold the wedding here," Sadie told him. "Right here in the courtyard. We can set up tables and serve the reception from our restaurant."

"We're not open," Justin pointed out.

"Which is why this is perfect," Sadie argued.

"I really think she's right," Sam said.

"Your wedding's in two weeks." Justin looked at Sadie. "We can't be ready."

"Of course we can. We're mostly doing finish work now and all of the plants for the courtyard arrive tomorrow." She waved one hand at the wide, beautiful space. "This will be gorgeous. And it's not like we have to have treatment rooms ready. It's a wedding and a party. That's all."

"My crew will finish everything that needs doing in plenty of time," Sam said.

Sadie watched Justin and could see that he was considering every angle. So, to help push her idea over the finish line, she mused, "We can think of the wedding as a sort of trial run for the grand reopening."

He looked at her and after a long moment or two, smiled. "That's not bad."

"Thought you'd like that."

Sam grinned. "So we're good? I can call Kate and tell her we're saved?"

"Absolutely," Sadie said, her gaze locked with Justin's. "She can come check it out, see how she wants things set up—"

"Tell her everything's going to be great," Justin interrupted.

Sam shook Justin's hand, then turned and hugged Sadie again. "You might be sorry for this. Kate's mom is a little picky. But too late to back out now!"

As he moved off to call his fiancée, Sadie watched Justin. "He's really grateful."

"Yeah I can see that." He flicked a glance at his friend, who was laughing and talking on the phone. "It was a good idea to offer him this place."

"It'll be fun," she said, then changed the subject. She'd been worried since Justin had left for Orange County. She couldn't help it. Once the Careys knew about Ethan, everything might change. She had to be prepared. "So how'd the meeting go?" And did she want to know? Did he tell them all about Ethan? Were they calling lawyers?

Justin laughed shortly. "Like I expected. About the

Cliffside, howling, shouting, my father acting like it's the end of the Carey family."

She blinked. Sadie couldn't imagine a family not standing behind one of their own. "Wow, that was a lot to throw at you."

"Dad's always had good aim, too," he said, dropping down on one of the iron chairs in the shade.

"Well, it's terrible. Were they all against you?"

He frowned a little. "Not really. Just my dad. Which I was expecting. He thinks the family's moving against him and it doesn't help that my mom is still living at Bennett's house."

"What? Why?"

"Long story," he said and thought about it for a second before adding, "Weird story. Very Carey."

Well, now she really wanted to know. Her curiosity must have been evident, because he said, "I'll tell you later."

"Okay…"

"Where's Ethan?" he asked.

"Right over there. In his playpen, sleeping."

Justin got up, walked over and simply stood there, staring down at the sleeping baby. And a niggle of worry sprouted in the pit of Sadie's stomach. His features were tight, his eyes shadowed, and he studied their son as if seeing him for the first time.

"What's going on, Justin?"

He shook his head. "Nothing."

"Clearly it's something, and if you don't tell me what it is, my brain is going to create all kinds of possibly apocalyptic scenarios."

He turned his head to look at her. "I don't remember you being this…nervous."

"I wasn't. Until I had Ethan." She glanced at her baby. "After, it's amazing how many scary situations my mind can conjure up. Everything from a tidal wave sweeping the hotel away to Ethan crawling off down the boardwalk and I don't notice until it's too late." She bit her bottom lip. "It's all about him now."

"Yeah," he muttered. "I get that."

"Hey, you two!" Sam strode up, took one look at them and asked, "Wait. Why the long faces? Did you change your minds? Because Kate and her mom will be here tomorrow going over everything. Kate's thrilled and grateful and cried again. The good kind of tears this time."

"Nope, no changing our minds. We're set." Justin slapped Sam on the back. "And don't worry. The wedding will be beautiful. We'll make sure of it."

"Thanks. Sincerely, thanks. Both of you." Sam nodded, tucked his phone into his pocket and said, "Now I'm heading to the third floor, to tell the guys to get a move on and finish everything just right. We've got a wedding to plan."

When he left, Sadie watched him go for a second before saying, "He's pretending it's all about Kate being happy, but Sam's really excited about getting married, too."

"Of course he is," Justin said. "Why else would he be doing it?"

Since he'd walked into the courtyard, she'd sensed the tension in Justin. Was it all over his father and the man's expectations being shattered? Or was there something else going on? She tipped her head to one side and looked at him. "Tell me what's happening, Justin."

"What do you mean?"

"You seem… I don't know. Not angry, but…something."

"I guess I am *something*." He ran one hand over the back of his neck. "The family knew all about Ethan when I got there."

"What?"

"Yeah. Bennett told Hannah, Hannah told Mom, and it was off and running."

"All of them?"

"Well," he said with a shrug, "all but my dad. He's sort of outside the loop these days."

"Oh, God." What did this mean for her? For Ethan? Yes, she knew the Careys were going to find out. Eventually. But it was here now and she didn't know what to do. Stay? Go to Arizona? Take an RV road trip with her parents?

"Come on, Sadie," he snapped as he read her expression, "they're my family. Are you expecting them to drive down here and kidnap Ethan?"

She wrapped her arms around her middle and held on tightly. "How do I know? I've never met your family." She shook her hair back from her face. "All I know about them is they have more money than I ever will and they gave you nothing but grief over wanting to live your own life."

Justin groaned.

"So why shouldn't I worry about them wanting to take Ethan from me and raise him as a Carey?"

"He's already a Carey," Justin said.

"His last name is Harris."

"For now," he said.

"See?" She jabbed her index finger at him. "It's

that kind of statement that can push every button and nudge me right over the cliff of my own fears."

Turning his back on her, he walked away from the sleeping baby so they wouldn't wake him, and headed for the chairs under the shade. "Why shouldn't they know about my son?"

Instead of taking one of the chairs, he paced, then leaned back against the hip-high terra cotta pot. "And he *is* my son."

"Of course he is." She threw her hands up. "I told you that."

He stared at her, his blue eyes shadowed. "Yeah, but before I came back here, I stopped by the lab to get the DNA results. It's official. He's my son."

Amazed, Sadie shook her head. "Did you really think I was lying about Ethan?"

"No. Of course not. There would be no point, since it would be easily checked."

"Oh, thanks very much."

"And hell, he looks just like me. But somehow," he said, rubbing his forehead, "that report just smacked me in the face with it and I'm still off-balance."

Panic tangled with that small curl of worry, and between the two sensations, Sadie's stomach turned and her mouth went dry. "It doesn't change anything, Justin."

"Doesn't it?" A short laugh shot from his throat. "You know, I used to think I'd be a father someday, but when we first met, I was a bad bet for fatherhood."

"Justin…" She didn't know what to say to him. He was right. He'd left her the moment his plans evaporated. The moment she told him she loved him.

"I'm not sure I'm a good fatherhood bet *now*,"

he said, glancing to where his son slept. "But," he added as he stood up to face her, "I want you to know, I'm not running again. I'm not walking away. I'm sticking, Sadie. He's my son and I'm not going to lose him."

"What are you saying, Justin? Specifically."

"I'll let you know as soon as I have all the angles figured out."

"Right. Angles." Nodding, she turned to go to the baby, but Justin's hand on her arm stopped her. She looked down to where he held her, where the heat of his hand pooled into her body and sank deep into her soul. Then lifting her gaze to his, she said, "You want your son, Justin. Not your son's mother."

"You're wrong. I do want you."

"In bed."

"Is there something wrong with that?" He didn't let her go, as if he understood that she would bolt if he did. "It's been more than a week since we had sex, Sadie. Why're you keeping your distance from me?"

"I didn't hear you complaining."

"Maybe you weren't listening hard enough," he said. "So why?"

"Because I can't do it again, Justin." She turned her face up to the wide, blue sky that she could see through the canopy of the potted tree. "I can't hop in and out of your bed with the ease I did the first time we met. I'm a mom. I have more to think about than just what I want."

"So you *do* want me," he said, and one corner of his mouth lifted.

"Justin," she said on a sigh. "I'll probably still want you six months after I'm dead."

"Happy thought."

"We can't do this."

"We excel at this," he countered, stepping closer.

In the dappled shade of the tree, she looked up into his eyes and saw more than desire. She saw pain and worry and heat and so many damn things she imagined her own eyes must look the same. So why complicate things even more?

He slid his hand up her arm, over her shoulder, to the back of her neck. His fingers rubbed and stroked her skin until she was practically purring. "Justin…"

"One kiss," he said, "after a hard, long day. One damn kiss, Sadie."

He lowered his mouth to hers, and at the first brush of his lips, she knew she was a goner. That spark of electricity that buzzed whenever he touched her. The slow burn inside that reminded her a bonfire was only moments away. The deep, throbbing ache that had settled low in her body and kept her awake every damn night hungering for him.

One kiss would never be enough.

And still, she wanted it.

She lifted her arms to encircle his neck and pressed herself into him as his mouth claimed hers in a tenderly desperate maneuver that had her trembling in his arms.

When he finally lifted his head and stared down into her eyes, Sadie knew they weren't finished. Not by a long shot.

"Tonight, Sadie," he urged. "I'll come to your room and once Ethan's asleep…"

She went hot and hungry in an instant. This would

never change, she thought. She would always react this way to Justin.

"Tonight, Justin," she agreed and hoped she knew what she was doing.

Justin brought dinner—pizza and wine—when he went to Sadie's suite. It had been a crazy day, but things were starting to look up. It had been more than a week since he'd been with Sadie and he'd spent every night of that time half-awake and aching. That ended tonight.

He'd taken care of business with the family. He was on the verge of finally making his goals and dreams come true. Now it was time to stop thinking about a future that was any further away than the big hotel opening. All he wanted now was to focus on finishing this project, getting to know his son and enjoying Sadie.

He knocked on the door and when it swung open, he found Sadie, her long, luxurious hair in a messy ponytail and some kind of orange stain on her pale yellow shirt. Her mouth was tight, her eyes flashing, and there was a frazzled look on her face as she held a crying Ethan on her hip. "Good," she said. "You're here."

Quickly, she took the pizza from him, then said, "Your turn," as she eased the crying baby toward him. Ethan reached out both arms and leaned, still screaming, at his father.

"My turn?" he asked, taking Ethan and staring into a tiny face, red with fury. Tears pouring down his face, the baby shrieked, and it was like a nail being driven through Justin's temple. He looked at Sadie as she took the bottle of wine from his free hand. "What's wrong with him?"

"Well, that's a good question, isn't it?" She shook her head and that long ponytail of hers swung like a metronome behind her back. "Why don't you ask him?"

She carried the wine and pizza to the coffee table, set the pizza down, then grabbed two glasses from a nearby wet bar before she dropped onto the sofa.

Why was she just sitting there? Why wasn't she helping? "What do you want me to do with him?"

She slanted him a look and there were dangerous glints in her eyes. "Settle him down. Give him a bath. Change him. Feed him. Put him to bed. Take him to Maui…dealer's choice."

"Sadie…"

She held up one hand for silence, then laid her head back, closed her eyes, and Justin was left to stare at his howling son in abject terror. Every other time he'd been around Ethan, the baby had been all smiles and sunshine. And his only other baby experience had been with his niece, Alli. Whenever she'd gone berserk, he'd simply handed her back to her mother and left.

Justin didn't think that was an option now.

While he was still asking himself what to do and how to do it, Ethan slapped both hands into his face and one small finger poked Justin in the eye. "Ow!"

"Yeah, watch those hands," Sadie warned a little late. "His fingernails need to be trimmed."

Justin looked over at her and saw Sadie opening the bottle of wine. "You're not going to help?"

She snorted. "Like I said. Your turn. You're Daddy… Have at it."

"Fine." How hard could it be? Was she expecting him to fail? Was this a test, somehow? Did she think he'd put Ethan down and walk away? He looked at his screaming son—the red eyes, the wide-open mouth, the flushed cheeks—and seriously considered doing just that.

But, Justin told himself, that would prove to her that he couldn't do it. That he would walk when things got tough. So, fine, he could do this.

She held a glass of wine, propped her feet on the coffee table and watched him. "Diapers are in his room," she said. "Food on the wet bar in here. Bathtub you should be able to locate."

"You think I can't?"

She smiled as she sipped. "I think you're mentally planning which route to take back to Orange County."

Yes, he was. But he would be keeping that to himself.

"Have some pizza," he told her and carried the screaming baby from the room.

"Good idea."

An hour later, Justin was exhausted and soaking wet, and he smelled bad, thanks to the ridiculously wet burp Ethan had dumped down the back of his father's shirt. But, he told himself as he eased out of the baby's room and pulled the door nearly closed, Ethan was clean, fed and currently asleep.

A miracle.

Stumbling back into the main room of the large suite, he found Sadie still on the couch, still sipping wine and watching him with an interested gleam in her eye. "How'd it go?"

"Funny," he said, sitting down beside her. He nipped her wineglass from her, took a long swallow and asked, "That was a test, right?"

"Yeah, it was." She smiled at him. "I wanted to see how you'd react to Ethan when he wasn't being adorable."

"Surprised I made it through?"

"Yes," she said, grinning. "I thought for sure you'd turn and run." Reaching for another wineglass, she filled it, then handed it to him and took back her own.

"Thanks," he muttered, then confessed, "I have to admit, running was my first instinct. Hand him off to you and get in the car. Drive. Fast."

"Congratulations," she said, lifting her wineglass in toast, "you are now officially a parent. We *all* do that. We *all* drive past a freeway on-ramp and think, *In three days, I could be thousands of miles from here.* But we don't go."

"You, too?" He sounded surprised.

Sadie laughed. "Of course me, too. I love him more than anything and sometimes, walking into the ocean and just keeping on walking seems like a solution."

"You know," he said companionably, "I never really gave my sister Serena enough credit. She was a single mom, too. Her bum of an ex left her—"

Sadie's eyebrows arched at that statement and immediately he knew what she was thinking. "Not the same. I didn't know about Ethan."

"True." Sadie nodded and gave a shrug. "Okay, I give you that. And now that you do know…"

"I'm still here, right?" Then he glanced at the baby's door. "Shouldn't we be more quiet?"

She laughed again. "No. Once Ethan's asleep, nothing wakes him up."

"Thank God." Justin took a long drink of wine. "How about some cold pizza?"

She studied him for a long minute and thought she'd never seen him look so...tempting. His hair was sticking up, the front of his shirt and jeans were wet, he smelled like stale formula and he was still keeping the eye Ethan had poked half-closed.

But, Sadie realized, he was more *real* to her in that moment than he'd ever been before. Her heart simply filled up and spilled over in her chest. She'd loved him before. Loved him still, and yet now, that love was suddenly richer, deeper and more terrifying than ever.

However, worry was for tomorrow. Or the next day. She wouldn't waste tonight.

"Cold pizza is always a good idea," she said. "But so is a hot shower followed by—"

He didn't even let her finish. "Sold." Justin leaned in to kiss her and when wine sloshed over onto her shirt, she gasped at the cold damp.

He pulled back, grinned and said, "Looks like we could both use a shower."

"Conserving water," she mused. "Good for us. Good for the planet."

"There you go." He set their wineglasses on the table, then stood and held out one hand to her. She slipped her hand into his and he pulled her to her feet.

"Thought you were tired," she teased.

He looked down at her and gave her a smile. "I think I'm getting my second wind."

"Glad to hear it."

In the expansive and beautifully remodeled bathroom, there was a soaker tub in one corner and a massive shower with a bench and six different showerheads. Turquoise tiles shone under the lights and made it seem as if they were stepping into the sea.

"It's more than big enough for two," Sadie said.

"Best offer I've had in a long time." He reached for her, but Sadie slipped out of reach. Turning the water on hot, she watched steam rise while she quickly stripped out of her clothes. Stepping into the walk-in shower, Sadie stood beneath the rainfall stream, pushed her hair back from her face and watched Justin. Her heart galloped as he came toward her, and when he joined her in the shower, she reached for him.

"Whoa!" He jolted and hissed in a breath. "Is the water temperature set to *lava*?" he asked, laughing as he pulled her out of the direct stream of water.

"I like it hot."

"Yeah, I get that." He grabbed her and pulled her in close to him until their bodies were sliding against each other, and then he said, "Let's see how much hotter we can make it."

He tapped the body soap dispenser and then rubbed his soapy hands all over her body. Sadie closed her eyes and concentrated on the nearly hypnotic feel of Justin's hands moving over her skin. Up and down her back, over her hips, then tracing the line of her spine down to her butt. Then he slid his hands to the front where he caressed her breasts until she was breathless, then he slid those talented hands down her rib cage, over her abdomen, and slowly, lower. She parted her legs for him and when he touched her, stroked her, Sadie gasped and leaned back into him while the water pulsed down onto her.

Finally, finally, he took her back under the rainfall shower until the soap bubbles streamed down their bodies to the tiles beneath their feet. Then he flipped off the water, reached for a bath sheet and wrapped them both up in it. Roughly, he rubbed that thick cotton towel over her skin and his own until both of them were nearly vibrating with need.

"You're killing me," Sadie whispered while her body burned and her blood buzzed in her veins.

"Not yet," he promised, continuing to rub that thick, luxurious towel up and down her body.

"No. We're dry enough," she said and took his hand, leading him into her bedroom.

The emerald green duvet was tossed aside, and she pulled him down onto the crisp, cool sheets. When she would have hurried because the need was so huge, he caught her wrists in one hand and held her arms back and over her head.

"Not this time, Sadie," he said. "There's no rush here. Tonight, I want to savor you."

He trailed his mouth across her breasts, taking the time to nip and tease her hard nipples, suckling at her until she felt the pull of his mouth right down to her bones. She arched up into him, and whimpered a little, unable to swallow back the sound. He released her hands but still took his time, exploring every inch of her body as if he'd never touched her before.

And, she thought, he hadn't. Not like this. Not as

if he were worshipping her. As if she were the most important thing in the world to him.

Helpless tears filled her eyes and she closed them, to keep him from seeing. But he was too busy to notice. He trailed his mouth down her ribs and across her belly to the juncture of her thighs, and Sadie gasped aloud. "Justin!"

"Savoring, Sadie…" he reminded her.

It was too much. Too much and not enough all at once. Her head dug back into the mattress as he parted her thighs and held her there. He dipped his head to her and his tongue and lips and teeth did things to her that drove her so far beyond pleasure she didn't know if she could ever find her way back.

Again and again, he drove her to peak, then pulled back, leaving her trembling, dangling from the edge of an abyss. Breath crashing in and out of her lungs, heart racing, Sadie choked out, "Justin! I can't take much more."

"Take it all, Sadie," he whispered, then slid up the length of her body until he was covering her. And as he kissed her, he slid his body into hers and she groaned because it felt so good. So right. So complete.

"I've missed you, Sadie," he whispered, burying his face in the curve of her neck.

"I missed you, too," she admitted and lifted her hips into him.

He pulled his head back and stared into her eyes. "I've missed you for a year and a half."

Her heart leaped and her breath caught in her throat. With his body buried deeply within hers, she didn't know how she was supposed to *think*.

"Justin…don't…" She said it brokenly, voice coming in gasps as he moved faster and faster, driving her toward the peaks he'd denied her only moments before.

He kissed her then, taking her sighs into him, cutting off whatever else he might have said. Instead, he devoted himself to pushing them both to the brink of madness, then, hands joined, bodies linked, they fell over the edge together.

Nine

When they could move again, Justin walked to the living room, grabbed the wine and pizza and carried it back to Sadie's bedroom.

She leaned back against the headboard and watched him, knowing she would never forget this image of him. Hair rumpled, cold pizza in one hand, with two wineglasses balanced on top of the box while he carried the bottle of wine in his free hand. Naked, his body was hard and muscled and tanned and made her mouth water, even though she'd just survived the most amazing orgasm she'd ever had. She wanted him again.

And always would.

He set the box on the duvet between them and she held the glasses while he poured the rest of the wine.

He clinked his glass to hers, kissed her and asked, "Hungry?"

"Sure." Sadie took a sip of her wine to ease the knot lodged in her throat. Food wasn't high up on her list at the moment. She had too much going on in her mind for that. But she couldn't really confess that, could she?

He flipped open the lid on the box, but instead of helping himself, Justin turned to look at her and said, "Before we eat... I've been doing some thinking, Sadie, and there's something I want to talk to you about."

"What is it?" She held her breath, unsure where he was going and not at all sure she was going to like it.

"Well," he started, then paused to sip at his wine, "we both love Ethan—"

"Yes." And she loved Justin, but he wouldn't want to hear that, so she kept it to herself and waited.

He flipped on a bedside lamp and a small circle of golden light fell across the bed. "We're his parents, Sadie, you know, between us, we have to find a way to do what's best for him."

Carefully, she set her wineglass on the bedside table and swallowed down the quick slash of fear that ripped through her. When she looked at him, she deliberately kept her voice calm.

"What's best for him?" she repeated. "In what way? The best schools, a fancy house, nice car when he's old enough? Just what are you talking about, Justin?"

"Why are you suddenly so hostile?" he asked. "I haven't said anything yet."

"I know what's coming," she said, "and I'm telling

you right now, Justin. You can't take Ethan away from me and say it's for his own good."

"What are you talking about?" He pulled back, clearly surprised. "I didn't say that."

"You didn't have to," she countered. God, how could they have been so close moments ago and at odds now? She loved him and couldn't tell him. Couldn't let him know just how close to the edge she really was. He'd been with his family earlier today and now, she was terrified of what that might mean to her. To them. "Your family is involved now. They'll want their grandson being raised the 'right' way."

He choked out a laugh and shook his head. "The right way? What the hell, Sadie?"

She wasn't listening. Her fear was driving her words and she had to make her position clear to him right now. She wouldn't risk Ethan. "You'll try to take him because you can afford the best attorneys and I can't. But I'll fight anyway, Justin."

He pushed one hand through his hair. "Who are you going to fight? And where are you getting all of this in the first place? I'm not trying to take him away from you, Sadie." Setting his glass down, as well, he took both of her hands in his, met her gaze squarely and said, "When I said we could do what's best for him, I meant that we could get married."

For several heartbeats, she simply stared at him. As if she wasn't entirely sure she'd heard him correctly. But the way he was watching her, waiting, told her she had. Still, it made no sense.

"Married?" Her heart pounded in her chest.

"Exactly!" He beamed at her like a teacher proud

of a student who had finally caught on to a confusing problem.

"When did you come up with this?"

"Well, Sam and Kate got me thinking about it, really."

"You're not making any sense, Justin." Her breath came in short, sharp gasps, but she didn't think he'd noticed at all. Sadie didn't know what to think, what to feel. So she listened and hoped for the best. Married?

"Give me a chance. I'm getting to it. We're hosting their wedding here—"

"Yeah?"

"They'll be married. Sharing everything. Living together."

"Well, yes, Justin. What's your point?"

He frowned, probably because he knew he wasn't getting his point across very well. "I just thought about it and realized that if we're married, Ethan has two parents and—"

"And?"

"And we'd be a team, Sadie. We're good together. You know that. We share a son." He blew out a breath and shook his head. "I don't know, I just think it would be best is all. For Ethan. And for us." He grinned at her, warming to his subject. "I know I'm not at my most convincing at the moment, but think about it, Sadie.

"Look, we've already proved these last few months that we work well together. Once the Carey Cliffside is open for business, we can get to work on the hotel in Newport Beach. And from there, wherever we want. We can transform hotels all over the state and do it as a team. You, me, Ethan. All three of us.

"Sadie, we like each other. We share Ethan. And damn it, we're *great* in bed. Why shouldn't we get married?"

And just like that, nerves and fear and hope collided in her chest and died miserable deaths. He was willing to marry her because it made things easier for him. Marriage itself didn't mean anything. He would get a partner at work, an eager bedmate and a son out of the deal. What wasn't to like?

But Sadie wasn't that desperate. That lonely. She loved Justin Carey. How could she marry him knowing that he didn't love her? How could she settle for a marriage that wasn't real? If she did that, her heart would slowly wither and die.

Reaching for her wine, she drained the glass, set it down again and turned to face the man watching her. The man she loved. The man she couldn't have.

"What do you say?" he asked, giving her the half smile that always showcased the dimple in his cheek. He was everything she wanted. And now she knew for sure that she'd never have him. Not the way she wanted. He offered her marriage, but he didn't love her. And knowing that, feeling that, hurt more than she could have imagined. But she wouldn't let him see that.

"Where do I start," she wondered aloud. "That was simply an *enchanting, romantic* proposal, Justin. Romantic enough that if I had a diary, I'd write it all down."

"Romantic?" He scowled at her. "Who's talking about romance?"

"Neither of us, as it turns out," she said quietly. "One day, I'll be sure to tell Ethan that his daddy loved him so much that he was willing to sacrifice himself on the altar of marriage."

"What the hell?" He pushed off the bed and stood facing her.

"You actually look surprised that I'm not happy about your idea of a proposal."

"No." He stopped and corrected himself. "Well, yeah. I am. It's a great idea, Sadie. Why can't you see that?"

"What I can see is that you're still running. The only difference is, you haven't left."

"You're not making any sense."

"Right." She nodded and stood up. "It's *me*. Well, thanks for that generous offer, but I don't need a pity wedding ring—"

"Pity?" He shoved both hands through his hair as if he couldn't understand how he'd lost control of the whole situation.

"That's not what marriage is, Justin. My God, your parents have been together more than forty years— just like mine. Do you think they did it all because they made a good team? Or because they were great together in bed?"

He held up one hand. "I do not want to think about that."

She sighed. "My point is, marriage is about love. That's why Sam and Kate are getting married. That's why our parents are *still* married. Remember what I said to you our last night together before you left a year and a half ago?"

His features went blank and hard. "I remember and I know you didn't mean it." He shrugged. "It's just the kind of thing you say after great sex."

"Right. Because I've heard you say 'I love you' many times after great sex, so, good point." Shaking her head, Sadie said, "I told you I loved you and I meant it, Justin. I loved you then. I love you now—though I couldn't tell you why at the moment—so no. I won't marry you. Because frankly, I deserve better." She slipped a robe on, turned her back on Justin and said, "I think you should go."

For a week, they were too busy to revisit that conversation even if they'd wanted to. Justin, Sam and the crew focused on finishing up the small touches left, while Sadie and Kate concentrated on turning the courtyard into a "fairy garden" setting for the wedding.

Kate was a nervous wreck, of course, but she simply radiated happiness that Sadie had a hard time not envying. It wasn't as if she begrudged Kate her happiness—she only wanted it for herself, as well.

But the odds of that happening with Justin were now zero. He hadn't spoken to her except in the most coolly polite terms since that night in her room. He visited Ethan, played with him, took care of him, but he had nothing to say to Sadie. It was as if they'd said it all that last night together.

Sadie's heart ached. How she wished things were different. She loved Justin and always would. If that proposal had been a real one, she'd have accepted in a dirty minute. Because he was right about at least one thing. They did make a good team. But without love, what was the point of marriage?

She took a breath, smiled and told herself, "It's going to be a gorgeous wedding."

"I think you're right."

Justin's voice. How had he slipped up behind her without her noticing? Because, Sadie thought, she'd been too busy wishing for what might have been.

"Kate loves all of this," he said, and she looked at the courtyard through a bride's eyes. Not only did they have the original plants that Sadie had ordered, but now there was an arbor covered with trailing, dark blue clematis. There were ornamental iron stands holding terra cotta pots filled with jewel-toned flowers. On either side of the aisle that Kate was to walk down were chairs that would, on the big day, be draped in pale green cloth, while pots of bright pink and white petunias lined the white silk runner. The ceremony would take place beneath the arbor, and once it was over, tables would be brought out for the feast prepared and catered by the hotel.

Sadie saw it all and realized that this was exactly what she would have wanted for her own wedding. A sort of casual sophistication.

"She's pretty happy about it all," Sadie said, still not turning to look at Justin. "Even her mother is pleased and loves the arbor. I'm glad Kate's going to have the wedding day she wanted."

"Yeah." He paused. "Well, Sam says she can't stop talking about all you've done. He's really grateful, Sadie." He touched her arm, turned her to face him. "You saved their wedding for them."

"We did," she said and avoided meeting his gaze.

"Yeah, we did." He tipped her chin up until she had no choice but to look at him. "I'm sorry I've been… quiet this last week."

"Have you?"

He smiled. "Fine. You didn't notice. Look, I don't like having my plans messed with, and you saying no threw me. Like I said. We make a great team."

She shook her head and bit her tongue. It was pointless to go over it all again. "Stop it, Justin. Just stop."

His hand on her arm tightened. "Why? You said you love me."

She looked up at him. "Yes, but I'll get over it."

He choked out a laugh. "You would, too. But what I'm saying is why try? If you love me, marry me. Good for you. Good for me. Good for Ethan."

"Don't you get it?" she asked. "A one-sided love is not a good time for the one doing the loving."

"Sadie…" He threw his hands up in frustration. "Damn it. You *matter* to me."

"Uh-huh. Your black leather jacket matters to you, too, Justin."

"Now you're being ridiculous."

"Am I?" She gathered up her long hair that was flying all over the place and did a quick braid that wouldn't last more than five minutes, since she didn't have anything to hold the ends, but she needed something to occupy her hands. "I don't think I am. I think we've run our course and one of us has to be the one to say it. Guess that's me."

"But you said you love me."

"Sadly," she said, staring up at him, "love doesn't solve everything."

"Damn it, Sadie." He tipped his head back, stared up at the cloud-studded sky briefly, then looked at her again. "Everything I've worked for the last few years is on the line right now. This hotel opening is it for me. Make it or break it. If it goes well, sky's the limit. If it doesn't…well. I'm not going to accept anything less than success. So don't you think there's a lot going on right now for us to be having these conversations?"

"Hey," she reminded him, "you're the one who gave me that tired, empty proposal. If you can't deal with my answer, then that's your problem."

Her eyes were stinging but she refused to cry. He couldn't see the truth because he didn't want to see it.

"It wasn't tired or empty," he told her flatly. "It was an offer to join me. To be my partner."

"If you want a business partner, you write a contract, not a marriage license." God, if her heart cracked one more time, it would simply shatter and tumble out of her chest.

"Now," she said sharply, "I really need to get Ethan. It's his lunchtime and like his father, he gets crabby when he's hungry."

Sadie skirted around the rows of chairs and walked to where a playpen was set up in the shade. She knew Justin was right behind her, because she could feel a buzz in the air.

Why wouldn't he let this go? Why try so hard to get her to marry him if he didn't love her? Was it all for Ethan's sake? A way for him to have his son without taking him from her?

And if she didn't agree, would he move on to an expensive lawyer and sue for custody? But how could she marry him knowing that he didn't love her? Or wouldn't, which was basically the same thing. That kind of marriage would be empty and it would slowly, daily grind her heart into dust. And hell, eventually, even Ethan would notice.

"Don't you have something to do?" she asked, tossing the question over her shoulder.

"I'm doing it. I want to see my son. Go take a break or something," he offered. "I'll feed Ethan."

"It's okay. I don't need a break." Nice of him, she supposed, but she needed this time with Ethan. To remind herself of how much she already had in her life.

She smiled down at her son as he kicked his legs and waved his arms. He never failed to make her smile and today was no different.

She leaned over, scooped him up and gave him a loud, smacking kiss that had Ethan giggling. That wonderful belly laugh was enough to remind her that life was pretty great. That she was a mom, with someone who depended on her. That it was up to *her* to make her life the way she wanted it.

She tucked Ethan onto her left hip and automatically started swaying as she reached down for his diaper bag.

"I'll get it," Justin said.

"Justin…" Before he could pick up the bag, Ethan laughed again and launched himself at his father. Sadie could only watch as Justin grabbed him, then swung him up in the air to make the tiny boy laugh himself silly.

Her heart ached to see them together. To know that they would never be the family she'd dreamed of.

Movement at the corner of her eye caught her attention and she said, "Someone's here. I guess they think we're open, what with all the activity."

Justin, still grinning, lowered Ethan to his chest and turned to look. Sadie watched his smile slowly dissolve. "That's my family. Well, some of them."

"What?" She looked at the three people walking toward them and saw that they were hurrying forward now. All Sadie could think was that her hair was a mess, she was dressed like a hobo and she was probably sweaty on top of it all. "Oh, God."

He grabbed her hand as if he thought she might make a run for it—he was right. "Come on, Sadie," he muttered. "You're tougher than that."

He was right about that, too, damn it. Tugging her with him, he walked toward his family. "Mom," he said. "What are you doing here?"

"There he is," the older woman said eagerly, her gaze fixed on Ethan. "I couldn't stand it. Had to come and meet my grandson!"

Justin sighed and Sadie had to fight the urge to grab her son and get out of there. Instead, she listened while Justin made introductions.

"Well," the woman said with a wide smile, "I just couldn't wait until Sam's wedding to meet my grandson! So I talked Bennett and Hannah into coming with me."

"This wasn't my idea," Bennett pointed out.

Hannah gave him a hard elbow nudge.

"You're coming to the wedding?" Sadie asked.

"Oh, yes," Justin's mother said. "We've known Sam for years. Now, Justin, don't you think you should introduce us?"

He sighed a little and Sadie thought it sounded like a surrender.

"Mom, this is Sadie Harris. My partner in this hotel." That sounded sad, but he probably didn't think so. "Sadie, my mother, Candace Carey."

"Call me Candace," she said and spared a quick

smile for Sadie. The woman was elegant. She wore a slate gray skirt and jacket with a deep scarlet blouse. Her heels were the same shade of gray as her suit and her short brown hair was expertly styled with streaks of a dark red running through it.

Sadie felt even shabbier than before, in comparison. "It's nice to meet you."

"Oh, that's a nice thing to say, though you're probably not enjoying it," Candace said, chuckling, "but I hope you understand it."

"Sure." *No.*

"Sadie," Justin said, "this is my older brother, Bennett, and his fiancée, Hannah Yates."

Bennett was tall and had on a suit that probably cost more than her car. Hannah, on the other hand, had short, spiky black hair and was wearing worn jeans, work boots and a T-shirt that read Yates Construction.

She liked Hannah already.

"Sorry," Hannah said, "but Ben snatched me up off a jobsite and didn't give me a chance to change."

"Why should you change?" Bennett asked. "You look gorgeous. As always."

Candace ignored the two of them giving each other moony looks and concentrated on Justin instead. "Can I hold him?"

"Sure, Mom." Justin handed the tiny boy over to his mother.

"He's not very good with strangers," Sadie said quickly and then watched as her son proved her a liar. The tiny boy looked at Candace, then reached up to tug her hair as he babbled incoherently.

"Oh, yes, you are your daddy's son, aren't you?" She glanced first at Sadie to say, "He's just adorable."

And before Sadie could say anything, Candace looked at her youngest son. "He has your dimple."

"Okay," Bennett announced, "if we're down to discussing my brother's dimples, I'm out. You guys do the baby thing while Justin shows me the hotel."

Sadie gave Justin a don't-you-leave-me-here-alone glare, but he only shrugged and walked off with his brother. For a long moment, she considered snatching up her baby and running, just to escape.

Instead, she plastered a smile she didn't feel onto her face and decided to stand her ground. For now.

"I can imagine you're not thrilled that I dropped in on you," Candace said, still smiling and cooing at Ethan.

"No, I... Well." She took a breath, then blew it out. "No."

Hannah laughed at that. "Know just how you feel. She 'dropped in' on me once, too. At a jobsite. She wanted to give me a talking to and explain what was wrong with Ben. I didn't like it, but that worked out okay."

"Oh, sweetie," Candace said, "it only worked because you loved Bennett. And," she added, with a considering look at Sadie, "I have the feeling that Sadie loves my Justin..."

Thankfully, Ethan chose just that moment to start fussing. Sadie used that excuse to say, "I'm really sorry but he needs to eat and—"

"Could I do it?" Candace asked. "It's been a long time since my granddaughter was this small, and I do miss babies."

Sadie looked at the older woman, really looked at her, and for the first time, saw beyond the elegance to the nice woman with kind eyes. Going with her instincts, Sadie said, "Sure. Let's go over here. His bottle's in the bag."

"Oh, isn't this fun?" Candace gave Hannah a nudge. "You'll have to give me one of these soon."

"We're working on it," Hannah assured her with a grin. "Every chance we get."

"Well, as I told Bennett not too long ago, a healthy sex life is important to any good relationship."

Surprised, Sadie stared at her for a second, then noticed Hannah shrugging. Justin's family was a little different than how she'd imagined them. She'd just assumed they'd be rich and snooty and too highbrow for her. So far, not so much.

Once Candace had the bottle, she laid Ethan back in her arms, smiled down at him and held that bottle while his little hands batted at hers. "Oh, Sadie, I'm so happy to meet my beautiful grandson. I hope you'll forgive me for just crashing in on you."

"Sure." That was knee-jerk polite, so she added, "Of course. I do understand. My mom would have done the same thing."

"Oh, I think your mother and I will get along famously."

"I doubt we have to worry about that," Sadie said. "Justin and I aren't together."

"Oh, I wouldn't give up just yet," Candace said.

The sea breeze tossed the leaves of the tree, sending dappled shade dancing across their faces. The mingled scents of the flowers gathered on the courtyard were almost overpowering. Surrounded by beauty, Sadie tried to enjoy the women talking with her.

"The second reason I wanted to come," Candace

said quietly, "was because I wanted to meet the woman who has my youngest son all twisted up."

Sadie laughed. Looking from Candace to a sympathetic Hannah and back again, she said, "Oh, no, I don't."

Candace shook her head and said, "I know my kids, Sadie. Justin has never been so protective. Not just of the baby but of you. He didn't tell us about you, you know."

"Because he didn't think I was important enough to mention."

"Oh, just the opposite, dear." Candace freed one hand long enough to pat Sadie's. "If you weren't important to him, he'd have told us everything. But because you are, he held back. Keeping you private. For himself. It's very Justin of him.

"Just as it was very Bennett to make an idiot of himself with Hannah. Isn't that right?"

Hannah sighed and grinned. "Have to say, she does know her children."

"That's why I wanted you to meet Hannah," Candace said. "She's marrying a Carey man, so she can really commiserate with you if you need it."

"And you will," Hannah said with a nod. She propped her elbows on the table and said, "I love Ben to pieces. But even now, he drives me crazy sometimes. He's opinionated and stubborn and sweet and loving. I have to say, the Carey men are kind of weird, but generally, they're worth the trouble."

"There." Candace beamed at Hannah before telling Sadie, "You see?"

"Look," Sadie said, "I appreciate the solidarity and

the advice and even the sympathy. But I'm not the problem. I do love him. But that will pass. Eventually."

Hannah and Candace exchanged a long, telling look.

Sadie sighed. "You don't understand. Justin proposed, but made it more of a business deal. He doesn't want love involved. Just teamwork."

"What did I tell you," Hannah muttered. "Weird."

"Weird or not," Sadie continued, "I'm not going to live my life that way. So there really isn't anything you guys can do."

Candace sighed. "It's very disappointing to hear that I have another son who is being shortsighted. Although," she added, "their father hasn't been much better lately."

"Look," Sadie said. "I really do appreciate all of this, but Justin and I aren't together and we're not going to be."

"You have a child together. Ethan is a Carey."

Sadie felt a quick jolt of panic at Candace's quiet words. Was that a warning? A threat?

"That means you and Justin will always be linked together," the older woman said. "And no one can read the future, Sadie." She smiled down at the baby. "He's all finished. Aren't you, my darling?" Lifting him onto her shoulder, she patted his back until he burped, then she gave him a proud smile.

"Babies change everything, Sadie. You'll see."

"Thanks, Candace," she said, "but I don't want to be married because of a baby any more than I want to be just a business deal."

"And I don't blame you a bit," Candace said, and

reached out to pat Sadie's hand. "Oh, honey. Patience is a must when dealing with a Carey male."

"She's not wrong," Hannah mused.

"What do you think they're talking about?" Justin shot a look out the windows at the women.

"Us, of course," Bennett said, strolling through the hotel, checking everything with quick eyes that never missed a thing. "What do women always talk about? The men in their lives and how to fix them."

Justin glared at his brother's retreating back. "I don't need fixing."

"Yeah, neither did I," Bennett said, turning to wink at Justin. "But I do enjoy having Hannah try."

"I should go out there."

"Are you worried?"

"Sadie doesn't trust the Careys."

"Neither did Hannah."

Justin sighed and pushed one hand through his hair. "How'd you change her mind?"

"By loving her. By letting myself love her."

Justin shoved his hands into his pockets. Love. It kept coming back to that one, small word. One emotion that so many people had tried and failed to define. What he felt for Sadie was stronger than anything he'd ever known. And could *probably* be described with that word she wanted to hear.

Well, he wanted to be with her. Wanted to give her what she needed. Wanted the partnership they'd built over the last few months, but that one little word kept stopping him because once it was said, there was no going back.

And he still couldn't risk it.

"I've never said that word to a woman before, Bennett. And I can't say it to Sadie yet."

"Why the hell not?"

He scowled at his brother. "I've got too much to prove."

"To whom?"

"You. Dad. *Me*."

"You've already convinced me. Dad's got his own issues," Bennett pointed out, "and if *you* don't believe in you, who the hell will?"

"I've got a *son*, Bennett," Justin said, and even hearing the words aloud still felt strange to him. "I owe him something, too."

"Yeah, you do." Bennett stared at him. "You owe him a family if you can give him one. If you love Sadie, step up. Hell, Justin, I almost lost Hannah because I was too stupid to see the truth." Bennett slapped his brother's shoulder. "Be better than me."

Justin nodded as his brother's words resonated with him. He had been stupid. But he didn't have to stay that way. "I hate that you're right, Bennett. But I don't hate that you said all of that." He was risking what he had with Sadie because he was afraid to risk Sadie's heart. Suddenly, it made zero sense.

A year and a half ago, he'd left Sadie because she had become too important to him and he'd had too much to prove. Now he loved her. Yes, that word. He loved her. And he'd been willing to walk away again because he couldn't risk her happiness until he was sure he would succeed. How could he make promises to her when the promises to himself were unfulfilled?

But hadn't he proved it? Hadn't he done what he'd promised himself he was going to do? The Carey Cliffside was a reality and in two weeks, it would be open and he *knew* people would flock to this amazing spa hotel at the ocean's door. He'd done it. The only thing he had left to prove was to Sadie. He had to prove to her that he loved her. That he would never leave her again.

Otherwise, how many hotels would it take for him before he could consider himself a success? Before he could offer Sadie what she deserved?

"I want Sadie with me," he said, nodding to himself, shooting a glance at his brother. "I want to be a permanent part of my son's life."

"Glad to hear it," Bennett said. "Because you two did a hell of a job on this hotel/spa—and we're going to need Sadie for the Newport Beach hotel."

Justin laughed out loud. "Leave it to you to talk business while I'm having an epiphany." Shaking his head, he let Bennett talk business while his own mind shot straight to Sadie. He had a lot he wanted to talk to her about. Once Sam's wedding was over, once the hotel was opened, he would give her all the romance she needed.

He wanted to build a family with the woman he loved. But could he do it? Could he convince her to trust him? To trust his family? He had to make a phone call. Get the wheels moving. So he could show Sadie he meant what he said. "I've got to call Jackson."

"The family lawyer? Why?"

"Because, Bennett…" Justin grinned at him. "I'm going to be better than you."

"Hah!" Bennett slapped his back. "Only this once, Justin."

"Thanks. For coming down here. For telling me what I needed to hear."

Bennett smiled. "Women will mess a man up, Justin." He sighed. "But I'm here to tell you, it's worth it. Hannah is...*everything* to me. Make the right moves, Justin. You won't regret it."

Justin thought about it. Thought about the last week, when he and Sadie were so close and yet miles apart. Thought about the long, empty nights without her. And he knew. He was willing, finally, to take the biggest risk of his life.

He hoped it wasn't too late.

Ten

An hour later, Bennett stepped out of the hotel, walked straight to his fiancée and kissed her. Then he looked at Sadie. "It's a great place, Sadie. I think we're going to do really well together."

She knew about Bennett and the Carey Corporation investing in the Carey Spa Hotel group and she was all for it. One thing she could give the Careys. They were very successful in business. If they could continue the partnership through other hotels, she would be making sure that Ethan's future was safe.

"I'm glad you like it," she said, and watched Candace swaying in place to keep a now sleeping Ethan happy. Did the little boy know somehow that it was his grandmother holding him? That sounded fanciful, she knew, but Ethan had really connected with Candace right away.

The Carey family showing up unannounced had worried her, but they were so nice. So…normal, that Sadie was relaxing and trying to remember why she'd been leery in the first place.

"Oh, I more than like it." He looked at Hannah and said, "We're going to put a bid in on the Newport Beach hotel in a couple weeks and *you*, my gorgeous contractor, are going to be running the remodel."

Hannah grinned at him. "I'll try to work you in. I've got to finish the castle at Jack's house first."

"Please. That's almost done." Bennett kissed her again. "Work me into your schedule. You're the only contractor I trust to do the job."

"Sweet-talker," Hannah said with a smile.

"Where's Justin?" Sadie asked, looking toward the hotel. He'd taken Bennett on a tour—why hadn't he come out with his brother?

"Oh," Bennett said, dropping one arm around Hannah, "he's making a phone call. Wanted to talk to Jackson."

Sadie smiled. "Who's Jackson? Another brother?"

"Oh, no," Candace said as she kissed Ethan's forehead. "Jackson is the family lawyer." She didn't notice when Sadie went completely still.

Swallowing hard, Sadie asked, "Why did he have to call a lawyer?"

"No idea," Bennett said, oblivious to Sadie's distress. "Mom, I know you're having a great time, but we need to head back before the traffic is more of a nightmare than usual."

Sadie heard them, like buzzing noises inside her head. Fear thrummed through her bloodstream with every beat of her heart. But she didn't let it show.

Couldn't. She knew it was important to smile and nod, and when Candace handed Ethan to her, Sadie cuddled him close, steadying herself by inhaling the soft, sweet scent of him.

"Fine," Candace said. "We'll go. But we'll be back for the wedding, Sadie, so we'll see you in a week, yes? And oh, wait until Martin sees his grandson."

"You care what Dad thinks?" Bennett asked.

"Don't be ridiculous, Bennett," Candace said. "I love your father very much."

"Right. That's why you're living with me."

"Us," Hannah corrected.

"Well, with any luck, I may be moving out of your house soon. I believe Martin may be coming around," Candace said with a tiny smile of satisfaction.

They were still talking, laughing, joking with each other. Sadie knew it, but she wasn't registering any of it. All she could think about was that Justin was calling the family lawyer. Why? Her stomach tightened and a knot of worry lodged in her throat. Somehow she smiled at Candace, said *something* to Bennett and Hannah and waved as they walked off.

Her mind racing, Sadie clung to Ethan. She wanted to take him and run. Lawyers? This could only mean one thing. Justin had been playing her all along. She'd begun to trust him and he'd simply been setting her up. That was why his family had come here today. To see Ethan. To make sure he was Carey-worthy before they took him from her.

Was she being paranoid? Or were all her fears suddenly springing into life? Sadie couldn't risk it.

"Oh my God, Ethan," she whispered, looking around as if she expected someone to leap out from behind the arbor to snatch her son from her arms. "We have to get out of here."

Panic rushed through her, stealing her breath, stinging her eyes with tears of betrayal. How could he do this to her?

"It's because I said no to his lame proposal," she whispered, stunned as the realization slapped at her. "Of course. He gave me a chance to keep my son. All I had to do was marry a man who didn't love me."

He'd called the Carey family lawyer to get a custody suit rolling. She knew it. Just as she knew she'd never be able to win in court against the Carey money. The Carey family reputation. So she wouldn't fight. She'd run.

A year and a half ago, Justin had walked out on her, leaving her broken. This time she would be the one walking.

"Hey," Justin called as he strolled out of the hotel. "Did they leave?"

"Yes," she said, and forced a smile that felt tight on her face. "They wanted to beat the traffic. What were you doing?" Would he lie? Would he be honest and tell her what he was up to?

"Oh," He shrugged. "I put a call into a Realtor I know in Orange County. Bennett and I want to move on the Newport Beach property right after the grand opening here."

Lies. He had looked her in the eye and lied. She swallowed back the pain, the humiliation, and said, "That sounds great. But for right now, Ethan's sleeping so soundly I'm going to take him up to our room, put him to bed."

"I'll do it," he said, stepping forward to reach for his son.

It was all she could do not to turn and run. Instead, her arms tightened instinctively around Ethan and the little boy stirred fretfully. "It's fine. I've got him. You should, uh, talk to Sam. Make sure we're on schedule for the wedding and the opening."

He frowned a little as he watched her, so she smiled again to ease his mind. "Okay. I will," he said. "We're running out of time, aren't we?"

"What?" Another spurt of panic.

"To get everything set for the wedding." He frowned again. "Are you okay?"

"Fine," she said sharply. "Just tired."

"Maybe you should lie down with Ethan."

"Not a bad idea," she agreed. "We'll see you in a couple of hours, then."

"Okay."

She turned to walk into the hotel and only paused when Justin called, "Sadie?"

Looking over her shoulder at him, she waited.

"When the wedding and the opening are over, we have to sit down together and talk about something."

A lead ball dropped into the pit of her stomach, but she didn't let him see it. Sadie knew what he wanted to talk to her about. But she wouldn't be here to listen.

Nodding, she walked into the hotel, forcing herself to take slow, steady steps.

Justin hadn't seen Sadie in hours. But he was giving her some space because of his family's surprise visit. Talking to Bennett had helped Justin out a lot.

But he'd seen the look on Sadie's face when they'd all arrived. When his mother had been holding Ethan.

Fear. She didn't trust him, he thought, and then considered it. Why would she? She didn't trust his family and again, why would she? Hopefully, after she heard what he'd talked to the lawyer about, that trust would come. Looking back now, he could see that his suggestion to get married because they made a great team at work had been the biggest mistake he'd ever made.

Justin could admit that he'd been stupid about that. But he'd been too scared to admit he was in love. Real love. Hell, that was a big admission for any man. Now he knew that the only way Sadie would ever believe that he loved her was if he gave her a real proposal. A real promise. And he was ready to do that now.

He walked into the lobby of the Cliffside and paused to take a look around. Cleaning staff was busy, polishing floors, dusting, setting out vases of flowers on the gleaming wood tables. Two women stood behind the reception desk, answering phones.

Apparently, all of the advertising was doing the job, because they were taking reservations now for the opening of the hotel. He walked over, waited for one of the women to hang up, then asked, "How's it going?"

"It's amazing, Mr. Carey," she said with a wide grin on her face. "We're almost booked out. Only a few rooms left and the treatment rooms are booked solid for the first week."

"Just what I wanted to hear," he said, then left when the phone rang and she answered, "Carey Cliffside."

It sounded good. Sounded perfect. Maybe he didn't have to wait for the wedding and the opening to be over. Maybe the time for a real proposal was at the precipice of their new beginning. After all, he wanted Sadie to know that win or lose with the hotel, he wanted to be with her. He was finished waiting, planning. Now was the time to act.

But even as he thought about going upstairs to propose, he realized he didn't have a damn ring.

"Can't propose without a ring," he muttered, and turned on his heel. Smiling, he left the hotel, headed for the best jewelry store in town.

It took Sadie a little over three hours to drive to her parents' house in Bullhead City, Arizona. Their house was brand-new and in an adults-only golf course community. For herself, Sadie would miss living right beside the ocean too much to make the move. But she knew her parents were loving the change.

She parked in front of their house and winced when she got out of the car. It was only June and already the heat was blistering. She glanced up at the brassy sky and smiled sadly at the two small clouds drifting lazily across it. Her parents' house was one-story, sitting on a knoll so that there was a view of the Colorado River in the distance. Desert landscaping surrounded the house, but there were two trees in the yard that would, one day, provide shade. While she stood there staring, the front door flew open and her mother ran down the walkway toward her.

"Sadie! What a wonderful surprise!" Monica Harris was tall, like her daughter, with chin-length, dark brown hair cut into a bob that suited her perfectly. She was slim and tanned and the white shorts and dark green shirt she wore looked great on her. "Hi, Mom." Tears stung her eyes as her mother wrapped her in a tight hug. This was what she'd needed. After a long minute, she said, "Yeah, I just had to get out of San Diego for a while."

Monica held on to her daughter's shoulders and pulled back, studying Sadie's face. "Something's wrong. So you come in and you tell me about it."

Sadie glanced at the house. "Where's Dad?"

Monica was opening the back door to get at her grandson. "Oh, he's golfing with his buddies. If he doesn't get heatstroke, he should be home in an hour."

"Okay..." Good. It would give her a chance to talk to her mom first.

"There's my boy!" Monica scooped him up out of the car seat. Ethan laughed and kicked, happy to be out.

Then, Monica spotted Sadie's suitcase and asked, "How long are you staying?"

"I don't know yet, Mom." Sadie took a breath, looked at her son, then met her mother's gaze. "I don't know anything."

Sympathy shone in her mother's eyes and Sadie's aching heart eased just a little. "Oh, sweetie, come on inside. You can tell me everything over a slice of cake."

"Chocolate?" Sadie asked with a smile.

"Is there any other kind?"

She'd needed this, Sadie thought. Her mom's steadiness—not to mention her cake. And to be here with people who loved her and understood her and, most important, the two people in the world who would support her, no matter what.

"You just disappeared with the man's *child*?"

Sadie sighed in the face of her father's outrage. If this was support, she wasn't loving it.

"Really?" Sadie asked. "Mom laid into me already and the minute you get home, you do the same?"

"Baby girl," her father said, moving in close enough to give her a hard, fast hug. "You can't take a man's child away. Hell, you can't take *anyone's* child away. It's not right. You're worried that's what he's going to do to you? But you just did it, to *him*."

God, he was right. In her defense, she hadn't been thinking. Sadie had been running on pure emotion.

"You're gonna scare the crap out of the man, too." Her father studied her closely. "Is that what you wanted?"

"Of course not," Sadie said, a little insulted that he would think so. "I just had to get Ethan out of there. Justin was talking to their family lawyer."

"That could have been about anything," her mother added while she bounced Ethan on her lap.

"No." Sadie had been thinking about this for hours and she knew she was right. He'd called the lawyer right after his mother and brother had seen Ethan. The Careys wanted her little boy and they couldn't have him.

She picked up her glass of iced tea and took a drink. "I can't believe I came to you guys and you're on Justin's side. What happened to unconditional support?"

Max Harris laughed shortly. "We're always on your side, Sadie. We love you. That doesn't mean we won't tell you when we think you're wrong."

"And you're wrong this time, sweetie," her mom said.

"No, I'm not." Sadie's gaze shifted to her son and everything in her told her that she'd done the right thing to protect him. The *only* thing she could have done.

Her mother smoothed Ethan's silky hair back from his forehead and a soft smile curved her mouth as she shook her head. "Imagine what Justin's going to think, *feel* when he finds out you two are gone."

"He'll be furious when he finds out that Ethan is gone," she acknowledged. "But he won't care about me," Sadie said, shaking her head. She really hated saying that out loud. Heck, she hated to admit it to herself at all. But the simple truth was, Justin didn't love her. He only wanted her because of their son. Hadn't he already offered her the least romantic proposal in history? And the kind of marriage he was interested in was so…lonely.

"Well, if that's true," her father said with a hard hug, "then the man's a fool."

She went up on her toes to kiss her dad's cheek. Sadie hated bringing trouble here. Her parents had a new, more relaxing life and her father hadn't looked this good in years. "I shouldn't have come and dragged you guys into this."

"Who else would you drag?" her father demanded, making her smile. "You always come to us, kiddo. We might not always think you're right, but we'll always love you. And Ethan."

"I know that," she said, leaning into his hug. He smelled like peppermint and sunblock and made her feel safe. "And I'll call Justin. I don't want him to be scared for Ethan."

"Or for you."

"Dad, I told you. He only proposed because he said we made a good team. Because we share Ethan." One tear escaped her eye and she swiped it away impatiently.

"Honey…"

"No." She turned and looked at her mom before shifting her gaze to the happy baby holding his own hands. "I have Ethan. And you and Dad. I'll be fine."

She'd turned her phone off when she left San Diego, so when she slipped outside and turned it back on and it lit up with a dozen texts and just as many voice mails, she wasn't surprised. She flipped through the texts quickly.

The same theme over and over. *Where are you? Damn it, call me.*

She didn't bother listening to the voice mails. What would be the point? Sadie paced around her parents' patio and dialed Justin.

"Where the hell are you?" he demanded, startling her. She hadn't even heard the phone ring.

"I'm at my folks' house. In Arizona."

"Arizona?" She heard anger and frustration and fear in his voice and she was sorry for the last. "Is everything all right? You and Ethan are okay?"

"Yes, of course."

"Good. How could you just leave? Without a word?"

"You did the same thing, remember?" Sadie countered, and let her own anger jump to the forefront. "A year and a half ago, I told you I loved you and you left. Well, this time, it was my turn to disappear."

"Your turn?" The outrage in his voice made her wince. "That's what this is about?"

She closed her eyes and could just *see* him, pacing, pushing his hand through his hair, a death grip on his phone.

"No, Justin," she said and fought to speak past the pain thrumming in her chest. "I left because I had to.

And I only called to let you know that Ethan is fine." She took a breath. "As for the hotel and our partnership, you can have it all. My twenty-five percent was a way for me to take care of Ethan's future. But that's pointless if I don't have him with me. So keep the hotel. I don't care. But you can't have my son."

"What are you talking about?"

"I'm staying in Arizona, Justin." She walked across the yard to stand under one of the young trees. "Ethan's safe and he's going to stay that way."

"Why wouldn't he stay safe? What the hell happened when you were talking to my family?"

"You know exactly what happened. Why else would you have called your family lawyer?"

"Is that what this is about? Because I called Jackson? For God's sake, Sadie—"

"Because you called a lawyer and then lied to me about it. I don't want to hear anymore lies," she said, cutting him off again. She couldn't hold back her tears for much longer, so she needed to get off the phone fast. Damned if she'd let him hear her cry. "I have to go. Ethan needs me."

Two hours later, Ethan parked his rental car outside the Harris house. When he turned the engine off, he just sat there for a minute or two, getting a grip on the fury that had ridden him all the way from California.

Sadie had walked away from him. Left him without a damn word and now he knew exactly how she'd felt when he'd done the same damn thing to her. He didn't like it a bit.

More than that, though, he knew he'd deserved this. Sadie had had every reason to take their son and leave. He hadn't given her any reason to trust him. To believe that now would be different from when they were together before. So she'd taken their son to protect him—from his father. And wasn't that a bitch?

It hadn't been hard to find her parents. A call to the Carey company had put three of Bennett's best employees on the task. One to find the Harris family, one to rent Justin a car and the third to get the Carey family jet ready. Which meant that by the time Justin left his car in short-term parking at the San Diego Airport—the Carey family jet was ready and waiting to take him to Bullhead City, Arizona.

Now he stepped out of his rental car, marched up the walk to the front door and rang the bell.

She opened the door and her eyes went wide.

"Surprise," he said and stepped forward. Pushing past her into the house, he walked into the great room, spotted his son on the lap of Sadie's mother and took his first easy breath in hours. Nodding at the older couple, he said, "Mr. and Mrs. Harris, I'm sorry to meet you this way, but I've got some things to say to your daughter."

"I'll bet you do," Max Harris mused.

"Mom, Dad, would you excuse us?" Sadie gave her parents a look that said, *Help me out here.*

"I don't think so," her mother said and sat back in the chair, cuddling Ethan close.

Sadie took a deep breath. "Fine. Why are you here, Justin?"

"You're kidding, right?" Justin walked in close to her, grabbed hold of her shoulders and forced her to look up at him. "You were *gone*. Ethan was *gone*. Then when I couldn't get hold of you—answer your damn phone from now on—the fear kept growing until I finally found out that you're here. With your parents. Then you tell me you're not coming back? I can have the hotel but not you? Not my son?"

"You don't have to repeat it all," she muttered, throwing an uncomfortable glance at her parents.

"Yeah I do. Just to believe it's real." His hands on her gentled and he asked, "Why, Sadie? Just tell me that much. Why?"

She lifted her gaze to his. "Because you called your lawyer. Because you're going to try to take Ethan from me."

Justin choked out a strangled laugh. "What are you talking about? Where did that even come from?"

He noted how interested Sadie's parents were. Well, that couldn't be helped. He was finally going to say everything he wanted to say to Sadie and he didn't care if they had an audience.

"Right after your mother and brother came," she was saying, "right after they saw Ethan, you called your family lawyer. Why else would you do that?"

Justin felt her words land like a slap in the face. He'd kept her at such an emotional distance that she actually believed he would steal their son?

"I'm sorry, Sadie," he whispered and watched her eyes fill with tears.

"So it's true?" she asked quietly.

"No, it's not true. I'm sorry I was an ass for so damn long that you can't trust me. I never should have walked away from you, Sadie." He smoothed the pad of his thumb over her cheekbone, wiping away a single tear. "And you should have told me about Ethan."

"Yes, she should have," her father said.

Her mother added, "We told her to."

"Yes," she said, as she rolled her eyes. "Everyone is right. I should have told you, Justin. And... I'm sorry we're doing this with an audience."

"I don't care who hears me," Justin said, meeting her gaze. "As long as you do. Look, I know you don't trust me and I don't know how to change that except by showing you that you can. It might take years to prove it to you, but I'll put in the time because I love you, Sadie."

Her breath caught and she bit down on her bottom lip. She looked like she wanted to believe, but was again afraid to trust.

"The reason I called the lawyer was because I wanted to start adoption procedures. I want Ethan to have my last name. Hell, I want you to have it, too."

"What are you saying?" Sadie whispered.

"I'm saying I want you and Ethan to be my family."

"Oh, Justin..."

"Just wait a second," he blurted out, rubbing her shoulders, simply because he needed to feel her. To know she was there. With him. Where she belonged. "I'm finally saying it, Sadie. So just... Hear me out. Please. I'll work my ass off to prove myself to you. To show you how much I love you and Ethan. But the next time you're pissed at me, I'd appreciate it if you'd just tell me what's going on instead of running?"

She gave him a soft smile. "I will. I think maybe we've both done enough running from each other. Maybe it's time we ran *to* each other."

"Good idea," he said as his heart seemed to fill beyond what should have been possible.

"I never meant to keep Ethan from you, Justin."

Sadie lifted one hand and cupped his cheek. Her touch filled all those empty, icy places inside him with warmth. "And you don't have to adopt your son because you're already listed on the birth certificate as Ethan's father."

"Thank you for that."

She smiled. "I couldn't take that from you or from Ethan."

"I do love you." He pulled her in close, wrapped his arms around her and gave her a quick, hard kiss. "We're going to make the best chain of spa hotels in the country. And we're going to do it together."

She smiled up at him and he loved seeing the sparkle back in those gold-flecked eyes. "Glad to hear it, since I own twenty-five percent of the business."

"No, you don't," he said and took her left hand in his. "From now on, it's fifty-fifty all the way." Holding her hand, he dropped to one knee and heard her mother gasp in delight. But all he could see was Sadie, watching him, her eyes glistening and that amazing mouth turning up into a smile.

Digging into his jacket pocket, he produced a square-cut, canary yellow diamond and held it at the tip of her ring finger. Waiting.

"Marry me, Sadie," he said. "Have more kids with me. Build a family, a legacy all our own. I swear I will love you forever. And if you ever feel like leaving again, you have to promise to take me with you."

"I think I can do that," she said, her smile wider, her eyes brighter.

"That's a yes?"

"Oh, yes, Justin. It was always yes."

He slid the ring onto her finger, then stood and

swept her into a kiss that had their son clapping tiny hands and laughing. Sadie's parents cheered. And just like that, the rest of their lives started.

It was perfect.

Epilogue

Sam and Kate's wedding went off without a hitch.

Even the weather cooperated, with a bright sun streaming out of a sky studded with white clouds. A gentle ocean breeze kept everyone from getting hot. The food was wonderful, the flowers glorious and the ceremony, brief and beautiful.

The best part of the day, though, for Sadie anyway, was the fact that she and Justin and Ethan were officially a family. She looked down at her gorgeous ring and saw more than a lovely stone. She saw the promise she'd longed for. Saw the love she'd dreamed of, and when Justin came up behind her and wrapped his arms around her, she leaned into his hold and smiled up at him, free now to love and be loved.

"It was great," he said. "The whole day. You and Kate really pulled it together."

Laughing, she said, "In spite of Kate's mom. It really was a wonderful day," she agreed, grinning up at him. "And you did a terrific job holding Sam together."

"It's pitiful," he said, shaking his head and smiling. "The man's nuts about Kate and nearly crumbled when he had to stand up in front of the crowd."

"Hmm. We'll see how you do when it's our turn."

He frowned a little and shivered. "Let's not think about that part yet."

Sadie laughed, hooked her arm through his and said, "We should probably get Ethan and give your parents a break from the baby."

"Yeah, good luck with that." Most everyone had gone, but there were a few people, obviously reluctant to leave, still swaying on the dance floor. Justin held on to Sadie's hand as he led her across the courtyard.

The Carey family sat around a large table and Sadie could smile now when she saw them all. The Careys were her family now. And the warmth she'd already received from them filled her heart. Justin's parents, Candace and Martin—with Martin holding Ethan and having what looked like an in-depth conversation with the tiny boy. Justin's sister Amanda sitting on her fiancé Henry's lap. His sister Serena's daughter, Alli, perched on her soon-to-be stepfather Jack's shoulders while Serena leaned into him. Bennett and Hannah holding hands on the table and watching Ethan with silly smiles on their faces.

As Justin and Sadie approached, Candace smiled warmly and said, "Perfect timing! We want to have a toast to all of the upcoming weddings in the family."

Justin sat down, and dragged Sadie onto his lap.

Across the table, Ethan spotted them and laughed, chewing on his fingers. Sadie held Justin's hand and gave it a squeeze. She was just so happy she hardly knew what to do with herself. She had Justin. Ethan. Her own parents and now this wonderful family, too.

"Mom," Bennett said, gathering everyone's attention, "if we're going to toast to all of us, there's one more thing to be excited about." He looked at Hannah and she nodded.

"We didn't want to say anything, but what the hell, we'll risk it. Hannah's pregnant."

The whole table erupted in cheers, laughter and a few tears.

"Oh, this is so wonderful," Candace said. "Soon, I'll have two new sons and two new daughters." She glanced at her husband and smiled. "And just imagine all the grandbabies we'll have!"

Martin rose and drew Candace up to stand beside him. He held Ethan close to his chest, even when the baby began to chew on his two-hundred-dollar tie. Dropping his free arm around his wife's shoulders, Martin looked around the table, at each of his children and the partners they loved. "We'll toast to your weddings, to Bennett and Hannah's baby…"

Bennett kissed his fiancée soundly, making her laugh.

"And," Martin continued, "we'll toast to your mother and me and retirement."

They all groaned and Candace laughed and raised one hand. "No, it's real this time. Isn't it, Marty?"

He looked down at her and kissed her forehead. "It is. I'll never risk losing you again, Candy." Looking out at his family, he said, "Thanks to all of you falling in love, building your own futures, I finally realized that this time with Candy is the one thing I can't live without."

She laid her head on his chest and sighed, even when Ethan leaned forward to pat her face.

"We're taking a round-the-world cruise—we leave at the end of the week."

"I'm getting him out into the middle of the ocean, just to make sure that *this* time, retirement sticks," Candace said, giving her husband a nudge.

"It'll stick, Candy. I promise." Turning to their children again, Martin assured them, "We'll fly home for every wedding. And when the cruise is over, we'll be doting grandparents who take occasional trips."

Candace laughed happily and hugged Alli, when the girl came rushing up to her.

Martin lifted his glass and waited until everyone else had done the same. "The business is yours now. I trust you all to work together. Help each other. Love each other.

"And I know that the Carey Corporation, the Carey Center and the Carey legacy...are in very good hands."

* * * * *

COMING SOON!

We really hope you enjoyed reading this book.
If you're looking for more romance, be sure to
head to the shops when new books are
available on

Thursday 6th
January

To see which titles are coming soon, please visit

millsandboon.co.uk/nextmonth

MODERN

Prepare to be swept off your feet by sophisticated, sexy and seductive heroes, in some of the world's most glamourous and romantic locations, where power and passion collide.

HISTORICAL

Escape with historical heroes from time gone by. Whether your passion is for wicked Regency Rakes, muscled Vikings or rugged Highlanders, await the romance of the past.

MEDICAL

Set your pulse racing with dedicated, delectable doctors in the high-pressure world of medicine, where emotions run high and passion, comfort and love are the best medicine.

True Love

Celebrate true love with tender stories of heartfelt romance, from the first rush of falling in love to the joy a new baby can bring, and a focus on the emotional heart of a relationship.

Desire

Indulge in secrets and scandal, intense drama and plenty of sizzling hot action with powerful and passionate heroes who have it all: wealth, status, good looks…everything but the right woman.

HEROES

Experience all the excitement of a gripping thriller, with an intense rom

Romance

For exclusive extracts, competitions
and special offers, find us online:

facebook.com/millsandboon

@MillsandBoon

@MillsandBoonUK

Get in touch on 01413 063232

For all the latest titles coming soon, visit
millsandboon.co.uk/nextmonth

GET YOUR ROMANCE FIX!

MILLS & BOON
— *blog* —

Get the latest romance news, exclusive author interviews, story extracts and much more!

blog.millsandboon.co.uk

Indulge in secrets and scandal, intense drama and plenty of sizzling hot action with powerful and passionate heroes who have it all: wealth, status, good looks…everything but the right woman.

MILLS & BOON
MODERN
Power and Passion

Prepare to be swept off your feet by sophisticated, sexy and seductive heroes, in some of the world's most glamourous and romantic locations, where power and passion collide.

Set your pulse racing with dedicated, delectable doctors in the high-pressure world of medicine, where emotions run high and passion, comfort and love are the best medicine.

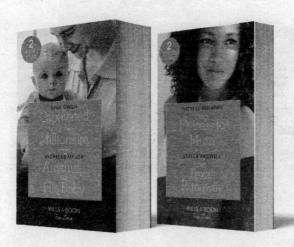

Celebrate true love with tender stories of beautiful romance, from the rush of falling in love to the joy a new baby can bring, and a focus on the emotional heart of a relationship